A GATHERING MIDNIGHT

Books by Holly Race

Midnight's Twins
A Gathering Midnight
A Midnight Dark and Golden

A GATHERING MIDNIGHT

HOLLY RACE

HOT KEY BOOKS

First published in Great Britain in 2021 by
HOT KEY BOOKS
4th Floor, Victoria House, Bloomsbury Square, London WC1B 4DA
Owned by Bonnier Books
Sveavägen 56, Stockholm, Sweden
www.hotkeybooks.com

A CIP catalogue record for this book is available from the British Library.

ISBN: 978-1-4714-1029-1
Also available as an ebook and in audio

2

This book is typeset using Atomik ePublisher
Printed and bound in Great Britain by Clays Ltd, Elcograf S.p.A.

MIX
Paper from responsible sources
FSC www.fsc.org FSC® C018072

Hot Key Books is an imprint of Bonnier Books UK
www.bonnierbooks.co.uk

To the 126,000 and counting
and those who cared for them

'No greater shame to man than inhumanity.'
– Edmund Spenser, *The Faerie Queene*

Prologue

Many years ago, in a time shaped from legends . . .

The forge burned sapphire in the many-sunned light of Annwn. The metal that was not metal threw flecks of inspyre into the shimmering air as it was shaped. The Fay bent over their masterpiece, taking turns to bring the hammer down upon the blade. Merlin, the oldest and strongest, thrust his bare hands into the fire to form the hilt from melting crystal.

'Is it complete?' The voice came from the darkness at the back of the hall.

'Soon,' Andraste answered, throwing her face up to catch her breath. A sea breeze whistled in through the open doors of the hall. The tang of saltwater and seaweed caught in her throat. She glanced towards her lover, waiting in the shadows.

'There is only one thing left,' Merlin said, as hilt and blade joined with a hiss. 'Are you certain you wish it?'

'I am certain,' he replied, shifting impatiently.

Merlin nodded, placing one withered hand on the hilt. The rest of the Fay followed him. Andraste was last. She should be happy to do this for him. A goddess and a mortal; she had fallen in love with many men and women of Ithr before, but never with one such as him. So why did she feel uneasy? Why did her bones – such as she had them – tremble at the prospect of this gift?

'I am indebted to you,' he said, seeming to address them all. Certainly Merlin thought he spoke to him, but Andraste knew that the words were meant for her alone. His voice was so sincere that she dismissed her misgivings as the insecurities of a proud woman. She did his bidding; bent her will to the task before them. The forging was the easy part.

They did it as one, untwisting the stories that bound them together and finding the common threads. From Merlin, the firstborn, was cunning. Nimue's thread was more delicate: fortitude. Puck's was gaudy: he gave desire. Andraste's twin, Lugh, gave strength. Andraste's gift was many-threaded, and it was power. There were other, lesser gifts too, from the myriad Fay: memory, foresight, charm. Each one spun out from the Fay in glistening inspyre, before sinking into the sword. Andraste could feel her own strength diminishing as she pushed her gift into the metal. *It matters not*, she thought, *for when it is done, there will be stories for us all.*

At last, when they saw that it was good, the Fay stepped back. Andraste went to her lover and touched her heat-glistened forehead to his. He looked into her eyes in the way she adored: the way that told her that he *knew* her, as no mortal had before.

'It is done, my love,' she said.

He kissed her cheek, then stepped past her to look at what they had made. The others, her family, were panting. The glow of inspyre that surrounded them was hazy. They were all weakened from the effort of their creation. They watched as he pulled the weapon from the fire. It hissed as it branded his palm, but he didn't mind the pain. He flicked his arm and inspyre flooded down his muscles, healing the burned skin.

His gaze was shrewd.

'It is perfect,' Andraste assured him. She had never made anything so beautiful, or so powerful. The Fays' threads had woven a pattern of violet and gold across the crystal hilt and down into the blade. When he moved it, the light from the open doors threw coloured patterns across the assembled faces.

'Yes,' he said, smiling at last. 'It is good.'

The way he said it made Andraste pause. She reached out to him, but he drew away, casually, moving towards the entrance.

'Our deal is done,' Merlin croaked. 'You are in our debt.'

'We will all have stories, will we not?' Nimue said, her high voice carrying around the chamber.

'We are hungry,' Puck said, flitting towards Andraste. 'When will we feed?'

But Andraste said nothing at all. She followed her love as he moved into the fresh air. Outside, the undulations of Dyvnaint stretched before them on one side. On the other, the hills of Sumorsaet reached out towards a sun-kissed sea.

'We were going to restore Annwn together,' Andraste said sadly.

On the fields below, imps and piskies frolicked. In the distance, a giant paddled in the shallows, fishing for sea-spirits. 'These are creatures of the devil,' he said softly, so that only Andraste could hear him. 'I will brook no danger to my subjects.'

'Please, my lord,' Andraste said.

But he turned away from her, holding the sword aloft. He roared – a roar the like of which she had never heard human make. In that moment, she knew for certain that the true love of her immortal existence had deceived her. As her heart shattered, she vowed she would one day, many years from now, make it right.

Chapter 1

Now, in a time when legends are forgotten . . .

'Get down, Fern!' Ollie shouts at me, and without waiting to check whether I've heard him, chucks his chakram straight at my head. I duck just in time and feel the blade whisk through the top of my hair. A thud tells me he hit his intended mark.

I'm about to reprimand my brother when an ungodly scream warns of another incoming nightmare. This time, it's a woman with sunken cheeks and matted hair. She reminds me of the little group of homeless who station themselves at the bus stops in Stratford, near my home. I can't think about that now. I turn Lamb on the spot with a press of the ankle, and thrust my scimitar into her chest. The blade sucks its way out with my pull, and the woman bursts back into inspyre.

Rachel's voice echoes through the earpiece in my helmet. 'There's more of them coming down the alleyway, Bedevere. From the east, moving fast.'

Samson's voice is next. He's close enough that our knees are nearly touching as we sit astride our horses, but I hear him through my helmet. 'Cantabrian circle.'

Our only acknowledgement of his order is to swing our horses to form a ring around the street, facing outwards. We're not far from the great museums of Kensington, and within hearing of an aria, emanating from the Royal Albert Hall a few streets away. When I first joined the knights, these roads would have been occupied by buskers, sphinxes and the occasional pack of rabid werewolves. Now unformed inspyre drifts listlessly, waiting for someone with enough imagination left to give it shape.

Our patrol was supposed to take us around Trafalgar Square and the maze of Soho, but the Gawain regiment were overwhelmed on their route, so Samson volunteered to cover both. That raised some eyebrows amongst the rest of the regiment, but I can understand Samson's reasoning: he's the Head Knight, and Ollie and I are the thanes' greatest assets – if anyone should shoulder more of the load, it's us.

The thudding of feet on tarmac is growing louder – our harkers have done their work correctly. That's getting less easy these days. Nightmares used to be simple to spot. They would be giants or sprites or huge bugs. Now, nearly every nightmare is human-shaped. It's not impossible to spot them, but it makes the harkers' work – and ours – harder in every way.

The cries begin – the wails and babbles of human-monster hybrids. Lamb whickers gently, and I press a hand to her neck, trying to reassure her.

I look over at Ollie. 'This time I'd appreciate a heads-up before you nearly decapitate me, 'kay?'

He raises his chakram in a mock-salute and smirks, but it's not the same smirk he'd have sent my way a year ago. I pull a face at him, and Vien and Linnea, sitting behind me, snicker. This is our routine; our way of bringing some levity to the dark work we now do.

The first of the nightmares scurries out of the alleyway and we swing into practised formation. Every one of them is human in shape, but their behaviour is anything but. Some of them swing from lampposts, others scuttle on all fours.

We go to work, silent for the most part, trying to ignore the fact that it feels as though we are killing people, not nightmares.

'A little help!' I hear Linnea shout. She's hemmed in by nightmares, a stone wall behind her and her weapon, a mace, lying just beyond her reach.

'I'm on it,' I say into my helmet.

I leap from Lamb's saddle into the air, escaping the clutches of the earthbound nightmares for a few moments. Calling upon my Immral is getting easier, but it still requires a degree of concentration I can't achieve if I'm in the middle of battle. The familiar crackle in the back of my head comes quickly, and I direct it full force at the nightmares surrounding Linnea. They resist me. I can sense hundreds of imaginations bolstering their forms; a wave of fear and prejudice lending them strength. I feel the inspyre that winds through the nightmares' bones and muscle and skin and pinch it with my mind, folding them like origami. Heads meet feet, hinging at the waist. Arms flatten and tuck back; joints pop. It's horrific, but effective. Linnea leaps out of the way, retrieves her mace and rejoins the fray.

The time was when the final blow dealt to a pack of nightmares would be cause for celebration. Now when Samson shoots the last dream – an old man with wild hair and an even wilder beard – no one cheers. None of us say it, but we all feel it. These nightmares mark a sea change in the minds of dreamers. Their imaginations are contracting, unable to conceive of anything more frightening than someone who looks like them but isn't.

'Bring the clear-up crew in,' Samson says into his helmet, and a few moments later the streets are swarming with apothecaries and veneurs. This is a recent measure. It's becoming more difficult to avoid hurting dreamers in our skirmishes, hence the apothecaries. The veneurs are an attempt to alter the nearby dreamers' minds a little – to give them a friendly nudge away from the polarised thinking that's become so prevalent of late. It's now common practice to see a morrigan pecking at a dreamer, the veneur guiding the creature to remove the fear and anger dotted there, like pockmarks. Or seeds.

'You alright, old girl?' one of the veneurs asks Lamb, bringing me into the present. A hooded morrigan sits on his shoulder, ruffling its beak through his hair. To anyone else this would be positively alarming – the morrigans feed off imaginations and memories, so keeping them away from your brain would seem like the sensible thing to do. This veneur, however, is unfazed.

'Don't call my pony old, Brandon,' I say to him, trying to keep a straight face.

'She doesn't mind, do you, ancient girl?' he says, patting Lamb's muzzle. 'Ow!' He looks up at me, astonished. 'She nipped me!'

'Told you.'

'No animal has ever nipped me before in my whole life.'

'Lamb's special,' Samson says, riding up behind me. 'I think you're wanted with a dreamer over there, Brandon.'

'Righty-ho,' Brandon says, giving Lamb another affectionate pat. She flicks her ears at him. I can tell that she regards him in the same way I do: he can be irritating, but he's basically a puppy, and as such will be tolerated.

'Ready to head back?' Samson asks me.

'So much yes.'

The return to Tintagel is quieter than it once was. It's not just the nightmares that preoccupy us. It's the silence. Annwn used to be so full of noise. It was a cacophony of birdsong, dragon roars, the conversations and shouts and whispers of millions of dreamers. It was dizzying and annoying and impossible to hear myself think at times. But it had energy. Life.

Now the only sounds we hear are our horses' hooves on the cobbles, or the mournful cry of a lonely seal on the banks of the Thames. The sole constant is the quiet murmur of thousands of dreamers: *One Voice. One Voice. One Voice*.

Our route takes us back along the river. Only a few months ago the waters would be peppered with dolphins, and sirens would call out to us from the wreckage of ships. Now the water is still. The sharks and kelpies haven't been seen since July. The rest of London isn't faring much better. The streets we ride down were once awash with hardened merchants and weary women plying their trades; with bears and dogs escaping baiting games. The buildings would switch between the stark 1970s concrete of Ithr's version and the buildings that were razed to make way for it – structures of timber and plaster, stone and straw. Now the area is an exact replica of the one in Ithr, except here the buildings feel a little greyer than they do in the real world.

'Sometimes I wish you could just blast every nightmare we meet,' Nerizan says as we move down the Strand. 'Do us out of a job. That'd be great.'

'Speak for yourself,' Ollie responds. 'Some of us like earning our keep.'

'Fern isn't a machine.' Samson looks back from his place at the front of the regiment and throws me a rare smile. He and Ollie are the only ones in Bedevere who know how much I chafe at my situation. I need to save my power for the truly dangerous situations, given I still can't use it without getting pounding headaches and nosebleeds. But I also hate it when people assume I'm this all-powerful god of all things inspyre. It only reminds me of my shortcomings.

'It's not easy, being the Chosen One, is it?' Ollie sometimes jokes and, even though I force a smile, I wish I could return to my old, grumpy self and snap at him. *What would you know? You got the shit half of the power. I'm the one everyone's looking to for hope.*

If I sound despondent and irritable, it's because I am. Every time I step foot in Annwn, I am reminded of my weakness. I love this world, but it's dying, all because I'm not strong enough to save it.

Chapter 2

As we approach Tintagel, the reeves on the walls pause to greet us. The stone at this part of the castle has been crumbling for months, the first sign of weakness it has shown since it was built in King Arthur's reign. Now repairing it is a daily task, and loose stone is proving more and more difficult to come across.

'We might need your help here soon,' one of the reeves calls as we pass.

I nod stiffly.

'Ask Lord Allenby,' Samson tells the reeve. 'I can't afford to lose one of my lieutenants for long.'

'We can't afford to lose anyone,' I hear another Bedevere knight, Milosz, say from further back. 'Samhain can't come soon enough.'

He is absolutely right. Our two battles with Medraut's treitres have left us hopelessly underpowered, and not just in the knights. The other lores joined the second battle last year and were punished sorely for it – they aren't fighters, after all, and they were easy targets for the monsters. We have seen to it that no treitre's going to risk coming anywhere near Ollie and me now we know how to bring them down – by finding their greatest fear – but we still don't have enough numbers to maintain regular, full patrols of London. Our only hope is to recruit a lot more thanes at Samhain.

As we skirt the castle walls and approach the gate, the drawbridge lowers to admit us. A dog, outlined in blue inspyre, barks as we approach and is gently rebuffed when it tries to run across. We have enough strays in the castle already; the veneurs don't want another added to their care. In the courtyard, apothecaries are tending to a group of dreamers brought in by Palomides. I used to be shocked by their appearance but it's now a common occurrence – mouths disappeared, holes bored into the back of their skulls to let out the independent thoughts. Medraut's work – part of his ongoing efforts to make everyone submit to his singular vision of the future.

We take our horses back to the stables and rub them down before letting them out to graze in the castle grounds.

'No eating the lilac,' I tell Lamb as I give her a farewell pat on the bum. 'The apothecaries had a real go at me for that last time. They need it for the morrigans.'

She wiggles her ears at me as if to say, *Yeah, yeah, whatever,* and I have never felt more empathy for my father.

Samson joins me as I walk from the stables towards the castle. I can't wait to get into the knights' chamber, where my usual armchair awaits beside a roaring fire. It's the perfect tonic for tonight's patrol.

'You okay?' he asks, moving over to my side of the path to let a gaggle of reeves past. His arm brushes mine, and warmth floods my cheeks. *God, Fern,* I think, *get a hold of yourself.*

'Are you?' I reply.

He half smiles at my refusal to answer the question. 'I used to hate waking up and going back to Ithr.'

'Now you don't?'

'No, I still hate it.' He smiles. 'But I hate coming to Annwn too.'

'Yeah,' I say, 'it's like watching someone you love die slowly, isn't it?'

'What do you mean?'

'Well, you support them, obviously, but really all you want to do is remember what they were like when they were properly alive. I'll do whatever I can to protect Annwn, I really will. But I wish I could go back to the way it was when I first became a knight.'

'That's exactly it, Fern. Exactly. Sometimes . . .' He pauses, as though he's not sure he should admit this. 'Is it awful that sometimes I wish I'd died instead of Rafe? Not,' he adds quickly, catching my alarm, 'because I'm suicidal or anything. I just . . . It's like you said. I'd just like to remember Annwn as it was, not like it is now.'

We lapse into silence as we walk up the steps. Samson hauls the door open and ushers me through first. Inside Tintagel, the bustle is as busy as ever. It's a hive in here, a quiet hum of activity and purpose. To my right is the hospital, where a steady stream of apothecaries carries dreamers and thanes in and out of treatment. To my left Maisie, the harker captain, is hunched over the Round Table. To the inexperienced eye, nothing has changed. But dread and anxiety hang over the castle in a permanent cloud.

'For what it's worth,' I tell Samson as we fall into step beside each other once more, 'I don't think Rafe would have liked that idea very much. And nor do I.'

It's the boldest thing I've ever said to him. My heart hammers, worried that I've misstepped; misread the nature of our professional relationship. But then Samson smiles. 'It's okay, Fern. I'm not one to give up on something. I'll see it through to the end.'

'That's not as comforting as you seem to think it is,' I say.

Rachel, a harker my age, raises a hand as we pass the cloisters where she works.

'Good reporting tonight,' Samson says to her.

She doesn't reply, her head buried in her notes. I raise my eyebrows at Samson: not long ago Rachel would have glowed at such a small compliment from the knight captain. At the very least she'd have tried to engage us in conversation: *her* regiment, she'd call us, as if she wasn't a harker and we weren't knights.

'So . . .' I try to restart the conversation, but Samson stops me with a hand to the shoulder.

'You go ahead, okay, Fern?' he says, and turns back. I hover in the middle of the cloisters, watching as he approaches Rachel. Guilt fills my stomach. This is why Samson is the leader and not me. My instinct had been to acknowledge Rachel's strange behaviour but move on – she's not my concern, even though I suppose we'd call each other friends. Samson, though – Samson cares.

That's why he could never like you.

I turn on my heel and march to the knights' chamber. I don't need Samson to like me. I don't want him to like me.

And anyway, he has a girlfriend. He told me so himself a few months ago.

In the knights' chamber, I deposit my scimitar into my locker and pull chairs into a semblance of a circle in one corner of the room. I throw myself into one and wait for the other regiment heads and lieutenants to arrive back from their patrols. Ollie's next in, accompanied by Natasha, Gawain's head. Behind them is Amina, Lancelot's leader.

'Thanks for your help today,' Natasha says as she slides into the seat beside me. 'Things got bad in Soho.'

Ollie takes the seat on my other side and kicks me gently under the table. 'No problem. Piece of cake for us.'

'It's not,' Natasha says, gripping my hand, 'I know it's not. Really, thank you.'

The heads of the day patrols join us, clutching mugs of warming, milky lotus juice in preparation for a difficult shift, and the conversation moves on to comparing notes from the night's patrol. As usual when Samson isn't around to keep things in order, the conversation invariably moves onto other matters. Medraut matters . . .

'. . . I really think we need to address the ghosts . . .'

'. . . did you see what he did to that group of dreamers the other day? It was as though he'd been trying to *plant* something in their heads. One of the apothecaries told me . . .'

'. . . my sister forgot her imaginary friend's name yesterday. I know that seems stupid but I can't help but think it's got something to do with Medraut . . .'

'Can we concentrate?' Samson interrupts, standing over us. When I see him from this angle I notice how different he looks. It's not tiredness, that's too simple a description. It's . . . worry? Fear? Frustration? Maybe a mixture of all three. I could ask Ollie what he thinks, but he'd only smile at me oddly and ask why I was so interested in Samson's emotions.

I'm about to start taking notes on tonight's patrol when a reeve pops her head round the door.

'Fern? You're up.'

Natasha grins. 'Lucky bitch.'

I pull a face at her as I rise. 'Want to swap? I'd take patrol notes over *Jin* any day.'

'Play nice,' Ollie says, grabbing my pen and paper.

'I'm always nice,' I say sweetly, eliciting a snort from every person round the table *and* the waiting reeve.

The reeve leads me into the warren of corridors next to the hospital, and directs me towards a room tucked away at the end of one. I knock reluctantly and open the door without waiting for an answer. The space beyond is cramped and dark, a high, small window the only source of light. Two armchairs face each other. One is occupied by one of my least favourite people in the world. It's a long list, but she's managed it.

Jin is thin-faced and thin-lipped and not the kind of person you'd peg as an apothecary at first glance. She sits, straight-backed, in an armchair designed for slouching.

'Get lost again?' Jin says. 'I'd have thought your Immral would lead you to the right place.'

'Nope. Still a regular person,' I respond.

'Sit down then.'

Jin and I eye each other with barely disguised hatred as I sink into the chair and curl my booted legs up onto the fabric, just to annoy her. These sessions run weekly, more or less, and I have tried everything in my power to get out of them. Mandated therapy for the knights and harkers involved in the battle against the treitres. There is nothing therapeutic about time spent with Jin.

'So, are you still getting headaches?' Jin asks.

I shrug, which is my standard response to any question she poses.

'Okay.' She raises her eyebrows at her notes. 'What about the latest news in Ithr? Anything you'd like to share about that?'

'I don't watch the news,' I reply.

'Really? You don't keep an eye on what Medraut's doing?'

'Nope.'

'And you don't think that's a bit neglectful? A bit disrespectful of your power?'

I hold her gaze. 'No, that's what *you* think.'

Jin purses her lips. Then she leans – no, hinges – forward. 'I can't help you if you don't open up, Fern.'

'I'm fine,' I say. 'I don't need someone like you poking around in my head.'

Jin all but sneers, 'Oh right, only Immrals are allowed to do that.'

I stand up. 'Are we done?'

Jin shrugs this time, which I take as acquiescence. I'm halfway down the corridor before the door is slammed shut behind me. Bursting out into the fresh air of Annwn, I make my way to the platform that will take me back to my bedroom in Ithr. The others like to tease me about the enmity between Jin and me, but the truth is, she genuinely did start it.

I had been cautiously excited about my first session with her. Natasha had told me how useful she had found hers. And I had so much that I needed to get off my chest. But I'd walked into one of those rooms and been hit instantly by the intensity of her dislike. The way she'd looked at me, the way she'd asked me if I felt I'd really done all I could to prevent the deaths of my friends. At first I'd been confused and hurt, but I soon found my way back to my comfort zone – the place where I can snap at people, secure in the knowledge that I owe them nothing.

Sometimes, I miss being that person. It's exhausting, trying to understand others and care what they think. It's exhausting feeling all the time as though I'm failing the people I've grown to like – even love. And in that sense, I suppose, Jin *is* helping me. More than she'd ever realise.

Chapter 3

Waking up in Ithr, I feel as bone tired as I would have if I hadn't slept at all. When I was first accepted into the knights I'd wake rejuvenated, even if it had been a tough night. This lethargy is becoming a common occurrence, for more than just me. My dad has deep bags under his eyes. That might, granted, be because Ollie and I now have a habit of needing to be rushed to hospital with blood coming out of our eyes and ears, but I don't think that's the whole reason. I think it's because Annwn is no longer the kind of place that helps dreamers to process everything that they've been holding on to in Ithr. Medraut is turning it steely grey, like his soul. Grey doesn't sustain anyone.

I pad down to breakfast still in my PJs. This, too, is a new development. I used to stay in my room until the last moment, but nowadays Ollie and I eat our cereal in companionable silence. Chatting is still beyond us – in Ithr at least, where so much of what we want to discuss concerns Annwn. Still, there are some things I can tell my brother, albeit in thinly veiled code.

'I'm going to Bow tonight,' I say, pouring milk over my Weetabix.

Ollie eyes Dad, who's munching on toast and peanut butter while watching the morning news.

'I can't tonight,' Ollie says. 'I'm going to FOTS.'

I roll my eyes. 'I'll see you at home then, I guess.'

FOTS is exactly as stupid as the name suggests. 'Friends of the Sleeping.' A ton of the groups were set up in the wake of all the deaths a few months ago. Counselling sessions for the friends and families of the people who were found dead in their beds, apparently having passed away in their sleep. Ollie and I, of course, know that the real cause was Medraut's treitres slaughtering them, but that's not information we can share.

I actually went with Ollie to the first session he attended, in a pub basement that vibrated with the bass music playing on the floor above. The group was small back then. Everyone knew someone who'd died, but as they talked about their loved ones, all I could think about was how insincere it felt to be witness to their grief when I knew what had really happened.

So tonight, while Ollie talks about his feelings with strangers, I plan on sharing mine with a friend. In the meantime, I have to get to school unscathed. You would think that should be simple, but the way I look, in the world Medraut is crafting? Not a chance.

'Don't watch the telly, Dad, it rots your brain,' I tell our father as I swing my bag over my shoulder and wind a scarf around my neck.

I wasn't being totally honest with Jin when I said that I never watched the news. I keep an eye on it partly because Dad has it on almost constantly now. There's a never-ending scroll of politicians and celebrities and journalists on-screen, and to my untrained eye they all seem to be saying the same thing at different volumes. The effect is the same as the greyness of Annwn: to suck a little colour from the world.

It's like a parasite. It's everywhere, and it's growing.

'Freak,' people hiss as I pass.

'Devil,' I hear them mutter on the tube.

One man leers at me and, when I get off, follows me up the stairs. I'm used to this kind of thing now, though, and I run up to one of the tube workers and ask for directions. Her presence is enough to put the man off for now. I know that if I can't stop Medraut soon, then not even that will save me.

London used to be the kind of city where you could prance around semi-naked and no one would do more than look away self-consciously. But now there's a stark difference between those who have submitted to Medraut and those who are holding out. A subtle uniform has pervaded, with a strength that Kensington's fashion houses could only dream of.

Everywhere I look, people are wearing a monochrome colour palette. Businessmen don grey pinstripe suits; women dress in demure, knee-length skirts. A few times I've spotted people frantically attempting to cover their tattoos with make-up on their way into work, ashamed of the decorations they once loved enough to get engraved onto their skin.

Those of us who don't conform stand out. Ollie has more than once encouraged me to wear contact lenses to disguise my eyes. If I was sensible, I would. My scar might still mark me out but it would be more acceptable than red irises. But it's the principle of it. 'That's exactly what Medraut wants,'

I tell my brother, but it's more complicated than that. I would feel like a hypocrite, working against Medraut in Annwn but pretending to be one of his followers in Ithr. It would feel as though I'd abandoned those strong enough to stand against him.

'You're so bloody moral.' Ollie rolls his eyes when I get into one of these rants.

I shrug. 'I got the morals . . .'

'I got the looks, I know, I know.' It's an old phrase, once wielded as an insult. The sting is gone from it now.

It's not just fashion that's been affected. The curved walls of the tube stations used to be plastered in a cacophony of coloured adverts. Beautiful book covers; humorous announcements for boring banks; garish statements about gyms and diets. It took me longer to notice the change than with clothes. It was Ollie who pointed it out, but once he'd shown me I couldn't stop seeing it. The adverts are more muted these days – not just in colour. Today, as I take the escalator up to street level, I notice that the font of every single advert is the same. The slogans are gone: all that remains is a factual statement of what they want us to buy.

I never thought I'd miss bad humour and overblown advertising, but here we are.

Padding up the steps to school, I wonder what fresh hell today's lessons have in store. Bosco College was, for a while, a haven. I may not have had friends, but I had peace and the teachers' protection. Now even those professional bonds are cracking. Hardly surprising, I suppose, given that Sebastien Medraut is at the school on a regular basis because his daughter goes here.

Lottie Medraut is another source of anguish for me. A few months ago I tortured her in Annwn in the hope of harvesting information about her father's plans. In Ithr, she might not remember what I did, but I can tell that somewhere in her psyche she knows that I'm dangerous. Rumours have been spread about me in Bosco. The walls in the girls' toilets have *Fern King Must Die* carved into them with deep strokes.

Today, I sit down at my desk and find a note stuck to it. *Evil evil evil* is scrawled in messy red pen. When I find these notes, something tells me from the way she looks at me – edge of her mouth upturned – that Lottie is behind at least some of them. There's no real bite in them, which matches her. Notes are hardly the worst thing that's been done to me. She'll have to go to some lengths to beat the burn scar that Jenny caused. Anyway, I deserve everything Lottie throws at me, even if she doesn't fully understand that. It's the others I have to worry about.

Luckily no one at Bosco has stooped to serious violence yet, but they're coming closer. Little things that are easily denied: an elbow to the ribs in a busy corridor, a foot stomped on, a hair tug. As I pull my notebook and pencil case from my bag, someone shoves my chair hard from behind, so that my forehead knocks against my desk. I look for the perpetrator, but whoever it is has already sat down. No one will meet my eyes.

These may seem like small offences compared to what some of my fellow 'freaks' are going through, but I know how easily small acts of violence can ignite. The tinder has been laid. All it needs is a match.

Chapter 4

I used to spend my breaks and lunches poring over my knightbook – my little notebook filled with information about Annwn. But I can't any more. My nights spent patrolling Annwn are so intense, so riddled with sadness, that I have nothing left to give when I wake up.

Instead, I do what I always used to do when I needed sanctuary: I draw.

The art room is tucked away in a dilapidated wing of Bosco. The classroom is cluttered with old desks resigned to ending their lives being defaced by paint. The earthy smell of clay comforts me. When I used to come here there would usually be a few others – mostly loners, like me – working quietly. Now, though, I am alone.

'You'll have to be quick to grab a seat,' the art teacher jokes when I arrive. Mr Nolan's a sweet, awkward man who sports a moustache that looks as though it wished it wasn't there. He busies himself washing paintbrushes while I retrieve my portfolio from a cupboard. The swathes of paper inside are covered in the faces of the dead. Ramesh and Phoebe, as I remembered them in Annwn: joyful, comfortable, alight with purpose.

'They look kind,' Mr Nolan says, making me jump.

'They were,' I say.

'Ah. Sleeping?'

I nod. The question has become a shorthand for asking about those who died in their sleep. I hate it. It's not just that I know they didn't simply fall asleep and never wake up; it's that it violates something positive. I know now how powerful dreams can be. I've seen what happens when people are denied them. Making that harmless word, *sleeping*, a platitude for genocide makes me want to scream.

I flick to the back of my portfolio. My latest artwork is quite different from the rest. Six squares dotted around the page, each containing a different pattern: one caramel flames; one geometric purples and silvers. I'm working on the third now – all mint and forest greens.

It might seem like doodles to most people, but this is the most important piece of artwork I own. It is my answer to Sebastien Medraut's mahogany puzzle box. His was filled with plans for the destruction of Annwn and Ithr. These squares are the first sketches for my own box. Mine won't literally hold my thoughts, of course – if it did it wouldn't be very pretty, given most of my headspace is devoted to despising Medraut. It will just be a trinket in Ithr. Each square represents something I love about Annwn. The flames for the strength I found within myself there. The purples and silvers for Tintagel and the thanes. The greens are for the beauty of Annwn itself, and all that grows there. It serves as a reminder to me, when Annwn is dying, of why I must save it.

'You know, if you need to talk to someone . . .' Mr Nolan starts, making me jump again.

'I'm fine. Thanks,' I say. The number of people who've tried to get me to *talk* to total strangers in the last few months makes me think they don't know me at all. The truth is, I don't need Mr Nolan or Jin or anyone else, because I already have someone to talk to. The ideal listener, because they cannot reply.

After school, I go to them.

Bow is just one stop before Stratford, where I'd usually get off to go home. The path to the cemetery is now as familiar as the one to my mum's gravestone. The place I'm looking for is near the back, where dozens of fresh graves sit; all those who died in their sleep in this part of London over the last few months, all buried side by side. Sometimes I like to imagine that if Medraut ever dared, or deigned, to come here that the injustice of it would make the bodies push through the soft earth and drag him underneath to join them.

The headstone was only erected a few weeks ago. There are still fresh flowers at the grave, and a garland of pink blooms has been laid over one corner of the stone.

Reyansh Halder, the engraving reads.

Loving son and brother.

Missed every day.

Sleep in peace.

It's been months since Reyansh – or Ramesh, as I knew him – was killed in Annwn, and I still miss him. Phoebe is buried somewhere near Bristol and I wasn't able to get to her funeral, so Ramesh's grave has become the place where I speak to both of them.

'You'd think we'd have got used to not hearing your loud voice in the chambers,' I tell him, 'but it's so quiet without you and Phoebe. I'm lieutenant now. Well, me and Ollie are joint lieutenants. We'd be your bosses. Bet you'd have liked that.'

I clear away some cut grass from the green stones that cover the grave. Ramesh died before Ollie and I really became friends again. I think about the message Ollie wrote to Ramesh after his death: *You knew who I really am and you liked me anyway*. Ramesh had that way about him – of needling out someone's secrets then holding them close, using them to make that person better. He knew who I really was too – he knew the worst of me – and he liked me anyway. I wonder what Ollie told him. Maybe he told Ramesh about what he did to me.

'I'm trying to let people in,' I continue. 'I feel like there are people I can trust now. Lord Allenby, maybe. And . . . and Samson . . .'

I trail off. I can't quite put a finger on what's going on between Samson and me. I've never been good at reading people so I'm probably finding all kinds of things in his behaviour that aren't there. Sometimes I sense a tension when we're riding next to each other; an elastic band connecting our knees. Sometimes his eyes flick towards me in the knights' chamber, when he should be writing reports. I feel each one like a pulse in my back, in my cheeks. In the deep places I am only just starting to explore.

'Sorry, this is stupid.' I smile at the grave. Ramesh and I never spoke about that kind of thing – we had better things to do, like saving humanity from its nightmares. Talking about a crush feels petty. I'm probably just projecting onto Samson.

After all, he's got a girlfriend in Ithr. And even if he didn't, who'd fancy a freak like me?

Something catches my eyes over the other side of the cemetery. In the distance, a shadow rises from the circular memorial listing the names of the dead from the world wars. Maybe it's my mind playing tricks on me, but for a moment I thought the memorial – and the shadow – glowed with a faint blue light. The light of inspyre.

I move towards it. Yes. There, very faintly, beside the monument, is a ghost. Well, to the uninitiated it's a ghost. To those of us who know about Annwn, it's a dream. One that has escaped through a portal between the worlds. It's been happening more and more frequently of late. This isn't the first time I've seen one. Even the newspapers are picking up on the strange occurrences.

One of the cemetery's groundskeepers moves past with a broom, casting me a doubtful look. When I turn back to the memorial, both the ghost and the blue light have vanished. Dreams cannot last for long in Ithr: the physics of this world aren't the same as those in Annwn. I turn back to Ramesh's gravestone, but before I can resume my conversation with him I hear a voice.

'Who are you?' It belongs to someone I recognise from Ramesh's funeral. Then she stood at the front of the church and glared at the congregation, daring us to grieve. She's got Ramesh's nut-brown skin and the same chin as him, but there's a flintiness to her expression that Ramesh never had – his eyes were always kind, even when he was disappointed in me.

I back away, but she follows. 'What were you doing?'

'I was friends with Ra– Reyansh,' I tell her, intimidated even though I'm older than her.

'He didn't have any friends,' she says.

I flinch, protective of Ramesh even though he can't hear her. I don't want to answer. I don't want to have to lie to my friend's sister.

'Maybe you didn't know him as well as you thought.'

It's a nasty answer to a girl still grieving her brother, but I can't help it. I'm annoyed at her presence even if she has more right to be here than me, and I don't like that she had so little faith in her brother.

'What do you mean?' she says, a hint of surprise bleeding through the coldness of her tone.

'It doesn't matter.'

'Wait . . .' she says as I dodge past her. 'I remember you. You came to the funeral . . .'

'Sorry for your loss,' I say over my shoulder. As I leave the cemetery, I look back. She's watching me still, standing lonely against the backdrop of rows upon rows of fresh graves.

Chapter 5

'How was it?' Ollie whispers to me as we wait for Dad and Clemmie to serve up dinner that evening.

I shrug. I don't particularly want to mention my encounter with Ramesh's sister. I'm already feeling ashamed of how I handled it, and I know Ollie will make me feel even worse. 'How was FOTS?'

'You don't care,' he says.

'True.'

But not even my nonchalance can dent a strange buoyancy in Ollie's demeanour.

'What's got into you?' I ask, nudging him with my foot.

'Nothing.'

'Something's happened,' I insist. 'Why are you so zen?'

He pulls a face at me. 'I've been meditating.'

'No, you haven't.'

'Smoking weed.'

'Stop it.'

'I'm just a naturally happy person, Fern, I don't know what to tell you.'

I snort, and drop it, for now. It's clear I'm not getting the truth out of my brother. His cheeks are flushed, his eyes sparkling in a way they haven't for years. Unease prickles me. I think I know what this means. It's not that I'm jealous. It's that this reminds me of Jenny, and the weird friendship Ollie had with her. Look where that led him – led us.

'We're still on for tonight, right?' I ask, hating the insecurity lacing my voice.

'Wouldn't miss it,' he says quickly, and we both lapse into silence as Dad plonks a bowl of steaming casserole in front of us. Clemmie pops a saucepan of mashed potato in the middle of the table as she settles into her chair. I keep watching Ollie as we all make small talk, but he won't meet my eye. My distraction means that it takes me a while to realise when the conversation turns a corner.

'I mean, my heart goes out to the families but it really was a provocation,' Clemmie is saying.

'What was a provocation?' I ask.

Ollie shakes his head at me.

'No one deserves a thrashing like that,' Dad tells Clemmie.

She just shrugs, then turns to me. 'There was a fight last night over in Romford.'

'What happened?'

'Oh –' Clemmie flicks her hand dismissively and takes another spoonful of casserole – 'it was six of one, half a dozen of the other.'

Something about the way she says it, and about the expression on my family's faces, makes me push further.

'Who was involved?' I ask.

'Just a group of idiots protesting a One Voice meeting. The

One Voicers didn't take kindly to being interrupted. Things got out of hand.'

'They attacked the protesters?'

'Yes,' Dad growls.

'Well, really, they were having a quiet meeting,' Clemmie says, clearly exasperated that she's not getting the support she was expecting. 'Can't people discuss their views without being shouted at any more?'

'How badly did they hurt the protestors?' Ollie asks quietly.

Clemmie huffs and turns her attention back to her dinner.

I raise my eyebrows at Ollie. We both understand what's happening. Medraut's mind control is getting to Clemmie. Keen to escape the glacial atmosphere filling our kitchen-diner, I finish my plate in double quick time. 'Homework,' I tell them as I bolt upstairs.

In the comfort of my bedroom, I look up the fight, certain that Clemmie was twisting the truth. A plethora of articles come up almost immediately. One shows a photo of a bunch of One Voicers. Their clothes and hairstyles are so similar they may as well be wearing a uniform. The protestors are dressed differently – a range of jeans and hoodies and t-shirts – but as I look at the photo the two groups merge into one. If I only look at their expressions, they look the same. Their faces are twisted, mouths snarling, eyes flinty.

Shaking off the feeling that I'm being disloyal to the protesters by having such thoughts, I read the article.

Three members of grassroots protest group Shout Louder are said to be in critical condition . . . Sebastien Medraut's One Voice party has risen from obscurity in recent years to challenge the prime minister's position . . .

I turn my attention from Medraut's photo to one of Shout Louder's founder, Constantine Hale. It's an elaborate name for a man who looks as though he spends at least half his time on an allotment.

Hale condemned the violence, the article says. *'We were protesting peacefully against a party with insidious and dangerous beliefs . . .'*

Well, at least he's got that right.

A little more searching takes me to a video of the incident. Just a few seconds in, I wish I hadn't watched it. The two groups are shouting obscenities at each other, the words lost in noise. Then someone – I can't even tell if it's a One Voicer or a protester – makes a sudden movement. And that's it: fists against heads, teeth into arms, knees into stomachs, feet into ribs. It's rabid. I stop the video, but not before hearing the crunch of bones breaking.

Clemmie's high-pitched laugh drifts up the stairs. I think of Clemmie's words – *It really was a provocation* – and my face crumples. She thinks the protestors deserved that beating. I've never been particularly kind to her, but that doesn't mean I don't like her in my own way. She's always seemed so harmless. And Dad . . . at least he didn't agree with what the One Voice thugs did. Instead, he just made some disapproving noises and, from the sound of the merry conversation coming up through the carpet, made up with his girlfriend at the earliest opportunity.

I can't help but wonder if I could have done something to

keep Clemmie and Dad on my side. I voice my worries to Ollie when we arrive in Annwn that night.

'Do you think – if I'd been nicer to Clemmie . . .' I begin.

Ollie shrugs, which is not quite the reassurance I'd hoped for.

'Come on,' I press him, 'you're the mind reader.'

Ollie sighs. 'I don't know. Maybe? I mean, I can only read Clemmie's mind in Annwn, and I haven't. Maybe she'd be more sympathetic, or more like Dad, if you'd been kinder. But I thought she was my friend and that doesn't seem to have done much good, does it?'

'But you look normal,' I say. 'She's got no reason not to like you.'

He glances at me then – a clouded, troubled glance – then looks forward again. 'Yeah,' he says. 'I'm normal. Great.'

We don't go straight to the stables, but pop into the knights' chamber in the hope of catching Samson. Sure enough, he's there, head together with Natasha and Nerizan. The group parts to welcome us in.

'Ready for the riverside route?' Samson asks Ollie and me. 'Nerizan had an idea –'

'Actually,' Ollie interrupts, 'do you think we could catch up with you?'

Samson's smile falters. 'Just for a sunset,' I say quickly. 'We'll be quick, promise.'

'Sure,' he says, as Nerizan nods.

'I can tack Lamb and Balius for you before I head out with Gawain,' Natasha says. 'That should save you some time.'

'Thank you,' I say, trying to show them how much I mean it.

'Come on.' Ollie grabs my arm, but I feel the need to say something more.

'You know –' I begin, but Samson places a hand on my shoulder.

'You don't need to explain, Fern,' he says. 'You guys have clearly got stuff going on, and you're not ready to share. We trust you. Tell us when – if – you can. Until then, we've got your backs, okay?'

Impulsively, I throw my arms around his neck, trying not to let myself linger in the hug. Then I pull away and don't let myself look back as I follow Ollie out of the room. My brother and I skirt the main hall and trot down the back stairs to the lower floor, where the dungeons and the archives are situated. We press against the wall and I cast my Immral round the corner, sensing a handful of reeves in the lobby.

'Ready?' I whisper to Ollie.

'Do your thing,' he replies, and holds out his hand. I take it, ignoring the electric shock that always accompanies us joining the two halves of our Immral. I sink into my power, spinning the inspyre around us into a veil; one that mirrors the wall behind us, blocking us from view. Needles prickle my skull as I pull Ollie across the floor. I don't want to spend all of my energy on this illusion when we have a full patrol afterwards. We dodge past reeves and dreams, finally pressing ourselves against the wall next to the archive door. I reach out a hand, making sure the veil of inspyre is still covering me, and test the handle.

Locked. Well, not for long.

Sending a tendril of inspyre into the lock, I twist and mould it into the right shape. There's a clunk as the bolt draws back, and a reeve turns around to check where the sound came from. Beneath our veil, Ollie stretches out his free arm. Through our clasped hands, I can feel a twinge as he tests the reeve's mind, pressing here and there until he finds the right point to twist. The reeve shakes his head, confused, and turns away. Ollie casts me a guilty look – neither of us like using our powers on our fellow thanes, but right now secrecy is more important.

Checking that no one is watching, I turn the handle, open the door and my brother and I slide into the empty archives.

The air is close in here, as though the millions of records and books, some of them thousands of years old, are breathing creatures, waiting to be awoken. I let the veil of inspyre dissipate, certain that we're alone.

'Down here,' Ollie says, and we race along the corridor to the end of the stacks.

'Stop,' I say, pointing to one of the labels on the tallest bookcase. 'It's here.'

Ollie sets about hauling the stack apart from its fellow, creating a narrow aisle. I follow him in, taking a deep breath, my fingers lingering on the label marking the information it holds.

Excalibur.

Chapter 6

Ollie and I have been discussing Mum's letter for months.

I have left a gift for you in Annwn. King Arthur's sword – Excalibur. I found it and have hidden it for you to use, when the time is right. If you have found this letter, you will have found the first clue and be on the path already.

My brother's immediate instinct was to tell Lord Allenby, but I asked him not to. I had been excited at the prospect of finding a legendary sword at first, but as the days went on, I found myself worrying that Excalibur would become just another way to set me apart me from the other thanes. Another pressure heaped on my shoulders. Maybe enough to crush me completely. And so I asked Ollie for a reprieve – keep Mum's letter secret for now.

And then there's the fact that keeping this between Ollie and me is bringing us closer. I have come to treasure the moments when we walk to school together, or meet up in the park, to discuss our plans for finding Excalibur. As soon as we tell anyone else that intimacy will be stretched. I don't want it to tear.

The last time I was in the archives I was looking illegally for information about my mother, and stumbled across a portrait of her, painted by the woman who would go on to murder her. That portrait still sits in my locker up in the knights' chamber. The fact that it was painted by her murderer doesn't bother me as much as it should – perhaps it's because I understand that what my mum did to Ellen led to everything that happened over the ensuing years. It's something that plagues me – maybe if Mum hadn't decided to experiment with morrigans, Ellen wouldn't have become a treitre, Medraut would have struggled to find one to exact his revenge, and then no one would have been loyal enough to him to train another several hundred treitres over the course of the next fifteen years. The ripples of Mum's actions haunt me, so if I blame Ellen, I have to blame Mum too.

'You take that end, I'll take this end,' Ollie says to me, heading deeper into the aisle. I run my hands over the folders, each one labelled in neat script that flickers and flows, growing bolder as I read them. I am getting used to listening to my Immral now, sensing the weight of history in each script. This one, light as a cotton ball, was written only years ago. This one is heavy like coal – centuries old. I pull out the older ones, hoping they'll give me a good start, and kneel on the floor to read them.

'What's The Great Betrayal?' Ollie whispers from further down.

I shrug. 'Dunno. Why?'

He holds up a huge tome. The title printed on the front of the leather: *The Great Betrayal*.

'Well, and this is just an idea, you could read it to find out?'

Ollie cuts his eyes at me, but opens the book. Then turns the page. And keeps turning.

'Fast reading there,' I comment.

Ollie looks up at me. 'There's nothing in here.'

'What?'

I scoot over to see what he means. The book's first pages are blank; not even the faintest impression of ink remaining on them. Ollie flicks through the rest of the tome. It is totally empty.

'That's weird,' I say.

'It's more than that.' Ollie frowns. 'I can sense something, but . . .'

He breaks off as a sound comes from an aisle a little further along from us. We look at each other, alarmed. We thought we were alone. I put one finger to my lips, and Ollie gives me another look, as if to say, *No kidding, idiot*. I place a hand against the bookshelf closest to the noise and close my eyes, reaching my power through the pages, trying to sense any movement beyond. A door that I didn't realise was there is opening on silent hinges – I can see its outline in inspyre. And there, peeking from behind the door, a human shape. I can't make out the face.

I signal to Ollie to move back into the shadow of the aisle, and whisk some inspyre together to make another veil. The person, whoever it is, pads through the archives like a cat. Evidently they don't want to be caught here either. Then they fill the space at the end of the aisle, reading the label on the heel of the bookcase, and I see who it is.

Rachel.

Ollie and I look at each other, confused, as Rachel makes

her way into the *Excalibur* aisle. Up close she looks haggard, her freckles prominent on her pale skin. She pulls at her plait as she begins removing folder after folder. I move the books Ollie and I pulled down behind us, hoping she won't come this far and bump into us, or notice the gaps on the shelves.

She begins to open the volumes in turn. The first one is also blank, just like the one Ollie found. But Rachel isn't surprised. She merely slots that volume back into its shelf and opens the next one in her pile. This contains a folder of documents labelled, *Immral Use in the 19th Century*. It's full of scribbled notes, and Rachel removes her own notebook from her pocket and sinks to the floor to start copying some of the passages.

Ollie nudges me and nods towards the door. He's right. Rachel seems to be here for the long haul and there's no way we're going to be able to find what we're looking for with her right next to us. I pull the veil more tightly over us and use a knight signal to tell Ollie my plan. He nods and grabs my hand. The spark of inspyre that always marks us joining our power can't be seen beneath the veil, but it makes a *crack* that causes Rachel to jump.

'Hello?' she whispers.

I pull Ollie up and together we fly over Rachel's head, lifting our feet to avoid kicking her. She looks up just a moment too late, and we land far enough away that she doesn't hear us. The last thing I see as Ollie pulls me onwards, back towards the main door of the archives, is Rachel returning to her work.

'What was she doing?' Ollie says once again as we ride Lamb and Balius out through the gardens and over the tower walls to avoid the harkers at the drawbridge.

I don't answer. Anxiety gnaws at my chest. She was researching Immral, and she'd been doing so for some time if she wasn't surprised by the empty pages. That means that she was probably researching something to do with Ollie and me, doesn't it? Or was she researching ways to bring Medraut down by herself? Does she not believe that I'm powerful enough to face him? I mean, I'm not, we all know it, but having someone you thought had your back make it clear that she doesn't believe in you still feels like a kick in the teeth.

'More importantly,' Ollie continues, 'we didn't get a single piece of useful information about Excalibur.'

'We sort of did,' I reply. 'We found out that something's happened to all those records. Before Rachel came in you said you felt something, didn't you?'

Ollie shakes his head. 'Not enough to really understand what happened. There was a lot of anger in them. Maybe if I had more time I could read the memories in the pages, but . . .'

We come into view of the rest of Bedevere. An apothecary is tending to a wound on Linnea's shoulder. On the other side of the road, more apothecaries tend to Samson, who is clutching the back of his head. Brandon is bandaging a nasty cut on Samson's horse's leg.

'What happened?' I say, leaping off Lamb and running over to them. There's no sign of any injured dreamers, and I can't sense any recent inspyre activity either.

'Ask *her*,' Milosz spits, pointing to Linnea.

'What?' Ollie says, walking over to Linnea. 'What's going on?'

'I saw it all,' Brandon says, his usually jovial face grim. 'Linnea was riding next to Samson, then she just reached over and tried to stab him in the head.'

'I'll be fine,' Samson says, although the blood gushing from his wound suggests otherwise. 'Is Linnea okay?'

'Why do you even care?' Vien says.

'Fern,' Ollie calls. 'We need you over here.'

I join him at Linnea's side. She stares forward vacantly as the apothecary dabs at the point where I can see Nerizan's rope was used to pull her off Samson. Ollie has one hand on her upper arm, and he holds his other hand out to me. I take it, closing my eyes to absorb whatever it is that Ollie's hearing.

One Voice. One Voice. One Voice.

I pull away. The name of Medraut's political party, in Medraut's own quiet, certain tone. It's reverberating around her body, through her bones and into her brain.

'No,' I whisper, 'he can't have.'

I bypass Ollie's hand this time, taking hold of my fellow knight's shoulders. I don't know Linnea well – not beyond the usual killing-nightmares-alongside-each-other way – but she has never shown signs of being Medraut's lackey before. She was friends with Rafe and Emory, who were both killed last year. I can't imagine her ever joining him voluntarily. I send my Immral into Linnea, searching for the source of that voice.

A taste – metallic, like petrol – seeps into my mouth. If there was any doubt before, there is none now – this is Medraut's doing. I send my thoughts through Linnea's veins, following the pulse of those words as they beat an anthem of rigidity into her soul. Up, through her heart, up through her chest and her neck and . . . there.

'It's in her ear,' I say, 'just inside the canal.'

As I pull away from Linnea, the apothecary retrieves a torch from his bag and peers inside. 'You're right,' he says. 'There is something here.'

He uses a pair of tweezers to twist at something wedged inside her ear. I couldn't get a good idea of its shape when I was looking for it – I could only tell that it was the source of the sound.

'I think . . .' the apothecary says. 'Yes. Can we get that veneur here now, please?'

Ollie looks over. 'Oi, Brandon!'

'What is it?' he asks, hurrying across the road.

'A present for you.' And the apothecary pulls out a bug. A cockroach, or something like it, except this cockroach has a proboscis designed to extend through an ear drum, deep into Linnea's head.

'Urgh,' Ollie says, giving voice to what everyone's thinking. I am watching Linnea, though. Awareness is returning to her vacant gaze.

At first she's bewildered. 'What happened?' she says. 'I felt something in my hair, and then . . .'

'There's something strapped to it,' the apothecary says, as he and Brandon peer at the creature. We all lean in closer to look.

A hole has been drilled into the bug's belly. From it, a tinny sound emanates: *One Voice. One Voice. One Voice*. A mechanical speaker, strapped to the inspyre that drives the bug, giving it a sole purpose, binding it in this shape.

'What has he done to you, you poor thing?' Brandon whispers.

Chapter 7

'We have to find Excalibur,' Ollie whispers to me later, when we're back in the stables. 'If we find Excalibur . . .'

'Then what?' I say. 'It's a sword, Ollie, that's all.'

'It's clearly not just a sword if Mum wanted you to have it.'

I don't need to hear this. I can't shake the look on Linnea's face as it was explained to her what happened, and what she'd done to Samson and his horse. She's in the hospital now, with Natasha stationed outside her bay; Medraut's cockroach may have been removed, but Lord Allenby isn't taking any chances.

'Do you really think me having a sword would have stopped Medraut from making that bug?' I hiss.

'I don't know, Fern, but isn't it the *only* thing we can do right now?' Ollie snaps.

I know he's right. We've got no way of finding out what Medraut is working on until he launches it upon us – all our attempts to get spies into his strongholds have failed since Samson and I took his puzzle box. I hate being constantly on the defensive. We have to find some way of getting an advantage, and Excalibur is the only thing I can think of that would do that. Even if it is nothing more than a symbol, symbols hold a power of their own.

'Maybe we should tell Lord Allenby –' Ollie begins.

'No,' I say, 'not yet. Look, let's try by ourselves for a bit longer, okay? Give it a month, and if we haven't found anything then we'll tell him, I promise.'

'A lot can happen in a month,' Ollie warns.

'I know. Please, Ols.'

He glares at me, but relents. 'Fine, a month.'

But as the days pass, I have to admit that it's looking more and more likely that we're going to need help. Ollie and I can't be spared for another trip to the archives, secret or otherwise. Linnea is kept in the hospital for now while the apothecaries run tests to make sure she's safe to come back to duty, which leaves Bedevere one knight down.

'Does anyone actually want her to come back anyway?' Milosz says one night as we loaf into the knights' chamber.

'Of course,' I pipe up, 'she's a good fighter. It wasn't her fault the bug got her.'

'Well said,' Natasha says, throwing her helmet onto a table. 'It could have been any of us. Some friend you are, Milosz.'

Milosz has the grace to look ashamed. Natasha's right – it could have been any of us, and sometimes it is. For the skies of Annwn are infected with Medraut's flying bugs. We find them most often in the ears of dreamers, so much so that it's become one of the many things the apothecaries check for after an altercation. But sometimes, often enough to make us wonder whether it's by design, the bugs aim for us. Knights, apothecaries, harkers – they're not fussy what lore they go for, but if there's a bug in the vicinity of a thane and a dreamer, you can be sure the bug will choose the thane.

'What are you up to, Sebastien?' Lord Allenby growls one night, after two apothecaries on the Lancelot regiment are brought back with the creatures stuck in their ears.

'Isn't it obvious, sir?' Brandon says. 'He's trying to kill us off.'

'If he wanted to kill us, he'd have made the bugs kill us,' I say. 'There's something else he's trying to do here.'

'Miss King is right, yet again,' Lord Allenby says, peering at the creatures as they're pulled from the apothecaries' ears.

Linnea eventually rejoins Bedevere, and Milosz cleaves to her. I wonder whether he's trying to make up for his lack of faith, or whether he now sees it as his personal mission to keep an eye on her.

The days tick by as Ollie and I rack our brains for a way to find Excalibur. I sequester myself in a corner most nights, after the patrol notes are done, and read Mum's letter over and over.

If you have found this letter you will have found the first clue and be on the path already.

Knowing Mum as I think I do, there's a hidden meaning to this, if only I were clever enough to work it out. I have never shown the letter to Ollie – it's too private, too wholly for me – but eventually I crack and hand it to him. Maybe he'll see something that I haven't.

As he reads Mum's words, his expression makes guilt crawl up my throat. He tries to keep a poker face, but I'm starting to know my brother. His eyes linger over the declaration of love that my mother left for me and not him. He isn't even mentioned. I imagine how that must feel – how I'd feel if Ollie were left such a letter and I wasn't.

Betrayed, alone, unloved. I'd feel exactly like I did for all those years when Ollie and I were enemies, except this time it would be worse because – well, because she's our mother. Mothers are expected to love their children equally, aren't they? Isn't that how it's supposed to work?

'It's obvious, isn't it?' Ollie says eventually. 'The clue's where we found the letter.'

'You think there's something else hidden in that hole?'

Ollie shrugs again. 'Maybe it's only something you can see, since you're the one she wanted to find it.'

'Would it really be that simple?' I muse.

'Don't overthink it, Fern,' Ollie says. 'Mum may have thought she was clever, but that didn't stop her from missing things that were right in front of her nose, did it?'

The sharpness in his voice doesn't escape me, but we don't have time to address it. We head back to the stables immediately. Lamb is unimpressed at being saddled up again so soon, and makes it known by refusing to do more than the most desultory trot. I try to make up for it with pats and carrots, but since she's not the one who's going to have to do a full day of school and homework later, my sympathy is limited.

Ollie remains quiet on the ride, and truth be told I'm not inclined to chat either. We are both lost in thoughts of Mum, and what we might find at our house. We haven't been back since the night we found her notes and the letter itself. When we arrive, though, I am curiously reluctant to go inside.

'Come on then,' Ollie says at the door. 'I can't change the house back without you, can I?'

We leave Lamb and Balius in the front garden and set to work, turning the house from what it looks like in Ithr now, into the version my mum wanted us to find.

We finish upstairs, in what would usually be my bedroom. In Annwn, it's almost totally bare except for the floral curtains.

'It would really help if we knew what we were looking for, wouldn't it?' I comment, prying up a floorboard and dipping my head inside the cavity. I'm trying to fill the void that has opened up between Ollie and me, so I'm not expecting an answer, and I don't get one. Ollie peers into the hole where he found the letter, reaching a hand inside and feeling around.

'Nothing,' he says.

I come closer. 'It's dark in there. Maybe . . .' I form a ball of inspyre in my palm, then shape it into a light bulb. Pushing it inside the cavity, I move it this way and that until . . .

'Look,' I say. It's in the bottom corner, barely perceptible against the grain of the wood, and entirely invisible without the light of my Immral. The curtains flutter, casting patterns on Ollie's inscrutable expression. Outside the open window, birdsong fills the air. Beneath the light, a tiny symbol has been etched into the oak.

'I can't see it properly,' Ollie says, his breath hot on my ear.

'It's an orchid,' I reply. Mum's favourite flower. She has left us her first clue.

Chapter 8

'The wallpaper in the dining room is covered in orchids,' Ollie says.

We stumble down the stairs and into what would be Ollie's bedroom in Ithr. There's no furniture at all in it now, just a single wall, opposite the window onto the street, that's decorated in a vintage wallpaper of exotic flowers. Ollie runs his hands across it, his eyes closed, reading its memories. When he steps away, he's sporting a nosebleed.

'Underneath the paper,' he tells me.

We each take a corner: me the bottom, him the top. He pulls away a great strip of wallpaper, and my soft artist heart breaks a little at the desecration.

As the paper comes away, letters are revealed piecemeal, painted on the plaster. It's Mum's handwriting, but messier than usual, as though she was rushing to complete her task. It's not long before the wallpaper is trashed and Mum's message is revealed in full.

Three tasks lie before you, seeker of the sword,
Three tests to prove your worth.

The great traitor used Excalibur for destruction,
You must use it to heal.
The first task is one of strength.
The second is one of faith.
The third task, the most difficult of all,
Is a task of humility.
In all are five, and five are in all.
Go well, protect us,
and let not the sword fall into another Arthur's hands.

'Wow,' I say to the silent room. 'Thanks, Mum, that helps a lot.'

'Well, that gets us no closer to finding Excalibur,' Ollie says.

'There must be something else,' I say, pulling away more of the wallpaper. 'She can't have just left that for us.'

'For you,' Ollie says pointedly. 'Let's not sugar-coat it. She wanted you to find the sword, not me.'

'It doesn't matter,' I say, but we both know it does. Maybe not to the search for Excalibur, but to everything else – to the fragile new peace between us – it is crucial.

Ollie goes to the wall now, searching for more memories; trying to find something we missed.

'Maybe there's something on the orchids . . .' I say, sifting through the discarded wallpaper now curled at our feet. But then something else occurs to me – something off the back of Ollie's remark. I don't know if I should say it out loud. I don't want to risk hurting my brother even more, when I know how much of a sore spot this is for him. But if it helps us find Excalibur . . .

'She didn't write this for me.'

'Her letter –'

'Look.' I point to the top of the poem. '*Seeker of the sword*. Not *Fern*, not *daughter*. This could literally be for anyone with Immral.'

'But she said she'd left it for you,' Ollie says.

I search for an explanation.

'Maybe she meant for me to find it, but she couldn't give that away?'

'Why not though?'

I look down at the shards of paper in my lap, trying to work out our mother's motivation. I know enough about her to know that everything she did had a purpose. I know she loved me, and I suspect that she knew I had Immral. So there must be a reason she didn't mention me at all in this message.

Then my stomach drops. There's something else I know about my mum; something I've been trying to gloss over. She was ruthless. If I'm right that she knew about my Immral, then she didn't share that information with anyone.

'Maybe Mum was working with someone else,' I say, 'but they didn't know she wanted me to find the sword.'

Ollie nods. 'That makes sense. It might explain something else I've been wondering.'

'Which is?'

'We don't know much about Excalibur, but we know Arthur was the only one who could wield it. It stands to reason it can only be used by someone with Immral, otherwise why wouldn't Mum have just used it herself when she found it?'

I start to understand where Ollie's going with this. 'So you think she was working with someone with Immral, who didn't know she wanted me to get the sword?'

'There's only one person we know who had Immral around that time, and he wouldn't be likely to share.'

We're both thinking of Medraut. Mum was instrumental in toppling him sixteen years ago. I can't exactly see them doing this together, as if they were partners on a school project.

'Let's keep looking,' I say, and Ollie returns to examining the wall. I'm just about to leave the room and go back upstairs to look at that cubby hole again, when he curses under his breath.

'Did you find something?' I ask.

'Yeah,' Ollie says grimly, 'we've got a problem.'

'Another one? Oh good.'

Despite my sarcasm, something heavy settles in my stomach, as if I know what's coming. I take his outstretched hand as he rests the other against the wall. A now familiar spark of inspyre electrifies us, and I let the memories in, closing my eyes to see them more clearly.

A woman enters, but she's not my mother. I hiss involuntarily. Helena Corday, or Ellen Cassell as she was known in Annwn. My mother's murderer; an assassin who was once under Medraut's spell. She looks younger, much younger, than when I last saw her a few months ago. Sixteen years younger, I think. Around the time she killed our mother.

Ellen wanders through the house, spending a long time upstairs. When she comes back down she stares long and hard at the wallpaper. In an instant she transforms into the golden treitre who killed so many of our friends last year. If I wasn't being held so tightly by Ollie, my instinct would be to flee, or fight.

The treitre uses one of its claws to slice into the wallpaper, neatly tearing it in lines. It changes back to Ellen Cassell, who carefully prizes the newly cut paper from the plaster to reveal the message beneath. Ollie pulls away from me, breaking the connection, and the memory disappears.

'There's more,' Ollie tells me. 'Medraut came back and secured the wallpaper in place.'

We look at each other, the weight of this discovery settling on us. 'He knows, then,' I say.

'He's ahead of us,' Ollie adds. 'A sixteen-year head start.'

'I think,' I say after a long silence, 'that it might be time to tell Lord Allenby. We're going to need all the help we can get.'

Chapter 9

Lord Allenby takes the news as well as might be expected. He stays silent throughout my stumbled explanation of Mum's letter and our search for Excalibur. Then Ollie tells him what he saw of Ellen and Medraut. I've very rarely seen Lord Allenby shout in anger, but he lets out a guttural roar of frustration at that moment. He calms himself immediately, but his chest is heaving and his fists clenched.

'I'm sorry,' he says. 'I shouldn't have done that.'

'I'm sorry we didn't tell you sooner,' Ollie says. 'We didn't want to get anyone's hopes up.'

'*I* didn't,' I interject. 'I asked Ollie not to tell you.'

Lord Allenby nods, and despite his words I can tell he's really angry with me. 'I understand, Fern. But I do wish . . . Well, it's done now.'

I'm okay with him being angry – I knew we'd have to come clean at some point and I've been preparing for his reaction. I can't help but worry that he – and Ollie – are blaming Mum for this, though. On the ride back to Tintagel, Ollie had said, 'Couldn't she have just left it in Tintagel for you? It's not like the rest of us would be able to use it and Medraut can't get inside the castle, can he?'

I had to bite back the desire to defend Mum, because honestly I've been wondering the same thing. Why did she try to make this so difficult for me? There must have been other ways to make sure that Excalibur didn't fall into Medraut's hands, even if she was working with someone else and couldn't tell them her true motives.

Looking at Lord Allenby now, I wonder what he's thinking about his one-time friend. I reckon I'd feel betrayed in his shoes. Why didn't Mum confide in him the way she confided in Ellen? Couldn't she have given him one of the clues, at least, instead of tying him up in riddles and oaths? It's as though she didn't trust him.

'What do you think our next move should be, sir?' Ollie says.

But Lord Allenby doesn't reply. Instead, he unlocks a cabinet set into the walls, behind which is what can only be described as a shrine. He's never struck me as a religious man before, so my curiosity gets the better of me. Figurines are bunched together in the centre, surrounded by candles of all sizes. As Lord Allenby lights each of them, a heady fragrance fills the room – frankincense, rose and apple. Everything else in the office – the sharpness of the lights, the sound of the apothecaries gardening outside the window – is muted.

As Lord Allenby returns to his desk to write something on a scrap of paper, I move towards the shrine. The figurines are moulded from glass and wax and iron. There's no detail to the faces, but nevertheless they feel familiar. Like an old doll retrieved from a cupboard.

'Excuse me, Fern,' Lord Allenby says in his deep voice. He is holding the scrap of paper. I can't see what he's written on it, and as I watch he holds it over one of the candles until it catches.

'Let's see what they have to say for themselves,' he mutters, then turns his attention to Ollie and me.

'Well, I'm glad you decided to come to me now. It's clear that we need to find Excalibur before Medraut does. And more urgently, we need to find out why Una thought it was so important for you to have, Fern.'

'Do you not think Medraut has it already?' I ask, voicing my innermost fear.

'No,' Lord Allenby says, 'I think if he had it, we'd know about it one way or another. That means we stand a chance.'

He sends Ollie and me back to Ithr, promising us that he'll have the start of a plan by our next patrol. 'In the meantime, don't say a word about Excalibur to anyone besides me, alright?' he growls. Given we've been keeping it a secret all these months, it's not a hard ask, but part of me is disappointed. I had hoped that Lord Allenby would at the very least tell his captains what was happening.

'It's going to be hard keeping all this a secret from Samson, isn't it?' I say, as nonchalantly as I can, as Ollie and I make our way to the platform leading out of Annwn.

Ollie shrugs. 'Not really. Lord Allenby told us to, didn't he?'

'Yeah, but Samson's a . . .' I was going to say *friend*, but that doesn't encompass all of it. I don't have a problem keeping this a secret from Natasha or Rachel. Why is it different with Samson?

'He's our boss,' I say decisively. 'That's why it's strange.'

Ollie casts an amused look my way. 'If you say so, sis.'

For the first time in many months, I find myself flicking through my knightbook in Ithr. I read my notes from the last year. They form a road map of my journey. Not just of what I've learned about Annwn and the way our minds work when we're asleep, but of the way I see the worlds.

At the start, my notes were all focused on the practicalities of being a knight. I wrote about how to fly and which battle formations were best for which type of nightmare. But then I started to write addendums to what I'd learned. *Is this because they can't escape their anger?* I'd written next to a description of a stalker nightmare. Then, a few pages later, beside a journal entry about shadowing a patrol: *This might be crazy but this dreamer reminded me so much of Ollie. Except this dreamer was clearly really lonely and afraid. And Ollie isn't either of those things, right?*

My throat closes with the threat of tears, and I hastily flip back to the start of the book. I can't cry in class. Then I notice the date at the top of one of the first pages: today's date. How could I have forgotten? Tonight is Samhain.

In the midst of everything that's been happening lately, the fact that it's a year since I found out about the thanes had escaped me. The Fern who stood in her sitting room in Ithr and watched her twin brother be taken by a strange light; the Fern who went into Annwn thinking she just wanted to find out what happened to her mother, and never wanted to make friends; how can that have been the same Fern as the one sitting at this desk now?

* * *

When I arrive in Tintagel, the new squires haven't yet been called. I head to the knights' chamber to gather my uniform and scimitar, but a reeve is waiting outside for me.

'Lord Allenby wants to see you and Ollie,' he says. 'He's told Samson not to expect you on patrol.'

Lord Allenby had told us he'd come up with a plan, and come up with a plan he evidently has. Sometimes I wonder whether Lord Allenby has a life outside of Annwn and the thanes. What does he *do* in Ithr? Bank manager? Estate agent? And how does he cope with the stress of a normal job *and* everything that's going on in here?

The reeve directs me towards the veneurs' tower, and my enthusiasm fades. The last time I went up this tower, it was in pursuit of my mother's murderer as she basically committed suicide. The effects of the morrigans, their eyrie far above us, can be felt even from the bottom of the tower – an airless oppression that pulls at my throat. I'm relieved when I spot Lord Allenby waiting only halfway up the tower, Ollie by his side.

'Good,' is all that Lord Allenby says, and without further comment, he knocks four times on a woodworm-filled door, *tap-a-tap-tap*, and a few seconds later the door opens.

Jin. Of course, it had to be Jin, the very apothecary who's made her dislike of me so clear. 'Oh,' Jin says, as if she hasn't been expecting us, 'hello, sir.'

Jin looks at me inscrutably as I enter behind Lord Allenby and Ollie, then closes the door smartly.

'You've met Jin already, I believe,' Lord Allenby says, 'and this is Easa.'

A reeve, taller than Samson, his long hair bound in a green turban to match his tunic, holds out a hand without speaking. As Ollie chats to Jin and Easa, I study the room more closely. We're in a circular tower, which is echoed in the furnishings. The table that sits in the centre of the room, piled high with files and boxes, is round. The shelves and cupboards that line the edge of the room are fitted to the walls. There's a solitary window facing the door, through which I catch a glimpse of the knife-like building known as the Shard, glittering amber in the sunset.

'Now,' Lord Allenby says in a way that means *shut up*, 'shall we begin?'

Chapter 10

'We all know what we're up against,' Lord Allenby begins, once the five of us are seated, 'or we think we do. We know how powerful Sebastien Medraut is. Or we think we do. My point is, we actually have no idea what Medraut's capable of. But earlier this year Fern and Samson found something that gave us a crucial insight into what his ambitions are for Annwn and Ithr. Ollie here helped us to decipher it.'

Lord Allenby opens a box. A small wooden cube, inlaid with rivulets of mahogany that snake across its surface. Ollie leans back in his seat. He knows better than anyone how dangerous that thing is.

'Inside this box, Medraut kept all of his ambitions. His endgame, his final plan. You know what that is now. The destruction of all free will and independent thought. Anything different or unusual stamped out. One Voice. That's what he wants – every single person to think and act with one purpose – his purpose. His will. I'll leave you to tell me how well he's doing.'

I look around the table at sombre faces. All of us, I'm guessing, have something unusual about us in Ithr; something to mark us apart from Medraut's narrow definition of acceptable. For

Easa and Jin it might be the colour of their skin. Me – well, I need no explanation. The only people in the room who don't have anything obvious marking them out for persecution are Ollie and Lord Allenby.

'But we've also been gifted an opportunity,' Lord Allenby continues. 'I don't want to put undue pressure on Fern and Ollie, because goodness knows they've got enough of that already. But with Medraut's Immral so strong, Fern and Ollie's combined power is one of the few things that saved us and many thousands of dreamers from total annihilation back at Beltane. And Fern's mother, my friend Una, left her a gift somewhere in Annwn. Excalibur.'

'King Arthur's sword?' Jin blurts out.

Easa frowns. 'I thought that was a legend.'

'It is a legend,' Lord Allenby agrees, 'but when has that meant that it couldn't be real?'

The reeve ducks his head.

'In any case,' Lord Allenby resumes, 'there's a reason Una wanted Fern to find that sword. My guess is that she knew about Fern's power and thought Fern would need it.'

'But there's no record of Excalibur being anything special except that it was King Arthur's sword,' Jin says.

'Perhaps that in itself is significant,' Lord Allenby says, 'but my guess is that Una found out something else. Something that means Excalibur wasn't just a weapon.'

'So you want us to find what's different about it?' Easa asks.

'In part, yes. If we find where Una hid it, we're going to want to know how to use it. But I also want you to help Fern with her mother's clues.'

'Our mother's clues,' I interject, feeling Ollie stirring next to me.

'Indeed.' Lord Allenby nods. 'Fern and Ollie are going to need all of your help to decipher these clues alongside their patrols. That's why I've chosen you two. Your heads of lore tell me you're reliable, smart and, most importantly, discreet.'

We all share glances. The spectres of Linnea and the bugs rise between us.

Lord Allenby looks out of the window, where the sun is beginning to set on the first of several cycles it will go round tonight. 'I have to go now. These files are just a few of many references to Excalibur that we have in the archives, to get you started on your research. Fern and Ollie can fill you both in on what they know so far.'

Here Lord Allenby pauses, and regards us all more seriously than he has up to this point. 'I don't think I need to reiterate this, but I will just in case. You will all report to me, but outside of me and this group what you are doing here must remain absolutely secret.'

We murmur our assent, and Lord Allenby leaves the room. He shuts the door behind him and there's an uncomfortable moment where we hear him turn the key in the lock from the outside. We are stuck together until someone decides to let us out again.

'It's okay,' Easa says. 'Locking it makes this room soundproof. He's doing it so no one can eavesdrop on us.'

That doesn't make me feel any more comfortable. It's as though, despite his words, Lord Allenby doesn't fully trust us either. Nor do I – Easa is an unknown quantity, and Jin . . .

well, it's clear that Jin's loyalties do not lie with me. Why did it have to be her? I'm still pondering this when I realise that everyone's looking at me.

'If you're expecting my sister to take charge, you're going to be waiting for a while,' Ollie pipes up.

Jin smiles and Easa raises an eyebrow. 'Well, this is your quest, we're just helping out.'

I shift uncomfortably. I'd imagined a proper team effort, headed by Lord Allenby. I'd be the muscle, like always. But he's right: Mum left me the sword, and I have most of the information. If I want this to succeed I'd better at least pretend to know what I'm doing.

'What do you want to know?'

'The beginning is the traditional place to start,' Jin says, and I have to bite back a snide reply. Easa steps in just as I open my mouth, though. 'Why don't you tell us about your mother, Fern? Why do you think she thought Excalibur would be useful to you? The better we know her, the more likely we're going to be able to help you figure out her clues.'

Before I can reply, Ollie starts talking. 'We went through all her notes earlier this year . . .'

And he's off. It's only right, I tell myself, as Ollie drones on about the things Mum was researching, her friendship with Ellen Cassell and Lord Allenby, and her time in the knights, that my brother's the one to tell this story. He's trying to make it his story as well: to own a little part of Mum. I understand how difficult it is to know that your parent loved your sibling more than you – don't I have daily reminders of that from Dad?

The problem is that as I listen to Ollie, I realise that he doesn't understand Mum at all. This is an alien concept to me because usually I'm the one who can't get into someone else's head, and my brother literally has the power to read minds. He's sensed Mum's feelings through her belongings. But here he is, talking about what she did and what she said instead of who she was.

Jin is watching me brazenly, a mix of emotions playing across her face. I can't work most of them out, but I'm certain that the one I do recognise is disappointment. I jut my chin. Her expression wouldn't hurt so much if I wasn't feeling disappointed in myself for not taking charge. But no one except Ollie and I understand the complex relationship that we have; how we have to tread carefully around each other's feelings; how we're both still tender from years of hating each other, and if we look like friends now it's only because we both work so hard at it.

'That's really interesting, Ollie.' Easa breaks into my train of thought. 'Can you remember anything else, Fern? I'm pretty sure I know everything there is to know about what your Mum did when she was a knight, but I'm not really getting a sense of . . .' He wiggles his fingers stupidly. '. . . A sense of her, you know?'

Jin raises an eyebrow at me; a challenge.

That makes me dig my heels in again. 'No, Ollie said everything there was to say.'

I push away the niggling thought that tells me that by appeasing my brother, I am betraying my mother.

'So how do we start this quest then?' Jin says, flicking through the files inside the first box.

'Figuring out the impossible riddle my mum left us would be a great start,' I say.

I find the piece of paper that Ollie scribbled the message down on and push it into the centre of the table. Jin and Easa lean in.

Three tasks lie before you, seeker of the sword,
Three tests to prove your worth.
The great traitor used Excalibur for destruction,
You must use it to heal.
The first task is one of strength.
The second is one of faith.
The third task, the most difficult of all
Is a task of humility.
In all are five, and five are in all.
Go well, protect us,
and let not the sword fall into another Arthur's hands.

'Have you considered the idea that your mum actually didn't want you to find Excalibur?' Jin comments.

'Have you considered the idea that Lord Allenby wanted you to *help* me instead of making snide remarks?' I snap back.

'Stop it,' Ollie says. 'Stop it.'

Jin and I shoot hatred at each other across the table, while Easa tries to sooth the tension. 'Why don't you leave this with us for a while? Jin and I will look at it with fresh eyes. We'll read through the files on Excalibur as well. See if there's anything useful to be found.'

'Sure,' Ollie says. 'Thanks.'

He knocks on the door and a waiting reeve lets us out. Ollie leads me down the stairs. I'm on the verge of asking him why he didn't stand up for me in there, when he mutters, 'How on earth did she become an apothecary?' which mollifies me a little. Then when we reach the main hall all thoughts of Jin are driven from my head. Samson is running towards us.

'Fern, you've got to . . .' He pauses, and for the first time since I've known him a glimpse of uncertainty darts across his usually strong features. 'There's something I think you'll want to see.'

Suddenly I remember what day it is. Samhain. This has to be to do with the new squires. 'Coming?' I ask Ollie. He shakes his head. 'I'll see you at home.' He's smirking at me for some reason.

I trot to catch up with Samson as he heads for the east wing.

'What do the new recruits look like?' I ask.

'You'll see,' Samson says, but there's no excitement in his voice. We've been holding on to this date like a lifeline. The day when we'll finally get a new injection of squires – new knights to take the place of our fallen comrades.

Samson and I pad across the castle hall, beneath the great domed roof, towards one of the training chambers. A gaggle of thanes is already gathered outside the room, peering in through the keyhole and the stained-glass panel at the top.

'I thought last year there were three rooms?' I say, remembering something Ramesh had told me about that first night.

'There were,' Samson replies. As we near the room I catch the mood of the group outside. None of them are smiling. Some shake their heads and mutter darkly to their companions. A few harkers break away to return to their desks, and as they pass I hear them whispering to each other, '. . . won't even make a difference . . .'

I speed up, dread pooling in my stomach like tar. As we approach, the other thanes make way for us – a by-product of my celebrity status in Tintagel is that I no longer have to queue. I nudge the reeve who's kneeling at the keyhole out of the way so that Samson can stay beside me, and put my face up to the glass.

'You know how Samhain works, right?' Samson says as I try to see what's going on inside.

'Of course,' I reply. 'On their fifteenth Samhain, the people with the strongest imaginations and ability to sacrifice themselves are called into Annwn.'

I can dimly see some shapes, but nothing clear. I try to edge my head round to a different angle.

'That's only part of it,' Samson says. 'The way Arthur set it up was that the number of people called into Annwn would vary each year.'

'Vary? Based on what?'

And then I find it – the piece of clear glass that allows me to see properly into the room. That allows me to see that the room, which only held a third of last year's intake, this year isn't even half full. Barely more than a handful of squires – shell-shocked, excited, petrified – sit on the pews watching Lord Allenby explain the truth about Annwn.

'It's based on the amount of inspyre there is in Annwn,' Samson is saying. 'King Arthur's logic was that the more inspyre there was, the more dangerous Annwn would be. Less inspyre – less danger – less need for new thanes.'

In the middle of speaking, Lord Allenby looks up and catches my eye. My first instinct is to draw away, worried that he'll be annoyed at me for peering in, but there's no anger in his eyes. Only defeat. He raises an eyebrow at me and I raise one in return. An acknowledgement that we're screwed. We may as well give up before we've even begun.

Chapter 11

I turn back to the assembled crowd. Every one of them is watching my reaction, waiting to see whether their panic is justified. I hate this – this is one way where life in Ithr is so much easier, because there no one cares about my opinion. Here, people follow my lead.

I shrug at everyone. 'We've got work to do, haven't we?'

Some of them wander off, but others are more persistent. Rachel collars me. 'Will there be enough knights to fill the patrols?' she says. 'None of you are safe out there with so few . . .'

'I don't know,' I tell her, raising my voice so the others can hear, 'but worrying about it isn't going to change anything. Are you just going to give up because it's not as many people as you wanted?'

'That's not what I . . .' She blushes.

'And this isn't all on me, okay?' I snap. 'Why does everyone keep looking at me for answers? I'm not the Head Thane!'

'Fern!' Rachel says, mortified. 'That's . . .'

But I've stormed off, to the platform that will take me back to Ithr. By the time I reach my bedroom I'm already feeling guilty, and that's only compounded when Ollie opens my door without knocking.

'I could have been changing!' I protest, but he just snarls at me.

'You didn't need to be so rude to her, Fern.'

Even though I was already planning an apology in my head, Ollie's aggressiveness puts me on the defensive.

'I'm so sick of everyone treating me like I'm some kind of messiah.'

'They're desperate,' he hisses back. 'They're desperate and they're scared. Do you not think that loads of them are getting stick in Ithr as well? Like us?'

'You mean like *me*. I don't see anyone harassing you for your perfectly normal face.'

'They just want to know that there's an end in sight.'

'But we don't know if there is,' I say, shoving my mirror portal into a drawer. 'We're not powerful enough, even together, to bring Medraut down. And who knows where Mum hid that bloody sword? We may never find it.'

'Yes, we're doomed – you think they don't know that? They just need some hope, don't they?'

'Fine, but why do they have to get it from me?'

'You know why.'

My voice takes on a begging edge. 'I'm not the kind of person who boosts morale, Ollie. Feelings are your territory, they always were.'

'I can do a limited amount,' Ollie says, collapsing on the floor next to my bed. 'But I can only read emotions, I can't change them. That's your power.'

'I've never been good with emotions.'

'You never used to have friends, or give a shit about other people,' he counters, 'but here we are.'

'Rachel might even be working for Medraut. We still don't know what she was doing in the archives.'

Ollie snorts. I think about Rachel's expression when I laid into her. Yeah, there's no way she's working for Medraut. I throw myself back onto the bed.

'Urgh, this was all so much easier when I didn't care about other people.'

Not that that's a courtesy shown to me by anyone else in Ithr. In fact, I'm coming to realise that a lot of people no longer regard me as human at all. That morning, I'm shoved to one side when waiting to get on the tube. That in itself isn't unusual at rush hour, but the force with which it's done reminds me of someone kicking a dog on purpose.

I lose it completely during the afternoon break at Bosco. I'm waiting in the queue for the toilets, reading through my Classics notes in preparation for a test, when Lottie Medraut enters, sees me waiting, and pushes straight past me as the cubicle door opens. I have been willing to take a lot from Lottie, but I'm bursting and after a day of being ignored and punished for looking weird I am done.

'Excuse me, I was here first,' I say.

She just shrugs, and opens the cubicle door. Before she can lock it, I have elbowed my way in and stand in the blocked entrance, arms crossed.

'Are you a lesbian as well as a weirdo now?' she sneers. The venom in her voice isn't hers. It's her father's.

'It's my turn. I'm asking you to leave.'

'If you'd just let me go I'd be done by now,' she says.

My face, my fingers grow hot. It's not anger, but it's not far off. A distant burst, somewhere behind my eyes. *'I. Am. Here,'* I say, my voice quiet but powerful.

Lottie falters. An odd expression crosses her face. Then she pushes past me in silence, her lemony perfume following in her wake. It's only once she's opened the door to the hallway that she finds her voice.

'Just stay away from me, witch,' she spits. The door bangs shut behind her.

I tell Ollie about the encounter with Lottie that night, as we're walking through the cloisters. I don't touch upon the strange rush of heat that flowed through me. I don't really understand what happened, nor do I like the way it made me feel.

'I think there's something weird going on with her,' I tell my brother.

'I'm not surprised,' he replies. 'You saw what Medraut was doing. He's probably ramped it up. It's bound to get to her.'

We skirt around the main hall, where the lore captains are trying to corral the new squires into the portal that will take them to Stonehenge and their Tournament.

'Poor bastards,' Ollie mutters under his breath. I agree with him – last year there was barely enough room for all of us to fit inside the circle. This year there's space for even the most antisocial of squires to feel comfortable.

'I think we should ask Lord Allenby if we can look for her again,' I say. There's been no sight of Lottie in Annwn since the night I tortured her. Medraut is evidently protecting her from us. Protecting her – or experimenting on her.

'Yeah, that worked out well for us last time,' Ollie says. 'Anyway, haven't we got enough to worry about at the moment without adding to our to-do list?' He jerks his head back towards the hall, where a deep *boom* tells us that the portal has been activated.

'Fair point.' Still, it doesn't sit right with me that we don't know what Medraut is doing to his own daughter. I file it away in the back of my head and vow to keep a closer eye on Lottie at school.

'Can you imagine though?' Ollie says. 'She's treated like an absolute princess in Ithr. Super popular, super smart. But in Annwn she's basically her dad's puppet, never gets to actually dream of anything. That's enough to mess with your head, isn't it?'

'Yeah. Yeah, it is.' I am suddenly struck by how different my experience is to Lottie's. We are opposites. If she's popular in Ithr and being persecuted in Annwn, I am regarded as the second coming in Annwn but the devil in Ithr. Ollie's right. It does mess with your head. Maybe that's why I'm so on edge all the time. Or maybe I'm overthinking it – I've got a lot of reasons to be tense without needing more to add to the pile.

As we pass the harker desks, I peel away from Ollie and approach Rachel. Once again, she's focused on her paperwork.

'I'm sorry,' I say. 'About last night. I was really harsh.'

She looks up at me with unfocused eyes.

'I'm just . . .' I don't want to make this apology about me, but I do need her to understand that I can't keep carrying everyone's hope on my shoulders. People make out that hope is light but it's not; when it all rests on you it's as heavy as lead.

'It's okay,' Rachel says. 'I shouldn't have panicked like that.'

She returns to her papers. That was easy. Apology accepted, apparently. But I can't shake the feeling that she's letting me off very lightly indeed.

'What are you writing?' I ask, moving closer.

'Oh! It's not important,' Rachel says, planting a hand over her work so I can't read it.

'Sorry,' I say, stepping back, inwardly cursing myself for intruding. This is why I don't talk to people unless I have to – I always make a mess of it.

'No,' Rachel says, 'it's not that I don't want to . . .' She looks down at the stack of paper, then holds a page out to me. In her neat, blocky handwriting she has written a series of questions.

Could we have stopped the treitre attacks?

How can we see the treitres before they transform?

Could we change the Round Table or the harker helmets to notice treitres?

'I started thinking about it after . . . after Ramesh,' Rachel says nervously, 'and then I kept thinking about it after the attack on Tintagel. I think there might be a way, Fern.'

'But we know how to take down the treitres,' I say. 'Ollie and I –'

'I know, you're both brilliant,' she says, 'but, sorry, but you're not always going to be around. And even if you are, we're still probably going to lose some knights before you're able to work out the treitre's weakness.' Her rabbit-like features look even more vulnerable. 'I know it was way worse for you, but I had to listen to . . .'

Suddenly I see what that first attack must have been like from Rachel's point of view. Listening over the helmets to Bedevere being slaughtered – the screams and shouts as Ramesh was beheaded; the shattering of weapons and the crunch as the treitres threw us across the streets like dolls. And she couldn't do anything about it.

'I get it,' I tell her, handing the paper back. 'I didn't even know that changing the Round Table was possible.'

'A lot of us have been talking about it,' she says. 'Some of the reeves have been helping us with the research, but everyone's so overloaded it's hard to find the time to spend on it.'

I open my mouth to reply, a lump building in my throat. But before I can say anything there's a flurry of feet on stone and the reeve captain bumbles up to us, red-faced.

'I'm so glad I found you before you went out on patrol,' he says. 'Fern, you're needed urgently.'

'Aren't you supposed to be at the Tournament, sir?' Rachel asks.

'I am,' the reeve captain says. 'That's rather the point.' He lowers his voice and steps closer to me. 'I don't want to alarm anyone, but we can't activate the Tournament, Fern. You might be the only way we can make it happen.'

'What do you mean?' I say, as I start walking with him back towards the portal.

'The Fay – they're not strong enough any more. Without them, we can't make the Tournament work.'

Chapter 12

'Careful now,' the reeve captain says, helping me step through the light, then assisting me onto the column. I know now how easy it is to move up this column – or along it – and with the reeve's help I'm able to do so rather more gracefully than last year. Before long, we are standing in the sunless brightness of Annwn's Stonehenge. In the distance, squires are ranged around the inner circle of the henge. The thane captains stand on the other side.

But there's only one person I really want to see. The woman who brought me into this world. I miss her terribly at times, even though I'm now surrounded by friends. She was the first to fight for me, to make me begin to believe that I could belong here. When other people talk about wanting to make their parents proud of them, she is the one I think of.

Andraste.

The Fay are, as they did for my Tournament, holding hands in a smaller inner circle. Even if I hadn't been warned, I'd be able to tell that something was wrong. I spot Andraste and my breath hitches. It's not the fact that her scars are weeping pus and blood, or the way she stands at an angle, as though her bones are too weak to support her. It's the fear in her eyes. I've never seen that before. She's a warrior – that's her essence; fear should be alien to her.

Lord Allenby escorts me to the central circle, where Merlin is gasping for breath. When they talk, they lower their voices. They do not want the squires to hear.

'We have a problem,' Lord Allenby says. 'It seems that the Fay are not as strong as they once were, and they're having trouble erecting the field needed for our squires to take the Tournament.'

Merlin scowls. 'We are just as strong . . .' he protests, but we all know he's lying.

'You think I can help?' I say.

Lord Allenby nods. 'The field requires the Fay's particular brand of, well, I suppose the best word for it is *magic*. It's not Immral, but it's not so different. My thinking is that you might be able to provide the extra strength they need.'

'Got it,' I say, and walk over to Andraste to mask how daunted I am feeling. Dozens of eyes watch me – lore captains who understand what's at stake; squires who need to be reassured that this alien world is where they belong.

'Thank you,' Andraste breathes as I reach her. I take her hand gently. Something tells me that any greater public display of affection from a mortal would be humiliating. Her skin is cold, despite the sunlight beating down upon us, and I can feel every bone beneath it. She gasps in pain: the slight pressure from my hand has rubbed out part of her skin. Beneath it there is no bone, no nerves, just a whisper of inspyre that fades into nothing.

'I'm so sorry,' I say.

Andraste smiles at me. I think she's trying to be reassuring but it comes out as a grimace. 'Shall we try to do this?' she says, nodding at the circle of Fay.

Holding lightly on to Andraste with one hand, with my other I take the hand of her twin, the warrior Fay known as Lugh. Immediately I sense the power flowing between them. It's not quite the same feeling as I get when I'm using my Immral – the lightning pull of willing inspyre that emanates from the back of my brain. It doesn't vibrate or tug at me in the same way Immral does. It's a gentler, steadier force. More settled. Ancient. The weight of the many thousands of years of human imagination that has created these gods and goddesses is an anchor. Next to that my Immral feels like an unruly colt.

I try to calm my power so that it's more in line with the Fays'. I send my Immral up and around the circle, leaping from hand to hand. That's when I feel it. The gaps in their strength. It's as though the Fays' power is an old, crumbling wall. There are holes in the fortress, and their life force is escaping through them. I concentrate on those holes, the throbbing in my head increasing. I pour my Immral into the gaps, plugging them, reinforcing them, and slowly the circle takes on a different energy. As is always the case when I use my Immral on another in Annwn, the connection is two-way – a flavour of each Fay seeps into my mouth. Bloody iron for Merlin; lavender for Nimue; something harder to pinpoint for Andraste, a complicated mixture of spices. I don't try to mimic whatever their power is doing. The way the inspyre moves for them is too subtle for me to understand, let alone mirror. At times I glimpse its intention, like listening to a foreign language: I feel it ebbing and flowing in accordance with the squire in the centre of the circle, its energy pulsing around the arena as they move. When their precious item transforms, the Fay seem to breathe in as one, their movement making me do the same, so that the inspyre that works between us swells.

Underneath it all is my growing headache, and the knowledge that I am not strong enough to keep this up for long. I try to take my mind off it by watching the Tournament. This is one advantage that I have over the Fay: they must enter a trance to produce the arena; I do not. One girl carries a pair of earrings, which turn into a compass, the points marked with rubies, that helps her find her way out of a maze. She is assigned to the harkers. One boy imagines an old lady, blue-rinse hair curled immaculately, and a man attacking her with a knife. Without hesitation, the boy jumps between the woman and her attacker, the blade sinking into his chest. The boy looks even more alarmed when the blade disappears, along with the set of medals he was holding. The act of someone who cares deeply but who carries no violence in their soul.

'There's no doubting this one's an apothecary!' Lord Allenby calls out, shaking the shell-shocked boy's hand and sending him to stand with the other white tunics.

I glance over at the remaining squires. There aren't many of them left, but I'm not sure how much longer I can hold out. The Fay are tiring too. Andraste sags, and I push one foot towards her, so that she can lean on my hip. The gaps in their power are widening, which means that I need to use more of my Immral to fill them. The problem is that because I don't understand the finer mechanics of their power and what they're doing to create this arena, I can't copy it exactly, and that starts to take its toll. One of the squires begins his fight, but can clearly see and hear beyond the circle to the thanes watching him. It throws him off his game and he almost doesn't survive his attacker – a huge bear that reeks of stale blood. More worryingly, the next squire nearly doesn't get her weapon – the brooch she takes in with her struggles to transform. I can feel the Fay pushing all their energies into helping her and I do my best to support them, but the inspyre isn't as willing to answer their call as it once was. It is deserting them.

Another squire finds their weapon, and the surge of energy it takes makes my brain explode. Blood erupts from my nose. The circle falters, but I am used to this kind of pain now. I simply wipe the blood on my tunic and kick my focus back. Lord Allenby strides over.

'Only one left to go, Fern,' he says. 'Is that going to be okay?'

I nod, not trusting myself to speak.

The final squire walks past me to enter the arena. There's something about her that's familiar. The dark, cropped hair. When she speaks to Lord Allenby, her voice is sharp and short. My stomach lurches. Then she opens her palm to reveal her treasured possession. A fountain pen, matte black with a gold tip. There's an inscription engraved upon it, but I don't need to get closer to read the words. I know already what they are, because I have seen that pen before. Its twin now lives in an amber monument to the dead, all the way back in Annwn's London, not far from Tintagel. It was Ramesh's pen. And now, it is his sister's.

Chapter 13

I'm not quick enough to duck my head. Ramesh's sister has seen me. I close my eyes against the pain coursing through my heart. It was only a few weeks ago that I met this girl in Ithr, beside Ramesh's grave. I was cruel to her. Now she's here. It hadn't even occurred to me that she'd be called. Siblings and children of existing thanes do get recruited regularly – maybe it's something in their genes, or something about the way they've been raised. But I didn't think it would happen in this case. For one thing, this girl seems so much harder than Ramesh. But I was in denial. I just couldn't bear the thought of it – of seeing someone so similar to him, every night, in the haven I have chosen. I grieve for my friend every day. Having this girl here will make that grief more visceral, even while it pushes it into secrecy – because what right have I to mourn Ramesh publicly when his sister is right here?

At last I feel the surge of energy that accompanies the transformation of a precious object into a weapon, and risk opening my eyes. Everything is blurry because of the growing migraine, but I dimly see that Ramesh's fountain pen has turned into a spear. The girl is thrusting it wildly at a shadowy force that looms over a body on the ground. I don't need to get closer to see that the body is Ramesh's. Then one of her swings connects with the shadow, and it disintegrates. She stands there panting, staring at her prone brother as he, too, melts back into inspyre. The energy running around the circle of Fay fades as they break the connection. Andraste sinks to the ground, and I catch her before she lands, some of the blood from my nosebleed joining the blood pouring from her scars.

'What a pair we are,' I whisper, and she smiles wearily.

'. . . a knight!' I hear Lord Allenby announce. I look up just as Ramesh's sister passes me. I know she saw me before she took the Tournament, but she doesn't look down at me this time. I can tell that she's aware of my presence though, by the way her hand is clenched and her eyes are fixed straight ahead. Samson shakes her hand but he isn't smiling. He bows his head to her and mutters something in her ear. Samson catches my eye, and I know we're both thinking the same thing: this is horrendous.

While the new thanes head back to Tintagel, I remain behind with Lord Allenby and the Fay. All of them are suffering for what they've just done. Nimue is shaking badly, veins pulsing visibly through the thin skin on her bare arms. Lugh removes his cloak and, with stiff fingers, fastens it at her throat. She pulls it around her body but then cries out in pain. The merest touch of the fabric has rubbed at her delicate skin. Swathes of it flake from her arms, leaving bloody grazes in some places, and grey nothingness in others.

'You have not answered my messages,' Lord Allenby is saying to Merlin. 'My lord, we only ask for information –'

'We shall never help an Immral,' Merlin snarls, shooting a look my way.

'Oh fine,' I reply, not even knowing what they're arguing about, 'but you don't mind me using my power to help you do your duty. It's alright when it's convenient for you.'

'Fern . . .' Lord Allenby starts.

'We should not have been bound to this Tournament!' Merlin screeches. 'Your traitor king made us take an oath, and we do not break our oaths.'

'Arthur is not my king,' I say. 'I hate everything he stands for. And Medraut. Why can't you see that?'

Merlin turns away, limping out of Stonehenge. The other Fay follow him, but this time some of them cast me uncertain looks. Andraste acknowledges what I've done with a squeeze of my shoulder and a smile. Only Nimue stops.

'A token of thanks,' she says, and offers me the belt from her dress.

'Thanks?' I say. The belt is woven from five strands of fabric, each one a different shade of gold. She smiles at me oddly, drawing Lugh's cloak closer around her frame.

Trudging back towards the portal to Tintagel, I wind Nimue's odd gift around my hands. I'm so busy studying the fabric that it takes me a moment to realise that I'm being followed. Half-hoping it's Andraste, I turn, but it's only Lord Allenby.

'I'm sorry about snapping at Merlin, sir.'

'Don't be,' he says. 'Neither us nor the Fay are wrong. Arthur was a terrible man, but he founded a great institution.' He hands me a handkerchief to wipe my nose. 'Do you need some time to recover?'

Yes.

'No, sir, I'm fine. I'll head back to patrol now.'

But the Tournament had evidently gone on longer than I'd expected, for by the time I return to Tintagel the night patrols are heading back in. Ollie dismounts Balius and runs over. 'Are you okay?' he says, noticing the blood still dripping from my nose. 'Rachel said you'd been called away and I needed to lead the patrol on my own.'

I take him to one side, aware that we don't want too many people to know what went wrong in case they panic. I'm filling him in when I sense someone approaching us. This is a new facet to my Immral that I've only become aware of recently – the inspyre moving and vibrating in such a way that I can tell when someone is nearby, even if I can't see them.

'It was you, wasn't it? The other day?'

Ramesh's sister is here. I don't want to talk to her. I'm tired and in pain and she is going to make things even more painful. But I owe it to Ramesh to do right by her, even if I've no idea what that might look like.

'Hi,' I say. 'I'm Fern.'

I hold out my hand and, somewhat reluctantly, she takes it. 'Sachi.'

'Well done for getting into the knights,' I say. I can sense Ollie making the connection between her and her brother.

'Was he?' Sachi says. Her voice catches in her throat, but I know what she means.

'Yes,' I say.

'His name isn't up on those columns,' she replies.

'It is.' I lead her back inside the castle, to the place where the names of thanes killed in the line of duty scroll endlessly, the year of their death inscribed beside them. The names with *2020* beside them go on for a long time, but then I point to Ramesh. 'Your brother didn't go by his Ithr name here. In Annwn we knew him as Ramesh, not Reyansh.'

'But . . .' Sachi is bewildered, and behind that, hurt and confused. 'Why would he do that?'

'It happens quite a lot,' Ollie tells her, having followed us in. 'It wasn't anything to do with how he felt about his family in Ithr.'

'How would you know?' Sachi says.

'It's kind of my thing,' Ollie says. 'I can read minds. Ollie, by the way.'

'I'm really sorry,' I tell Sachi, a bit peeved with Ollie for being here. This was my moment to do right by Ramesh, and Ollie's hijacking it. Sachi looks between us, measuring us. I study her more closely. The last time I saw her was at Ramesh's grave, but we had kept our distance from each other then. Now, I see how she's even more similar to her brother than I'd thought – the same weak chin, the same eyes. I don't think there's any difference between the way she looks in Annwn and Ithr, which in itself tells me something. Sachi knows exactly who she is. She's absolutely confident in her body. As she surveys me, I realise that I look very different in Ithr – here, I don't have my burn scar. No one besides Ollie knows about that in Annwn, and I want to keep it that way. Given the way Sachi's looking at me, I think my time is up on that front.

'Did he look different too?' she asks me, ignoring Ollie.

'A little,' I say. Then, hoping it will tell her to keep quiet about my burn scar, add, 'Sometimes you don't have any control over how you look between the two worlds. Sometimes it's a chance to . . . reinvent yourself. Or at least to not be defined by the kind of things that define you in Ithr.'

She considers this, then nods, catching my eye in a way that tells me she will keep my scar a secret. I find myself warming to this hard, younger version of Ramesh.

'How did he die?' she says quickly.

I'd been expecting this, but I don't know how much any of the squires have been told about Medraut. We weren't taught about him until a few months into our training. I can't see how we can hold off telling this intake for long, but equally can't imagine Lord Allenby telling them exactly what they were getting into on the first night – after all, we can't afford for any of them to decide they don't want to become thanes. But can I really fob her off when it comes to the death of her own brother?

'He died protecting people,' I say lamely. The truth is that Ramesh never had a chance to actually protect anyone. He never saw the treitre coming. In fact his death was entirely in vain, a more complete waste of life than any of my other friends who've died in the last few months. I think Sachi can tell I'm fudging too, because she gives me a stare of such contempt that I cringe.

'Bullshit,' she hisses, and stalks away. I don't follow her. I know I didn't say the right thing, but I don't know what I could have told her that would have been any less painful.

'That probably could have gone better,' Ollie remarks.

'She's going to be impossible, isn't she?' I say.

'Oh, you mean she's going to be bitter and hurt and angry and convinced that we're all her enemies?' Ollie says. 'Yeah, probably. Oh no, wait, that was you.'

I glare at him. 'I was different.'

'Were you?' Ollie says lightly. 'Anyway, my point is she'll come round. Just like you did. The tough cookies always end up having the softest centres.'

We both shove our hands in our pockets as we wander towards the knights' chamber.

'That's not even remotely true about cookies,' I say, nudging him with my elbow, 'and also – eww.'

Chapter 14

Despite our best efforts, word that the Fay are growing weaker spreads around the castle faster than a trickster nightmare. Some of the squires mentioned me helping at the Tournament, and the rest of the thanes put two and two together.

Most go into barely-suppressed-panic mode, but there are pockets, here and there, who take it as a challenge. One of them is Brandon the veneur. He has always loved his animals – it goes with the territory of his lore – but he takes the news the most personally.

'Nothing's going to happen to you, okay?' he tells his morrigan, feeding it a little dream mouse. 'I won't let them disappear *you*.'

The other person it affects is Rachel. She redoubles her efforts to research the possibility of changing the Round Table. I end up spending more time with her after patrols than with the other knights. It's become our routine – I'll stop for a chat on my way out of Tintagel after patrol notes. She'll ask me questions and I'll interrogate her research in return.

'The thing is,' she tells me one night, 'the Round Tables *have* been altered since King Arthur built them, but only in a superficial way. We're able to change the map on their tops pretty easily, but the mechanics inside? Not so much.'

'What's so special about the mechanics?' I ask. 'Besides the fact they're kind of magic.'

'The trouble is, there's so little information about King Arthur's reign in . . .' She trails off, evidently realising that I'm not supposed to know about her secret trips to the archives.

I take a leap of faith. 'You mean, all the information missing from the Arthur files?'

Her eyes widen, making the deep circles beneath them even more pronounced. 'You know about that?' she whispers.

I just nod, aware of the fact that we're surrounded by harkers and reeves.

'I've looked and looked, but I can barely find anything on how Arthur made the Round Tables. The only thing I've found is, well – look.'

Rachel rifles through her notes and pushes a diagram towards me. It's a cut-out of a Round Table, segmented to show the inner workings. Cogs and wheels are drawn in minute detail.

'This bit here,' Rachel says, pointing to a platform just beneath the surface, 'It's a sensor. It's connected to the map but also to the corresponding parts of Annwn. Whenever inspyre forms a dream or a nightmare, it sparks the sensor, which then mirrors the inspyre movement on the map above.'

'So you were wondering if we could alter the sensor to make it recognise treitres, right?' I say, but I'm not really listening to Rachel's answer. Something else has drawn my attention.

'That's what I was hoping, but I don't see how.'

'What's this?' I say, pointing to a part of the diagram beneath the sensor. A black shape, like a raincloud promising thunder, seems to reach up out of darkness.

'I don't know,' Rachel says. 'That's the problem. There's nothing in the records to say what that shape is, or what powers the tables at all. And if I can't work that out then I can't find a way of changing it.'

'We'll figure it out,' I assure her, although I'm far from certain myself. I'm learning that there's a lot about the thanes' history that is shrouded in secrecy. Whether that's for our good, or the good of someone else, I'm not sure.

The other thing I'm not certain of is the Excalibur team. My therapy sessions with Jin have, thankfully, been cancelled for now. She's too busy researching Excalibur, or at least that's what she tells Lord Allenby, and I'm perfectly happy to have the excuse to stop seeing her in that cramped room in the hospital wing.

Instead, I have to see her in a cramped room in the veneurs' tower. Jin remains as hostile as ever, but Easa seems content to act as our go-between.

'I've been going through your mum's stuff,' Easa tells me one evening, 'and I think you should take a look at this.'

He hands me a silver box, the kind my dad's mum keeps her pills in. The lid is covered in a geometric pattern, and when I flip it open, there's a verse inscribed inside.

When all men saw this sudden change of things,
So mortal foes so friendly to agree,
For passing joy, which so great marvel brings,
They all gan shout aloud, that all the heaven rings.

* * *

The box contains nothing but a plain silver coin. I tip it out into my hand. The other side actually does have some ornament: five crystals embedded in a star shape: four of them clear, one of them blue.

'I thought, because of the poem – *In all are five, and five are in all . . .'* Easa begins.

'But what does it mean?' I say, my annoyance with Mum rearing its head again.

'We'll find out,' Easa says. 'It's not supposed to be easy, Fern, otherwise everyone would have found Excalibur and we'd be in real trouble.'

I wish I could believe him.

If we'd imagined that getting a new influx of squires would take some of the workload off our shoulders, we soon find out just how mistaken we were. Traditionally, squires are taught by retired thanes, who give up their time to teach in exchange for not having their memories of Annwn wiped by the morrigans. But some of the teachers have chosen to leave the thanes entirely. 'If I'm going to die, I want to die ignorant, thank you very much,' one of them said in his rousing farewell speech.

Then there's the problem that a lot of the teachers who specialised in training the knights were killed in the battle against Medraut's treitres. The upshot is that the few teachers left are pushed to their limits, and current thanes need to plug the gaps. Lord Allenby does his best to mitigate the pressure on us by rotating us between patrols and training. Still, it's an extra strain that we could have done without.

I take the squires for a few hours each week, and suddenly have a new appreciation for my teachers at Bosco. Teaching people my age is *hard*. There's only fourteen new knight squires this year, and they're either trying to impress each other, trying too hard to impress me, or in Sachi's case trying too hard *not* to impress me. I'm supposed to be helping them with weapons training, but that's made more difficult by the fact that there are so few of them. When I was being taught last year, there were enough squires to get a variety of weapons fighting against each other in pairs. I take it in turns battling them with my scimitar, and occasionally I'll manage to recruit one of my colleagues for a demonstration. This always elicits squeals from the more eager squires, who love 'watching the experts duke it out' as Vien puts it. I try my best to do what Rafe did last year; providing a running commentary on the decisions we're making as we fight.

'Watch as Samson moves out of my reach,' I pant, feeling like a fool as I chase Samson around the gardens. Samson uses one of his arrows to tap me on the shoulder as he darts past. The squires are laughing; even Sachi is smiling a little. This would all be so much easier if I could use my Immral.

Samson knows it too – his eyes are twinkling with mischief, knowing this is his sole opportunity to face me in combat and stand a chance of winning. A rare joy flows through me – this is my chance, I realise – a chance to fight without fear of being hurt. And, perhaps, to impress Samson.

Slowing down, I duck as one of Samson's arrows flies over my head, and pretend to trip over in the process. A couple of squires are cheering Samson on – the ones who want to suck up to the knight captain, not knowing him well enough to know that he'd never want praise or adoration like that. 'If Fern was a nightmare, which let's face it she sometimes can be,' Samson calls out, 'she'd be on the back foot and now would be my chance to take her down.'

I hear him stride over and I wave a hand feebly in surrender.

'You okay?' he says, genuinely concerned.

For a fleeting second I feel guilty for what I'm about to do . . . then it's gone, and I swipe a leg out to trip him up. His surprise doesn't stop him from doing a back roll as soon as he lands, but it's enough to give me an advantage. I leap high into the air and land astride him, my scimitar mere inches from his face, our bodies connected in a way I have daydreamed about for months. He stares up at me, betrayal and admiration warring over his expression. There's an energy in the air that I can't account for. A twanging beat that pulses between us.

'Never let your guard down,' I say to the squires, my eyes not leaving Samson's. 'That's something we've learned all too well lately.'

There. Samson's expression shifts and whatever confusing thing had been between us pops. *That's good,* I tell myself. *Keep things simple between you two*. But I of all people should know that starting to trust people – starting to love them – is never, ever simple.

Chapter 15

It's only when we're packing up for the night that I realise how much of a mistake I made with that fight. Sachi is waiting for me as I leave the training area. 'Is that how he died?' she asks, falling into step with me. 'Did those treitres trick him?'

'No, it wasn't like that . . .' I trail off. Shit. This cannot happen here. I'm not ready. I don't know how to have this conversation. The squires have only been given the barest details of what happened over the last year, and of Medraut's involvement. They'll undoubtedly be starting to put together the full extent of what happened already – it's not as if the mysterious deaths of thousands of people have gone unnoticed in the news.

I cast around for help. Samson is just behind us. 'Sachi?' he says, speeding up to join us. 'Now's not the time. I'm sorry, I know how –'

'You don't,' she spits. 'None of you know what it's like. You don't understand that I . . . I see . . .' She looks from Samson to me, trailing off. Then she runs ahead of us, dashing tears from her cheeks.

I glance at Samson. 'Thank you.'

He sighs. 'We're going to have to tell them all soon, aren't we?'

'You think that's a bad thing?'

'Yes and no.' Samson swings his bow over his shoulder. 'They should be told what's going on, but I don't want them to . . . I want them to love Annwn, the way I've loved it for years. I don't want everything that's happening now to tarnish that for them.'

I look up at the turrets of Tintagel, where angels once flew. I look over at the walls of the castle, where huge horse chestnut trees used to drop conkers the size of my fist. All gone, or dying.

'What's more important, though?' I ask. 'Giving them a romantic notion about this place, or making sure they know what's at stake?'

'You tell me,' Samson says. 'You're the one who brings most of the joy to Annwn now.'

He says it in such an offhand way that I don't quite know how to take it. He must have meant that my Immral can create joy.

'Maybe we should just tell them and get it over with,' I say. 'Then they can join us in being deeply traumatised whenever Medraut's name comes up in Ithr.'

'It's out of our hands anyway.' Samson smiles. 'Nationwide decision – all the thaneships agreed that they wouldn't tell the squires the details of what went down. I guess they're scared to lose any of them before they've even got through Ostara . . .'

Much as I disagree with keeping the extent of the truth from the squires, I can understand why the decision's been taken. Ithr's so bleak now that the thanes are doing everything they can to keep some of Annwn's magic for those who never knew it when it was truly magical.

More and more often I find myself drawn to Bosco's art room. I sequester myself in there at every break time. The designs for my own puzzle box are completed. Now all I have to do is make it. Medraut's box is made of an amalgamation of wood and metal. Hard, unforgiving materials. Mine is going to be made of clay, which means I won't have much time once I start to make it. The clay will dry quickly, and I want to make sure the patterns and textures are perfect. So I do a mock-up out of cardboard, piecing the squares together in different formations to figure out which way will work best.

I'm sitting on a bench one lunchtime, trying to decide whether green will look better next to blue or orange, when Lottie walks past, sees what I'm doing and stops dead in her tracks.

'What is it, Lottie? I'm busy.'

She gapes at me, her usually composed face slack, then blurts out, 'Pandora.'

'No, my name's Fern.'

'You're going to . . .' She seems to struggle to understand her own thoughts. 'You're going to stab . . . and let them out.'

Lottie's friends try to drag her away, but I spring to my feet. 'Is this something to do with your dad?' I ask her. 'What's going to happen?'

'Leave her alone, bitch!' one of her friends spits at me, and another pushes me back onto the bench.

'Pandora!' Lottie cries out, raking at her friends' faces, pulling at her own hair. 'Pandora!'

A teacher runs up. 'What's going on here? Miss Medraut?' He turns on me. 'What did you do?'

'Literally nothing,' I say, gathering my things. 'She's the one with problems. You need to get help for her.'

'She doesn't need help,' the teacher sniffs. 'Don't you know who her father is?'

I relay the exchange to Lord Allenby as soon as I get to Tintagel that night. The way Lottie stared at my box design, as though she was connecting it to her father's, has to be significant.

'She kept saying *Pandora,*' I tell Lord Allenby. 'I thought – Pandora's box?'

'The Greek legend?' Lord Allenby says. 'Pandora opened the box and all the world's evils escaped. I suppose there's some parallels with Medraut keeping his plans inside the puzzle box, but I must confess I'm not sure how much that helps us.'

'It was the way she looked, sir,' I say. 'Like she was terrified of what I was doing.'

'Well, maybe it's worth investigating. I'll drop my Greek counterpart a line, see if she can shed any light.'

As it happens, the Excalibur team are already in touch with Greece's answer to the thanes. In fact, they're already in contact with thanes all over the world. The veneur tower that's become our base of operations is gradually filling with documents sent from Brazil, France, Japan and Russia; just a few of the countries who have already answered Easa and Jin's call for help, even though they haven't been told what exactly they're helping with.

'This is all they had on Pandora's box,' Easa says, handing

me a crinkled scroll. The writing has been erased, but the images adorning the margins remain. In one panel a woman, voluptuous and strong, is given a box by a god. In the next, she takes a knife and hacks at the latch that locks the box shut. In the final panel, she has wrested the box open. The evils of the world erupt from inside. In all the versions I've read of the legend, Pandora is remorseful, but in this illustration she looks triumphant.

'What happened to the text on this?' I ask.

'That's the problem,' Easa says. 'Something weird is definitely going on.'

'What do you mean?' Ollie says, as I hand back the scroll and flick through a folder written in Russian.

'Well, it's not just our archives that have been cleared out of information,' Jin says. 'It's happened all over the world.'

'What?' I say, my intention to avoid talking to Jin shattered in the face of this news.

'Yeah,' Easa says darkly, 'it's like a conspiracy. Someone *really* doesn't want us to know what went down at the end of Arthur's reign. Or, apparently, about Pandora's box, although I can't work out the link between the two.'

'So what *do* we know?' Ollie says.

'Not very much,' Jin responds, placing a hand on a small stack of papers. 'This is everything that anyone could find so far. There's nothing that directly references Excalibur – but these are all papers and books that other thaneships thought might help.'

'And? Has it?' I ask.

'We're still going through it,' Jin says, 'which obviously takes a while since it's just the two of us and we have to spend so much time updating you even though you're not –'

'Jin,' Easa warns.

Jin turns away, and Easa continues. I take the opportunity to pick up one of the books from the pile. It's the one Ollie found down in the archives. The one titled, *The Great Betrayal*.

Betrayal. That's what Merlin always says when he talks about King Arthur. As Ollie and I had already discovered, most of the pages inside are blank. There are only a few illustrations left, and none that look as though they're useful. Mostly they're of a fictionalised version of King Arthur holding Excalibur aloft, or standing next to the stone he pulled the sword from.

'Ollie?' I say, remembering something about our secret trip to the archives. 'Did you say you felt something when you touched this book?'

Ollie runs his fingers over the pages. 'Yeah,' he says slowly. 'Anger and . . . there's a memory there, but it's not useful to us. I think it's the reeve who wrote this, daydreaming about what he was going to have for breakfast.'

'What are you thinking, Fern?' Easa asks.

'I'm wondering if we can find a document that *Ollie* can read, even if we can't. Whoever erased the words in these books didn't erase the memories of the people writing them, did they?'

'So if we find a document old enough . . .' Jin says, trailing off as she realises that I might actually have had a good idea.

Easa sighs. 'We've been looking in the wrong place then. We've been looking for words. Instead, we need to look for the oldest books we have.'

'Better get to work then,' Ollie says, fist-bumping me.

Looking for missing information becomes something of a theme over the coming days – a frustrating one. Jin and Easa scour the archives for ancient texts, but none of them yield what we're looking for. Rachel's research keeps hitting dead ends too.

'I thought I could help, but I'm just wasting your time,' she says one night.

'It was a good idea,' I tell her. 'Maybe we'll find something. Maybe we're just looking at it the wrong way.'

But the more I think about Rachel's aim to help us track the treitres, the more uneasy I feel about it. I can't put my finger on why until I mention it to Samson while we're out on patrol.

'Do you think it could be done?' I ask him as we ride along the canals of Little Venice, watching shellycoats – harmless trickster dreams made of shells – try to leap onto the narrowboats.

'Probably,' he says, frowning, 'if we could work out the mechanics of the tables. It's a good idea in theory.'

I smile. 'But?'

'You know me too well,' he replies with a wry grin. '*But* . . . they're trying to fight the past.'

'Yes, that's it,' I say. 'We should be looking to the future.'

'You think Medraut's got more up his sleeve?' Nerizan pipes up from behind us.

'He's already shown us he has,' Samson says. Linnea makes a quiet sound of distress. She's been jumpier and more morose than usual since rejoining patrol. I can't say I blame her.

‘It would be nice,’ Ollie said, ‘if for once we knew what he was planning, wouldn’t it?’

‘It would,’ I agree. ‘I’d love to be one step ahead of him, instead of always feeling like we’re on the back foot.’

And, as if Annwn itself heard our prayers, the next day, we get the lifeline we asked for. But it comes at a price.

Chapter 16

A few days later, as I'm walking back from Bosco, something new happens. I'm nearly home, walking through the town centre, dodging between fruit stalls and prams and scooters, when someone approaches me.

'Excuse me,' the voice says to my hunched back, and I prepare myself for an attack. These days the best I can hope for is that it's verbal rather than physical. 'Excuse me, miss, can I walk with you for a while?'

I look up. I recognise the man, but can't for the life of me remember where from. He's a little older than Dad, with a neat beard and the look of a strict grandfather. Where have I seen him before?

He offers me a leaflet from the pile he's carrying. 'Can I give you this? We'd love to have you join us . . .'

The paper features a group of faces, all beaming up at me, cult-like. Across the top of the leaflet in balloon-like letters are the words, *Shout Louder!*

'You're Constantine Hale,' I say, finally placing him from the website I looked up a few months ago after the fight between Shout Louder and One Voice.

'Oh, you've heard of us already, have you? That's excellent,' Constantine says. 'We're really growing, you know. You look like you'd be perfect to join the fight.'

He swings his arm, elbow bent, in the manner of a pirate. It's an affected gesture, and does nothing to quell the sudden anger in my belly.

'Why me?' I ask him.

'I'm sorry, dear?'

'I'm not your dear. I asked, why me? What makes you think I'd be perfect for your group?'

Constantine is wrong-footed. 'Well . . .' He makes a feeble gesture towards my face. 'I can't imagine you're having a great time at the moment, given . . .'

I move in front of him and stop, blocking his path. This is the end of the line for him and me, and I want to make that clear.

'This isn't for me.' I hand the leaflet back.

His expression shifts from amiable grandpa to sneering old man. 'Too afraid of the fight, maybe?'

I step forward, into his space, forcing him back. 'You have no idea what fear is,' I say. 'Who are *you* to tell me where I belong?'

I turn on my heel and march away. I carry my anger into patrol that night, although I don't mention my encounter with Hale to anyone else, not even Ollie. A quiet voice tells me that I handled it wrong. I leaped to take offence. Yes, his reaction wasn't great, but did I need to accuse him immediately?

It plays on my mind all night, so by the time we finish patrol, and Samson and I are trudging back to the castle, I am twisted with the circles I cannot square.

'Do you think there's a way back from anger?' I ask Samson.

'That's a big question for this time of night,' he replies, smiling.

'Sorry. I just . . .' I trail off.

'What is it? Has something happened, Fern?'

'Not really.' I feel stupid now, trying to articulate something that's so much bigger than my brain can compute. 'I just don't know where the line is any more, I suppose. Between people like Medraut, who are beyond salvation, and . . .'

'And people who could be changed?' Samson asks.

I nod. 'Not just that. But, who are we allowed to get angry at, you know? I'm so furious, all the time, with Medraut and what he's doing to the world. But he's not on his own any more, is he? Maybe he never was. How do we work out who needs to be punished and who was just brainwashed? And is it okay to be brainwashed, or does that make you weak?'

Samson takes a long time to reply. Long enough for us to make our way up the steps of Tintagel and past the hospital wing, past the harker tables where, to my surprise, Jin is talking to Rachel in a low voice.

'I don't think we'll ever know, to be honest,' Samson says. 'Maybe it isn't about anger. Maybe it's about mercy. Accepting that some people deserve punishment but choosing not to, instead of thinking of them as the ones who got away. I hope you know that . . .'

Samson stops in his tracks. I follow his gaze to the golden banner that's been thrown over the side of the balcony in the central hall.

'Secret meeting?' he says lightly.

'Sorry.' We have never spoken directly about the quest for Excalibur, or the reason that Ollie and I sometimes have to disappear into the veneurs' tower. Samson has always made himself scarce whenever an explanation might have been needed.

'It's okay, Fern,' he says. 'I had to keep my mission a secret from everyone for nearly a year, remember? It didn't cheapen my friendships. It needed to be done.'

I remember the way I first met Samson – he had been inside Medraut's headquarters as a secret agent for months, with no way of communicating with Tintagel. It must have been such a lonely existence, and in no way comparable to what Jin and Easa are doing up in that tower. It's sweet of him to try to reassure me, though.

'Go.' He smiles. 'Save the world, brilliant girl.'

I can't help but grin as I run across the hall and through the door beneath that golden banner. It is our signal that the team has found something important.

Only Easa is in the tower room when I enter. He's more animated than I've ever seen him.

'I told you we'd figure it out,' he says.

'You worked out that coin?' I say. The little pill box with its five-jewelled coin has been the subject of much conversation over the last few days. It sits in pride of place on a separate table, with a handful of items that we've deemed *of interest* to the Excalibur quest. A collection of silver spoons with another verse inscribed on their stems. A christening mug that looks similar to the ones my mum's parents gave to Ollie and me when we were born.

'Well, no,' Easa admits, 'but we think we've done better than that.'

Ollie clatters up the stairs behind me and topples into the room. He still has the sweat of a heavy patrol on him, and his tunic appears to be covered in horse shit.

'Did you fall off Balius?' I ask him innocently.

'It was a *fight*,' Ollie sneers. 'I was saving a boy's life.'

'Ah, he looks so heroic, yet smells so disgusting,' I singsong.

'We think we've discovered something that might tell us more about Excalibur and the Great Betrayal,' Easa interrupts.

Silence descends. This is it. This is the moment we find out why my mum was so dead set on me getting Arthur's sword.

'You found a document old enough?' I say.

'Yes,' Jin replies, entering the room behind Ollie and closing the door. 'In the end your mum led us to the right place.'

'How?' Ollie asks.

'We looked back over everything she'd removed from the archives in her final years at Tintagel,' Easa says. He points to a mass of papers sorted into tottering piles on one of the tables. 'It took us a while to find it because we thought it would be more efficient to look at the papers that had some kind of relation to Arthur or Excalibur. Look.'

As Easa hands me a torn scrap of paper, Jin tells him, 'Lord Allenby knows.'

Ollie and I peer at the writing. It's nearly faded – a sure sign that this paper has never in all its long existence been deemed important. In Annwn, things don't fade with age. They fade with forgetfulness – if a book had been read daily, it would look as new as if it had been bound yesterday, even if it was thousands of years old.

'There's nothing on here though,' Ollie says.

'There is,' I say, holding the paper up to the light. 'See? Right in the bottom corner, very faint.'

'Here.' Easa hands Ollie a magnifying glass, but I have a better idea. I send my Immral into the paper, feeling the power leaping along the ancient pen grooves, filling them with inspyre. Two words leap out at us in blue light.

Sir Bedevere.

A chill runs down my spine. 'You did it,' I breathe. Something about it feels *right*. The knight who gave his name to my regiment – one of King Arthur's favoured few – is the one who might hold the answer.

'We hope so,' Easa says, 'because the writing on the page hasn't just been erased. It's been drowned. It's covered in tears. Jin ran some tests on the parchment.'

'Salt water.' Jin nods. 'Over a thousand years old. We thought, if anything was going to have memories, it's a piece of paper covered in grief.'

I look at Ollie. He's not thrilled, I can tell – the emotions he gets from these items always take a toll on him, and not just in the nose-bleeding way. But he takes my hand, and places his free one on the parchment. Our Immral connects quickly. Tastes seep into my mouth. Stale and faint at first, but then growing stronger and fresher.

The tang of a sea breeze. The bitterness of steel. And something much more complicated behind it all: an earthy, sodden smell. The smell of grief in righteousness. Then the memories come, through Ollie's hand and into mine, and I raise my spare hand to project them into the room.

A group of knights stands ceremoniously on a cold mountaintop, waiting. The mountain is in Annwn, I see now – the memory shows huge birds swooping around the knights' heads. Then there's a stirring amongst the company. Someone is approaching. From the steep path emerges a tall man, glowing with inspyre, the same way Medraut glowed with it when I last saw him in Annwn. In his hand: a sword. Excalibur.

'My lord,' the knights murmur, falling to their knees.

Arthur doesn't look at them. He holds Excalibur aloft, and inspyre sparks around it and between him and the sword, as though wishing to meld them into one being.

'It is done,' he says. 'It is mine now. We will have no more devils.'

Most of the knights stare up at Arthur devotedly. But Bedevere shares a look with a dark-haired knight who kneels on the edge of the group. I can taste his fear. But King Arthur doesn't care any more. He plunges the sword into a bare rock perched on the very precipice of the mountain. The inspyre in the sword, in the snowy earth around them, is pulled towards him as though Excalibur were a black hole. All down the mountainside, the grass is ripped from its roots, leaving the earth bare.

Arthur laughs, his voice echoing into the cold air. 'It works!' he cries. 'My power is increased. My power is magnified. Now no one and nothing will stand in my way.'

He roars, and with a blast of Immral from Excalibur, he lays waste to the landscape. The birds in the sky disintegrate; the monsters in the uplands far below crumble. Soon, the knights can see all the way down the barren mountain to the ocean. A giant had been playing in the sea. It falls, too, into nothingness. The sea is stripped of its water, leaving an endless shell of dust. The knights cower, all of them. Bedevere's eyes fill with tears and his heart with grief.

So. This was King Arthur, and this was the Great Betrayal.

Chapter 17

'If Medraut gets Excalibur first,' Easa says, 'that's it. That's his endgame. Everything Ollie saw in that box would come true.'

The implications of what we've found floods me. So this is why Mum left Excalibur for me. It amplifies our power. She knew that I had Immral and she thought I'd be able to wield it. Did she know that Medraut would still be a threat, fifteen years later? She must have suspected it. Then, with a drop in my stomach, I have another realisation – she didn't think she'd die. She left me that letter as a failsafe, but she hoped not to use it. She thought she'd have all this time to teach me, so that when I was called to Annwn I'd be ready. All that time, stolen from me by Sebastien Medraut.

'We need to talk to Lord Allenby,' I say, forcing myself away from my spiralling thoughts.

'He's waiting for you,' Jin says, nodding towards the door.

I look back down at the empty piece of parchment. Could this really be the answer we've been looking for?

'You're welcome,' Jin snarks.

I don't respond.

Lord Allenby opens the door to his office before we've even

knocked. It doesn't take long to fill him in on what we saw in Bedevere's ancient memories. But instead of answering us, he simply goes to his desk and scribbles something on a scrap of paper.

'One moment,' he says, gesturing towards two chairs.

I sink into one, only now realising how bone-tired I am. As we watch, Lord Allenby takes the scrap of paper and unlocks the wooden panel that houses the shrine I saw a few weeks ago. As he did then, he lights the candles and burns the paper over them.

'Maybe this time we'll get their attention,' he says quietly. He turns towards Ollie and me. 'Well, what do you make of it?'

'There's something that doesn't make sense, sir,' Ollie chimes in before I can speak. 'Mum told Ellen that she'd found something that would defeat Medraut forever. But that can't have been Excalibur, because she wouldn't have been able to use it – she didn't have Immral.'

'She wanted me to use it,' I point out.

'She couldn't have known you'd have Immral though. Not at that point. She must have told Ellen about Excalibur before Ellen faked her death, right? Well, we hadn't been born then.'

I ponder Ollie's words. He's right. We were born shortly after Ellen seemingly died. So how was Mum planning on using the sword? 'Maybe she didn't know exactly how it was used?' I suggest. 'I mean, we've only got this memory to go on, it's not exactly a comprehensive guide to King Arthur's weaponry.'

'I think it goes deeper than that,' Lord Allenby says, 'but we're not going to find anything more today. Good work. Now you both go home and rest.'

I'm surprisingly okay, beyond the usual headache that comes from using my Immral, but Ollie isn't. He sways as we leave Lord Allenby's office, and I have to catch him before he falls. 'You okay?' I whisper.

'Yeah, I . . .' Ollie vomits up some blood. A passing reeve sighs.

'Sorry,' Ollie mumbles.

'It's fine,' the reeve says. 'Go get checked out at the hospital while I clear it up.'

We move onwards. 'I don't need the hospital,' Ollie tells me in a low voice, 'I just need to get out of here.'

'Are you sure?'

Rachel rushes over from her desk. 'What's going on?' she asks, taking Ollie's other arm and shouldering some of his weight.

'It's because the magic was so old,' he slurs. I glance at Rachel, listening closely to what he's saying. She's not supposed to know anything about the quest for Excalibur, but Ollie's too far gone to remember that.

'The memories,' Ollie says. 'The older they are, the harder it is to see them . . .'

'Shh,' I say, pulling him away from Rachel and down the steps to the platform that will take us home. 'Thanks,' I call over my shoulder to Rachel. She just stands in the doorway, the giant arch making her look even smaller than usual.

By the time evening rolls around again and we're due back in Tintagel, Ollie is mostly recovered. He'd vomited blood onto his pillow in Ithr, and I'd made an exception to my I-don't-do-laundry-for-anyone-other-than-me rule to get it washed before Dad noticed and panicked.

'I owe you,' he says over dinner, stuffing nut roast into his mouth.

I grin. 'I'll add it to your tab.'

We return to Tintagel with fight as well as food in our bellies. Knowing Excalibur's capabilities has confirmed the urgency of our quest. Lord Allenby collars us as soon as we step foot inside the castle.

'Follow me,' he says, hurrying back towards his office. 'They've replied, at last.'

He presses on one of the wooden panels that lines his office, and it springs open to reveal a shallow cupboard, in which an array of doorknobs is arranged. They are all different sizes, shapes and colours – one even glows bright purple. As I watch, a final doorknob materialises – tarnished gold, covered in enamel that knots over the metal. Lord Allenby plucks the new doorknob from its resting place. Removing the little copper knob from his office door, he replaces it with the gold. The outline of the door glows for a moment, as though a bright light is being shone through it from the other side, then it returns to looking exactly as it did before.

'Are you both ready?' he asks.

'Ready for what?' I say.

'I've been trying to get an audience with the Fay ever since you told me about your mother hiding Excalibur,' he replies. 'They've been ignoring me, and wouldn't talk about it at the Tournament. My note last night, telling them that we know what Excalibur can do, seemed to get their attention.'

'We're going to see Andraste?' I say. I'm longing to see her again. I want to make sure she's okay.

'I don't know how long they will permit us an audience,' Lord Allenby says. 'We have to stay focused. Find out everything we can about Excalibur, and how much they know about what Una did with it. Understand?'

'Yes, sir,' Ollie and I parrot.

Excitement flares up in my chest. I might be about to get answers. Then Lord Allenby opens the door, and it's not a stone staircase and a tunnel behind there any longer. It's a broad hall lined with huge candles. At the other end a line of thrones sit on a dais. Upon each throne is seated a king or queen. The entire hall is lined with lesser thrones, each one occupied by a Fay. A three-eyed crone; a man made of leaves; and one Fay who flits between adult and child form depending on which angle I see them from.

As we duck through the doorway and into the hall, the first thing that hits me is the musty but not altogether unpleasant smell of a damp building being warmed by a large fire. The fire in question roars in the centre of the space, heavy stones encircling it so that it doesn't set light to the rushes that are scattered across the rest of the floor. I look back and see that the door we've come through isn't narrow or concealed as it was on the Tintagel side – it's a huge, iron monstrosity. Beyond the open doors I can still see Allenby's office, looking modern in contrast with this medieval affair.

As Lord Allenby leads the way up to the dais, something above catches my eye. We're not under a thatched roof as I'd initially thought. There are fish on the ceiling. We're in an underwater palace. Above us, held up by the magic of Annwn, is a vast lake. Seaweed clings on to an invisible roof. Sharks and seals dart after trout and carp, and for one bone-thrilling moment I spot a huge, lithe, worm-like creature slicing through a dark patch of water.

'You're wasting your time,' Merlin says in a wheezy voice, pulling my gaze back to the Fay, and to the matter at hand.

Merlin is hunched in the central throne, his naked torso and wooden skirt incongruous against the grandeur of his surroundings. Nimue is on his right-hand side, her arms bare once more, and scarred from the trial of the Tournament. I look down the row. There she is, her eyes lighting up as they land on me. Andraste is seated at the far end. Her warrior twin brother is at the other end, as though they are poised to protect their family from attack on either side. I want to hug her, but I settle for sending her a grin and a thumbs up instead.

As Lord Allenby kneels before Merlin, I study Andraste from my standing point. Usually she is so upright, so proud. Now, though, she leans on her throne's velveted arms. Every one of the Fay shows similar signs of sickness. Merlin's chest heaves with the effort of breathing. Andraste's twin brother Lugh nurses a warped arm, as though it's been broken several times and never properly set. Nimue raises a hand to her head and when she returns it to her lap she clutches a long braid of hair, leaving an empty patch on her skull. They have grown sicker even in the short timespan between now and the Tournament.

'We received your messages,' Merlin says. 'Perhaps with this audience you will finally leave us alone.'

'We only ever sought information,' Lord Allenby replies. 'A few minutes in your long lives.'

'The Fay have many responsibilities and many lives. We cannot always be present to answer your whims.'

'I understand,' Lord Allenby says, and I can tell that he's trying to hide his annoyance. 'As you know, we've found information about Excalibur . . .'

'Whatever you think you've found out about the Great Betrayer's –' Merlin begins.

'Grandfather, let them speak,' Andraste says.

Merlin purses his lips, but falls silent.

Andraste nods at Lord Allenby, but Lord Allenby doesn't speak. Not at first. He turns to me, and holds out his hand. 'Would you mind, Miss King, if we showed them the letter?'

I hesitate. I keep Mum's letter in the little pouch that holds my other weapons – fire-quenching marbles – but to share it with people like Merlin? I don't like it, but I trust Lord Allenby. If he thinks this is the best way to get what we want, then I must agree. Reluctantly, I pull out the letter. Merlin snatches it from my hands and peers down at my mother's spiked handwriting.

'This is the letter I informed you about some weeks ago,' Lord Allenby says.

'I told my family that you did not speak the truth,' Andraste says, her eyes glittering strangely. 'I told them that you couldn't possibly have found anything about Excalibur, since we erased all records of it.'

'But why?' I ask. Why would Andraste accuse me of lying?

'Impossible,' Merlin spits. 'We hid Excalibur and its secrets too well for any mortal to steal it.'

That exclamation is taken up by the other Fay; up and down the thrones they whisper furiously.

'Ridiculous.'

'Not even an Immral . . .'

'Presumptuous mortal.'

Only two Fay do not express surprise. They glance at each other, and then they look at me, their gaze steady, their eyes blazing. One of them, I would have expected. The other, I would not.

'You helped her, didn't you?' I say, loud enough to silence the rest of the Fay. 'You helped my mother take it.'

'Yes,' Andraste says, standing with difficulty.

'Yes,' Nimue says, standing too, her honeyed voice otherworldly. 'Yes, we did.'

Chapter 18

Heavy silence falls over the hall. Lugh is looking at his sister the way Ollie used to look at me: with disgust and hatred.

'You helped the mortal?' Merlin sneers. 'You helped her take the sword?'

'It was the right thing to do,' Andraste says.

'It was safe!' spits the trickster Fay, Puck. 'No mortal could find it without us.'

'And therein lay the problem!' Nimue says, turning on her brother. 'What if it were needed and we weren't there?'

'Why would it be needed?' Merlin says, his voice low, and more dangerous for it. 'Why would it be needed, eh?' He gets to his feet, and although he still clutches one of the throne's arms, there is power in him. It radiates from him, through his voice and eyes and the tension in his arms. 'Have you both grown so soft that a thousand years makes you forget what was done?'

'We forget nothing,' Andraste says, her voice vibrating with equal power. I take a step back. The atmosphere in the hall is the pinch before a thunderstorm.

'Did you forget,' Merlin says, his voice rising, 'what we pledged to each other once the Grail was found and the Great

Betrayer was defeated? We vowed that no mortal would wield the sword again.'

'Things change,' Nimue says. 'My sister and I understood what you cannot. That there may come a time when we need the sword to be wielded by one who will use it to save us.'

'No mortal can be trusted,' Puck spits, and I resist the urge to say, *That's a bit rich, coming from you*.

'Especially one with the power to command Excalibur,' Lugh says.

'My lords, my ladies,' Lord Allenby says, 'forgive my interruption, but –'

'Do you forget that we are dying?' Nimue shouts. 'Look!' She wrenches another clump of hair from her scalp and casts it at Puck's feet. 'Our stories are being forgotten. Do you think that we can ride this out? No, we must do something.'

'Do not lie to us,' Merlin says. 'Medraut had been defeated when you thought to take Excalibur from its resting place. Tell the truth: your acolyte made you a pretty promise and you betrayed us for her.'

That word, *acolyte*, startles me. Mum – Nimue's follower? The Fay of love and softness. Everything I know about my mother tells me that if she was anyone's devotee, it was Andraste's, not Nimue's. The Una I have come to imagine was weaved in darkness and ambition and always ready for the fight. Is Merlin just making things up, or does he know more about Mum than I do?

'Even if that were true, have we not been proven right?' Andraste says. 'Another threatens to kill us, and Gorlois's girl is the only one who might be able to stop him.'

I shift uncomfortably, very aware of Ollie standing right

beside me. He has not moved, but tension balloons between us. We both noticed, then, that Andraste talked about me having Immral, as though his part of the power was irrelevant. Andraste is parroting what our mother felt – that I'm the important one, not him.

'Who's to say she will, though?' Merlin exclaims. 'Who's to say she would not use us to get Excalibur, then betray us, just as *he* did.'

'Sorry,' I interrupt, 'but I am right here. I get you not trusting me, I really do. But what are your options right now? Either you help me get Excalibur and risk me killing you, or you definitely get killed by Medraut.'

The Fay are appalled at me speaking to them. Ollie coughs nervously. 'I'm not wrong, am I?' I say, less confidently now.

'You admit that you would betray us then,' Lugh says.

'I never said –'

'I have seen her,' Andraste says, loudly enough to silence everyone. 'She could have destroyed a nightmare, but instead she changed it into a dream. The Betrayer would never have done such a thing. Nor would Medraut. She passed the test.'

I am floored. The moment Andraste is referring to was never framed as a test to me – she was supposed to be helping me access my power, that was all. I was struggling to use my Immral, and she made me face down a nightmare. Instead of destroying it, I turned it into a little girl; odd, but harmless, much as I saw myself. But now I think about it, she did look relieved, and she shared that look with Allenby. Maybe they were both in on it. I should feel betrayed but actually I'm secretly pleased. They knew at that point, even if I didn't, that there was hope for me.

'It matters not,' Merlin says. 'No mortal will ever wield the sword, not while I live.'

'Nor I,' Lugh says. 'Tell us where it is, sisters, and silence these humans, or we will be forced to turn against you.'

In an instant, the rest of the Fay are on their feet. The hall is charged with inspyre; like spikes of static, it radiates from the Fay in flickers of anger and fear.

'Enough!' Andraste says, just as Nimue stamps one of her feet and the floor quakes with the power of their combined rage. The other Fay sink back onto their thrones. Only Andraste, Nimue and Merlin remain standing.

'It is done,' Andraste tells Merlin. 'We will not obey you. You cannot take it back now, grandfather.'

Merlin moves so quickly that I barely have time to react. He crosses the room and strikes Andraste so hard that she is brought to her knees. I run towards her, but Merlin holds a hand out and I am brought up short, the force of his power pressing against my chest, squeezing my lungs tight.

'Fern!' Lord Allenby calls out, warning me to step back, but I won't. Ignoring the tightness in my chest, I pull at my Immral and throw it towards Merlin in a great ball of energy. As it hits him, he only lets out a puff of air, but I can tell that I've hurt him. The band around my lungs releases instantly. I don't stop there, though. Another swipe of Immral and I throw Merlin from his feet, toppling him so that he lands crumpled at the foot of the dais. In a second more I'm cradling Andraste.

'Are you okay?' I whisper.

'You should not have done that,' she replies softly, but she doesn't look up.

'Fern.' Ollie is behind me, his hands pulling me away. 'Fern, we have to go.'

'Andraste?' I say, more urgently. I can feel that something's wrong. There's a prickling in my hands and feet, as though my power is warning me of a rival. Something drips on the back of my neck.

'Fern, *please*,' Ollie says.

More footsteps, then Nimue's cool hands are upon my arms. 'I will care for her,' she says. 'You must flee. Now.'

I look up at last. Merlin is getting to his feet, achingly slowly. But it's not him who is the threat. Not right now. The other Fay are gathering around him. Their faces are pure fury, and all of it is directed towards me.

Lord Allenby, to his credit, is standing between the Fay and me, his hands outstretched. 'She's young, my lords,' he's saying. 'She does not understand . . .'

Then Puck reaches up and plucks one of the spikes that grows from his head clean off. He brandishes it at Lord Allenby like a knife.

'Alright,' Lord Allenby says at last. 'Alright.' And he draws the crossbow from his back. We are about to battle with the Fay, and it's all my fault. I look towards Andraste and Nimue. 'Come with us,' I say.

They shake their heads. The walls of the hall are trembling. There's another drip from above. I look up. The ceiling is giving way. The lake above us is poised to flood the room.

'We need to know about Excalibur,' I say urgently.

'We made sure that you wouldn't need us,' Nimue says. 'That was the point.'

'What do you mean?' Ollie says. 'Where is it?'

'No.' Nimue shakes her head. 'If you are worthy, then you will find it. I have given you all that you need.'

'Run, Fern,' Andraste says. 'We will hold them off.'

At last I let Ollie pull me back towards the door. Lord Allenby isn't far behind us. The Fay are advancing. Cracks form in the floor and run up the walls, leaving little puffs of plaster in their wake. The inspyre that was crackling around the hall pulsates, as though the Fay are preparing to use it. In the distance, I see Nimue pull Andraste to her feet, and they turn as one towards their family. And I realise why Andraste didn't want to look at me.

Merlin's blow didn't just send her to her knees; it tore off a great chunk of her face. Where her cheek and jaw once were, now there's just a gaping grey hole. I want to run back to her, to try to heal her or at least protect her from further harm, but we're nearly at the door now and I can tell from the raw energy filling the hall that I am not strong enough on my own to hold the Fay off for long. But I have to try, don't I? Andraste's already risked so much to help me; it's the least I can do for her, and for Nimue.

Nimue pushes Andraste towards one of the cracks in the wall. The Fay haven't noticed yet; they're so focused on me. So they can escape – thank God. But then Lugh spots them. He doesn't have to say anything. As though the Fay are bound together as one force, they turn to look at their fleeing sisters. No. I can't let them hurt Andraste any more.

An arrow whisks through the air, past my cheek, and embeds in Lugh's arm. He roars with fury. Lord Allenby fits another arrow to his crossbow and reaches for me, pushing me behind him. 'Get through, quickly,' he tells me. 'Destroy the key. Don't wait for me.'

I'm not done, though. I'm certainly not going to leave my commander behind when I've still got my power. As we reach the door back to Tintagel, I raise a hand and call the inspyre rattling around the hall towards me. It flocks to my outstretched palm.

'No,' Merlin snarls, reaching out his own hand to call it back.

'Oh yes.' I say grimly, and throw off Ollie's grasp. Squaring up to Merlin, I bring my fist, filled with inspyre, swirling with it like a tornado, down into the shaking earth. My punch moves through the straw and the dust as though it were quicksand. Lord Allenby stumbles back as the ground beneath him cracks open, the earth collapsing. I push the inspyre out towards the gathered Fay like a tide of water. With a deafening rumble, the ground gives way right as the ceiling does. The Fay fall with it, their shouts unheard beneath the sound of freshwater bursting through the cracks in the ceiling, pouring down into the abyss in pursuit of them.

I run the final few steps to the door, craning to see past the flood. There they are. Andraste and Nimue, slipping through the crack in the wall on the other side of the hall. Andraste meets my gaze and I am sure, despite her poor, broken face, that she offers me a smile.

Chapter 19

As Lord Allenby slams the door between Tintagel and the Fay's hall shut, I collapse into a chair. I can only watch as he takes the doorknob and hurls it onto the floor, the impact leaving a deep dent in the metal. It is useless now; the way back to the Fay's hall is locked. If any vengeful gods want to find me, they'll have to take a longer route.

Panting, Lord Allenby, Ollie and I look at each other. It's Ollie who breaks the silence. 'That went well.'

I'm still trying to process everything I've learned. The news that not just Andraste but also Nimue – a Fay I'd previously dismissed as being superficial and irrelevant – were working with my mum to hide Excalibur, is big enough. I should be thinking about what Nimue said – something about needing to be worthy – but all I can see is the image of Merlin hitting Andraste. Hitting her with such force that half her face came off.

'It could have ended better,' Lord Allenby says, 'but at least we got the information we needed.'

'Did we?' Ollie asks, casting a glance my way.

'What?' I snap back. 'You wanted me to just stand there while he hurt her?'

Ollie holds up his hands in defence, but it's Lord Allenby who speaks. 'The ways of the Fay are different to ours, Fern. I didn't like it either, believe me, but it would have been better for us to keep Merlin on side.'

'So just because that's how it's always been done, that's how it's got to be forever?' I say. 'Because Merlin's *powerful* we'd better shut up and let him do whatever he wants?'

'It's politics.' Lord Allenby says.

'Of all people, I didn't think you'd be one to stand back and let something like that happen because of politics, *sir*,' I say. I ignore Ollie's sharp intake of breath. I'm ready for Lord Allenby to snap back at me, raring for the fight, but he's thoughtful.

'You make a fair point, Fern,' he says instead, 'but then I think all three of us know that I don't always get things right.'

He's referring to something that only a handful of people know he did when he was much younger – the part he played in creating my mother's murderer. Without him to argue with, though, a terrible guilt settles inside me. *You should not have done that*, Andraste had said. This is all on me. If Mum hadn't wanted to hide Excalibur for me then Merlin would never have attacked her. If I hadn't turned on Merlin then the Fay might still be on our side.

Did I really do the wrong thing by throwing Merlin off Andraste? I can't see how I could have done anything different, but there's no denying that we're in a precarious position. We've made enemies of most of the Fay, and who knows what Andraste and Nimue will do now that their betrayal of their family has been uncovered.

'Well,' Lord Allenby says, 'at least we know how Una got Excalibur. I suspected, of course, that it had something to do with the Fay, which is why I was so keen to talk to them. I didn't think it would have this outcome though.'

'Do you think we can contact Andraste and Nimue?' I ask. 'They'll be able to tell us exactly how to find the sword, won't they?'

Lord Allenby shakes his head. 'We'll certainly look for them, but without their hall, and with them separated from the rest of the Fay, I'm not sure it's possible.'

'Also,' Ollie says, 'they're probably lying low on account of, you know, their entire family wanting to kill them.'

'Quite,' Lord Allenby says. 'Now, Nimue said that we had what we needed to get started. Una's letter did too. So I think we should keep looking on our own.'

'We've been trying to work out that first clue for ages,' Ollie complains. But I am already remembering something. Nimue hadn't said *we* had what we needed. She had said, *I have given you all that you need*. I mention this to Lord Allenby and Ollie. 'That seems quite specific, doesn't it?'

'She gave you something at the Tournament, didn't she?' Ollie says.

I am there already, running out of Lord Allenby's office towards the knights' chamber. I push a knot above the mantelpiece, where my locker is hidden, and pull out the belt Nimue gave me. The braided fabric glistens in the firelight. Five pieces of soft rope entwined around each other. *In all are five*. It had seemed like an odd gift at the time, but the kind of tone deaf present I'd expect of Nimue. Of course, now that I know she was in cahoots with Mum and Andraste, I am having to rethink every unkind thought I had about her.

'I think you should keep that belt with you from now on,' Lord Allenby says when I show it to him and Ollie. 'If it's pertinent to the quest, there's no telling when it might come in useful.'

I can't quite see a belt being useful for anything other than holding my trousers up, but I wind it around my waist, beneath my tunic.

'It seems to me that we have a lot of the puzzle pieces now,' Lord Allenby says, holding up a hand and folding each finger down as he goes through his points. 'We know why your mum wanted to find Excalibur – because she had discovered what it's capable of and she wanted her daughter, who she knew had Immral, to be able to wield it. We know how Una retrieved Excalibur and how she went about hiding it again – with the help of the Ladies Andraste and Nimue. We have the message she left you, the coin with the crystals and now this belt. We know that there will be three tasks to complete, and we know that five is the key number in each of them.'

'When you put it like that, sir, it does sound like quite a lot,' Ollie says.

I can't muster their enthusiasm. We may have a lot of puzzle pieces, but we don't know how many we're missing, or which of them are the corners. And I may have just burned our bridges with the only people who have the information we desperately need.

'You're just tired,' Ollie says when I voice this frustration to him in Ithr. 'Although . . . I'm not going to lie that you could've been a bit more tactful to keep the Fay on side.'

'It's *too much,*' I tell him. It's not just the constant anxiety of wondering what Medraut is planning and knowing that the clock is ticking on our chances of stopping him. It's that I'm only sixteen. I'm supposed to be worrying about GCSEs and boys and how to get fake IDs, not about whether a mass-murdering politician is going to find Annwn's equivalent of a nuclear bomb before we do.

My realisation about Nimue's belt, and her and Andraste's confession, lights a fire beneath the Excalibur team. Jin and Easa trawl through the archives and ancient maps of Annwn for any mention of the number five. They cross-reference their files for references to golden belts and jewelled coins. Before long, the little tower room's walls are covered in lists, notes and theories. I find myself playing with the belt during meetings, or at quiet points during patrol. The ancient Fay magic held in its depths is dormant, waiting for me to utter the right words, like the witch Jenny once accused me of being.

I start to see why Lord Allenby chose these two for this job. They have an attention to detail and a different way of looking at things than the knights, who by nature tend to be more gung-ho, act first, wonder-whether-it-was-a-great-idea later. But that doesn't stop me from getting frustrated at our lack of progress.

'Well, have you got any better ideas?' Jin asks one night, when I express this, 'or are you just going to complain?'

I stare at her. 'I thought apothecaries were supposed to be kind?'

'No, we're supposed to want to help. And I'm not going

to sit here and let you put down people who are doing their best for you.'

'I wasn't putting anyone down.'

Jin shrugs. 'Sure sounded like you were, Chosen One.'

'My point,' Easa says loudly, before I can retort, 'is that we're working on it, and for now you two don't have to be here. Go and focus on doing your heroic, bad-ass thing.'

'Thanks,' Ollie says, leading me away.

It's no secret that Jin and I don't like each other, but Easa is growing on me, even if I don't show it. He may be quiet but when he speaks it's with consideration. Sometimes I think he and Jin have been assigned to the wrong lores – Easa's the kind of person I can imagine having a good bedside manner. Jin, not so much. There are others, too, who are starting to wriggle their way in through the cracks in my emotional walls. I find myself growing protective of Rachel, who always seems so eager but so fragile. And Brandon, the veneur who dotes on Lamb almost as much as I do . . . Well, he's just fun to be around. In some ways he reminds me of Ramesh, or the kind of capable joker Ramesh could have become.

I've just got to hope that I can keep all of us alive long enough to give them the chance our fallen friends didn't get.

Chapter 20

In the days that follow our disastrous visit to the Fay, life almost goes back to normal. By day I go to school, by night I patrol Annwn. Only those in the know would be aware that anything more dangerous was happening. Dad and Clemmie don't seem to notice the drip-drip-drip of Medraut's ideologies becoming more frequent on the news. If anything, they claim that the media's giving Shout Louder a bigger voice, using them to discriminate against Medraut: 'That poor man, hasn't he been through enough?'

If I thought that the dull clothes his supporters wear and the unimaginative adverts he's inspired weren't enough, there are, I'm ashamed to say, some aspects of Medraut's rise to power that I do enjoy. The National Gallery, a huge building that looks down on Trafalgar Square in the centre of London, has long been one of my favourite haunts. I'm used to having to dodge tourists and other people like me – those seeking a moment of calm amidst the London bustle. But now when I visit, I can walk through entire galleries without seeing another soul except for the volunteers who guard the paintings. It's lonely, and melancholy, and blissful. No one cares for art or music or history or discoveries any more. The museums and theatres and concert halls of Ithr fall silent. Only the white noise of industry grows.

In Annwn, Medraut's bug-like creatures have all but disappeared. Some semblance of normality has returned to patrols. Linnea and Milosz's friendship is rekindling. But Samson, Ollie and I remain alert. Everyone knows that if Medraut has given up on his bugs, it's only because he has something else up his sleeve.

And we are right.

Bedevere is on the underground patrol route tonight, but we stay above ground for as long as possible. No one enjoys the underground patrol, and I'm told that in past years knights used to bargain ridiculous things to allow their regiment to swap out of this route – barrels of lotus juice, patrol notes done for a month, even their horses. It's not just that the kind of nightmares you get down there are usually worse than the ones above ground; it's the feel of it. The tube stations might still be crowded, but as soon as you go onto the tracks, or into the abandoned tunnels where some lonely dreamers venture, it gets very frightening indeed. Our helmets emit a dim sort of glow down here, but it's still difficult to see far and nightmares or trains can loom up alarmingly quickly. Using lights to illuminate the path is a no-no as well: it has a tendency to attract inspyre and, therefore, nightmares . . .

Rachel tells us over the helmets that something's been spotted beneath Hammersmith station, so we dismount and leave our horses to graze on turnips and swedes from the market stalls nearby. Darting past dreamers, we fly over the escalators and into London's depths.

'They're to the south of the station,' Rachel's voice echoes through my helmet.

It's not long before we hear the sounds of fighting. It's never as dramatic as I think it's going to be – no screams or shouting, just a low, intense roar.

The sounds are coming from an old tunnel that I recognise from a tour Dad once took Ollie and me on. An old war room, now turned into a museum to memorialise the brave from World War Two. My stomach sinks. Museums have some of the worst nightmares. They fire up too many imaginations – not necessarily a bad thing if they inspire good dreams, but when the dreamer's frightened or spooked by what they've seen it can get dangerous.

We race around a corner and spot an open door, through which light and shadows play. Great. A single door – that makes whichever of us enters first a sitting duck. Samson signals to me and I feel my way along the wall until I reach the opening. Closing my eyes, I send my Immral from the back of my skull, across my arms and down to the tips of my fingers. *Wider*, I command it and, groaning under the weight of thousands of memories, the door at last does as it's told.

Samson is just signalling to the rest of the regiment to move in, when a dreamer comes flying out and hits the wall on the other side of the tracks. I hear the whizz of the knife before I see it, and thrust a hand out to knock it off course. A sharp little blade embeds itself into the concrete, a whisper away from the dreamer's ear.

Another signal from Samson, and we slip into the room.

Inside, it's a melee of people. At first, I can't see any

nightmares. There's no blue edging of inspyre to tell me who I should be attacking. And there are bodies on the floor.

I catch a glimpse of a female face bearing tattoos and blue spiked hair, another of those little knives stuck in her ribs. There is something else – a sound, too low for me to hear it underneath the clank of weapons.

'Medraut,' Samson breathes next to me, his eyes wide with horror. 'Can't you hear them?'

Then, with that piece of context, I suddenly understand what they're saying, and what's truly happening here.

One Voice. One Voice. One Voice.

The name of Medraut's party. His endgame. That's what some of these people are chanting. The last time I heard that chant was in Ithr, and that was when a group of people were trying to kill me too. There are no nightmares here, or none made of inspyre.

They're all dreamers. And we cannot kill dreamers.

It's against the most fundamental code of the thanes. These aren't trained assassins who know what they're doing; they're brainwashed humans who would probably be horrified to discover that they'd killed someone. For that's what's happened, I realise now. One set of dreamers have happened upon another set who Medraut wouldn't approve of – outsiders, people who don't fit his idea of acceptable – and they are attacking them. They have killed two already: two dreamers who will join the legions of those quietly, deniably murdered. They simply won't wake up, and the people who loved them will think that they died in their sleep. I have never been able to work out which is kinder: the cruel truth or the tragic lie.

'Neutralise and wake up,' Samson says, unstringing his bow in one swoop and tying it swiftly around one dreamer's wrists.

Ollie uses the blunt handle of his chakram to pin a dreamer against the wall beside us. 'Where's the nearest portal to Ithr?'

'Rachel?' Samson says.

It's only a second before Rachel responds. 'The closest one's above ground, by the market.'

Samson looks at me. He doesn't need to tell me what he needs – a clear path out of this hellhole, so we can get the dreamers back to Ithr.

'On it,' I say. 'Just keep them off me for a few minutes, okay?'

At a word from Samson, a few of the Bedevere knights swing round to protect me while the rest protect the dreamers being attacked. Now that I'm inside the room properly I can distinguish the two groups more easily – Medraut's dreamers are going for a couple who, despite everything, won't let go of each other's hands. The women cleave together, shielding each other. The knights push the attacking dreamers back, but they're rabid, determined to get to the couple at any cost. Every one of them is armed with one of those sharp little knives. The couple have nothing but their hands, which are covered in their own blood. One of the attackers lunges and, out of time to intervene with his weapon, my brother steps in front of the couple and takes a knife to the shoulder.

'Ollie!' I shout. There's a burst of inspyre that I feel in the back of my head. Like lightning, it arches towards my brother, flicking against the attacking dreamers. They fall away, stung, which gives Ollie enough to time to roll out of the way and more knights to step into his place. I push down my terror. I have to focus. Trying to ignore the fighting around me, I call to my Immral and reach out my hands. I close my eyes, sensing the inspyre in the room. There's something strange about it, but I don't have time to dwell on that just now. Instead, I latch onto the only solid shapes made of inspyre: the little knives. Holding them all in my consciousness, I twist my hands, curling them into a different shape, telling them that they are no longer made of steel. As one, the knives disintegrate. I feel them falling away into swirls of light.

Nerizan unspools the rope she uses as a weapon and winds it around the attackers, first around their waists and then looping around their arms, until they are neutralised. The ache in my head triples, except this time it's not just in my head – it reaches into my very bones. The thoughts that had conjured those knives were stronger than they'd seemed.

As the others escort the attacking dreamers up into daylight, I sink back against the wall, giving in to my headache. Ollie is looking after the couple, who do not seem to realise that they are safe. The terror of the attack is still written on their faces. It doesn't help that the attackers, even though they no longer pose any danger, keep uttering their mantra: *One Voice. One Voice. One Voice.*

'Can you shut them up, Fern?' Linnea says. 'If I have to hear that phrase one more time I'm going to kill them myself.'

I approach the attackers. I see no malice. That's the frightening thing: one of them is about the same age as my grandmother, a balding man wearing a shirt and jacket, as though he was on his way to a fancy restaurant when he got diverted. The other is a woman around Samson's age. She, too, looks polished. Her hair is straightened and she wears diamond studs in her ears. They stare at the couple in Ollie's care with purpose. As though they don't see them as people, but as bugs to be stamped on; no need for any emotion as important as anger or hatred. And they keep murmuring those words: *One Voice. One Voice. One Voice.*

With some trepidation, I place my hands on the woman's head. The last time I messed with a dreamer's brain, I ended up torturing her, so this is not a happy place for me. I've also never done it with so many people watching. Trying to block everyone else out, I close my eyes and focus on the woman's mind. I send my Immral into her skull, looking for the inspyre that must be lurking there. For a long time, it's all dark. I can't sense anything, which is strange because usually even the most boring of dreamers has a brain sparking with the stuff. Perhaps this is what I had sensed was so wrong earlier.

'Anything?' I hear Ollie say.

'Can you come over here?'

I feel Ollie's hands next to my own, and the familiar jolt as our two Immral halves become whole. And there they are – the dreamer's memories. Flashes of her life in Ithr play out before me.

'There's a block here, like the one in Lottie's mind,' Ollie says.

'Should we take them back to Tintagel?' Samson says, his voice strained. We are all remembering what I did to Lottie.

'Yes, I think that would be a good idea,' I start, then add, 'Wait . . .'

There. I felt something in the brain. A tick. A flicker.

'What is it, Fern?'

'Hang on. Maybe it's nothing . . .'

It's not nothing, I know it isn't. This dreamer's imagination isn't like anything I've felt before. When I tortured my old bully, Jenny, her imagination was solidly black. She didn't have the ability to conceive of anything outside her own experience. That's not what's going on here. This dreamer's mind feels soft. Empty, yet not empty, as though there's an invisible sponge where the mind should be. I try squeezing that sponge with my power, and that's when I feel it again. The flicker. Like a leech, living independently inside the dreamer's head, gorging itself on her thoughts. I squeeze again, and see what's there, and nearly fall back in shock.

'Fern, what's going on?'

'Do not take them to Tintagel,' I say, keeping my hands on the dreamer.

'Why?'

I look at the thing resting in the ruins of the woman's imagination, and it looks back at me. A pair of eyes, with no body, staring at me through violet irises.

Medraut is watching.

Chapter 21

January 2005

The archives were empty, thank God. Una had used all her strength to push aside the wooden panelling that hid the narrow doorway, and she'd been worried that a reeve would hear her. She was prepared with an excuse, but this would be the third time they'd find her down here without permission. They'd undoubtedly grow suspicious. And with suspicions, came consequences. Like informing Lord Medraut . . .

Hurrying along the bookshelves, she wished she'd spent more time down here when she'd first become a knight. In the beginning, she'd turned her nose up at such a dusty, stuffy place – what interest could books and paperwork hold when Annwn's delights were outside the castle walls? It was only once she was no longer a squire, when she had fewer excuses to explore the stacks, that she began to realise how useful they could be.

There. *King Arthur Pendragon*. The engraved brass was nailed into a bookcase at the far end of the stacks. She hauled it away from its neighbour and slipped into the shelves' embrace. But she didn't spend time looking through the files. Instead, she moved to the very end and reached underneath the bookcase, for the folder she'd hidden there on her last visit.

Some of the accounts were so forgotten that they'd degraded too far to be readable, the penmanship faded and the paper disintegrating. Una flicked through them as quickly as she could. A poem – no. A recipe – no. A love letter – no.

Una froze. She was certain she heard something move nearby. It was padding ever-so-softly towards her end of the stacks. The near-silent tread of a hunter. Clutching the parchment in one hand, Una flattened herself against the shelves and inched her way up towards the opening. If it came to it, she'd have to push past whoever it was and make a run for the secret entrance.

'*Riaow?*'

A bloody cat. Una almost laughed out loud as the tension left her body. This tabby, made of inspyre, was in search of cuddles, not mice. Una gathered it up and retreated back into the shelves. She crouched down and scratched the dream's head.

That's when her eyes caught on the next piece of parchment. It had been torn from an ancient book, one corner entirely missing. The writing was very faint, but if she held it up to the light she could just make out some of the words. It was written in Old English. She had never learned the language formally, only picked up words here and there over the years, both in Ithr and Annwn. She couldn't be certain that she was translating it correctly. There was something about *power* and something about a *vessel*. The two were related; entwined together like two sides of a scales. She wasn't adept enough to fully understand it. Her frustration bubbled to the surface, emitting itself in a huff. If only she had more time.

She put the torn parchment to one side and rifled through the rest. Nothing. She got up, upending the tabby onto the floor. It clawed at her in rebuke.

'Needy,' she whispered absent-mindedly to it as she ran her hands over the labels on the folders. She could feel how close she was to finding the key. She had gathered, piecemeal, the history of the object, and had some idea of what it could do if wielded by the right person. She just needed to find out where it was . . .

'You're here again.'

Una barely heard it at first. It was like a whisper close to her ear, though the speaker was at the end of the aisle.

Sebastien Medraut was watching her, one hand resting on the bookcases. It was a nonchalant gesture, but Una knew what it meant: he was blocking her exit.

'My lord,' she said. The tabby curled around her legs, mewling. She picked it up and held it to her chest, craving the comfort of the warm body next to her hammering heart.

'Have you found what you're looking for?'

He knows he knows he knows, she thought. But all she said was, 'One of the downfalls of being a journalist in Ithr. Curiosity strikes randomly and then I can't rest until I've researched it all.'

She shoved the papers back into a shelf and smiled cheerily at Medraut. 'I suppose I'd better head back home.'

Medraut didn't move. Then she felt it: a *tug* at the centre of her mind. So this is what it was like to have your mind read. She covered her thoughts in a dampening blanket. She'd been practising meditation for her bipolar for years, and now it came in useful.

'I'm not hiding anything from you, my lord,' she said, injecting as much sincerity into her voice as she could.

'You're looking for Excalibur,' Medraut said softly. 'Why?'

Una hoped that she had managed to keep her expression neutral. He had guessed, from the jumble of thoughts he'd found in her head. And he had guessed wrong. Better to let him think it, though. Better than for him to realise the truth. That she was looking for something to defeat him, not something that would strengthen him.

'I love a mystery, that's all.' She shrugged. 'Haven't you ever wondered what happened to it after Arthur's death?'

'*King* Arthur.'

'Yes, of course.'

Una moved forward, letting the cat drop to the floor. She nudged it behind her. She had heard the rumours of what Medraut did to animals that irritated him.

'I really should be going h–'

Medraut moved so suddenly that Una hadn't any time to react. His fingers curled around her throat, and though his grip was firm, it was the otherworldly power behind the muscles that truly frightened her. Inspyre crackled into her veins like electricity, each shock a needle through her skull.

They stood like that for what felt like an age. She refused to beg, she refused to try to claw his fingers away from her. Both would be fruitless. He roved through her memories. She tried to allow it. She fed him her life in Ithr: her work, her friends, even Angus. But she filed away her true purpose, praying that he was not yet strong enough to find it buried so deeply in her soul.

At last, when she thought she couldn't take any more, he released her.

'Better go and give your husband his morning tumble,' he said, a sneer lifting one side of his mouth, 'while you still can.'

Una didn't wait. She fled, not looking back, and she didn't stop until she reached the safety of Ithr, and Angus's embrace. She couldn't go back to Tintagel now, not after that. She hadn't found what she'd been looking for – a way of defeating Medraut – but surely she had enough. She thought of the binder of evidence in her locker in the castle: Maisie's gift, testimony from veneurs and harkers. Tonight, she would take it to the other lords and ladies of the thanes, and pray that they'd believe her. Otherwise, she was a dead woman walking.

Chapter 22

We bring the dreamers to the walls of Tintagel and no further. We can't risk Medraut seeing what's inside the castle. Nerizan takes the injured couple into Tintagel to find out whether the apothecaries can mend the wounds on their hands.

'Maybe we can get the morrigans to remove the nightmare as well,' Ollie comments.

'Don't be stupid,' Vien replies. 'Why would you want them not to be afraid of people like this? We should all be afraid.'

'Shouldn't you go to the hospital too?' I ask Ollie.

'Oh, this?' he says, looking down at the wound in his shoulder, which is turning his blue tunic black. 'It can wait. Besides, you might need me.'

Lord Allenby is striding over the drawbridge towards us, side-stepping the dream dog that darts past him to get into the castle. With him are Maisie, the harker captain, and Jin. *Great*. We tell them what happened while a group of reeves erects a makeshift canopy to prevent prying eyes. I secretly think it might be a bit late for that if what I suspect is going on is true. Jin takes one look at Ollie's wound and digs around in her apothecary bag for a cold poultice, which she makes him press against the bleeding.

'Can you go back into their minds, Fern?' Lord Allenby says. 'Without it hurting you too much? I think we need to take a closer look at what we're dealing with.'

I nod and place my hands on the man's head. Ollie rests a hand on my shoulder. Ollie's Immral, even though it's not at work, bolsters my own, allowing me to ignore my headache more easily.

It's the same in this man's head as in the woman's – the dark sponge where the inspyre should be, then if I manipulate it the right way, the appearance of Medraut's violet eyes. I relay this to Lord Allenby.

'And it's just eyes?' Allenby asks. 'Nothing else?'

If I find his questions odd, I don't say anything. 'Let me see. I think it's just the eyes, yes.'

Lord Allenby sighs, and I can't tell if it's with relief or something else.

'Can you remove them?'

I experimentally pull at the eyes with my mind, and find resistance.

'Hang on,' I say, 'I think there's something holding them in place.'

I pull again, and the dreamer lets out a groan. I draw back, immediately releasing him. 'I'm scared of hurting him,' I tell the others.

'So am I,' Lord Allenby says, 'but let's see if we can at least find out what it is.'

A shout goes up from the gatehouse, outside the canopy.

'It's going to be a lot harder for me to do that with a racket going on,' I say pointedly. A moment later, Samson's head appears through the opening.

'Sir, we need to get you all inside.'

'What is it, Samson?'

'Dreamers, loads of them. They're heading this way.'

'Medraut's?'

'Seems likely.'

Samson opens the tent flap further and the distant sound of marching feet creeps into the canopy. It's a base note to the chant that's now become so familiar: *One Voice*.

'Should we go, sir?' Ollie asks.

'No.' Lord Allenby frowns. 'No, I don't think so. Samson, how long do you think you can hold them off?'

'Not long. A few minutes, maybe?'

'Good. We'll try to work quickly.'

'Sir,' I say, 'I can't guarantee –'

'I know, Fern, but I'll be damned before I let Medraut force me to take these dreamers into Tintagel with those things still inside them.'

'You think this attack is timed just for this?' Maisie says, pressing a hand to her chest.

'You don't?'

The five of us look at each other. If Lord Allenby's fear is correct, then something bigger is going on. To get to the bottom of it, our best bet is finding out exactly what Medraut has done to these dreamers.

'Can you use your Immral to show me what's going on in there?' Jin asks. 'I might be able to help.'

I nod, secretly dreading the extra drain on my power.

'Take my hand,' Ollie tells the apothecary.

Immediately I feel the extra weight of Jin's mind connected

to my own through Ollie. I try to channel what I'm seeing in the dreamer's brain through my brother. The marching footsteps are closer now. The ground is vibrating with their weight.

'Is it working?' I say.

'Yes,' comes the reply. 'Can you show me the bottom of the eyes in more detail?'

'She's not a camera,' Ollie says sharply, but I try to do as I'm told. I push the bottom of the eyes up with my mind, to show the space beneath them.

'Do you see?' Jin says. 'There, at the base, where the spinal column would be in Ithr.'

Now she's pointed it out I do see. Something darker than the black sponge, tethering the eyes to the skull.

'You might be able to extract it without hurting him,' Jin says, 'if you're able to widen the gap –'

'I understand,' I cut Jin off, because the way she's talking about it, as if it's a surgical procedure, is making me feel ill. I ease my mind around whatever it is tethering the eyes there, gently pushing against the man's skull, against the sponge beneath, to widen the gap. The man's breathing quickens.

'It's okay,' Ollie tells me, 'he's not in pain.'

'Can't you go any faster?' Maisie says.

'No, she can't,' Ollie snaps, but I don't blame Maisie for her panic. A cool breeze on one side of my face tells me that someone has left – I guess Lord Allenby and Samson have gone to hold off the dreamers.

I focus now on the base of the eyes, pressing from all angles to loosen them. Gradually, with more effort than I'd like, they begin to come away, and whatever was holding them in place comes too. It slides out from a well that reaches deep into the dreamer's spine. The man groans again.

'Can someone open his mouth?' I say. 'My hands are kind of busy.'

'Done,' Jin says, and slowly I edge the eyes and whatever was holding them out of his mouth. I hear three gasps as something squelches onto a medical tray.

On the tray Jin is holding lie the pair of violet eyes, sparking with inspyre, and a long, coiled tail. That's not the most horrifying thing, though. The tail is knotted with thinner tendrils, like the nightmarish roots of a tree. Some of the tendrils are still pliable, but most of them have hardened into thorns.

'This was inside him?' Maisie breathes.

'It must be Medraut's design – he plants it there and it grows down instead of up,' Ollie says.

Another shout goes up from the gatehouse. Ollie peers out of the tent. 'Quick,' he says, 'let's get inside.'

'What about the other dreamer?' I say, looking at the dreamer who still must have that curled, violet-eyed serpent rooted in her skull.

'No time,' Maisie says. 'We'll have to let her go.'

'But . . .' Jin starts. And then the decision is taken from us. The dreamer seems to click to life, as though someone has flicked a hidden switch. She looks to the open tent flap and lunges for freedom.

'She's racing for the drawbridge,' Maisie shouts. 'She's trying to get into the castle. Quickly! Go!'

Ollie and I dash after her, ignoring the pounding in our skulls. This is why Medraut's doing it, I think: he wants to get inside Tintagel. Medraut himself can't get inside because he means us harm – the power of Tintagel would never let him in. But dreamers who don't consciously mean us harm – they *can* enter. And if they're controlled by Medraut then who knows what havoc they could wreak.

Samson and Lord Allenby are beside me now. I reach out a hand, trying to stop the dreamer with my Immral, but I've used my power too much tonight already, and my brain isn't in the right place to make it work. Samson pulls an arrow from the sheath on his back and leaps into the air, giving himself space to shoot. But I can see it in his eyes, in the bearing of his arms, which are usually so steady: he can't bring himself to injure a dreamer. It's against our code. It's not something Samson could ever do. But it's something *I* can do, if it protects the ones I love.

'Throw it to me!' I shout at Samson, and he does without hesitation. I may not have the strength to stop the dreamer by myself, but I can direct an arrow, and I direct it true. It hits the dreamer in the nook of her knee, toppling her to the ground. She'll live, but she won't be getting into the castle before us. Jin and Maisie overtake us, each carrying the healed dreamer between them, while Samson retrieves his arrow from the wounded dreamer with a crunch. The dreamer's going to have a sore leg tomorrow, that's for sure.

The sound of feet is deafening now – dozens of dreamers under Medraut's influence are flooding into the square outside Tintagel's walls. The drawbridge begins to creak shut.

‘Quickly!’ Lord Allenby shouts, already there, waiting for us. Samson takes Maisie’s place carrying the dreamer, powering forward as though he was no heavier than an idea. Ollie and I bring up the rear, fending off the dreamers who are on our heels. We make it to the drawbridge and throw ourselves onto the wood, rolling down the other side as it rises. The dreamers try to clamber on, but they’re too late. The drawbridge closes, leaving us panting in a pile inside Tintagel’s walls, with a zombified dreamer and a rope of thorns.

Chapter 23

With the drawbridge closed and no way of getting in, the dreamers outside Tintagel evaporate back into the rest of Annwn within minutes. It only cements Lord Allenby's suspicion that all of this was planned.

'Take the dreamer to the hospital,' he tells Jin, 'but I want two knights guarding him at all times, understand? He's not to step a foot off his bed until we're escorting him out of the castle.'

Lord Allenby eyes the jar containing the eyes and thorns. Jin is filling it with thick, dark liquid that smells like paint.

'Resin of a guardian tree,' Jin tells Ollie. 'It preserves things so we can study them. It sets quickly so there's no chance of this – whatever it is – escaping.'

The liquid is bubbling, belching air pockets, but sure enough it begins to set so that tiny bubbles are captured mid-escape, next to the eyes and their terrible roots. Jin covers the jar in thick fabric. If the eyes still work they won't see anything inside Tintagel.

'You knew it would look like this, didn't you, sir?' I ask Lord Allenby.

Lord Allenby shares a look with Maisie. 'I think you'd better come into my office. We can talk better there.'

Ollie and Samson follow Lord Allenby straight away, but I pursue Jin instead.

'Brandon,' I blurt out.

Jin stops, raising an eyebrow.

'You should talk to Brandon. He's a veneur,' I tell her.

'Yes, I know who he is. You don't think I'm able to study this myself?'

'I'm not saying that,' I say, trying to keep my temper in check, 'I think he's really good with animals and the more experts we have looking into this, the better, okay?'

Jin looks as though she wants to fire another insult my way, but instead she nods reluctantly, and heads off to the hospital, where the injured couple lie not far from the dreamer who attacked them.

The thought of that dreamer being so close to the ones he attacked makes me unexpectedly angry. Logically, I know that he's been the subject of Medraut's experiments – it's not his fault. But, I think as I trudge past the harker desks towards Lord Allenby's office, did Medraut experiment on those dreamers because he knew they'd be more amenable to his brainwashing? What came first? Were those dreamers inclined to hatred to begin with? Were the women they attacked the kind of people they'd usually be friends with in Ithr, or would they sneer and make comments even before Medraut planted those eyes? I find it hard to imagine that someone like Samson would have endured having Medraut inside his head like that. He would never allow those roots to dig so deep.

When I enter Lord Allenby's office, the air is charged. Ollie's jaw is set in a way that tells me he's furious.

'What's happened?' I ask.

'Sit down, Fern,' Lord Allenby says. 'I was telling Samson and your brother about something that has come to our attention recently.'

I take a seat between Ollie and Samson, and find myself eyeing up the decanter of lotus whisky Lord Allenby keeps on a side table. My head is pounding from the fight and the extractions, and I have a feeling I'm going to need to clear it to hear this. Following my gaze, Lord Allenby goes to the decanter and pours five measures.

'Perhaps I should start,' Maisie says, holding her glass as though she'd rather not have the stuff anywhere near her. 'A few weeks ago we got word from a number of thaneships around the country, to say that their harkers had witnessed some odd behaviour from dreamers.'

'Behaviour like tonight?' I ask. 'Dreamers attacking other dreamers?'

'Please let me finish,' Maisie says. 'No, they weren't attacking other dreamers. If that had been the case we'd have acted more decisively before now. They were simply more aware of their surroundings.'

'Conscious? Like aventures?' I say before I can stop myself.

'Somewhat, yes. They were aware of everything, even other dreamers, but they weren't moving around Annwn with purpose. And inspyre didn't seem to want to interact with them like it normally does.'

'That fits with Medraut,' Samson says.

'It does indeed,' Lord Allenby replies. 'That's what we all thought too. But we couldn't work out what he was trying to do with them. Was he simply draining their inspyre, and their awareness of Annwn was a side product? It wasn't clear because they didn't seem to be dangerous. Perhaps that's when we should have got you in to look at them, Fern, but you've got such a lot on your plate at the moment.'

'I understand, sir,' I say, and I do – I'm grateful. If he'd landed this on me right after the Tournament, I'm not sure I could've coped. There have been so many times these last few weeks where I've had to find a quiet corner to myself and have a cry at the state of everything. Now, though, having seen what I've seen, I am focused. Then something else occurs to me.

'But that doesn't explain why you were expecting to see something else underneath those eyes, sir.'

Lord Allenby smiles grimly. 'You're right. For that we need to go back much further.'

As he talks, he goes to one of the wood panels that line his office – one beneath the huge stained-glass window that looks out over the herb gardens. He presses on it, and the panel fades away to reveal a cupboard.

'Nearly twenty years ago now, before your mother was recruited to the thanes, I was a new recruit myself, alongside Medraut. It didn't take long for us to work out that he had Immral – only a matter of weeks, unlike you two. It was a novelty for all of us, and he was a very charming man, as you know. But quiet. A lot of people took that to mean that he was humble. Some of his friends enjoyed asking him to experiment with his power.'

Lord Allenby catches my expression – this is no different

to what I did when I'd just found out I had Immral. Who wouldn't experiment?

'These friends wanted Medraut to experiment on them.'

'But why?' Ollie says.

'Immrals were the stuff of legends,' Maisie says, a little defensively, 'and we were young and naive.'

She's blushing. I've never seen her flustered before.

'Don't blame Medraut's friends,' Lord Allenby says, placing a reassuring hand on Maisie's arm. 'You know how convincing he is. As Maisie said, none of us had come across an Immral before. There hasn't been one recorded for generations in the UK. The closest anyone had come to an Immral when I started in the thanes was a woman in Argentina who turned away from her power and refused to use it. All the warnings about Immral were so remote or so part of ancient history that none of us thought it would happen here.'

'So he started experimenting on his friends,' Samson prompts.

'That's right. Just small experiments at first. Things like seeing if he could stop them from moving, or move them when they weren't expecting it.'

I remember something I once did to Ramesh. No, I am not Medraut. I am not on that path any more.

'Then it escalated,' Maisie continues. 'I wasn't a knight, obviously, so it was a while before I understood what was going on. It seems Medraut had kept his most extreme experiments to his close friendship group. Maybe he was worried that showing it to anyone outside the knights would risk Lady Caradoc finding out what he was doing. Maybe it was easier for him to do the experiments when he was on patrol with his regiment. Whatever the reason, I only found out when I was watching their patrol from the balconies. I'd seen him make his regiments bigger or stronger when they were battling nightmares, and that was fine. No one had a problem with that. But then one day he took his regiment underground, and I lost sight of them.'

'But you can still see underground when you're wearing the harker helmets.'

'That's the point, Fern. Afterwards, Medraut told me that they had run into some interference – a different kind of inspyre. I reported it to Lady Caradoc and she sent reeves to investigate and warned the other thaneships. We were all so trusting of him. Of course there was no such inspyre. Medraut had used his Immral to stop me from seeing him.'

'I didn't know that was possible,' Ollie says.

'I don't think I could do it,' I tell them, 'but we all know how much stronger Medraut is, right?'

'So what was he doing when you couldn't watch him?' Samson asks.

'I found out a few months later,' Maisie continues. 'I was taking a break and fooling around in the gardens with one of the knights.' There's the blush again. I find myself blushing too. I can't imagine Maisie fooling around with anyone and having Samson present only adds to my embarrassment. 'And he . . . I . . . well, I felt something on his back, and I told him to hold still while I looked. He told me not to worry about it, but I can be quite persistent. I suppose because he knew I was a fan of Medraut, he thought it would be okay for me to see it.'

‘What was it?’ I ask, leaning forward, although I think I already know.

‘It was this,’ Lord Allenby says, ducking back into the cupboard and producing a jar like the one Jin had used earlier. The resin is solid but transparent. Lord Allenby places the jar on his desk, and Ollie, Samson and I lean forward to study what’s inside.

The vessel contains a long tendril that, even encased in resin, sparks with imagination. But at its centre there’s a thread of dark, compressed inspyre. Along the tendril’s length, tiny thorns protrude. I put my hands around the jar and try to send my Immral through the resin. The tendril tastes of tar and something else – something sweet and addictive. It’s the same taste I got from the thing inside those dreamers just now. It is fear and certainty and purity. It is power.

Chapter 24

'When I saw that thing, embedded in his spine, I insisted he got it removed immediately,' Maisie tells us. 'I threatened Medraut – I told him that if he didn't take those things off straight away I would tell Lady Caradoc. He didn't like it, and I certainly wasn't welcome in his group after that, but he did as I said. I took this one as insurance.'

'I'm surprised he didn't just make you forget about it,' I say.

'So am I.' Maisie exhales shakily. 'I don't think even then that I had a clear idea of how dangerous he was. Maybe he didn't either – maybe he hadn't got as far as thinking it would be okay to silence me that way. Anyway, when he was made Head Thane I didn't like it one bit, and I knew I needed someone else outside his circle to know what he'd done.'

'So you told Lord Allenby?' Ollie says.

'No,' Maisie replies, 'I told your mother.'

Ollie and I stare at her. The thought of this woman confiding in the mum we hold in our heads – the wild, rule-breaking Una Gorlois – doesn't make any sense.

'*Why?*' I breathe.

'I see things, it's my job,' Maisie says. 'I could see that Una was as unsettled as I was about Medraut's promotion. So I approached her and found that she was trying to dig up dirt on him. I showed her this, and she took it to the other thaneships. It was a key part of the reason Medraut was thrown out of the thanes, in fact.'

I had known that Mum was one of the people who helped overthrow Medraut, but I didn't realise how central she was. I can't imagine how stressful that must have been for her – working to bring down your own boss, having to see them every night. But more than that – Medraut has Immral, so he was able to read minds. How did she keep her motives from him all those months? A great surge of pride wells up inside me. She must have had such strength of mind and character to not just stay strong against his mind control, but to do everything she did without him knowing about it until it was too late.

Then something else occurs to me – if Mum knew that I had Immral, even as a baby, that must have happened after Medraut was thrown out. By that time she'd seen how dangerous and destructive Immral could be. She had no way of knowing that I wouldn't turn into another Medraut. Despite all the love in her letter, I wonder whether that's why she set three tests for me to get Excalibur – to make sure I wouldn't use it to do what Medraut's planning on doing.

'What did this thing do?' Samson asks, gesturing to the rope of thorns in the jar. 'It must have been something awful to have got Medraut thrown out.'

'Not at all,' Maisie says. 'I was told that it was designed as a shield. So that when they were under attack from nightmares, it allowed Medraut to use his Immral to protect them.'

'Really?' I say. 'Did you ever see them use it like that?'

'No.' Maisie frowns. 'And to be honest I was suspicious, but the person I was with –' there's that blush again – 'was very sincere. I'm certain he believed that's what it was for.'

'What makes you think otherwise?' Lord Allenby asks me.

'The feel of it,' I tell him. 'It has the same feel as the ones we found today.'

'Yes, that's what I thought,' Lord Allenby says. 'When I was made Head Thane I inherited this, so to speak, and I spent a bit of time studying it. I was sure Medraut would regain his power one day, and I thought that the key to bringing him down properly would lie in what he'd done on his first rise. Perhaps you could take another look, Fern? I'd like to confirm my suspicions.'

I nod, and take the jar once more, casting my mind through the resin and into the coiled rope of thorns.

'There is a little-known legend about one of Arthur's knights – Gawain, in fact – who won a skein of rope that allowed him to cross a dangerous river,' Lord Allenby says.

'I've read it,' Samson says.

'Of course you have,' Ollie smirks.

Lord Allenby smiles. 'What you won't have read is the true story. It's recorded deep in the archives, in the records of the Round Table. A lot of the Arthurian legends have been corrupted from the truth. Of course they have – the legend is that he was a benevolent king, a saviour – so the things he did with his Immral have been changed to make them more palatable.'

'So Gawain didn't win the rope?'

'Gawain didn't win it, and it wasn't rope, and it wasn't a river,' Lord Allenby says.

'So nothing about the story was true?'

'I didn't say that, Ollie. The truth is that when King Arthur first took power, there was a rebellion in the land. He was trying to conquer Ireland and the southern coast of France, and as you can imagine, the people there didn't take too kindly to that. So he sent his knights – his closest followers, who knew about Annwn, out to those countries, with an invisible weapon.'

'A rope made of inspyre that would entangle their minds, not their bodies,' I say, connecting the dots.

'Exactly, Fern. A rope welded to King Arthur's will. That's what the records suggest, anyway. The knights cast the ropes over hundreds of the rebels in Annwn, ensnaring their minds and making them compliant to Arthur's rule.'

'And you think Medraut knew about this,' Samson says.

'If he didn't it's a mighty big coincidence, wouldn't you say? When I became Head Thane and inherited this jar, I remembered Medraut talking about the story when we had just taken Ostara. Even back then, and that would have been a few years before he became the knight captain, he was studying Arthur's reign.'

I've been casting my mind into the resin. 'You said Arthur's rope was made of inspyre?'

'*Compressed inspyre*. That seems to be the translation of the records, yes.'

'It wasn't compressed,' I tell him. 'It was woven.'

'Woven?' Ollie asks.

'I can count three different threads here,' I tell them, sifting through the skeins of rope. 'And they each have a different purpose.'

'How can you tell?'

'They taste different.'

'What do you think they're doing?' Lord Allenby says.

'Well, one is designed to protect, so your friend wasn't totally misinformed, Maisie,' I say, feeling the metal of a chain in one of the threads. The second thread is heady with perfume. 'I think this one is about power – but the kind of power that people give up freely. Then there's a third one – it's thinner than the others, but it's really strong. It smells sharp.' I send my mind into the inspyre, probing it, asking it to change so that I can get a sense of its purpose. 'This one's about . . .' I push deeper, and the thread turns on me, snapping like a demon to throw me off, sparking with violet inspyre. I pull back, away from the jar. The others don't seem to have seen anything. It must have moved only for me.

'The third one's the strongest. It's about fear.'

'So I was right,' Lord Allenby said. 'Medraut was planning these things decades ago, and this new development is only an improvement on what he did before.'

'If I'd known the full extent of what he was doing . . .' Maisie starts. She is on the verge of tears.

'You knew that something wasn't right,' Lord Allenby says. 'You did what you could. Without you, Una may not have got the proof she needed to get Medraut thrown out, and then just imagine where we'd all be. I'd wager Medraut would have conquered Annwn and Ithr long before now.'

'And you think he's doing this all over the country?' Samson says.

'I do,' Lord Allenby replies, 'which means that we have a much bigger problem on our hands.'

'It's my nightmare,' Maisie says.

'What is?' Ollie says.

'The harkers find nightmares by looking for the blue inspyre that surrounds them,' Maisie explains. 'And now we have no way of knowing which dreamers are dangerous.'

The way she says it makes me think of Rachel, and her desperation to find a solution to spotting the treitres before they transform. I suppose that, in a way, Medraut has simply created a new form of treitre – one that may not have the skill of an assassin, but does have a greater ability to hide in plain sight. One that uses the thanes' own code against them: can we really justify harming dreamers who aren't conscious of what they're doing?

'We thought the treitres were bad enough,' Maisie is saying, 'but at least there were only a few hundred of them. Now . . . well, there's no limit to the number of dreamers he could turn into murderers, is there?'

I imagine one of those ropes inside Dad's head, a pair of Medraut's violet eyes staring out at me from my own father. My own father unwittingly trying to kill me for looking different. I'd know, I think; surely I'd be able to tell from the way he treated me in Ithr?

'So what do we do about it?' Ollie says.

'Right now?' Lord Allenby replies. 'We wait. We study, we listen, we learn. Something will come to us. It always does, if we keep our minds open.'

'So, nothing,' I say, trying to keep the irritation from my voice.

'Is the gathering of knowledge nothing?' Lord Allenby says. 'We'll work it out, Fern. But not now. Not today.'

I wish I had his faith.

Chapter 25

I can't walk through Ithr now without remembering what I've seen in Annwn. Maisie had said that dreamers turning on us was her worst nightmare because she wouldn't be able to tell who was a threat. That's exactly how I'm starting to feel in my everyday life.

School is a daily trial. My concern for Lottie is outmatched by the growing antagonism from her friends. But the worst place is home. Whenever Clemmie comes to stay, Ollie and I have to endure her thinly veiled digs at our people.

'I just wish everyone would get on with each other,' she'll say. 'It's not that hard to agree to disagree, is it?'

'I imagine it gets quite hard for the people who're being told they're disgusting for just being who they are,' Ollie replies.

'No one's saying that, Ollie,' Dad says.

'Maybe not out loud, but you'd have to be blind to not see that's exactly what they really mean,' I snap, casting Ollie a grateful look for having my back. This doesn't need to be his fight.

'Oh, you people see conspiracies everywhere,' Clemmie sighs. She rubs her eyes, her palm facing outward. A subconscious movement, if I needed any more proof of who Clemmie supports, that reminds me of the One Voice gesture. 'Most people are simple folks, wanting to live their lives,' she continues, waving an arm at my burn scar. 'They don't want to have their faces rubbed in whatever trendy look you've decided to adopt this week.'

'Did you really just call my eye colour and burn scar a *fashion choice*?' I say, gobsmacked.

'Leave Fern alone, Clem,' Dad says sternly, then turns to me. 'She didn't mean anything by it, love.'

I push my chair back and dump my food onto Clemmie's plate. 'Grow a spine, Dad. Ollie managed it. But then, maybe he got it from Mum.' As I leave, I look back at Clemmie's sputtering face. 'Eat up, Clemmie – I made sure to put extra Fern cooties on my portion. With any luck you'll grow a conscience too.'

Thankfully Dad never got round to taking the lock off my door, even though he'd wanted to because of my tendency to start bleeding from my eyeballs while asleep. So I'm able to ignore him knocking angrily, telling me I owe him and Clemmie an apology. It's a little while later when Ollie knocks instead.

'Did I go too far?' I say as I let him in.

'You went pretty nuclear,' he admits, 'and just so you know, I've got mixed feelings about the way you brought me into that.'

'It was a compliment.'

'Funny, didn't sound like much of one. Not everyone thinks that being compared to Mum is a good thing.'

I flop back on my bed and throw Ollie a pillow to use as a cushion. 'Do you think I should apologise?'

'To Clemmie and Dad? No way.'

I sit up in bed. 'Why *do* you hate Mum so much, Ols?'

'Why do you hate Dad?'

'I don't hate him.'

'You did.'

'Maybe a bit, when I thought he was always taking your side after, you know . . .'

'After I almost burned you to death.'

'Can you blame me?'

'No,' Ollie says, looking at me thoughtfully. 'Course I don't blame you. But I do blame Dad a bit.'

'You do?'

'He made things worse between us, didn't he? I didn't mean for you to get hurt but what I did was still just . . . beyond awful. And he never really acknowledged that. When it happened, I was grateful that he didn't punish me properly, but after we got into the knights and started hanging out together again, I wondered whether if you'd seen him punish me, it would have made things better between us sooner.'

I can't think of a way to respond to this unusually open admission from Ollie that won't make me sound like a jerk. Our newfound friendship is so fragile that I don't want to risk jeopardising it by admitting that he has a point. I don't want Ollie to get defensive. And if I'm honest with myself, I haven't truly forgiven him for what he did. I've moved past it, yes, but that's not the same. If Dad had come down hard on him? Maybe it would have helped.

And who am I to bestow forgiveness when I can't claim it from others? Sachi remains as defiantly hateful towards me as she ever has. I can understand that. I still can't give her the answers she wants. She obviously feels as though I could have saved Ramesh with my Immral. Part of me agrees with her, even if the rational side of me knows there's nothing I could have done.

But when I see her taking her frustration out on others, I get really angry. One night as I'm heading out through the castle to the stables, I spot Sachi beside Rachel's desk. She's leaning over the harker, and although I can't hear what they're saying, I recognise the pleading tone in Rachel's voice.

I stride over. 'What's going on?'

'It's nothing,' Rachel says as Sachi steps back. 'It's fine.' But she's on the verge of tears.

I round on Sachi. 'What have you been saying?'

'I'm just trying to get answers!' Sachi says heatedly. 'Why is that such an ask around here?'

Her raised voice attracts the attention of some passing reeves and, to my dismay, Jin. She runs over but stops when she hears what's being said.

'If you have a problem with the way things are done then you should talk to Lord Allenby about it,' I say. 'What you don't do is bully someone who *adored* Ramesh. Who was probably a better friend to him than you ever were, if what I've seen is anything to go by.'

Sachi looks like I've slapped her. Rachel stands, reaching out to her. 'She didn't mean that,' she's saying. 'Please, I'll tell you what I can . . .'

'His name was Reyansh,' Sachi whispers, and flees into her classroom.

'You probably shouldn't have said that to her,' Jin says, but her usual spikiness is absent. She turns to Rachel. 'Are you okay?' Rachel's nodding but shaking, and Jin guides her back to her seat. As Jin orders a passing reeve to fetch a glass of lotus juice I look, unseeing, at the papers on Rachel's desk, shame flooding me. I really shouldn't have said that. No, Sachi shouldn't have been bullying Rachel, but how could I ever think it okay to accuse Sachi of being a bad sister to a dead brother?

'I just . . .' I say, trying to defend myself even though no one's listening. 'I couldn't bear to see her talking to you like that, when you've only ever been . . .'

Then I really do see what Rachel's been working on. It's all about the Round Table. She hasn't given up her attempts to stop the treitres. I pick up the papers, my eyes skimming over the words. *Round Table recognises inspyre due to sample on sensor. Could we capture treitre and get the Round Table to recognise that too?*

An idea forms. 'Rachel,' I say, ignoring Jin's glare, 'is this all true? The stuff about the Round Table recognising inspyre – is that researched?'

'Yes,' Rachel says, 'I read in quite a few accounts that there's a vial of inspyre on the sensor, so it knows what to look out for when it scans its surroundings. But there's no way we could find a treitre and, I don't know, hack part of it off or something . . . Fern?'

I am already dragging her from her chair, pulling her towards Lord Allenby's office. 'Get Maisie!' I shout back to Jin. 'Oh, and Samson. And Ollie, I guess. I suppose you and Easa should come too!'

* * *

Not ten minutes later, Rachel is stumbling through her ideas, nervous in front of Lord Allenby and the harker captain. '. . . You see, the records say that the Round Tables have been modified over the years, and I thought, now we have Fern and Ollie . . . well, they might be able to train the sensor to recognise a treitre. But obviously we'd need to find a treitre first . . '

'Could it be done, Maisie?' Lord Allenby asks.

Maisie nods slowly. 'Perhaps. The theory's sound. The Round Tables' sensors have never been modified before, but that doesn't mean it couldn't be attempted.'

'You did all of this work by yourself, harker?' Lord Allenby asks.

Rachel blushes. 'Well, there were a few of us who –'

'She was the mastermind behind it,' I say, determined for Rachel to get the credit she's due.

Lord Allenby nods. 'Excellent work.'

'Yes,' Maisie says. 'Very good. Rachel, was it? I'll be keeping an eye on you.'

Rachel looks fit to burst with pride, casting me a look of gratitude as she leaves.

'I thought,' I explain, once she's gone, 'that instead of treitres, we could use Rachel's idea –'

'To train the sensor to see when Immral is being used,' Lord Allenby finishes. 'Yes, I was thinking the same thing.'

'One step ahead, eh?' Samson smiles at me.

'And the best part of it,' Easa says, 'is that Medraut might well have given us the best thing we could use for the sensors. That rope of thorns.'

'Exactly,' I say.

'I'm not sure it's wise to try altering Tintagel's Round Table first,' Maisie says.

'No,' Lord Allenby replies, 'and I don't think we have the depth of knowledge here to be able to work out the details. But I do know someone who might.'

He turns to me. 'What do you say to a little trip, Fern?'

Chapter 26

'Cambridge? Really?'

When Lord Allenby raised the idea of exploring more of Annwn, I had been reluctant. The thought of meeting new people, leaving behind the group of friends I have cultivated with such difficulty, was intimidating. But as the plans for my 'tour', as Ollie put it, took shape, excitement gripped me.

I'd been hoping to go to Edinburgh, where the castle has the ability to detach from its foundations and rise into the air, or Cork, where it's said that a particular stone in the highest turret was once touched by King Arthur and imbued with some of his Immral. Cambridge feels too close to London, too small.

Nevertheless, the harkers and reeves fall over themselves to make sure I'm prepared. I think it's a matter of pride, to ensure that I know enough about the Round Tables to not disgrace Tintagel. Even Lord Allenby comments that I should be given a new tunic. 'One that looks as though it's been washed in the last year please. We don't want them thinking we're savages.'

The fifth time a reeve tries to give me an updated schedule, I snap.

'I literally don't give a shit any more,' I tell him. 'Just point me at a portal and I'll go through it, okay?'

I'd been worried that Ollie would be jealous of me being sent without him, but in the end he is assigned to the small group who are going to come with me. 'Your Immral is stronger when you're together,' Lord Allenby reasons, 'and I think you're going to be needing your power a lot.' Samson takes the news that his two lieutenants are heading off on a round-the-country tour with his usual stoicism. He puts Linnea in our place – a vote of confidence given what happened with Medraut's bug – and they spend long evenings discussing strategies. I try not to flinch whenever Linnea laughs at one of Samson's jokes.

To my shock, Jin took my advice on consulting Brandon about Medraut's rope of thorns. Not that she'd ever let me know. It's down to Brandon to pull me to one side after patrol and tell me that he's taking good care of it.

'Why would you do that?' I say, horrified.

'Well, it's a living thing, isn't it?' Brandon replies. 'It's not its fault that Medraut created it. It's just trying to go about its business.'

I stare at him. 'Please don't tell me you cared for those ear bugs as well.'

Brandon smiles proudly. 'I've got a little collection of them in a cage outside the castle walls. They're delightful if you wear ear mufflers so they can't, you know, burrow into your head . . .'

Maybe it wasn't such a great idea to get Brandon on board after all.

Then it's time for me to take my last patrol with Bedevere. The regiment gives Ollie and me a send-off, taking us for a picnic on one of the narrow beaches that line the south of the Thames. Samson and Ollie spot a dream of a busker and lure it over to us, and before long everyone is having an impromptu jig to a folksy violin. Eventually, drunk on exhaustion and happiness, we fall to the ground and the conversations start. I watch from a distance as my regiment shows me everything that I'll miss. Linnea and Ollie are skimming pebbles, with Nerizan as scorekeeper. Samson is handing out food with Vien, and then he sees that I'm on my own and comes over, clutching a glass of ambrosia for each of us.

'Budge over, this bit's pebbly,' Samson says, and I shift along, heat spreading through me at his proximity.

'Are you prepared?' he says.

'It's going to feel really weird not patrolling with you every night.'

'It's going to be even weirder not having you here.' He smiles at me, then his expression clouds.

'What is it?'

'Maybe it's a good thing,' he says, looking out towards the river. I'm grateful for this as it means he can't see how stricken I must look. 'We're going to miss you, of course, but I often wonder whether we've become reliant on your Immral. Maybe it's making us bad knights. Lazy. I don't know. I don't like that I keep asking you to use your power when it hurts you so much.'

'It's not that bad,' I lie.

'Yes, it is, Fern,' Samson says, looking at me directly. 'I see the pain on your face every time you use it.'

Over to our left, Ollie skims a stone and an exotically

coloured fish leaps out of the water to swallow it right before it scores him a record. He and Linnea laugh and make far more noise than necessary. Samson hasn't taken his eyes off me.

'You'll be alright out there,' he says.

'Yeah,' I reply, 'it's not like we're having to go into Medraut's fortress for months on end. I can't imagine what that must do to your sanity.'

For a while, Samson doesn't speak, to the point where I think he might have clammed up. Then he does say, very softly, 'I think the hardest part was trying to act normally in Ithr. The nights were difficult, don't get me wrong, but the fact that I was in danger, that I could be found out and killed at any moment, gave me a lot of focus.'

He starts drawing in the sand.

'In Ithr I had to pretend that everything was normal. And I know we have this big secret to keep with the thanes, but that's different because it's shared. I've got friends I can talk to – all you guys. When I was in there it was so lonely, not being able to talk to Natasha or . . . or Rafe . . . about what was happening. And I'd see these people being experimented on and be terrified that one of them would be someone I knew. I'd be having dinner with my family and have these thoughts going round and round in my head. *What if you're brought in tonight, Auntie? What if it's you next, little brother?*'

Something opens up between us. There's an unspoken rule in Annwn that you don't talk about your lives in Ithr – it's easier to keep the two separate for your own sanity. That's been shot to pieces for Ollie and me, since everyone knows we're twins. But Samson doesn't need to divulge this. I imagine him, sitting at a crowded table amongst a family so much bigger and more approachable than my own nuclear unit.

'Were you ever tempted to confide in your girlfriend?' I ask. Samson told me about her a few months ago, and she has felt like a spectre peering into my soul every time I'm around him.

Samson glances at me piercingly. Then he looks down, biting his lip in a way that makes me want to bite it for him.

'Of course,' he says. 'I wanted to tell her everything, but I reckon on some level the people who know us the best just know.'

I think about Dad's cluelessness. 'Your family and girlfriend operate in a different way to my family, but sure.'

The party doesn't seem so fun now. Vien waves cheerfully at us from his spot beside Milosz.

'I suppose I'd better go and join them,' I say.

'Yeah, I guess I'd better do some captaining as well.' Samson smiles.

As Samson starts to gather up the detritus of the picnic, I join Ollie and Linnea, successfully breaking their skimming record with one of my own.

'Twenty-six!' Linnea claps.

'You used your Immral! That's cheating!' Ollie cries.

I shrug. 'Nothing in the rules against it, bro.'

Then we head back to the castle and do our final patrol notes with the other regiment captains and lieutenants. For once, I'm actually looking forward to this – a routine amongst friends – a safe moment in a chaotic night. But it seems I'm not going to be allowed even that, because Jin and Rachel, who are going to be accompanying us, are waiting outside the knights' chamber.

'Aren't you guys supposed to be incognito?' Ollie says as they push away from the wall.

'Cat's out of the bag with you two going away,' Jin says. 'Everyone's *very* concerned. It's almost as if they've forgotten that they coped just fine before you came along.'

Rachel ignores her with all the enthusiasm of a spaniel. 'Road trip!' she exclaims. 'I've never been outside the castle before. This makes me a knight, right?'

'Well, not quite,' Ollie says.

'Honestly, though,' Rachel says, her green eyes earnest, 'we've got your backs, Jin and I. Whatever you need.'

'Thanks,' I reply, then something makes me say, 'And we've got yours, you know.'

We all agree on our final plans for Cambridge, and then part ways. As I take the portal back to Ithr, I cast one last look towards Tintagel. Samson is there, standing on the porch steps. I raise a hand in farewell. Then I do something I have never done before. I close my eyes, and let myself see the inspyre that swirls around him in hidden eddies. I see the way it outlines his shoulders, the way it picks out the bone of his jaw. I see the way it floods towards his heart. Then he moves, his hand raised in reply, and the inspyre reaches between his hand and mine, connecting us. I wonder if he feels it too.

Chapter 27

We don't return to Tintagel for some time. The reeves have engineered our portals to connect directly to wherever our schedule is due to take us. I land inside Cambridge's castle, instead of outside as we do in Tintagel. That's the first shock. The second is how much smaller it feels. The place is round, like all thane castles, but the roof is low and the harker desks that have a separate area in Tintagel are ranged around the central portal here. I'm the first to arrive. I'm being stared at by a load of strange thanes, and already beginning to feel like I'm not the right person to be doing this, when there's a pop next to me on the platform and Rachel appears, hunched with nerves.

A bespectacled reeve hurries over. 'The London lot, right?' she says. 'Where are the rest of you? I was told to expect four people.'

'They're not here ye—' I begin, just as two more pops signal Ollie and Jin's arrival.

'So you don't coordinate times in London? Fair enough,' the reeve says, and gestures for us to follow her. Ollie casts a gleeful glance back that's contagious, and soon all of us are trying not to giggle at the fact that this reeve puts Maisie's officiousness to shame.

She leads us through a narrow maze of corridors. It's a far cry from the wide spaces of Tintagel, but it's not without charm. Portraits and ancient documents are framed and hung on every available surface, making the castle feel like a museum. Rachel falls back to join me. 'Have you ever been to Cambridge before? In Ithr, I mean?' she asks.

I shake my head.

'I have. Once, to look round for uni. I can't wait to see what it's like in Annwn.'

She turns to address Jin and Ollie. 'How about you two?'

Ollie shakes his head. Jin blushes, though. Ollie, Rachel and I take this as a sign not to push, but the reeve looks back and sneers. 'Oh, you *go* here, don't you? What are you studying?'

'Anthropology,' Jin says after a while.

'Well there's no need to be ashamed of it. I'm surprised you didn't request a transfer to *our* castle. Most people do.'

Jin glares at the reeve.

'I don't think it's okay to out someone's Ithr persona like that,' I tell the reeve, for once feeling quite sorry for Jin.

'Here we are,' is all she says, ignoring me. 'Can you be quiet? I need to check she's free.'

She knocks on a heavy wood door. I'm prepared for another stuffy woman like this reeve – in fact, if Jin goes to Cambridge University I'm starting to wonder whether spikiness is a city-wide trait – but when the reeve ushers us through, we are greeted by the most candid, friendly face I've ever met.

'Hello there,' Cambridge's Head Thane says, coming round from behind her desk and shaking our hands with bone-crushing enthusiasm. 'I'm Carys. I'm so glad you arrived safely.' She nods at the reeve. 'Thanks, Frankie, I can take it from here. Please, do take a seat,' Carys says, pulling chairs in from the side of the room. 'Or . . . wait, shall I give you the tour first? It's not as grand as Tintagel, but you'll have realised that already. Come on.' She abandons the chairs and bounces to the door, pushing us all out in front of her. And then we're led back through the maze of corridors, except this time our guide is the opposite of silent. Carys keeps up a steady commentary of where we are, what's happening behind each door we pass, peppering in several hundred names as she goes. Then she takes a sharp turn down a corridor I didn't notice before. 'And hup, hup, hup we go!' she says merrily as she leads us up a narrow spiral staircase. Soon we erupt into the open air and the city is spread before us. A couple of solitary harkers stand at each end of the rooftop.

'You only have two sentinels?' Rachel asks her.

'No, no, no,' she responds. 'Lookie over there. Oh wait, you'll be wanting a helmet, won't you?'

She collects a couple of spare helmets from a box and hands them out. I've never seen a sentinel helmet up close. It's different to the ones the knights wear. These aren't designed to protect. They're more like silver caps that extend to cover the eyes and ears. I slip one over my head and realise it's like wearing a pair of binoculars.

'You use them the same way you knights fly and get smaller and bigger,' I hear Rachel say, and I'm struck by the fact that this is the first time she's sounded joyful about something since she and I were squires. 'You can control how much you see, how far, whether you want sound as well. They're like a remote control.'

I focus on a distant tower and push my thoughts onto that. The helmet zooms in suddenly, until I find myself staring straight into the eyes of another helmeted sentinel.

'Cambridge is so flat, you see,' Carys says, 'and our space in the castle is so limited that we have sentinels on the highest towers around the city. The one over there is on the top of King's College. Can't keep them there for long though, they start getting delusions of grandeur, don't you, Lizzie?'

'Yes, ma'am,' one of the sentinels mutters.

'Of course, all the sentinels in the world aren't going to be much help if we can't work out which dreamers Medraut's got under his control,' Carys says, her voice taking on a more sober edge.

I remove my helmet. 'Have you had many here?' I ask.

She shakes her head. 'Not many, no. There's a lot who don't hold truck with Medraut's ideas in this city. But that doesn't mean he doesn't have supporters, and as you know his Immral is persuasive. Some of the villages south of Cambridge are a worry. My plan was to take you down there as soon as you were settled. The harkers have seen some activity that concerns them.'

'We can go now,' Jin says, and Rachel, Ollie and I nod in agreement.

'Righty-ho,' Carys says, back to her former jovial self. I start to wonder whether the jollity is forced or her natural state. I had assumed the latter, but perhaps she's being upbeat to stop everyone from panicking. It's an armour, every bit as strong as Lord Allenby's staunchness.

'Where are your stables, my lady?' Ollie asks, as we trip back down the staircase.

'Oh, we don't have horses in Cambridge,' Carys replies. 'We have bicycles and . . . something else.'

She leads us out of the castle and up the street. I look back at Cambridge's castle. It is a lot smaller than Tintagel from the outside, too, and not as tall, but it still has the distinctive round shape – a pudding of a building sitting right on the street, with a tiny front garden that's bursting with herbs.

'I wonder what that place is in Ithr?' I say out loud.

'It's the round church,' Jin replies, not making eye contact.

'How does it work?' Ollie asks Jin. 'If you live in Cambridge most of the year how come you're still a London apothecary?'

'You get the choice: you can either transfer or stay with the thaneship you were assigned to when you were called up,' Jin replies, 'as long as you're in the same country. If you move abroad it gets trickier.'

We follow Carys round a bend in the road and come upon a small bridge. At its base sit long rows of punts, all different colours and sizes. Packs of dreamers and dreams cast off from the shore, using long poles to steer through the shallow riverbed.

A reeve and a knight are chatting on the decking next to the punts. The reeve stands to attention when she sees us. The knight wheels herself over and looks at Ollie and me baldly. 'So, you're the Chosen Ones, huh?' She studies us, amusement dancing in her eyes. 'Tall, good-looking, serious. Figures.'

'Play nicely, Niamh,' Carys says warningly.

'I'm going to be your guide while you're here,' Niamh says, offering us a hand. 'Come on.'

She lets us climb into a punt first, then with a twist of her arms, flips her wheelchair into the air, landing it with a thud.

As Niamh shoves the pole into the water and pushes us away from the bank, some hidden power takes hold of the boat, and it accelerates more quickly than any pole-propelled vehicle has the right to do.

'Wahey!' Carys says, ducking as we speed under the bridge and past a couple of dreamers on a romantic date. 'You might want to hold on!'

Ollie and I take a good grip of the sides. We zoom along a straight part of the river. On one side a stretch of lawn leads up to a grand, stone college. Like the angels of Tintagel, huge winged creatures flock around its towers, but they're not angels – as far as I can tell, they're hawks, with wingspans as wide as the punt is long.

'When the lady said hold on, she meant it,' Niamh shouts. 'We're about to go up!'

'What do you mean, u—' Rachel starts, but before she can finish we're in the air, Cambridge stretching out below us. I crane over the side of the punt. I've flown before in Annwn, of course, but never like this – I have never experienced flight that made me feel at peace. I catch Ollie's gaze and see my emotions mirrored there. For a brief moment, we are exactly as we should have been all these years: companions. For a brief moment, I glimpse what we could be in the future.

Chapter 28

The punt speeds through the air far faster than I can take everything in, beyond the bounds of the city centre and out into the flat farmland beyond. Ahead of us stands the only hill for miles, and we are making straight for it. Craggy protrusions extend from the hillside. Ollie points to one. 'Is it me, or does that look like an ear?'

'Nearly there!' roars Carys.

The punt flies lower, over roads and roundabouts where worm-like creatures dart over the tarmac, and there at last I spot a fort, surrounded by oak trees that rustle with life. Hundreds of eyes stare out from the leaves.

In the centre of the fort stands a folly. It's only three storeys high, made of red brick and dotted with stained-glass windows; a fantasy version of a castle turret. We land on the wide lawn beside it.

As I climb out of the punt, already wobbly-legged, I swear the ground moves.

'Did anyone else feel that?' Rachel says.

'Oh, don't worry about it,' Niamh says. 'It's just Magog having a stretch.'

We look at her.

'Who's Magog?' Ollie asks.

'The giant,' Niamh says, pushing past us towards the folly. 'This isn't a hill. It's okay, though, Magog's a pretty good sleeper. It's his brother Gog you've got to watch out for.'

Ollie stares. 'So that rock I thought looked like an ear . . .'

Niamh shrugs. 'It's Annwn, right?'

The folly is far larger inside than it seems on the outside. The ground floor holds a single, spacious room housing a gaggle of apothecaries; the first floor is given over to supplies of herbs, food and equipment, and on the top floor another group of harkers keeps watch from four equidistant windows.

A fifth harker stands in the centre of the room, poring over a smaller version of the Round Table we have in Tintagel. Cambridge and its surroundings are mapped out in detail. Inspyre darts across it in different shades of blue. I've never been close to Tintagel's Round Table before, although I've always been hypnotised by its beauty from a distance. I place a hand gently on the edge, closing my eyes to sense what the table is made of. The inspyre inside it isn't hard, like wood normally is. This material morphs as the landscape it mimics alters; the hills eroding and buildings sprouting with dreamers' collective imaginations. I sense the delicate links between the inspyre of this Round Table and the inspyre that surrounds us, sparking with connections that stretch as far as Cambridge and out the other side. There's something else, though. Something that sits deeper in the table. Something that makes goosebumps rise on my arms. I pull away, disconcerted.

Light sparks across one section of the table, and the harker watching it tells the sentinel at the east window where to look.

'That means there's dream activity,' Rachel says, her voice reverent.

'You could be overseeing one of these one day,' I tell her. 'Remember what Maisie said.'

Rachel smiles nervously. 'I've got to get a lot stronger to get promoted.' She runs a hand over the table as another spark of inspyre rolls across it.

Carys joins us, and she too is quieter than normal. 'As you know, the table only tells us of dream activity. We've no way of knowing whether there are dreamers out there who are posing a threat. It's all new territory for us. Obviously it never occurred to King Arthur to set the tables up in the way you're proposing.'

'Or it did occur to him and he didn't care,' I say.

Niamh moves forward. 'If there's a way of changing the table, we'll work it out. Do you have the thing you found in the dreamer's head?'

Jin produces the jar. In this small space, it's hard not to draw back from the rope of thorns, even when it's encased in resin. It's too malevolent for this cosy room. But Frankie moves closer to it, as does Carys.

'The eyes . . .' Carys says.

'Creepy, right?' Ollie says.

'Fascinating.'

Over the next few nights we go back and forth between the central Cambridge castle and its satellite forts. Carys eventually lets us make our own way there, although Niamh accompanies us at all times.

'You do know we're the two most powerful knights in the country right now?' Ollie tells her one night. 'I'm pretty sure we'd be fine if we were attacked.'

'You haven't seen me fight,' is all Niamh says in reply.

We barely see Rachel: she spends all her time sequestered away with Cambridge's reeves and harkers, having her research studied. I had been given a crash course in how the Round Tables are operated before coming here, but now I'm shown their inner workings too. Something makes me avoid touching them too much, though. Something about what I felt on that first night repels me.

It's only when it comes time to test our theories that I cannot put it off any longer. We assemble in Cambridge's main castle. The Round Table has been moved to sit in the centre of the portal, right at the heart of the building. Niamh appears beside me with a chair. 'Here,' she says. 'I remember you saying it gets tiring. Thought you should do this sitting down.'

'Thanks,' I say, caught off guard. The thought of sitting when everyone else is standing is a bit off-putting. Niamh raises an eyebrow. 'Hmph. I didn't peg you as the self-conscious type. You do know that emperors sit on thrones and everyone around them stands, right? That's what I remember when everyone's towering over me.'

'Good point.' I smile, and take the seat. She's right in so many ways: this is going to take it out of me and not having to stay on my feet will definitely make it more bearable. Ollie pulls up his own chair and settles down beside me. He glances back at Niamh. 'I'm not an emperor, but is it okay if I sit down anyway?'

Niamh grins and makes a show of bowing to Ollie and me. But for once Carys is the serious one. 'Concentrate, please, everyone,' she says. 'I don't want my precious tables messed up because some of you are too busy flirting.'

I blush that Carys could think that I'm flirting, and nod my readiness. Frankie shouts down to the basement below us. There's an almighty creak of cogs turning and gears cranking. The earth shakes, there's a distant *boom*, and I am bathed in light. It's the very same light that usually takes me to Stonehenge – a gravity-defying tunnel that breaks Ithr's rules of distance and space. This time, though, the white light above my head is split into six tunnels, each one linked to the subordinate thane fortresses that skirt Cambridge. At the end of each tunnel I glimpse six Round Tables, each one manned by a harker.

'Stage one complete,' Frankie says, raising a hand to the harkers. They all raise a hand in return: it's working as predicted at their end.

'Over to you then, Fern,' Carys says.

'Remember,' Jin says, 'keep talking to us if you can. We might be able to help if anything unexpected happens.'

I nod. On my signal, Ollie places a hand on my shoulder. 'You've got this,' is all he says.

Closing my eyes, I grasp the sides of the Round Table, immediately feeling the inspyre inside it reacting to my Immral. I try to take each element, from the hardened wood through to the sparks that play across the surface, and hold them in my mind. When I'm certain that I've got it all, I do what I've never done before. I've only ever, in fact, seen the Fay do it with the stone columns in Tintagel. I dig my fingers into the table, willing the wood to part beneath them, ignoring the familiar sense of dread that makes me want to pull away. At first the table resists, but with some pressure from my mind – a sharp little nudge that sends a spasm of pain through my whole back – the wood becomes sand-like, allowing my hands to sink inside. There's an intake of breath from the Cambridge thanes. They've never seen me use my power like this before – as far as they're concerned I've just been doing a lot of touching things and closing my eyes pretentiously.

'Focus,' Ollie warns. I allow the inspyre inside the Round Table to play along my fingers. The taste of the Round Table, and the power that fuels it, seeps into my mouth. It's woody, but not unpleasant. I've sensed something like this once before – at the Tournament, when I was trying to help the Fay. This is their magic.

Or is it . . . ?

There's something behind the Fay power. Something darker, sharper. It's the source of that dread, I know it. Something more human than the ancient source of the Fays' magic. It has a spirit and a strength to it, despite its age. I stretch my mind out and the thing uncurls, like a dragon waking from a thousand-year sleep.

'Arthur,' I breathe, as understanding hits me.

'What, Fern?' Jin says, close by.

'King Arthur is here.'

Chapter 29

The dragon-like creature and I examine each other. It's not made of inspyre; it's made of Immral. My own power made tangible, in a form far more beautiful than Medraut's rudimentary ropes and bugs. The sparks that play across it; the way it stretches and compresses in the same way that my Immral tugs at my mind and leaps from my hands. Arthur's has survived hundreds of years inside this table. The sheer power of his Immral, to have lasted this long without him alive to wield it, is dizzying. So this is the thundercloud on the plans Rachel was trying to decipher.

'Focus,' Ollie says again.

I draw back from the monster. I'm going to need to do something about it if I'm to enact my plan. I hadn't anticipated a creature here, especially not one as powerful as this.

'I need Brandon,' I say.

'Who?' Carys asks.

'He's a veneur back in Tintagel,' Jin tells her.

'We've got excellent veneurs here,' Frankie says. 'I can order –'

'No,' I repeat. 'I want Brandon.'

There's whispering, then someone leaves the room, slamming the door behind them. Carys sighs, and mutters, 'Such a drama queen for a reeve.'

'We're trying to get Brandon now, Fern,' Rachel says. 'Do you want to stop?'

I weigh up my options. It's taken me quite a bit of effort to get into the table. I don't want to risk backing out now. Better to press ahead, and hope Brandon can get here soon.

'Get it out,' I tell Jin. I hear glass being drawn from a bag, and a lid being unscrewed.

'Ready?' Jin says.

I nod, and inside the table I open my hands out, imagining them as a magnet.

There's a sticky thud, and the rope of thorns, still encased in resin, lands on the table. We haven't been able to work out how much access Medraut has to these creatures, so I have to act quickly. I melt the resin and force the table open, so that the tendril drops into its bowels, then close the wood, trapping it inside.

'Keep talking to us, Fern,' Niamh says.

'Give her a second,' Ollie replies. He can tell that there's an almighty battle going on in here. The dragon containing King Arthur's Immral reacted immediately to Medraut's rope. If it was mildly curious about my arrival, it is deeply threatened by Medraut's. The rope, it seems, does have some kind of independent thought, because it begins to pulse with Immral, as though warning Arthur's dragon away – a show of strength. The two whip around each other.

'Fern? There's some fireworks going on here, were you aware . . . ?' Carys says.

'It's pretty steamy inside here as well,' Ollie tells her.

'Whatever King Arthur used to make this table isn't reacting well to having Medraut's Immral in with it,' I say.

'Can you control them?'

'That would be a negative.' There's no point in varnishing the truth – I have no power at all over these two beasts. They are now sending sparks of inspyre at each other, one a deeper violet than the other. I had always thought that Medraut must be the most powerful Immral the world had ever seen – anyone who could do the things I'd seen him do had to have been. But Arthur is his match. The two creatures twine around each other, and even though neither of them have mouths or a head, it's as if they're trying to consume the other one whole, to eliminate the threat. I, the half threat – am ignored.

'Are they distracted enough for you to do what you need to do?' Jin says.

I bite back the snappy retort on the tip of my tongue. As if I don't know what I need to do.

Ollie squeezes my shoulder, just once. *Calm down.*

The two creatures thrash against the mechanisms. King Arthur's dragon pulls at its bonds, desperate to reach Medraut's snake. It takes all my energy just to keep the creatures from smashing the table apart.

'She's bleeding,' I hear Carys say.

'Yeah, she does that a lot,' Jin replies.

'Quiet,' Ollie says sharply. He's leaning into me now, trying to send all of his Immral my way. But we both know it's not enough. I need to wind Medraut's rope creature into the sensor, to make it understand that the Immral that powers it is a potential enemy as well as an energy source. But it's more complicated than we'd anticipated – we hadn't known that the ancient force of Arthur's Immral would be there, ready to eliminate any rival.

I try to grab at the creatures with my mind, to control them. 'This is impossible,' I hiss.

There's the distant *bang* of a door flying open, and then two panting bodies enter the room.

'I'm here. You're here. What am I doing here?' Brandon's voice says. 'Fern? Are you okay?'

'Hopefully I will be now you're here,' I reply.

There's a pause, then Brandon says, 'That's maybe the nicest thing anyone's said to me. Right. How can I help?'

I open my mouth to speak but it fills immediately with blood. I can't tell whether I've vomited it, which would be a new kind of hell, or whether my nosebleed is gushing more than usual. Ollie leans into me, reading my thoughts, understanding the problem. He builds chains of Immral in my head. He's trying to draw out the images.

Ah. I see where he's going with this. I try to visualise everything that's happening, and send it back through my hands, across my chest, and into the hand that is resting on my shoulder.

'Oh wow,' Ollie says, his voice pale. He describes King Arthur's power, then adds something I hadn't sensed. 'It's really old, and it's angry. That's what drives it. It's Immral that's channelling pure anger.'

The creature sparks against the Round Table's inspyre again, and I realise that Ollie is right. This is a new aspect to our connection, though – that Ollie is able to read an emotion second-hand through me.

'Arthur's power is like a creature?' Brandon's voice says.

I nod, not trusting myself to speak.

'Could you make your Immral into a creature too?' Brandon says. 'Use it to distract them while you get everything in place? Sometimes two predators will work together to overcome a larger predator.'

'You're overestimating her power if you think she's stronger than Medraut *and* Arthur,' Jin says.

While Jin's comment stings, she has a point. Still, Brandon's plan is worth a try.

I sink into myself, trying to draw my Immral out, to give it a shape. This is different from crafting inspyre, which is like sculpting clay. This is like painting with my own blood. A flash in my brain tells me that something's gone in there. It won't be long before my eyes start to bleed, and at that point it's a ticking clock on me passing out completely. If that happens, all of this will be for nothing, and I might well have broken Cambridge's Round Tables.

I pull at my Immral, weaving it as though I were making a tapestry with my own veins. Gradually, it takes shape. If Medraut and Arthur's creatures are grey, mine has no colour and every colour. It twists, flashing blue-blush-black depending on which way it turns, glimmering in a light that doesn't exist. At times it's a moth, then a beetle, then it has no shape. It flitters before the other Immral creatures as they wind around each other, vying for dominance.

Ollie tells the others what's happening.

'Okay, go with the small-creature look,' Brandon says, as if I had a choice. 'Try to annoy them a bit. You only want to stop them from damaging the mechanisms, right?'

I do as he says, preserving my strength for the task of converting the Round Table. Brandon's right. As soon as I send my moth in to dart around the creatures, they snap at it but don't focus so much on each other. It gives me time to do what needs to be done. Ever so delicately, I manipulate the sensor, moving it, adding to it. It's some of the finest craftsmanship I've ever seen: as thin as a child's hair, as smooth as mercury, as absorbent as an open heart.

At last, I feel sure I've made the sensor understand, tilting it towards Medraut's creature, impressing upon it the same kind of feeling as the one it uses when it senses inspyre activity. But Medraut and Arthur's creatures are finally understanding the threat I pose to them. And if I thought managing them was hard up till now, it's starting to get a whole lot worse. Arthur's serpent winds its way around my Immral creature, throttling it. Medraut's digs its thorns deep into my hands. Ollie's sharp intake of breath tells me he is feeling every prick as keenly as I am.

But this time, the sensor itself comes to my aid. A confused jumble of inspyre that now knows it needs to be wary of Immral, it sends out sparks that form threads, attaching themselves to the grey skin of Medraut's thrashing creature. If it were only fighting the sensor, Medraut's rope might have won. But the sensor has me helping it, making each knot as tight as heartbreak. And, finally, it succumbs. That's when the sensor, seeing that Arthur's creature is still tied inside its own cage, turns its attentions to me. Time to make a speedy exit.

'Ready?' I ask the room, my eyes still closed.

'Ready,' Jin says.

I lift my hands up, wrenching the wooden part of the table open and dissipating my little Immral moth in one movement. Once I'm out, the wood closes in on itself with a sucking noise. My hands are sore from channelling so much Immral. Ollie is wiping away a nosebleed. Brandon offers me a handkerchief and I turn my face away as I clean up my nose and ears.

'Shall we see if it works?' Carys says, unusually serious.

We all stare at the Round Table. To look at it you wouldn't think it had just undergone the table equivalent of major surgery. Luckily inspyre darts across it as usual, which tells me that the ancient engine of Arthur's power is still doing its job properly.

'So we're looking for purple light, instead of the usual blue?' Frankie says.

'If I did it right, yes,' I tell her.

We stare some more. Nothing.

'Well, maybe he hasn't turned any dreamers in Cambridge yet,' Carys says. It's something of an anti-climax.

'Oh for heaven's sake,' Ollie says, and grabs my hand. Immediately a spark of inspyre arcs over us, reacting to the joining of our Immral halves. At the same moment, the others gasp. A dart of violet light is playing like a flame across the Round Table, on the part of the map where the castle would be.

Ollie lets go, and we both nurse our aching hands. 'So it works.' He shrugs. 'Seemed like the simplest way of testing it.'

'Some warning next time would be nice,' I remark.

'This is extraordinary,' Carys says, staring at the table in wonder. 'This is a game-changer. Fern, Ollie, do you realise what you've just given us?' She looks at me, her eyes shining. 'You've given us hope.'

Chapter 30

With the Cambridge mission a success, we're able to continue our tour of Annwn as planned. One Round Table modification down: fifty or so to go. Ollie had joked about a road trip, but now it's actually happening.

Over the next few days I become used to the routine: land in a new place; extract a thorny rope from the many dreamers now being caught across the country or, in their absence, create a creature from my own Immral, each one feeling as though I'm carving off a limb; give myself a migraine – and sometimes worse – by altering the table. It's not long before it starts to take a toll on me. I constantly have a headache, in Ithr as well as Annwn. One day I lose my sight in the middle of a chemistry class and nearly set my uniform alight on a Bunsen burner.

The hardest thing, though, is the emotional cost. As usual it's my brother who vocalises it before I can. 'It's like being shown just how pathetic you are every single day,' he says.

Every night I go through the same fight and every night I understand a little better how weak my Immral is compared to what we're up against. Arthur and Medraut were evenly matched. I don't compare. I'm the bait dog who gets torn to shreds before the real entertainment starts. And every time I successfully manage to change the Round Table, the thanes who are witnessing it cheer and congratulate themselves and I can see in their eyes that they think this is a victory. Poor, deluded fools.

The only thing that keeps me going is that being away from my usual group of friends isn't as horrendous as I thought it would be. Brandon has joined the team permanently and is relentlessly upbeat. When it comes time for me to 'do my thang' as he puts it, he sobers, and is by my side should Arthur's creature cause any problems. Once we leave Cambridge, he's always the one who brings me a chair, and if anyone questions the process he'll hush them.

'You're my bodyguard,' I jokingly tell him one night.

'I'll be anything you want me to be,' he jokes back.

Jin may be prickly still, but sometimes I catch her watching Ollie and me as we come out of each trial. Sometimes I wonder if she's thawing towards me, then she'll make another snarky comment, and I realise my naivety.

So we work our way around the country. We go west, zigzagging from Brighton where circus performers fill the streets, across to Bristol, where trade ships dock on the shore, sending forth waves of nightmares in the forms of slavers and rats. Then we work our way up the middle of the country, from Oxford where the thanes are mad as hell that Cambridge helped us to develop the idea first, up to York and Newcastle, swinging by Liverpool where the river glows red and you can't move for footballs. By the time we cross into Scotland I am reaching the limit of my abilities. In Ithr, I have dark bags around my eyes and my skin is taking on a greyish tinge. Combined with my red irises, it makes me look more like a zombie than ever before. I'm just grateful that in Annwn I look vaguely healthy, even if I don't feel it.

Once we've dealt with the tables of the Edinburgh thaneship, we head into the Highlands, towards the lochs where kelpies frolic. It's there that Brandon ambushes me.

'We're escaping,' he says, dragging me off the portal platform as soon as I land in Annwn.

'What? No!' I say, wondering why none of the thanes seem remotely bothered by my imminent kidnapping.

'It's okay,' he replies, 'Everyone's in on it.'

'Well, that makes me feel better,' I snap. 'Once again I'm the last to know.'

'Are you always this moody?'

'Have you not spent the last week with me?'

'Good point.'

He leads me out of the castle, a gigantic tower that stands on the edge of a cliff and looks out over endless wilderness. The first time I climbed the turrets to meet the sentinels, I had to catch my breath, both from the force of the wind and the rageful beauty of it.

Brandon leads me to the hangar where the knights' transports are kept. In this part of Annwn, the knights have to cover vast distances in such varied terrain that horses aren't as useful as they are in the cities. Instead, they use a variety of flying machines, from helicopters to hang-gliders. Just outside the hangar, a hot-air balloon waits for us, the thanes' sigil embroidered on its side.

'In you pop,' Brandon says, helping me into the basket.

'I've never flown in a hot-air balloon before,' I say.

'Damn, neither have I. I was hoping you'd be the pilot.' Then, seeing my face, he adds, 'Joke.'

He expertly deals with the ropes and the flame that's keeping the balloon inflated, and before long we're lifting off. The castle slides past, floor by floor, turret by turret, until we're level with the crenelations through which the sentinels keep watch. I spot some familiar faces. Rachel is leaping up and down, waving her hands in seesaw motions. Jin and Ollie are both far too cool to wave – but they're smiling up at us. Jin lifts a single hand by way of goodbye, and if I was closer I swear I'd see my brother smirking. Then we're above them, the castle shrinking beneath us.

'You know I could've just flown anywhere you wanted to take me,' I tell Brandon.

'Tonight you get a night off. That means no flying, no using your power in any way, shape or form,' he replies, adjusting our course. I join him at the edge of the basket and look out over the Highlands. Beneath us a pack of dream wolves flow across heather. Brandon points at something in the distance – in the air, just a little below us. A dragon, green as a summer leaf, spikes running along its back, flame flickering through its nostrils with every breath. I should be frightened, but after the horrors I've seen enacted by humans over the last few months I can't think of anything purer. Brandon is equally awestruck. 'I've never seen one before,' he says quietly. 'Isn't she gorgeous?'

I reach a hand out, trying to sense the inspyre inside the dragon with my Immral, but Brandon pats my hand down. 'No superpowers tonight, remember?' he says.

'You don't know that I was going to use –'

'Yes, I do. I've been watching you do crazy, amazing things for months now. I know what you were doing, knight King.'

'You can't get to know me in a few months, veneur . . . Brandon,' I reply.

'You don't even know my surname!' he crows.

'I . . .' And then I feel bad. The truth is, while I've grown fond of my Excalibur team, I haven't put any effort into getting to know them. I have my group of friends. Making new ones is hard, and it comes with heartache in my line of work. Perhaps my reserve hasn't just meant that I've been rejecting people who could be friends; I've been outright rude in some cases. Brandon already knows enough about me to understand that I will try to find out the inner workings of something. What do I know about him except his lore and that he's a bit of a joker?

'It's Wilson, by the way,' he remarks, still smiling genially.

I'm about to respond when he points towards a distant hill. 'That's where we're going,' he says, and turns his attention to the controls on the hot-air balloon.

'How did you learn to fly one of these things?' I ask, unsure whether I should be distracting him or not.

'One of the knights back at the castle gave me a quick lesson,' he replies.

'A *quick* lesson?' I repeat. 'So this is your first time?'

'Yep,' he replies, then seeing my expression says, 'Don't worry, I'm a very fast learner.'

As a natural-born worrier I am not convinced by this, but he hasn't killed us yet. I'll reserve judgement until he returns me, preferably in one piece, to the castle, and then I am never getting in a vehicle with him again. We crest the hill and the hot-air balloon lurches to one side as he brings it down. I'd make a biting remark, but I'm too busy staring open-mouthed at the view.

We're looking down over a loch surrounded on all sides by brightly coloured trees; copper, dusky pink and burgundy. The loch itself is serene but for the occasional mermaid that sunbathes on the shores. But the really stunning part is the sky. If the ground is reds and golds, the sky is purples and greens, the light dripping like wet paint.

'One of the harkers told me about this spot, and I thought to myself, *That sounds like the kind of place a tired, aching Immral could find some peace,*' Brandon says, bringing the balloon down with a bump.

He helps me out of the basket, then busies himself fetching things from a pack stowed inside. There's a rug and a couple of velveteen cushions; another rug – 'To go over your legs' – and lastly a picnic hamper packed with cheeses, breads, pastries and a type of fruit only found in Annwn. It's not unlike a pomegranate, except the seeds are larger and less likely to get stuck in your teeth.

'This is amazing,' I tell him, tucking into a Cornish pasty. I've lost my appetite in Ithr thanks to all the migraines, but the journey here has returned it. 'Thank you.'

'Thanks for letting me explore Annwn with you,' Brandon replies. 'I knew I wanted to be a veneur the moment I learned what they were, but part of me's kind of jealous of the knights.'

'Sorry,' I reply, not really knowing what to say.

'Nah, it's for the best,' he lies back on one of the cushions. 'I don't think I'd be cut out for fighting. I wouldn't be able to take my horse into battle – I'd be too worried about them getting hurt. And I *definitely* couldn't kill a dream shaped like an animal. But I'd always said that when I retired I'd offer to become a teacher just so I could explore Annwn.'

'That's why most teachers do it, right? So they get to keep their portals and can do whatever they want here in their time off.'

'Mostly, yeah. Not Miss D.'

I nod. 'That woman is horse mad.'

'There's nothing wrong with loving horses,' Brandon retorts.

I look back out over the lake. Brandon cuts some cheese with his penknife and hands me a slice. In the distance, the dragon we passed roars and a spike of flame scorches the heather below.

'Why did you do this?' I ask him directly.

'You needed a break.'

'Sure,' I reply, 'but all of this –' I gesture at the blankets and the picnic – 'and bringing me here. You didn't need to go to all that effort.'

Brandon sits up, serious. He's watching me intensely. Too intensely.

'Isn't it obvious why?' he asks. I'm suddenly very aware of how close we are, sitting side by side on this rug. His eyes are so green. Something shifts in my stomach. The way his mouth curls as he smiles, as though he's teasing me. Oh God oh God oh God. He leans towards me.

And I move away, fumbling an excuse, looking down at my lap, adjusting the blanket over my knees. My cheeks must be bright red, but that's nothing to the burning awkwardness inside. I don't regret pulling away from what was going to happen next. I wasn't ready. It would have been my first kiss, and I don't want my first kiss to be with him.

I allow myself to admit it at last. I want my first kiss to be with Samson.

Samson who's my boss. Samson who isn't interested in me. Samson who has a girlfriend in Ithr.

I'm such a fool.

Chapter 31

The rest of our tour passes largely without incident, except for a lingering self-consciousness on my part whenever I see Brandon. My embarrassment is made worse by the fact that he is obviously trying very hard not to let things be awkward between us. He does exactly what he's always done; fetching me a chair, defending me if someone questions anything. But there's a formality to his behaviour that was never there before.

Ollie spots it first.

'So did things not go as planned on the picnic?' he asks, the day after we leave the Highlands, as we head out to school.

'You knew what he was going to do?' I say.

'Well, he didn't put it in words as such but it was pretty obvious.' Ollie smirks. 'Also, I can read minds . . .' He shrugs, like, *Sorry 'bout it.*

'I just . . . I didn't really see him that way until he leaned in, and then I panicked,' I tell Ollie.

'Do you even know what feeling that way is like?' he asks bluntly.

I stick a foot out and kick him in the calf. He laughs, but then stops as we come to the junction where we peel off in different directions to go to our separate schools. 'Well, do you?'

'Of course I do,' I say, although I don't admit that it's Samson I think about in that way. The teasing would never stop. Something odd flickers across Ollie's face: a hunger. But the next moment it's gone.

'Is it not worth a try?' he asks. 'I mean, someone likes you. That's pretty great, right?'

My hackles rise. 'So just because someone likes me, I have to be grateful to them? It doesn't matter if *I* fancy them, because they're all the chance I'll get?'

'That's not what I'm . . .' Ollie raises his hands in defeat. 'Whatever, Fern.'

As Ollie and I stalk our separate ways to school, I can tell that he's fuming as much as me.

I just want you to be happy, he'll say, justifying himself. But I don't see why I should go out with Brandon because of someone else's notion of what will make me happy.

Why won't you let your guard down? he'd say. And, if he were here, I'd probably retort with something petty about not wanting to be burned alive again. Because the truth is, I can't separate the idea that I'm not attracted to Brandon from the thought that even if I was, I'd never be able to trust that he wasn't with me because of my Immral. In Ithr, I'm too ugly for anyone to genuinely want me. In Annwn, I'm too powerful.

With the Round Tables picking up Immral use all over the country, the extent of Medraut's reach is becoming obvious. We knew it was bad. We just didn't know it was *this* bad.

Reports start coming in of nightly sparks of Immral appearing on the Round Table maps. They are everywhere, and as we move through the castles and see the modified tables at work, the violet light is often more commonplace than the blue.

'We'd thought it was just the inspyre diminishing,' Rachel says one night, as we watch purple sparks flashing across a map of Manchester, 'but it's like they're inversing. The more Immral there is, the less inspyre.'

'That's Medraut, not me,' I say.

'Historically speaking, Rachel's right,' Jin chimes in. 'Whenever an Immral comes to light, there's a dip in inspyre.'

'I don't remember inviting you into this conversation,' I say. 'How come you know so much about it, anyway?'

I stalk off before she can reply, but can't help myself from throwing one final barb as I leave the room. 'At least people with Immral can actually *do* something. What do you do all day, Jin? Except act like a massive bitch.'

I don't get far down the corridor before the door behind me bangs open. Jin pushes me up against the wall. My head cracks on stone. I thought I'd seen her angry before, but I was wrong. She looks demented.

'Get off me,' I hiss, but that only makes her lean on me harder.

'You really are blind, aren't you?' she says. 'There is someone back there who is already feeling *useless*, and the person she admires most in the world just confirmed it for her.'

I stare at Jin. 'Rachel?' I say stupidly.

'*Yes*, Rachel,' Jin says. 'God, how can you be so self-absorbed? How can you think that everything is about you when you're surrounded by people who are trying to make a difference?'

'I don't think it's all about me.'

I shove her, and a spark of inspyre flicks from my wrists, stinging her. She steps back, eyeing me with more hatred than I've ever seen.

'I've watched you from the day you found out you had Immral, Fern. I watched the way you martyred yourself. The way you act like you're *so* different from everyone else that no one can *possibly* like you. And I heard about what you did to Medraut's daughter. If that's what being an Immral means, I . . .' She trails off.

'You what?' I ask. 'Don't stop now when you were just getting into your stride. You've been dying to get this off your chest for ages.'

'Forget it,' Jin mutters, and leaves me on my own.

Ollie sidles up from the other end of the corridor. 'What's going on?'

I shrug. 'Jin being Jin again.'

Ollie watches her disappear round a corner. 'Don't be too mean to her,' he says.

'Why?' I eye him suspiciously. 'What have you seen in her head?'

It's his turn to shrug. 'What happens in the head, stays in the . . . Well, stays in my head.'

'You're so weird.'

The argument with Jin is still pumping through my veins, so it takes me a while to remember what caused her to follow me in the first place. Rachel. *The person she admires most*. That can't be me. She's mistaken. Rachel doesn't put that much stock in what I think, does she? It's a preposterous idea – we're the same age. We're basically equals.

Except you have Immral.

I bang my head against the stone wall, on purpose this time.

'Woah, don't go even more crazy,' Ollie says.

'Do you ever just want to be someone else?' I ask.

Ollie frowns, but before he can reply, Brandon runs up. 'I've been sent to get you. It's urgent.'

We follow him through the castle, towards the central hall.

'What's going on?' I ask, as Rachel and Jin fall in behind us.

'They think they've found another of your mother's messages.'

'What, here?'

'No, back in Bristol.'

Ollie motions towards Rachel and Brandon. They have been kept in the dark about the search for Excalibur until now. 'Exceptional circumstances?' I say.

Ollie shrugs and Jin purses her lips, but her words about Rachel are still sitting uncomfortably. Wouldn't telling Rachel be a vote of confidence? I decide to risk Lord Allenby's wrath, and fill the others in, as we say our farewells to the Manchester thanes and take a portal back to Bristol. We're met by a reeve, who hurries us into the wing where their Round Table is kept.

'But why on earth would a poem turn up here instead of Tintagel or your house, or even Manchester?' Brandon says.

'You haven't made the connection?' Jin says smugly.

'Please, grace us with your wisdom,' Ollie says, just as I understand.

'Five,' I say. 'This was the fifth thaneship we visited, wasn't it?'

Brandon does the maths on his fingers. 'Blimey. You think it's been here all this time, and we just didn't notice it?'

The reeve leads us right up to the Round Table. 'We spotted it under the table just an hour ago, as we were cleaning.'

'You haven't cleaned in here for a fortnight?' Ollie says incredulously.

'We've been busy.'

The reeve lights a lamp and holds it beneath the table. I kneel, feeling foolish, and crane my head to see the letters etched onto the bottom of the wood.

Well done, knight of strength, it reads,
You have found the first.
You have tested your mettle
And sensed its worth.
The second clue is trickier:
Reach out to them, I implore.
Is this the faith? she said, and said no more.

I stare up at my mother's handwriting. And begin to cry.

Chapter 32

It must be because I'm absolutely exhausted – I just don't have the brain capacity to deal with this turn of events. Ollie places his hands on my arms, and I step into a hug. It's only while I'm sobbing that I realise that this is the first time Ollie and I have hugged in years.

'I'm all out of handkerchiefs I'm afraid,' Brandon jokes lamely.

'Why is she doing this to us?' I say. If Mum wanted me to get Excalibur why did she make this so damn hard, even if she was trying to conceal her true motives from Andraste and Nimue? I've spent so long trying to understand my mother, and I thought I was getting closer to working out who she was, and now . . . she's so distant again.

'I just want this to be over,' I sniff. 'And I can't see . . .'

'You can't see the end,' Rachel finishes.

There's a long silence. The reeve shuffles awkwardly. 'So did you want to go back to Manchester or . . . ?'

Altering the Round Tables in the remaining castles will have to wait. This is more important. By the time we reach Tintagel, Lord Allenby has already been notified of our arrival, and he and Easa are waiting for us in his office.

'How are you holding up, Fern?' he asks. 'I've been getting reports of the incredible work you've all been doing – the lords and ladies of the other thaneships have barely had a bad word to say about you.'

'Barely?' Brandon asks.

Ollie grins. 'Hey, for someone with Fern's attitude that's a miracle.'

I stifle a smile.

'Let's have a look at this poem then,' Lord Allenby says, and Jin pulls a copy from her pocket. Lord Allenby studies the writing for some time.

'And we think it was found there because that was the fifth castle you visited?' Lord Allenby asks.

'I have a theory,' Easa says. 'What if Fern and Ollie completed the first task unknowingly – by changing the Round Tables? The first task was about strength, right? Well, what better show of strength than taking on King Arthur's power five times?'

'But there's no way Mum – or the Fay – could have known we'd end up doing that,' Ollie says.

'Maybe they didn't need to,' Easa says. 'I've been doing a *lot* of reading while you've been away. There's something I think you should see, down in the archives.'

'Let's go, then,' Lord Allenby says, but instead of leading us out of the room, he takes a solid wooden doorknob from his collection, and fits it to the back door of his office. The door glows white, and when Lord Allenby opens it there is no longer a candlelit passageway out to the herb gardens, or a long medieval hall where the Fay reside – there's a set of steps that circles round and down, leading, I'd guess, right into the archives.

'Let's not clue everyone out there into what we're doing, eh?' Lord Allenby remarks.

We enter the archives from the opposite end to the usual entrance. Ollie and I glance at Rachel: so this is how she got in that time we spotted her.

'How did you know about this way in?' Ollie whispers. We told her while on our tour about seeing her down in the archives – now she's on the Excalibur team there are no secrets between us.

Rachel frowns. 'I'm not sure. Maybe someone told me about it?'

'Who?'

Confusion clouds Rachel's tired features. 'I can't remember.'

We fall silent as Lord Allenby goes to talk to the reeves who usually man the archives, telling them to take a break. Something worries at my stomach; something's not right with Rachel. I make a mental note to mention it to Jin, since she seems to have appointed herself Rachel's therapist.

'I think it was here,' Easa's saying. He's standing next to the stack labelled, *Quests*. He pulls on it and the shelves, each one sitting on rollers, wheel apart like an accordion. We follow him down the passageway between bookshelves.

'Yes, here it is,' Easa says, pulling out a file labelled, *The Book of Taliesin*. 'Does this sound familiar? *And King Arthur did hunt for the cauldron of the Fay, but no matter where he looked he could not seek it. Then upon a full moon he rested upon a fulsome grassy mound, and in his anger he struck the mound with his fist, and the mound did break open, and there inside was a fortress. King Arthur ventured into the fortress and, finding it empty, struck the stone with his fist, and the stone did break open, and inside was a glass cage. And King Arthur, seeing that something rested behind the glass, did strike it with his fist, and the glass did break open, and with these three shows of strength, the cauldron did appear to him.'*

'Great story,' Ollie says.

'Oh my God, I get it,' I say, understanding dawning. 'Arthur went looking for the cauldron but the cauldron came to him –'

'When he demonstrated his strength,' Jin finishes.

'Exactly,' Easa continues. 'It's not that we ever had to go looking for particular places – it's that Fern had to prove herself worthy of the next stage.'

'So the clues aren't telling us where to go?' Brandon says.

'No, they're telling us what I need to do to get to the next level,' I say.

'But how did it know you had even started the quest?' Rachel asks.

'I guess finding the letter?' Ollie says. 'Maybe it had some kind of tracking device on it?'

I pull the letter from my pouch and examine it closely.

'There's nothing on the letter itself,' I say.

'What about the envelope?' Easa says. 'If your mother was trying to conceal her true motives from the Fay, she'd hardly ask them to enchant a letter written directly to you.'

He's right. The envelope looks normal, but when I run my fingers over the sealant, I detect something I hadn't noticed before: Fay power. The same ancient strength that ebbed and flowed through me at the Tournament. 'They charmed it so the quest would start when I opened the letter,' I say, looking at the others.

'And the show of strength was you changing all those Round Tables,' Rachel says, her eyes bright. 'Well done, you.'

I feel floored, but something else is stirring inside me uneasily.

'This is great!' Ollie's saying. 'We just get you to perform some kind of test of faith and then, *boom*, next clue. Thanks, Mum.'

I look to Lord Allenby, and see that he is having the same doubts as me. 'It's not going to be that easy,' I say, loudly to shut Ollie up. 'Don't you see? A location we could work out. But these tests – they're designed to make sure I'm worthy of the sword, aren't they?'

'Well, yeah,' Brandon says.

Jin is watching me closely.

'Well . . .' It feels as though I'm baring my insecurities before a jury. 'What if I'm not?'

No one has anything to say to that. Oh, they give me bland reassurances, but the truth is, they've all seen what Medraut can do. They know how difficult I find it to use my Immral. And even if I have passed a test of strength, there are two more tests to go. One of faith, and one of goodness knows what. We all know that my qualities as a person are limited. There is every possibility that I'm not going to be worthy.

As if to compensate for this uncertainty, the Excalibur group takes its list-making to the next level. Lord Allenby even recruits Samson into the team, hoping that his vast knowledge of thane lore might help us. If 'faith' is the next clue, the group scours maps, imaginations and stories for anything that might constitute a test. And even though I grumpily tell them that it won't be as easy as working our way through a list, Ollie and I still spend hours inventing scenarios that might help us to complete the second task.

'Maybe you have to learn to actually trust someone?' Ollie suggests, raising an eyebrow at me.

'Maybe people should actually be trustworthy,' I fire back. Once upon a time we'd both have meant it.

I'm oddly nervous about going back to patrols. It's only been a few weeks, but it feels as though a lot has happened in that time. The distance between me and the other knights was physical, but it's become more than that. Samson had said that keeping secrets didn't change anything between us, but it has.

The first time I enter the knights' chamber, Milosz is sitting in my chair. It shouldn't bother me, but I immediately feel it as a sign of things to come.

'Fern!' Natasha shouts, the first one to see me, and soon I'm surrounded by a scrum of knights.

'Did you go anywhere glamorous?'

'We're expecting souvenirs.'

'Thank God you can take over the patrol notes again.'

Then, 'Welcome back.'

Samson is standing behind me, quiet and warm. But I can tell that something's off, even if I can't put my finger on what it is.

'I'm pleased to be back,' I say truthfully, albeit more formally than I had planned.

As the others catch Ollie and me up on the events of the last few weeks, I spot Sachi on the other side of the chamber.

She is sitting in the corner I used to haunt, back when I didn't want friends, holding a book with one hand and scratching a dog's ears with the other. Her eyes keep flitting towards the other squires chatting around the fire. Her lip curls disdainfully as one of them invites her to join them. She shakes her head, but I can see from the way she keeps watching them that she wants, desperately, to be a part of their merriment. She is doing exactly what I did last year, until Ramesh broke down my barriers. I want to shout at her and shake her – tell her to just go and talk to them for God's sake, because there may not be much time left for her, or them, or any of us.

'Hang on,' I say, doing a double take. 'Isn't that the dog that's been trying to get into Tintagel for ages?'

'Oh yes!' Natasha says, whistling towards the creature. 'You need to meet our new addition.'

The dog scrambles to its feet and bounds over. It's some kind of poodle mix – fluffy and a bit ridiculous. Its coat is spotted, like a cow. It's clearly someone's pet, either living or dead – a memory held together by a lot of love. I look at the tag hanging from its collar, but instead of a name, there's a sentence: *I belong to Charlie*.

'He just barged in here last week and we haven't been able to get him out,' Natasha tells me.

'Not that we've been trying that hard,' Amina says.

'You're pretty cute,' I tell the dog, scratching its chin. It drools on me in reply.

Apparently that was the right thing to say, because the dog, who the others have affectionately nicknamed Cavall, follows me out to the stables.

'That's the first time he's left the knights' chamber since arriving,' says Samson. 'He must like you.'

'Mad creature,' says Ollie.

Lamb is most unimpressed by the dog, nudging Cavall out of the way with a gentle hoof as he cavorts in front of her. But this doesn't put him off. He trails Bedevere on our patrol of north London, happily nipping at trickster nightmares and begging for treats off dreamers.

And, apart from Cavall, everything sort of goes back to normal. Except it doesn't.

Chapter 33

Cavall isn't the only new addition to the London thaneship. One night we find her waiting in the knights' chamber, chatting at, rather than with, Natasha.

'Niamh!' I exclaim.

'Chosen One!' she says cheerfully.

'You moved to London?' Ollie says.

'Well, it sounded like you were having all the fun here,' Niamh says, 'I was getting FOMO. Besides, the access in Tintagel is so much better than in Cambridge. I'd been there five years, you would've thought they could've installed a bloody ramp or two.'

Samson introduces himself. 'I hear you're going to be Lancelot's new lieutenant?' he says. 'Amina will be thrilled. We've heard a lot about your fighting skills.'

And they're off, talking about people I don't know from happier times, when different thaneships had the luxury of meeting socially and sharing skills freely.

'How about you?' Niamh asks me suddenly. 'Are you going out with that veneur boy yet?'

Ollie snorts.

'Errr . . . no.' I blush. 'I didn't want . . .'

Samson studiously avoids the gaze of every human being in the room.

'Ha! And how about you, twin?' Niamh looks at Ollie shrewdly. 'Are you done hiding yet?'

It's Ollie's turn to blush. Niamh laughs good-naturedly, and sets about introducing herself to the rest of the knights just in from patrol. I watch Ollie, though, wrong-footed. What did Niamh mean, hiding?

While I'm pleased to have Niamh here with us, I cannot shake off my time spent in the rest of Annwn. I love London, and I love being with my friends. But I've seen the wider world here now, and part of me longs to explore it. More than that – I have now truly seen what's at stake. It was easy, before, to believe that Medraut's influence was confined to the capital, to my own little bubble. My tour has shown me that so much more than this city is in danger.

I take to reading the newspapers in Ithr, even though it makes me angry and sad and feel useless and puts me in a bad mood for the rest of the day.

'I wish you wouldn't,' Ollie says one morning as I pore over yet another interview with Medraut. 'Or at least give me some warning so I can clear the room first.'

'It's important that we know what's happening.'

'We know what's happening. It's all going to shit.'

'Language, please,' Dad says, coming up behind us.

'Sorry,' Ollie and I say in unison, and I close the paper and pop it on the dining table. Medraut's face is emblazoned across the front page, the headline, *One Voice For Our Time*, mocking me with the hidden import that only the thanes truly understand. Ollie spots it too and flips the paper over.

'You two. You don't talk for years then suddenly you're thick as thieves,' Dad says, busying himself in the kitchen.

I smile at Ollie but he doesn't return it. Once again there's that sense that he's holding something back from me, and then he seems to come to a decision and says, louder than he needs to be heard, 'Actually, Dad, can I have a friend over for dinner tomorrow night?'

'Of course,' Dad says, not turning round. 'Will they like pasta?'

'Everyone likes pasta, Dad.'

I look at Ollie curiously. He hasn't brought any friends over for years. Not even Jenny came round – our house was always too cramped compared to hers. But now Ollie's got a friend he wants us to meet. I can't help but feel curious.

'Someone from school?' Dad's saying.

'No. FOTS,' Ollie replies. 'He lost his sister.'

He darts a glance at me and shakes his head almost imperceptibly. I know what he's trying to say: *She wasn't a thane, don't worry*.

'Name?'

'Kieran.'

'Well,' Dad says, turning towards us, 'I look forward to meeting him.'

Admitting a stranger into our house feels like a huge step. Aside from Clemmie and our family, barely anyone's been invited over for as long as I can remember. I almost feel sorry for Kieran – does he have any idea how weird everyone's going to find his presence? Does he know that he's walking into a test? Because that's what this is, I realise the next night, as I change out of my hoodie into a simple blouse. It's a test of Kieran – how's he going to react to me, to how I look, to my weird social skills? But more importantly it's a test of us as a family. Do we hold together? Do we work, to an outside eye? Or will Kieran see the fractures between us?

Dad must feel something similar to me, because he's on extra special behaviour when I come downstairs. He's trimmed his beard and is faffing more than usual over dinner.

A key turns in the door. Ollie comes through first, brushing windswept hair from his eyes and looking flushed. He ushers another boy into the hallway, and before I'm ready Kieran is offering me his hand. He's bright and open-eyed in a way that reminds me of Ramesh, but there's nothing of Ramesh's nervousness about him. I had always thought that Ollie was confident, but I now realise that I was wrong. Ollie's bravura was always a show – his swagger is affected. When Kieran moves it's with an assuredness that tells me that he is absolutely comfortable in his own skin in a way that Ollie isn't.

'Come in then,' Dad says, beckoning Kieran and the rest of us into the sitting room, where the smell of ragu, heady with wine and thick sauce, makes my mouth water. 'Delighted to meet you, Kieran.'

Kieran's smile is infectious. 'I've been pestering Ollie for ages to let me see his place. I don't know why he was so shy about it.'

'Ollie, shy?' I snort.

Ollie pulls a face at me, but then Kieran firmly cements

his place in my regards by saying, 'Now, Ollie, this is the moment where I bond with everyone by ganging up against you. But it's okay, because everyone here loves you so it's not meant meanly, alright?'

Laughing, I pull out a chair for Kieran and Dad serves dinner. Within a matter of minutes our house feels as it never has before. It feels full. Cosy. *Normal*, or what I imagine normal must be for any family that hasn't been through what we've been through.

Kieran begins to talk, and I am quite happy to listen and watch. He tells us about his schoolwork and his hobbies, and asks us in turn about our own lives. It becomes clear that Ollie has told Kieran a lot about Dad and me, and Kieran isn't shy in asking some pretty personal questions considering it's our first meeting. He asks Dad about Mum, and he asks me about my time at St Stephens, giving Ollie a hard look that tells me my brother hasn't sugar-coated his own role in what went down with Jenny. Ollie chimes in occasionally, but more often than not I catch him throwing hesitating glances towards Dad and me. Checking to see if we're okay. Checking whether we like Kieran.

Realisation dawns on me, far too slowly. I should have realised months ago. I should have realised *years* ago.

Ollie's never had a girlfriend, despite so many making their interest abundantly clear.

Ollie's never been comfortable in his own skin, in a school where being perceived as different in any way is punished with . . . Well, just look at my burn scar.

Ollie and Kieran are in love.

How could I not have seen this part of my brother before? I'm wondering whether Dad's realised too when Kieran unthinkingly squeezes Ollie's leg under the table. Ollie's eyes widen, and we both unconsciously look to our dad.

He's seen too. I can tell just from the expression on his face. He noticed the leg squeeze, and he knows what it means. I have a strange, out of body experience. I am looking down on our family from a great height, acutely aware that this moment could fracture it along different fault lines. Then Dad smiles and continues the conversation as if nothing's happened, as if he didn't just pass the test.

As we carry on talking, Ollie's smile returns. No, it doesn't just return, it grows wider and wider, until he's like the Cheshire bloody Cat who got the cream. I'm so happy for him. Medraut hasn't got to Dad that much, then. But while I'm happy for Ollie, I really am, seeing him and Kieran sitting so easily next to each other? It's making me feel *awful*.

Not because I don't like Kieran. I like him a lot. And I can see that he's a good match for my brother. It's because of that spark between them – I want it. And I know that I could have that with Samson. If only he could ever like me back. If only I didn't look the way I look. If only I didn't wear my bitterness like a shell. If only he didn't have a girlfriend already.

'Fern, you go to school with Medraut's daughter, right?' Kieran asks, breaking into my spiralling thoughts.

It takes me a moment to realise that it's not just Ollie who suddenly looks tense. Kieran does too. His jaw is set, his eyes focused on me, as if this is what he's been wanting to talk about all along.

'Yeah.' I shrug. 'But we're not friends or anything.'

'Not a fan of Medraut then?' Kieran smiles.

'No, she's not.' Dad says. 'Nor is Ollie, unless something's changed since his last rant.'

'Good,' Kieran says. 'I wouldn't be friends with him if he was.'

There's an intriguing steeliness to his voice.

'Well, I wouldn't be with you if you did, so that's that,' Ollie replies. We all catch what he just said, accept it, and move on.

'I should warn you,' I tell Kieran, 'Dad and his girlfriend quite like Medraut.'

'Ah,' Dad says, throwing his hands up affably. 'If it's three against one I'll leave the table. I don't see the harm the man's doing, that's all. He's just trying to bring us together, isn't he? Is that so bad? There's far too much arguing nowadays, when we should be minding our own business.'

I have to bite back my retort spelling out exactly how much harm Medraut has done, and I can see that Ollie is doing the same. The cheek of Dad to say that in the presence of someone whose younger sister was killed on Medraut's orders is almost too much to bear.

'So you won't be joining the Shout Louder cause anytime soon, Mr King. What about you, Fern?'

Ollie whispers Kieran's name, trying to rein him in.

'You're part of Shout Louder?' I say. I think of the protestors who were injured by the One Voice members. I can't imagine Kieran being in their ranks. I can't imagine him standing next to the self-important bumble of Constantine Hale.

'Of course,' Kieran says. 'I can see what Medraut's doing. He's trying to divide us. Turn everyone against people like you and me.'

Dad releases a little sigh and sets about gathering up our plates.

'What kind of things do you do?' I ask. Ollie looks as though he wishes the ground would open up and swallow him.

'Well, it's only just getting started,' Kieran admits, 'but we're gaining members every day. There are people out there who can see that Medraut getting into power would be disastrous. I mean, the man never engages with any arguments. Have you seen him on TV? He doesn't answer questions, he just makes out like it's all the fault of people who look a bit different to him.'

I laugh. 'You see it too?'

'Of course. Not everyone's a sheep.'

Ollie gets up and helps Dad wash the dishes. Usually I would too, but something's ignited in me. Even with my Immral I can barely stop Medraut's progress in Annwn. This could be my chance to make a difference in Ithr.

Chapter 34

After Kieran's left, Dad takes me to one side. 'I understand if you don't like Medraut, Fern, but please don't go to any of these Shout Louder meetings.'

'Why not?'

'I don't want you getting caught up in anything dangerous.'

The irony is not lost on me – I am in danger just by existing. But I don't want to argue with Dad. Not today. Instead, I reach up and kiss his cheek. 'Thanks for not getting weird with Ollie,' I say softly.

'What? Oh, Kieran?' Dad laughs. 'I've known my boy likes boys since he was ten. I just wish he'd come out with it sooner.'

'You knew?' I say, feeling like even more of a failure as a sister. If Dad knew – Dad, who remains wilfully ignorant of anything that might inconvenience him – then I really should have. Then another thought occurs to me: is that why Dad let Ollie off so lightly after the fire? Because he knew that my brother was struggling too? I don't know what to make of that if it's true.

'I mean it, about Shout Louder,' Dad says. 'Please think about it, Ferny.'

'I'll think about it, I promise.' I don't think he catches my double meaning.

Once the dishes are dried, I knock on Ollie's door.

Now that I've had more time to process that Ollie is gay, more and more things are making sense. Not least the fact that I'm fairly certain Ramesh knew – Ollie wrote a note to him on a piece of coloured paper that hangs at the memorial to the dead: *You knew me, and you liked me anyway*. I am starting to appreciate that despite surrounding himself with friends, Ollie has probably been just as lonely as me.

'You could have told me, you know,' I say, trying to keep the hurt from my voice. This isn't about me, but I can't help but feel as though I've lost months of Ollie's companionship – months we can ill afford to lose thanks to our baggage – because he was keeping this a secret.

'Well, I didn't,' he says.

I trace the patterns of his quilt with a finger. 'Did you think I'd judge you?'

'No,' Ollie says. 'No, I really didn't. I just wasn't ready.'

I nod. Some truths are too tender. They need to be nurtured close to our hearts until they are strong enough to survive in the light.

'Then when I *was* ready,' Ollie continues, 'I thought you might be jealous. And I didn't want to make things awkward between us again.'

'Why would I be jealous?' I say. 'Hang on . . . Is this why you were so set on me going out with Brandon?'

'I wasn't –'

'Don't lie,' I say. 'You got really weird about it.'

Ollie shrugs. 'I thought if you had a boyfriend, it would be okay for me to have one too.'

'What made you bring Kieran over in the end, then?'

Ollie ponders this, as if not even he really knows. 'Well, mostly because Kieran was getting antsy about meeting you guys. He thought I was ashamed of him. Ridiculous.'

He plays with his pen, determinedly not looking at me. 'Niamh guessed.'

'Is that why she asked if you were still hiding?' I say.

He nods. 'She sees a lot. She told me that I shouldn't push you away again. What was it she said? *Don't let the anger of the past make you carry on making mistakes, or you'll spend your whole life being angry.* I've been so angry about everything lately – angry at Mum, angry that I didn't know how Dad would take it.' He looks at me slyly. 'Angry that you won't admit you're head over heels for Samson when no one would blame you.'

'I'm not –'

'Don't lie to me, sis. Mind reader, remember?'

'You little . . .'

I shove him good-naturedly, and he holds his hands up in surrender, both of us laughing hysterically, far more than is warranted by the situation. When we've calmed down, I bring things back to Kieran.

'So, you two met at FOTS, huh?'

'It's good dating ground,' Ollie smirks. 'Lots of bereaved, emotionally vulnerable young people.' He clutches his heart and throws his head back, and it's the most free I've seen him in ages.

'His whole family come to the meetings,' Ollie continues. 'His dad and I got talking first, then he introduced me to Kieran and, well . . .'

'So his parents know?'

'Yeah.' Ollie has the grace to look a little guilty at this admission. 'Kieran came out a few years ago and his parents weren't very happy,' Ollie goes on, 'but then Jo died and they said they realised what was important. So it hasn't all been plain sailing for him.'

'Is he your first boyfriend?'

Ollie nods. 'Well, kinda. There was someone at school – you remember Liam?'

'The guy with the –?' I twiddle my finger against my hair. Liam wasn't one of the cool kids, but he had a lock of hair that fell over his forehead, which made him look moderately cute.

'Yeah,' Ollie said. 'I mean, nothing ever properly happened, obviously . . .' Neither of us mention Jenny, although I imagine that both of us are thinking of what she'd have done if she'd discovered Ollie's secret.

Impulsively, I flick Ollie on the nose. 'No secrets any more, okay?' I say.

He smiles. 'Deal.'

'So . . . he's part of Shout Louder?' I ask.

Ollie nods. 'I went with him once, one of the first meetings.'

Another secret; another gut punch.

'What was it like?'

'Weird. Really intense,' Ollie says. 'I hate Medraut, but this was like he couldn't do anything without them saying it was motivated by evil. Or bringing his family into it. They were vile about Lottie, and I don't know her, but after what we did . . .'

He trails off.

'They were just so *angry*,' Ollie says. 'It made me feel really uncomfortable. Like I said, I've spent a lot of time being angry, and I don't like who I am when I feel that way.'

I nod. I, too, have been angry for a long time. I, too, understand how important it is sometimes to let go of that anger. But it can also be useful if trained in the right direction.

'I just feel so powerless,' I tell him, 'and if this gives me a way to feel like I'm making a difference in Ithr then I reckon that will help me with the anger.'

Ollie shrugs. 'I'll hook you up with Kieran's number then. You two can go and bond over some shouting.' He looks at me from under long lashes. 'You liked him, right?'

I smile. 'Yeah. I really did.'

Anger. That word plays in my head for days afterwards. There's so much of it going around, like a current getting stronger until it pulls you under and fixes you there, drowning in your own bile.

'It's like the anti-inspyre,' Easa says, when I mention this to the Excalibur team.

'You're not far off, scientifically speaking,' Jin says, looking up from her notes. 'Some research suggests that true Immral creates a counter-inspyre. A kind of by-product, I suppose.'

'What do you mean?' I say.

'You should probably have looked this up already,' Jin says. She's been marginally less snarky to me ever since I asked her to keep an eye on Rachel after the harker's strange behaviour in the archives, but apparently old habits die hard. 'Inspyre is imagination, isn't it? But Immral is all about controlling imagination. And what's the opposite of imagination?'

'Lack of imagination?' Ollie suggests.

'Noooo,' Jin says annoyingly. 'Think about it properly. Imagination is what happens when you're exhilarated and open-minded and free. Immral is the opposite of that, so it's . . . ?'

'Fear,' I say suddenly, 'and anger. Negative emotions. Ones that close you off from empathy.'

'Yes,' Jin says, looking surprised that I got it.

'But anger can be useful, can't it?' I say, thinking of Shout Louder's purpose. Thinking of the rage and sense of injustice that is so often my fuel.

Jin stares at me. 'Can it? I don't find it very helpful to me.'

Ollie and I snort simultaneously. The idea that Jin doesn't think of herself as an eternal ball of unreasoned anger is amusing.

'Anyway, how *do* you know so much about this? You're supposed to be researching Excalibur.' I say.

Jin blushes, but refuses to answer. But there's something about her reaction – and what she said, that sticks with me, although it will be a while before I understand why.

Chapter 35

Christmas may be approaching, but this year there is no hint of festivities outside the castle. Icy winds blow through Annwn, making the slates on Tintagel's domes whistle and jitter. The holly bushes that sprout up produce leaves sporting long spikes, but no berries. Last year, you couldn't round a corner without happening upon a Santa or an elf. This year, even the paltry snow is grey.

Inside Tintagel, the reeves do their best to make us feel Christmassy, but it's a poor showing compared to my memories of last year. The castle is decked out with wilting ivy. Brandon knits elf costumes for the dogs and cats. Watching Cavall wrestle his costume off affords us a good night's entertainment. Niamh negotiates with Lord Allenby for a hot drinks table in every lore chamber, so when we get back from patrol we can grab a mug of hot chocolate. 'Not that awful powdered stuff either,' Niamh says, happily sipping hers, 'proper chocolate soup. Bliss.'

Despite these efforts, though, I can't help but feel sorry for the squires, who are getting none of the fun of the training that we had last year. They shadow our patrols more often than we did – they need to be able to hit the ground running when they graduate at Ostara.

It's on one of these evenings that I decide to do something about Sachi. A handful of squires have been assigned to Bedevere for the night. I fall in beside her at the back of the group. Her companions aren't as forgiving as Ramesh and Phoebe were to me when I was doing my 'brooding loner' act at the start of our training. No one's being mean to her but they're not trying to include her any more either. I guess either I got lucky with my friends last year, or Sachi's better at emitting the leave-me-alone vibe than I was.

'If you're expecting me to start a conversation then you're in for a shock,' Sachi says.

'Yeah, it's pretty obvious that you're nothing like your brother.'

'Can we not talk about my brother?' she says shortly.

'Alright,' I reply.

'He's all my parents ever speak about now,' she continues. '*Ah, our Reyansh was the only good soul amongst us. Reyansh was so clever. Reyansh was so kind, our family is broken*. But have they been to his grave since the funeral? Have they shit.'

She side-eyes me again. 'How often do *you* go?'

I check that no one else is listening.

'Maybe once a week. It's pretty close to where I live. Ollie visits too, just not quite as often.'

Sachi nods. 'This lot –' she gestures towards the other squires – 'think it's really cool that my brother was a knight. They practically wet themselves when they found out he was killed by Medraut's treitre. *Ah, your brother's a hero, girl, what a legend*. It's the only reason they even talk to me.'

'Yeah, it's tough having a relative who was in the thanes.'

Ollie glances back at me, and I wave elaborately at him. It's designed to make the squires laugh, but Sachi just frowns.

'Is it true your mum was a knight?' she asks.

'Yeah.' I don't want to talk to Sachi about Mum. She's private. I don't need anyone else picking over my mother's memory, tearing it to pieces. I've got Jin and Ollie for that.

'What happened to her?'

I let the silence stretch out between us before answering. 'She was murdered.'

'By another knight, is that true?'

'Why do you want to know?' I say, more aggressively than I'd intended.

Sachi shrinks. 'Sorry. It's just all the squires can do is talk about you and your amazing power and this legacy you have. I thought at least half of it was made up.'

'It probably is,' I tell her, 'but that part's true.'

We ride on in silence. Samson signals for us to take the next alleyway, which will lead us through the hustling markets and locks of Camden and up towards Hampstead Heath, where packs of feral dogs roam and birds of every colour shelter in the scrub.

'It's difficult,' she says, 'finding out that someone you thought you knew turns out to have a secret life, and by the time you find out you can't talk to them.'

'Tell me about it,' I reply. 'I don't remember my mum but I read so many of her diaries and heard so much about her over the years that I thought I had some idea of who she was. It's still weird to me that my dad doesn't know this huge secret of hers.'

I don't hear Sachi's reply because Rachel's voice is echoing through my helmet. 'Trouble to your east, Bedevere,' she says. 'Looks like some tricksters are causing mayhem near the Roundhouse.'

Samson raises his hand again. I look to Sachi. 'It was good to talk to you,' I say as I urge Lamb forward, and I almost mean it. Milosz and Linnea flank the squires as we canter through streets, leaping over cars and carts, avoiding dreamers as we go.

As we pass over a bridge, the Roundhouse comes into view. It's a huge building and, as the name suggests, circular. Ollie went to a concert there a few years ago, with Jenny and her gang, and came back buzzing. I've never been inside. It looks as though I won't get the chance now either, for the trickster nightmares are crawling up the walls and plucking tiles from the gabled roof. They shatter into inspyre on the ground below. Trickster nightmares can take many forms – these ones are pixie-like, but they have needle teeth and spikes protruding from their backs, like mongrel hedgehogs. Any dreamers that venture near are set upon, and while the tricksters aren't strong enough to be fatal, there are going to be some odd-looking marks on those dreamers' bodies when they wake up.

We all know what to do; we've dealt with tricksters often enough. They're chaotic things, and will generally attack whatever makes the loudest noise. Ollie twists Balius' reins around one arm and raises a chakram in either hand. On Samson's command he begins to bang them together, the metal making a high-pitched drum.

It works, at first. Some of the tricksters turn their attention away from the dreamers and focus on the regiment stampeding towards them. Vien and I veer off from the others to herd the dreamers away; me using my Immral to move them; Vien using his weapon in more physical fashion. We direct the dreamers towards the squires and their guardians – this is something they can help with and learn from in the process – how to keep dreamers out of trouble while the rest of us take out the nightmares.

As I wheel Lamb back towards the scuffle, though, I realise that something's not right. For only a handful of the tricksters are fighting Bedevere – the rest of them remain focused on the Roundhouse.

'What's going on?' Nerizan's voice comes through our helmets. 'Their heart's not in it at all.'

'Fern, can you figure it out?' Samson says, skewering a few tricksters with one of his arrows.

I approach the Roundhouse on Lamb's back, holding out a hand to form a shield around us. But Lamb is such a small, quiet animal that the tricksters don't view us as a threat anyway. It's only when we get closer that I realise that they're not clambering over the building aimlessly. They're prodding it, delving their claws into the mortar, as though looking for weaknesses in the structure.

Then one of them raises a piercing cry and its friends scamper to join it. Together they insert their claws into the same spot and heave. I feel a jolt in my very core, as though the earth has lurched beneath me.

Behind the brick is not the inside of the building. Through it streams a bright white light. I know that light. I know it because I am pulled into it every night from my room, and every morning when I leave Annwn. The tricksters have ripped a hole in the fabric between the worlds. A makeshift portal.

The nightmares shriek, their voices relieved rather than delighted, and throw themselves into the light. At the same moment, the tricksters who had been holding off Bedevere leap away and flee towards the light, all inexplicably hoping to find a new home in Ithr.

'Fern!' Samson says. 'Can you stop them? Can you close the portal?'

I urge Lamb forward, using my Immral to throw off the nightmares still hoping to get through. But even as I leap from Lamb's back and place my hands on either side of the gap, I hear a sound like an avalanche. A stampede of dreams and nightmares are streaming towards us. It's more collective inspyre than I've seen in Annwn for many months. They, like the tricksters, want to get through this portal to Ithr. Why, I can't yet fathom, but that's not the most pressing matter.

'Some help holding those guys off would be nice,' I say into my helmet.

'Got your back,' Samson responds. The regiment moves into place, some on the ground behind me, some leaping off their horses and landing on the roof and walls above. I focus my efforts on the gap. I feel the pull of Ithr and my senses shifting, acclimatising themselves to the familiar physics and laws of the real world as opposed to the laws governing Annwn. My eyes are sharply open but I'm in that dozy state of waking up from a deep sleep. Shaking my head to clear it, I call to the inspyre, but it only slips through the portal. Suddenly I understand that this isn't necessarily just dreams and nightmares that want to get to Ithr; it's all inspyre, everywhere. This is like a kalend – the deadly, sanity-sucking black holes that Medraut is so adept at creating – except this is a kalend of the inspyre's own making. It's a sheep mad with fear, caught between a cliff and a wolf, choosing to dash itself on the rocks below rather than be eaten.

'Fern, any luck?' Samson calls.

I use all my might to stop the next drift of inspyre from escaping through the gap and catch it with my mind. I press it together, forcing it to congeal and then to harden. It resists, but I am used to inspyre fighting me, and I know how to command it. Gradually, it takes on the form I desire – the shape of the missing brick. I slot it into place, and that's the hardest part, because it knows it is so close to escaping, but I cannot let it.

'Fern, look out!' Ollie cries.

I look up just in time to see the avalanche of dreams upon me. They're too many. I can't stop them all . . .

Then a high, clear voice lets out a ringing note that shimmers in the air like a hummingbird.

Some of the dreams pause, long enough to give me time to catch one. The voice changes note – a soaring pitch that arches, a dolphin leaping. More dreams slow now, their tide pulled back by the beauty of the wordless song.

With one hand on the brick, I take the dream that I have caught and, whispering my apologies, crush it into its component inspyre. I press the inspyre into the gaps, turning it into mortar, sealing off the portal. The white light vanishes.

Like a switch, the nightmares and dreams that had been

focusing all their efforts on the portal lose interest. They drift away, some tumbling back into inspyre, some morphing into other forms, some returning to hunt their prey, either dreamer or dream. More drift towards the source of the song.

Sachi.

She sits, tall and alone, on her horse, her fellow squires watching in awe. The rest of Bedevere limp towards her. Linnea is sporting a painful cut on her shoulder and Nerizan curses as she pulls a spike from her thigh. Through it all, Sachi continues to sing. More dreams flock towards her, eager to feed. I push between them and reach up to her.

'You can stop now,' I say. 'Thank you.'

Her song peters out. 'The teacher said they liked imagination. I thought it would help.'

'It did. It gave me the time I needed to close the portal.'

Samson joins us as the dreams fade away once more. 'Some voice you've got there, squire.'

'Hear, hear,' Vien says. 'Saved our arses.'

The other squires surround Sachi on the way back to the castle, reclaiming her as one of their own. They don't seem to mind that she's not taking part in their conversation. It gives the rest of us a chance to discuss what just happened.

'Well,' Samson says, 'I think we've found the reason for all those ghosts.'

Chapter 36

When we tell Lord Allenby what happened at the Roundhouse, I spot his eyes flick towards the Fay's shrine. But he doesn't light any candles or burn any notes – that door is closed to us.

'The reports of ghosts in Ithr make more sense at least,' he says. 'All we can do is keep on trying to find Excalibur and hope that you can use it to help, Fern.'

It haunts me for days. I keep thinking of those dreams, fleeing their world because of the oncoming darkness. They were forcing themselves into Ithr for a few moments of freedom before they dissipate, like dust moving from sunbeam to shadow. Do they know that the end's inevitable? Have they accepted something that we have not? Are we blindly battling a war we cannot win?

Distraction from the anxiety comes in the form of a message from Kieran, inviting me to the next Shout Louder meeting. I arrange to meet him beforehand in the Olympic Park. As I leave the house, I realise that this is the first time I've ever actually met a . . . not a *friend*. Kieran isn't that . . . a *potential friend* in Ithr. I have spent the last year wishing that I could live every moment in Annwn, where my entire friendship group exists, but could that be about to change?

I spot Kieran first, sprawled out on the grass, talking on the phone.

'Here she is!' he says as I approach. 'Gotta go, gorgeous. Oh wait, do you want to say anything to your sister?'

Kieran hands his phone to me.

'Ollie?'

'Don't let him talk you into doing anything stupid, okay?' Ollie's voice comes down the line.

'What's he saying?' Kieran asks.

'He doesn't want you to talk me into doing anything stupid.'

'What? That's the only reason he's with me!'

I reassure Ollie and hand the phone back to Kieran.

'Ready?' he asks.

'I'm not sure,' I say. 'I've never really been involved with groups . . . or people . . . before.'

'It'll be great,' he says, tucking my hand in his arm and leading me down the path. I am acutely aware of the impression we must be making on passers-by. Kieran cuts a fine, confident figure with his ash blond hair and easy smile. I on the other hand have resting bitch face, demonic eyes and a burn scar. People are wondering why Kieran is happy being seen with me.

The cafe we're going to is on the side of a footpath, in an old shipping container. I've only been in a few times, despite passing it on a weekly basis, because it's too small for me to remain anonymous, to be overlooked. My anxiety peaks as we enter. The place is packed, not just with people from

Shout Louder but with what looks like a regular weekend brunch crowd.

'Don't panic,' Kieran says. 'We're upstairs.'

We climb to the first floor, where the container has been cut away to make a window that looks across the park. There are far fewer people upstairs, thankfully. And in here, Kieran is the odd one out. No one else in the room looks like they would pass Medraut's test for 'acceptability'. With a few exceptions, though, they're all around my age, or Samson's.

They flock to Kieran, and I am reminded of the way Ollie attracts people. They must be dynamite when they go out as a couple. I am welcomed into the group by association. Kieran shows me to a bench and before long the proprietor comes up to take orders.

'This one's on me,' Kieran tells me, 'for being my bodyguard.' He opens his wallet so I can see a few notes stuffed in there. Ah. So his family's rich, too. I bat away a nasty thought about Ollie.

'I'm not hungry,' I lie, and pour myself a glass of water.

Kieran may know that we're not exactly rolling in cash but that doesn't mean I'm going to accept his charity. When his order comes, though, he's got enough for a feast, and silently pushes a plate of pastries and several portions of chips into the centre of the table.

'Ollie told me you'd be too proud to let me buy you anything.' He grins. 'So you can share mine instead.'

'Ollie's such a snitch,' I say, helping myself to a chocolate chip muffin.

Once everyone's seated, the door opens and someone I recognise enters. I should have expected him, I suppose, but

I wasn't prepared for the instant recognition that flashes between us. Constantine Hale. The leader of Shout Louder.

'I thought the party was big enough that he wouldn't come to all these meetings?' I whisper to Kieran. I haven't told him what passed between me and Hale a few months ago.

'I'm as surprised as you are,' Kieran says, but he's excited, not nervous. 'He said he'd try to come but I didn't think he would.'

Hale shakes hands amicably enough, but there's an air of self-importance about him – a feeling that he is gracing these people with his presence.

When everyone's seated again he begins to speak, his eyes skating over me. 'Thank you all for coming,' he says. 'It's good to see so many of the east London brigade here – not all of us have been brainwashed!'

A cheer goes round and, with it, the certainty that it was a mistake for me to come. Everyone thinks that I belong here, because of my eye colour and my burn scar and my lack of social skills. I don't. I know I don't – and with that realisation comes another. The way I look doesn't define who I am. It's just a part of me, like the little mark on my knee from a fall onto gravel, or the patch of itchy skin on my elbow. I am more than the way I look. So much more.

The door behind Hale opens again and someone else skulks in. I freeze. It's Sachi, her hoodie pulled up to cover her hair, a scarf pulled over her mouth and what looks like three layers of tights on underneath a denim skirt and thick platform boots.

'Ah! Another one of us!' Constantine says. Sachi pauses a second before tensely perching in the space beside me.

Kieran whispers, loud enough for Sachi to hear. 'You two know each other?'

Sachi glances at me. I shake my head, trying to warn her not to give the game away. 'She knew my brother,' she says finally.

'Oh . . . Ramesh, was it?' Kieran says. 'Yeah, Ollie told me about him. Really sorry. I lost a sibling too.'

Sachi just stares at him as though he's gum on her boot. Constantine is now in full flow – a speech full of rage and hatred: at Medraut, but also at those who follow him. He rails against the police, against the politicians, and then he rails against ordinary people who can't see what Medraut is really like. 'These are the lemmings who are our enemies,' he says. 'If we take down Medraut's followers then he won't have anyone to preach to.'

Everyone is murmuring their agreement. I can't help but think about my dad and Clemmie. If Constantine is right, then they're my enemies too, and I can't believe that. I may disagree with Dad but it doesn't mean he's as bad as Medraut. Sachi is inhaling Hale's rhetoric, though. Her eyes are alight with fervent energy.

Then Constantine grows quiet and Kieran stands. 'I don't know about you all, but I'm tired,' he says. 'Really tired of trying to show people what's right in front of their faces.'

All around the room, people nod. 'But that's when we have to keep fighting,' he continues, 'we have to shout louder than any of them. Medraut's got one voice, but we've got hundreds! We can drown that bastard out, before he goes even further than provoking violence against us – before he gets one of us killed!'

Everyone's on their feet, shouting triumphantly, ferally,

venomously. Sachi pounds her boots on the floor so hard the cafe owner has to ask us to keep the noise down.

I'm done. This is not the salve I was hoping for.

I squeeze Kieran's arm by way of goodbye and try to push through the throng. Constantine steps in front of me.

'Leaving?' he says, his eyes flinty.

'I need to get some air,' I lie.

'It takes a warrior to stand up and be counted,' Constantine says, 'but you've made it clear you're not a warrior.'

We stare at each other, unmoving. Did this man, who looks as though he's never seen a hardship in his whole life, really call me soft? Anger prickles through me, heat following.

'Excuse me,' I say, my voice deeper than usual.

Constantine looks as though he's about to argue further, but finally steps to one side. I push through the group and make my way out of the building, down the stairs and into the fresh air of the park. I can still hear the uproar from outside. *Too loud*, Medraut had once said. For once, I agree with him.

Chapter 37

It's as I'm making my way down the slope that will lead me back home, that I hear footsteps.

'Avoiding the truth again?' a voice calls.

I turn around. Sachi is standing there, her face streaked with tears, her chest heaving.

'They're just not going to give me what I want,' I reply.

'What? A chance to actually make a difference? A chance to do something to that . . .' Sachi can barely speak, she's crying too much. Then she surges forward and hisses, '. . . to the people who did that to my brother?'

'You really think they'll change anything?' I say gently.

'At least they'll try! What do the thanes do all day except skulk around *gathering intelligence* and fighting nightmares when *he's* still walking around, spreading his poison. What use are any of you?'

That's too much for me to take, even from her, despite what she did the other night with the nightmares and dreams. I step forward to close the distance between us. 'You have no idea what I have seen, or done, to take down Medraut. You have no idea what it has cost me, or how hard we have worked to try to stand a chance against him. Don't accuse me of doing nothing *ever again* or I will have you thrown out of the thanes. Just because we don't shout about what's going on does not make us silent.'

We stand there, staring into each other's eyes, panting and furious. Then something seems to break inside Sachi. 'Did you even try to save him?' she whispers.

The first words that leap into my throat are defensive. But I cannot utter them. For the first time I see Annwn through Sachi's eyes. She wasn't there last year, before the treitre attacks. She didn't see the angels soaring above Tintagel, the dolphins playing in the river. Annwn was dying already when she was recruited. All she has seen of it is a greying world that is more danger than beauty. She cannot understand the drug of rescuing dreamers from their nightmares, because all she has seen the knights do is rescue dreamers from each other.

'Let's walk,' I say.

'Go to hell.'

'Sachi.' I look at her, holding out a hand, and the same hot rush as I get when I use my Immral floods into my body. 'Come with me. Please.'

She teeters between the easy anger behind her and the hard truth I am offering. Her jaw clenches.

'Fine,' I say, and walk away, stuffing my hands in my pockets. A moment later, I hear her heavy boots running to follow me.

In silence, I lead her down into the park, away from the narrow path where we risk being overheard. I have to get it right this time. I've flunked it with her so often in Annwn, and

I've been given another chance. And there, as we look over the slow, steady flow of the river, I tell her everything. Or nearly everything. I tell her about how Ramesh welcomed me. I tell her how he helped me find out what had happened to my mum. I tell her about how kind he was, and how silly he was, and how I miss him every day.

Then I tell her how he died.

'I couldn't try to save him, because none of us saw it coming,' I say. 'He was the first one to be attacked.'

'So he didn't get a chance to fight back?'

'No. I'm sorry.'

Sachi is dry-eyed now, and softer.

'Was he good, at least? At being a knight?'

'Your brother was meant to be a knight,' I tell her. 'It wasn't about being *good at it*, even though he was a good fighter. He was chosen – it was in his blood.'

She nods, and we walk on, through the winding levels of the park, over a river. I realise that there's something Sachi can tell me as well. Something I've only ever really guessed at.

'What was Reyansh like in Ithr?' I say, using Ramesh's real name for the first time in ages.

'He was a dork. Always desperate for people to like him. So bloody desperate.' She pulls at a low-hanging branch until some of the dying leaves come away in her hands. 'But he was good. Kind. He didn't deserve any of the shit that happened to him. He deserved better friends at school.' She crumbles the leaves in her fist. 'He deserved a better sister.'

I can imagine Sachi being cruel to Ramesh at home, making fun of him for his softness. I can't reassure her that he didn't mind, because even though Ramesh was more forgiving than I am, I know from bitter experience how much those kind of words can hurt.

'Family is weird,' is all I say instead.

'I just thought he needed to toughen up,' she says. 'And then I find out he was this warrior in Annwn and I can't . . .'

'You can't work out how?' I ask.

She nods.

We come to a road that bridges the river, and I lead her back down towards the water, where a bench looks out towards the canal boats. A realisation has been growing in my mind as we've walked – about the thanes, and the Tournament, and the kind of people we are in our hearts instead of the people we are on the outside.

'The thing is,' I say, 'I don't think being a knight is about being a fighter. Not *just* about that, anyway. Lord Allenby told me something when I first met him – he said it was about being willing to sacrifice yourself so your worst enemy could live.'

'He'd sacrifice himself for Medraut?' Sachi says, eyebrows raised.

I smile. 'Maybe not that far. I think he meant that we need to be able to understand where other people are coming from, even if we don't agree with them. That helps us to realise that they're worth saving.'

'Yeah, I understand,' Sachi says, kicking up gravel. 'Got to understand that they're all just brainwashed sheep who can't help themselves.'

'A lot of them are.'

She shakes her head. 'I can save their lives in Annwn. I can do that. But asking me not to speak out against them in Ithr? I think that's something separate.'

'So you're going to go back to those meetings?'

She nods. 'Yeah, I am.'

'I wish I'd liked it more,' I say.

'That guy you came with – he's your brother's boyfriend, right?'

'How did you guess?'

'Eh, he seems like he'd be your brother's type. Posh but pretending he's one of us.'

I look at her oddly. 'Well, he kind of is. Have you not seen the people Medraut's targeting?'

She scoffs.

'He's on our side, Sachi,' I say.

She shrugs: that's not enough to get her to accept him. Then she looks pointedly at my burn scar.

'You've been keeping that quiet.'

'I just haven't got used to it yet.'

'You should be proud of it.'

I snort. 'What?'

'Shows you're one of us.'

I stand. 'It's not like a tattoo, Sachi. I didn't *choose* to be burned. It's not a badge of honour that I *won*.'

'I didn't mean it like that,' she says, stumbling over her words. 'I thought . . .'

'You thought I could be a trophy for the misfits? Like I'm a trophy for the knights.'

Sachi is on her feet now too. 'I'm sorry, okay? I just thought you should know that I don't think anyone in Annwn would see you any differently, that's all.'

We stare at each other, flushed. Inside my pocket, my phone buzzes. It's a message from Ollie: *You okay? Kieran said you bailed.*

Sachi reads it over my shoulder. 'You better go,' she says, and indicates with a shrug which road she's going to take. I nod that I'm going in the opposite direction. She trudges off without saying goodbye.

'Sachi?' I call after her. She turns around, walking backwards. 'If you know no one would judge me, why are you so off with us? The thanes?'

She shrugs again. 'I just don't let people in. It's safer that way.'

'When I joined the knights I was the same,' I say. 'I had walls up a mile thick. But sometimes it's worth letting the drawbridge down.'

'It's not,' she replies. 'Not for me.'

'I wouldn't have survived if I hadn't,' I say, holding her gaze, wishing I was better at conveying my meaning. Because it's true. I might have Immral, but without Ollie's partnership, without the apothecaries who salved my bleeding eyes and the captain who believed in me and all the thanes who sacrificed themselves in the fight against the treitres, I wouldn't be alive now.

'It is worth it,' I say again.

Sachi doesn't stop walking, but I catch her silent nod as she processes what I've said, turns, and passes out of sight.

Chapter 38

Christmas Day marks a year since I discovered that I have Immral. Not many people would remember that, but Ollie does. He wakes me up on Christmas morning with the first present he's given me in years.

'I didn't want Dad to see and ask questions,' he explains quietly as I pull off the ribbon. Inside the box, on a pillow of velvet, rests a bronze figurine. I pick it up, admiring the workmanship.

I smile. 'A horse.'

'It reminded me of Lamb,' Ollie says. I see what he means: the slightly wonky ears and the spread-eagled legs. Like Lamb, this horse isn't quite in control of its extremities.

'It's part of a set,' Ollie says. He produces a second horse. 'See?' He pushes the horses against each other, and I realise that the odd stature of mine is because they fit together. Joined, it looks as though the horses are resting their heads on each other's backs. Friends.

'Those are happy tears, right?' Ollie stammers.

'Of course they are, dimwit. I thought you were supposed to be able to read minds?'

'In Annwn, yeah. Last I checked we're in Ithr.'

I hug him awkwardly. 'I'm so sorry,' I say. 'I didn't get you anything.'

'It's okay.' Ollie shrugs. 'I wasn't expecting you to.'

But that doesn't stop me from feeling wretched. Despite his words, I'm sure Ollie's disappointed. I'm racking my brains for anything that I might be able to gift him when he points to something on my desk. 'What's that?'

It's the puzzle box I've been making, brought home for the Christmas holidays. It's only six clay squares at the moment, but I show Ollie how I plan to fit them together, glad of the distraction. I've managed to glaze five of them, each one a different colour palette.

'This one's plain because it's going to go on the bottom,' I tell my brother.

'It's really beautiful, Fern,' Ollie says, turning the shapes over in his hands, running a finger over the different patterns. Then he frowns.

'What is it?' I ask.

'Five,' he says slowly, 'there are five pieces.'

'Well, six, just one goes underneath.'

'Did Medraut's box have a pattern on the bottom square as well? Do you remember?' Ollie says.

We both search our memories, our eyes glancing towards my mirror portal. The temptation to check for ourselves is strong, but we can't risk Dad catching us.

'I think, maybe it didn't?' I venture. 'So that leaves five panels that were decorated.'

'It always comes back to five, doesn't it?' Ollie says. 'Five strands on Nimue's belt, five jewels in that coin, five elements to each task.'

'Five lores,' I add.

'What does it mean, though?' Ollie sighs.

I shrug. 'If we knew that, we'd have Excalibur already.'

Ollie looks back at my puzzle box. 'Every one of your panels has a different colour, a different pattern.'

'Yeah, to represent all of Annwn.'

'Medraut's just has one pattern, though, doesn't it? That weird grey lava, like a web stretched over it.'

'I guess,' I say. 'Do you think that's significant?'

Ollie shakes his head. 'I haven't got a clue, Fern. Not a bloody clue.'

Ollie's words play on my mind all day. They roll together, like a snowball, building momentum, gathering strength. As I pull crackers and pass cranberry sauce I remember Lottie's words about Pandora's box. As I open my dad's gift of a new hoodie, I think about what the Greek thanes sent us – the images of the woman cutting through the latches of the box that held evil in its heart. I remember Bedevere's memories of Arthur entering the glade with Excalibur, and the way he thrust the sword down into a rock. As we watch the Queen's speech and Ollie argues with Clemmie, I think about Jin's research into Immral.

By bedtime, the snowball is nearly ready. I enter Tintagel at a run, darting towards the hospital wing and dragging Jin away from her hushed conversation with Rachel.

'Jin, you know what you said about anti-inspyre?'

'I was busy –' she starts.

'This is important. You said Immral was the anti-inspyre. Medraut's rope of thorns and Arthur's dragon in the round tables - they were anti-inspyre as well, right? Like an inspyre kryptonite?'

'I guess. Purpose without imagination. Look, what is this about?'

'We've got to find Lord Allenby,' I say, starting down the hallway, then call out to Rachel, 'You'd better come too!'

Jin and Rachel keep pace with me. Samson and Ollie are coming the other way, chatting happily. 'Time for patrol, sis,' Ollie says, 'or did you forget –'

'Can't,' I say, striding past them. 'Come on.'

Samson and Ollie barely hesitate before following me, Samson shouting instructions to Linnea to take over patrol. 'Get the others,' I tell Ollie, and he immediately curves off to the veneur tower, to collect Brandon and Easa.

'What have you realised?' Samson says, as I bang on Lord Allenby's door.

'Fern? What's wrong?' Lord Allenby says, looking at the group gathered outside his office.

'Where do we keep Medraut's box?' I ask him, breathless with urgency.

'Somewhere safe,' he replies helpfully.

'Please, sir,' I say, 'I think I know why he made it, and why he wants it back.'

Lord Allenby leads us towards a turret that is usually kept locked. He retrieves a set of keys from his pocket and uses a small golden one to open the door.

Ollie runs up to us with the rest of the Excalibur team.

'Do you want to explain your theory?' Lord Allenby says as we head through the door.

'Easa,' I say, 'the Pandora's box myth. She broke open a box full of evil, right?'

'Right. Some reeve scholars think she was an Immral herself.'

'And we know that Immral can be compressed to create a kind of anti-inspyre.'

'Yes.'

'Do you all remember that memory of Arthur and Excalibur? The one we found on that Bedevere parchment?'

'Yes,' Jin says.

'Fern, what's this about?' Samson asks. 'What's Medraut's puzzle box got to do with Excalibur?'

'Everything,' I say. 'Do you all remember what happened in that memory? When Arthur got to the top of the mountain?'

'He used Excalibur to destroy everything,' Ollie says.

'No,' Easa says, comprehension dawning. 'He pushed Excalibur *into the stone*.'

'What if the stone wasn't *just* a stone?' I say.

'Pandora's box,' Lord Allenby says. We reach the top of the tower and come upon a second locked door.

'There was a reason the Fay removed the information about Pandora as well. She was doing the same thing. Break the stone, and the poison flies out,' I say.

'Excalibur was the key, but the stone – the box – that's what holds the power,' Lord Allenby says, unlocking the door.

'I still don't get it,' Brandon says.

Lord Allenby opens the door, and we file into a small, windowless room beneath the eaves of the turret. Empty shelves line the walls.

'I'm willing to bet that rock was created by Arthur,' I say, looking for that beautifully crafted box of mahogany and resin, 'and I bet that the stone held Arthur's dreams. Everything he planned for Annwn and Ithr.'

'Just like Medraut's box,' Samson says.

'Yep,' I say, watching Lord Allenby become increasingly restless, 'and if Excalibur can amplify Immral, what do you think would happen if it was forced to amplify an Immral's dreams?'

'And what would happen,' Lord Allenby says darkly, turning to the rest of us with a look of despair, 'if it was stolen?'

For the tower is utterly empty.

Chapter 39

'Nothing,' Rachel says, slamming her hands down on the desk in the tower room, where she's been looking through security footage. She pulls her helmet off and throws it across the room. I've never seen her angry before.

'Woah,' Ollie says. 'Calm down, Rachel.'

'What's the point of having security if it doesn't see anything?' she says. 'It's all useless.'

I catch Jin's eye, the memory of our argument about Rachel rising between us.

'It just didn't work this time,' I say, trying to sound measured and authoritative. 'It doesn't make it useless. Why don't you take a break, Rachel? You've done so much, let someone else take over for a bit.'

Jin shoots me an appraising look.

'Medraut must have got it out some other way,' Easa says. 'No one who means harm to the thanes would be able to get inside Tintagel. He must have levitated it through a window or something.'

He didn't levitate it through a window. We all know this. The magic keeping Tintagel safe is older and stronger than King

Arthur. We are all dodging around the obvious solution: that the thief had permission to enter. That's the only way it could have happened. But only Samson is brave enough to raise that possibility with Lord Allenby. It does not go down well, and things are frosty between Samson and Lord Allenby afterwards.

With Ostara approaching, I'm spending more time with the squires. It won't be long before they are assigned to regiments. There's a certain amount of competition that Amina tells me wasn't there in previous years. 'I wasn't a commander then, of course,' she says, 'but Rafe and Emory told me.' Her breath hitches. It feels like both a lifetime ago and only yesterday that Emory and Rafe were killed in the two treitre attacks. Amina was particularly close to Emory, the commander she replaced. 'The thing is, there were enough squires to go around back then. And we weren't expecting a big attack – we thought we'd just be fighting nightmares. This year we've got a shortage of squires and we're on high alert. It's not a great combination for trying to work together.'

Where previously only the regiment commanders would watch the training sessions, this time every knight takes a keen interest in who they want as their comrades.

'Bedevere shouldn't really get any new squires in my opinion,' I overhear one of the Palomides knights saying to murmurs of agreement.

'Why's that?' I ask.

The knight colours. 'Well, they've got you and Ollie, haven't they? An Immral can offer way more protection than a squire.'

'Wow,' Niamh says, as she passes. 'Have you never thought

that maybe Fern and Ollie being in Bedevere makes them more of a target for Medraut, and therefore they should have more squires than the rest of us?'

The knight splutters further justification, but I'm not listening. I hate what Medraut has done to us. We used to be a tight unit – all the regiments working together to cover London, giving here, taking there, secure in the fact that we had each other's backs. Now I enter the knights' chamber to see regiment cliques dotted around the room, each one more frightened than the next. And the worst thing is, despite Niamh's words, I know that the knight was right. Medraut might want to target me, but that doesn't mean that the other regiments weren't hurt more than us by the treitre attacks.

Samson feels the same way, and it leads to some heated arguments in Bedevere.

'Just because you're the knight captain doesn't mean we should suffer from you being a martyr!' Nerizan argues on the way back from patrol, when Samson expresses his intention not to request any of the squires.

'We work well together,' he replies calmly. 'We don't need anyone else.'

Of course, the squires themselves have a different idea. Nearly all of them are desperate to be placed in Bedevere. The other regiments use Niamh's line against us, arguing that it would be far too dangerous to be placed with us because of my presence, but the squires aren't biting. They've seen what I can do out on patrol. They go all out to impress Samson. Those who have scimitars and bows and arrows for weapons even try to change them so that we won't automatically discount them on account of Samson and me already using those weapons.

Sachi is the only one who doesn't try harder for us. I watch her training carefully when I'm in charge of sessions. She's not the best fighter – that honour goes to a squire called Bandile, whose talent for acrobatics combined with the set of knives he uses as weapons makes him nearly as deadly as me. But while Natasha and Amina argue over which one of them should get Bandile, I notice that Sachi is industrious and hard-working. She fights with a determination that makes her efficient in a way that Bandile's showiness is not. And I can't forget her song to the dreams, her beautiful voice rising above the fray.

'I think we should take Sachi,' I say to Samson one night, collaring him as he rides into the stables.

'Ramesh's sister?' Samson says, raising an eyebrow.

'Not because of that,' I say. 'She uses a spear, which we don't have now in Bedevere. She thinks outside the box. And she's good but she flies under the radar, so you're not going to get flack for picking her.'

'She's quite a strong, surly personality, though, isn't she?' Samson says.

'So?'

'Don't you think we have enough of those in Bedevere already?' He smiles at me, pulling the bridle from his horse's head. I hand him a bucket of hot water and a sponge, and slip into the stable with a brush. Together we scrub down his horse.

'Are you talking about me?' I say, faux-indignantly.

'I'm talking about me, actually,' Samson replies.

He's definitely been grumpier of late, but nothing too

noticeable. Samson sighs at the same time as his horse lets out a satisfied whicker. We both descend into giggles.

'Seriously, though,' Samson says, 'I'm sorry I've been such an arsehole.'

'You're under a lot of pressure.'

'It's not because of that. It's not because of anything in Annwn.'

'Oh?'

Samson glances at me. 'I broke up with my girlfriend.'

I swear the squires training outside the stables should be able to hear the thumping of my heart. 'I'm sorry?'

'Thanks.' He smiles, shooting me another one of those fleeting looks. 'So. Sachi? Really?'

'I think she'd be good,' I tell him sincerely, glad for the change of subject.

'I'm sure she would, but . . .' He pauses. 'I know you and Ramesh were close.'

'Yeah.'

'Are you not worried you'd take anything that happened to Sachi a little too personally? I need you to be focused on the fight, not on protecting another knight.'

'I know what my job is,' I say.

'All I know is that I wouldn't want Rafe's brother on my regiment,' Samson says. 'I'd be thinking far too much about making sure his parents didn't lose a second child.'

Samson has nailed exactly why I want Sachi in Bedevere. Our conversation in Ithr the other day has made me protective of her.

'I just think you should consider her,' I say again.

Samson nods, and moves on to a different topic of conversation, but the next night he collars me as I lead Bedevere in from patrol. 'You were right,' he says. 'She is good. A little raw, but that comes from wanting to prove herself. There's a lot of potential there.' He fixes me with a hard stare. 'Are you sure this is the right thing to do, Fern? You promise me you think it's right for the regiment?'

I squirm inside. 'I promise,' I say, not quite meeting his eyes.

And it's done. The next week, Samson announces that Sachi is the only new knight who will be joining Bedevere. The other squires cast her jealous glances, or congratulate her for getting the 'prize'. It's a very different atmosphere to this time last year. Back then everyone already knew that Ollie and I had Immral but it hadn't mattered as much. Back then, there was only excitement at the prospect of getting to know our new colleagues. Sachi, for her part, accepts the assignment with grace. She smiles at the people who congratulate her, and ignores those who mutter about favouritism.

As we all walk to the stables to saddle up, ready for our new squires to accompany us on their first 'proper' patrol, I overhear some of the new Gawain knights bitching.

'I bet they only took her out of pity.'

'I know. What's someone got to do to get into the cool regiment?' That's Bandile.

I glance back over my shoulder. 'She had to have her brother killed. Can you do that?'

Bandile sputters an apology, but I'm not listening. I stride on to the stables and have Lamb tacked up and ready to go before they've even entered. As I swing into the saddle, I spot

Sachi coming out of the stables, Ollie beside her. They are deep in conversation. *Yes*, I think, *she's already making friends.*

'You should give it another go,' Sachi's saying. 'Kieran's a good speaker. A few of us are pushing for him to take over as leader of the regional group . . .'

'It's really not my thing, but thanks,' Ollie's saying.

I've read the situation completely wrong – Sachi is trying to get Ollie to join Shout Louder, and Ollie wants nothing more than to get away from her. So much for my supposed improvement in reading other people. As we all mount up, Ollie whispers, 'Whose idea was it for her to join us again?'

'She'll be fine,' I say, although I'm not sure who I'm reassuring. 'It'll all be fine.'

Chapter 40

'Welcome to Bedevere,' Samson tells Sachi as we ride. 'We're going to have a bit of a slacker night to begin with – we'll head over to Hyde Park and give the horses a graze. Then you'll go back to Tintagel, Sachi, and the rest of us will finish our patrol.'

It feels a bit pointless celebrating one person joining us. But it's tradition, so we all try to ignore the fact that when it was my turn, and Ollie's and Ramesh's, everything felt a lot more joyous.

As we go, I listen to Brandon chatting away to Sachi. Sachi's giving monosyllabic answers, but I get the impression she's not displeased. We have to take a few detours – packs of Medraut's altered dreamers are now commonplace in Annwn. Thanks to my modifications to the Round Tables we can usually spot them quickly. All we can do for them now is to move them to guarded areas, where they can't do harm to the dreamers who have escaped Medraut's influence.

We dismount next to the lake in Hyde Park, a distance away from the fountain where schools of exotic fish swarm. 'Head over there,' I whisper to Lamb. 'I'll make sure it's the best grass.' She nuzzles me conspiratorially and follows my outstretched hand, where I send a little inspyre into the ground to make the grass extra lush. Lamb makes little grunting sounds of pleasure.

'You're spoiling her,' Brandon remarks.

'Immral's prerogative,' I answer.

We spread blankets from our saddlebags on the ground and lounge in groups. I lay back and look up at the sky. I'd rather not talk too much today. Inside my saddlebag is the belt Nimue gave me. I wind it around my fingers, feeling each of the five strands, letting my Immral trickle into the fabric. It's become a habit now. There's something soothing about the material. Medraut and Arthur's creations were fraught with purpose. The inspyre inside this belt, woven through with Fay power, is blank, as if each piece is waiting for someone to write on it. I send a spark of Immral into the belt, and it scuttles along one of the strands, lighting it up a warm blue. Strange. I had meant for my Immral to go into the whole belt, but only one of the five accepted it. I file that snippet of information away to discuss with the Excalibur group later.

I listen to Nerizan and Vien jokily arguing about the best way to tackle a trickster nightmare: 'I've literally written a paper on this subject, Vien, why are you mansplaining this to me?' And Brandon is demonstrating a forward roll to a trying-to-look-unimpressed Sachi. Ollie flops down beside me. The inspyre that arches between us when we touch is never far away now. Even when he's close I feel my hands vibrating. We watch the heavens empty of clouds. They don't move across the sky here like they do in Ithr. They spark into nothingness, or twist into whirlwinds that consume themselves, or morph into dragons or planes or plumed birds. *This is blissfully peaceful,*

I think, right at the moment that a small, anxious voice rears its head. *Too peaceful.*

Then Lamb's muzzle looms over me as she nibbles at my nose.

'Ugh, Lamb, no!' I say, rolling over. She nuzzles my head, catching my hair in her mouth.

'Fern,' Ollie says.

Lamb starts chewing on my hair.

'Lamb, stop it, you div!'

I laughingly bat her away, but she doubles down. The other knights start cheering Lamb on.

'Fern!' Ollie says, more urgently now. Lamb releases me, aware of the change in atmosphere, and I turn to my brother. He's looking out over the skyline. 'Something's wrong,' he says.

That's when I feel it too. A low, rumbling sensation deep in my chest. The other knights are still laughing, feeding Lamb some of the salad from our picnic. Only Sachi and Samson have noticed that something's not right, and that's only because they're watching Ollie and me.

Samson comes over. 'What is it?' he says.

'I don't know,' I say.

'Is it a kalend?'

'No,' Ollie says, 'I don't feel sick. It's just . . . something terrible is about to happen.'

'Are we going to be attacked?' Sachi whispers.

'Oh God,' I say, my chest lurching, as though I've been thrown up in the air on a rollercoaster. Ollie reaches out to me and I clutch his hand for stability. The arc of inspyre that usually greets us touching doesn't behave normally, though.

It arches up, away from us, all the way across the park – a curve of pure white light that stretches over the trees. South, it heads; south towards Kensington and the strip of museums that sit along the edge of the park.

A hush descends. A silence that floods across the rest of London.

'Let's go,' Samson says, and within seconds we're saddled up and galloping across the park, around the lake, south, south, following the arc of inspyre and the growing sense of dread. As we clear the trees lining the park and gallop into view of the buildings that should line this street, we see exactly what has happened.

'What the –' Linnea breathes.

'Rachel,' Samson says into his helmet, 'put another regiment on standby. We may need back up.'

Up ahead is no nightmare. There's nothing to say 'danger'. In fact, there's nothing at all.

The Royal Albert Hall, a great ring of a building, should sit here. But where the hall should be, there is a tear in the fabric of Annwn. This is no kalend or portal. It is the emptiness of heartbreak. The ache of solitude. Blue inspyre swirls like dust caught in a tornado. What's even stranger is the hush that descends the closer we get. It's as though we're heading into a vacuum, where all noise, all existence, has been suppressed.

Samson rides ahead of the regiment, silhouetted against that blue devastation. Ollie tries to say something to Sachi. But no sound comes out. He frowns and tries again. Milosz talks to Linnea, who shakes her head in confusion. Then I open my mouth and scream.

Nothing. No one can talk. No one can make a noise. Medraut has taken our voices.

Samson signals a retreat. Sachi, wide-eyed, canters past me, her fear and confusion mirroring mine. As we move away from where the Royal Albert Hall should be, sound returns to Annwn. At first it's just the little things – a dislodged pebble clattering across the street; a solitary bird calling for its friends; then Lamb's hooves echo once more on the asphalt.

'What was that?' Sachi asks. The shock of hearing words makes me jump. No one answers her. Samson is talking into his helmet, updating the harkers. I am unsettled in a way I have never been before. Not when the treitres attacked or when I witnessed the way Medraut was torturing dreamers. This is different. This is the very foundations of this world being eroded by an unstoppable wave of Immral. No other power could have laid waste to Annwn like that.

'He's getting stronger,' Nerizan repeats, over and over again.

'He's showing off,' Ollie says. 'Trying to tell us how powerful he is.'

'Well,' I say, casting a final look back at the blue tornado where the Royal Albert Hall should be, 'message received.'

Chapter 41

'Do you remember when Mozart actually played there, and we could lie across the seats listening?' Amina says to Natasha.

'It almost made me like opera,' Natasha replies.

The shock of Medraut's most recent move is muted. We all knew he was going to do something, and we're just thankful it didn't cost any lives. Instead, there's an overwhelming feeling of sadness at what we're losing. If nothing else, this has brought the regiments together once more. There are no cliques now: we sit in a huge circle in the knights' chamber, reminiscing.

'Can you bring it back? The hall?' Niamh asks me. 'You made the Thames rise up once, didn't you?'

I start to shake my head but then notice the way Ollie is looking at me. I can't put my finger on how I know what he's thinking. Maybe it's a twin thing. Maybe it's an Immral thing. But I absolutely know what he's saying, *Fern, give them some hope*.

'Maybe,' I say, 'but we should wait and see what Lord Allenby thinks. It might not be the best thing for me to do.'

'What do you mean?' Amina says from her perch in the corner of the room.

'Well, it might be better to let Medraut believe that I'm not strong enough to change it back.'

'Make him underestimate us.' Natasha nods. 'Like he did last time.'

'It's basically his one weakness, right?' Ollie says.

'Really?' Sachi says, fire in her eyes. 'I can see a lot of weaknesses in a man like him.'

Others ask Sachi what she means, but I don't hear her response because at that moment a reeve pops his head round the door and beckons silently to Ollie, Samson and me. The three of us slip out of the room.

Lord Allenby's office is full of the people from the Excalibur quest.

'The question we have to ask ourselves,' he says, 'is whether this new development has anything to do with the puzzle box. Do we think he's found a way to use it without Excalibur, or do we think he already has the sword?'

'If he had Excalibur then he wouldn't spend his time doing this,' Samson says. 'He wants power first. He'd use Excalibur to open the puzzle box and seize control of Annwn.'

Lord Allenby turns to me. 'Fern, only you can tell us just how much this means his power has grown.'

I look at Ollie, a look that says I'm not going to sugar-coat things now, not in this company. 'I couldn't do it, sir, not even with Ollie's help. But then we always knew that my Immral's nowhere near as strong as Medraut's.'

'We might have something on that,' Jin says, plonking a

heavy book down on Allenby's desk, along with a packed file of notes. 'In the accounts we know of where these boxes have been opened, it's always been done from a height.'

'Arthur was on a mountainside,' Easa says, 'Before Arthur, Pandora was on top of a building. It seems that if the power is going to spread as quickly as they want, it needs to be done from high up. So that's where Medraut would go if he has Excalibur and the puzzle box.'

'The puzzle box . . .' I muse.

'What, Fern?' Lord Allenby says.

'Well . . . *I've* made a puzzle box,' I tell them uncertainly, hoping they won't jump to judgements. 'In Ithr. I wanted it to be the opposite of Medraut's. I'm just wondering – what if I make it in Annwn? And fill it with all of *our* hopes and dreams? Everyone's imaginations in one box –'

'Ready to be broken open,' Jin finishes. Her eyes are shining. 'Inspyre everywhere. The antidote to Medraut's Immral.'

'Exactly.'

'That's brilliant, Fern,' Rachel whispers.

'Genius,' Samson says. 'A box filled not with one person's purpose, but with everyone's.'

'I'd need all of you to help,' I say. 'It can't just be me who makes it, or that would defeat the point. It has to be as many of us as possible. Dreamers, too, if we can still find some who've escaped Medraut's influence.'

Lord Allenby is watching us, working it through in his head. Finally, he nods, and a smile breaks out on his lined face. 'Excellent. Let's start making it right away, so when we find Excalibur, we can be ready. We might be able to take

Medraut down without needing to fight him at all.'

We're all riding the wave of exhilaration that comes with a new lead – a new purpose. It doesn't take long for me to transfer my designs from Ithr to Annwn, and to craft the bones of our box. Injecting it with our hopes and dreams is a harder task. Ollie's power is used to its limits, since he's the one who reads minds. We spend long nights sifting through the dreams of our colleagues – the ones who have agreed to such a violation – and folding them carefully into the box.

'I feel like a morrigan,' Ollie remarks one night as we lean over Samson. Ollie feels his way through our friend's mind while I resist the temptation to look for clues as to Samson's feelings about me.

'Morrigans are a lot more painful than this,' Samson smiles, his eyes closed.

'Here,' Ollie whispers and, inside Samson's mind, shows me a quality. It is diaphanous, yet weighty. I examine it, turning it this way and that with my power, until I understand it. It is a particular kind of steadiness. Loyalty that is not blind. A moral compass without judgement. The best of this man.

Gently, I extract a gossamer strand and lay it in the box, beside Lord Allenby's regrets.

'You're done,' I tell Samson, my hand lingering on his chest.

He opens his eyes and they hold mine for a moment, before I pull away and gesture to the next thane to come forward.

From Brandon we take his love of any living creature, no matter how insignificant it may seem. We take Natasha and Niamh's bravery – one quiet, one bold. From Sachi and Easa comes a love of patterns, and from Rachel the wish to do justice for those she loves. Everyone has something small but beautiful to give. And the box, which was once blank, becomes coloured. It is so much more beautiful than the one I created in Ithr. Ombrés and marbles glaze its surface; the embodiment of hundreds of dreams.

But underneath all of our work is a soul-sucking fact that we can't escape. All of this will be for nothing if we can't find the sword.

Easa and Jin go all out trying to unravel the next clue. And that's how I end up doing some of the stupidest things I've ever done.

Faith in the knights and thanes? Kneel before the Round Table in Tintagel and swear fealty. Faith in Annwn? Use my Immral to plant trees over the country. Faith in myself? Throw myself off a building.

'Nothing,' I grumble to Ollie as we return to Ithr after weeks of doing this stuff. I'm still bruised from my latest attempt. We pass a group of apothecaries who are trying not to snigger at me, still finding the noise I made upon landing in the herb garden absolutely hilarious.

'Mum really could've given us an extra clue, couldn't she?' Ollie says. 'It's getting a bit silly now.'

'You're telling me,' I remark.

At home, I traipse downstairs in my pyjamas and continue the conversation with Ollie, who is already filling the kettle for tea. Without asking, he finds the Earl Grey sachets for me. I sniff the heel of a bit of bread for mould and, finding it acceptably stale, pop two slices in the toaster.

'Do you think she knew that I had any of the Immral?' Ollie says after a while.

I look at my brother. He's talking with the kind of studied nonchalance that he always adopts when Mum is the subject of our conversation.

'She was just focused on defeating Medraut,' I say carefully. The truth is, I do get the sense that Mum loved me more than Ollie, and I know from years of thinking that Dad favoured him over me how harmful that can be. But I also don't want to lie to my brother, and I don't think I'm lying to him now. Mum *was* fixated on Medraut, especially at the end.

'She didn't mention me at all in that letter to you,' he says.

'Does it really matter?' I say, with forced jollity. 'She's not here now. You've got Dad and me. Don't tell me you're getting sentimental now you've got Kieran to turn you into a big softy.'

I bump my elbow into Ollie's side, but he doesn't smile.

'Do you ever get the feeling that Mum wasn't a very nice person?' he says at last.

'What? No!'

'Look at the facts, Fern. She had this massive secret she kept from Dad. She experimented on her best friend – no, I don't care that she was trying to help Ellen – she did a really risky thing because she thought she was better than everyone else and it backfired. Then she sets us these impossible tasks – for what? So she can make her own daughter prove that she's worthy of Excalibur? Why wouldn't she believe that anyway?'

'She was being cautious. She grew up watching Medraut.' But I know that Ollie has a point.

'Or maybe she was worried you're more like her than Dad,' Ollie says pointedly.

'Well, I'd be proud to be like Mum,' I say. 'She was damn

clever. She figured out how to get at Excalibur when no one else could. She was investigating Medraut and fighting him even after she left the thanes.'

'So she was clever and obsessive,' Ollie sneers. 'Those two traits aren't as great as you're making them out to be.'

'She loved us, Ollie. She loved us and Dad.'

'Did she?' Ollie says, back to acting as though he doesn't care. 'Don't you think if she'd genuinely loved us she'd have told Dad what was going on? Or left us all better clues? Seems to me all this is just her trying to be the most impressive person in the room.'

'Stop being such a jerk,' I say. 'She's dead. Leave her alone.'

I stalk up to my room, and Ollie doesn't try to stop me. Here we are, fighting again, and it always comes back to Mum. She was the reason I used to feel so alone. I built all of my hopes on the idea of her loving me more than Ollie. Now I know that she did, it's causing even more problems. But I have to defend her against my brother's accusations. She has to have been better than Ollie is making out. Doesn't she?

Chapter 42

July 2005

Una shook as she approached the Chelsea townhouse. Her fingers slipped from the doorbell when she rang it. She may be in Ithr, but she couldn't forget all that Medraut had done. It was one of the things that rankled the most with her: that they would never be able to bring him to justice in Ithr for his crimes. Their only hope was to find him in Annwn, and that was looking more and more unlikely.

A young woman in a conservative grey dress ushered her in. Somewhere in the house, a baby wailed and the young woman shot a frightened look at Una as she rushed to take care of it. *Medraut's wife?* Una wondered, then dismissed it – a nanny, more likely. Or a nanny *and* a mistress, if he followed in the usual ways of rich, pampered politicians.

'Mrs King,' came the voice she recognised so well. It sent shivers down her spine in Ithr, the same way it did in Annwn.

'Mr Medraut. Thank you for agreeing to speak with me.'

'*The Maverick* has always been a faithful supporter,' he replied. 'I'm glad to be of help. Please, do come in.'

Una followed him into his office, just off the main lobby. Like the rest of the house, it had high ceilings and wood panelling. The walls were bare, except for one portrait, right behind Medraut's desk, looking down on him.

'An ancestor?' Una nodded towards the man. He looked austere, calm, out of his time.

'My father.'

Una saw the similarities between them – the same curl to the hair and carved cheekbones. The eyes were the same colour too: slate grey. Medraut's had once, of course, been violet.

Una retrieved her notebook from her bag, and then her voice recorder. She hated showing the back of her neck to Medraut. Her throat prickled from the memory of his hand. Then she straightened, and set her items on the desk.

'Do you mind?' she said, indicating the voice recorder.

'Not at all. But you'll find it won't work.'

'I'm sorry?'

He smiled slowly at her. 'It's a strange effect of my presence, I'm afraid. They never pick up what I'm saying for some reason.'

Una understood. His Immral prevented the recordings, even in Ithr. Maybe it was the same mysterious power that made people forget exactly what he said when he spoke on television. The revelation that Immral could affect machinery should have shocked her, she supposed. Maybe it would have shocked someone who underestimated Medraut's power. Una, though, had always known that Immral was dangerous in both worlds. But this man was stripped of his Immral a few months ago, and by the colour of his eyes it had not yet returned.

'Even these days?' she asked, risking the anger she knew it would inspire. 'Do you know, I think it might work now. Shall we try it?'

Medraut's mask didn't slip. 'Yes, it's always worth trying.'

Una pressed a button, and they both watched as the red light appeared, signalling that it was recording.

'So, Mrs King, what can I tell you that you don't already know about me?'

'Oh, it's not going to be that kind of article,' Una said. 'It's more of a personality piece. Everyone knows all the facts about you, don't they? I'd love to know what makes you tick. What are your values? What qualities do you admire most? Things like that. When you were running for prime minister people only wanted to know about your policies. Now that you're out of the race and One Voice has been disbanded, I thought it was time to get to the bottom of who *you* are.'

She was deliberately goading him. Partly because it was all the revenge she would be able to wreak on him for now. Partly because she knew it was the best way of getting honest answers. She was right – just momentarily, he stared at her with undisguised hatred.

'Come on, Sebastien,' she said softly, so that no one could hear them if they were listening from the door. 'What have you got to lose? You're powerless, reduced to scrapping for interviews from the only newspaper who pities you enough to give you some limelight.'

'Not totally powerless,' Medraut replied, just as quietly. 'I still have gold.'

His eyes bored into Una. The golden treitre that had killed

her friends and colleagues; the treitre that had almost killed her and driven her out of the thanes.

'It seems to me,' Una said, trying to claw back some control, 'that that isn't *your* power, is it? What does it feel like, to rely on someone else to do your work for you?'

'I control it. It is my doing.'

'What if it turned against you? I imagine that must be a fear, since your breakdown.'

Medraut didn't have an answer for that. Una saw his weaknesses laid bare. The need for sole control, the inability to allow others to take credit. And the total loss when he couldn't bully or brainwash someone into doing his bidding. That was all she needed to know. The last pieces of the puzzle, to take back to Andraste and Nimue.

'Thank you, Mr Medraut, you've been so helpful.' She gathered her belongings and stood up. 'I'll see myself out.'

Upstairs, the baby let out a single wail before it was silenced. Una caught Medraut's eyes flicking to the portrait of his father, expecting an admonishment. Medraut caught her watching him.

'Goodbye,' she said, but as she opened the door he spoke again.

'I could have killed you. Have you never wondered why I didn't?'

She knew what he was referring to – the moment in the archives all those months ago, the night before she turned in her evidence to the Thanes and began the process of taking his Immral. The truth is, she often asked herself why he let her live. They had been totally alone in the archives. He could easily have killed her and brainwashed the others into forgetting her. She knew that he wanted her to ask the question. Was she strong enough to resist?

She was not.

'Why?'

'Because I haven't *mined* you. As soon as I know what you know, I'll have no more need of you. Bear that in mind, Una Gorlois.'

Chapter 43

I can't afford to dwell too much on Mum: not with Medraut, Excalibur and, worst of all, GCSEs looming. And then something happens that drives all of that out of my mind.

I am already on edge when I enter the classroom: there's been an unusual atmosphere in Bosco today, like the void between lightning and thunder. The first thing I notice is the stillness, despite the fact that nearly every seat is occupied.

'Hurry up, Miss King,' the history teacher says, just as the bell rings. Lottie smirks.

The next thing that hits me, as I walk to my seat, is the stench. A deep feeling of impending humiliation settles in my stomach. But I can't stop – that would be admitting that I'm vulnerable. My desk is clear. Then I take in what they've done to my chair. Someone has taken the bin from one of the girls' loos and strewn its contents over the seat like bunting. A sweep of scarlet has been painted over the backrest; the pad it came from stuck to one corner, just to make sure I know that it's not paint.

'Sit down, Fern,' the teacher says.

Most faces are turned away from me. Some are shaking

with barely concealed laughter. A few meet my gaze with hard smirks. The kind of smirk I remember from St Stephen's. The kind that led to a match being struck on Wanstead Flats. That thought steels me. In the woods, when I had been tied to a tree, I had begged and pleaded. I won't do the same now.

'Please may I be excused,' I say to the teacher, polite but firm.

'You may not,' she says. 'Sit down, Fern, you're holding up the class.'

She still won't meet my eyes. She rubs one hand over her mouth absent-mindedly. But the way she does it – palm facing outwards – reminds me of the sign used by the One Voicers. That's when I know for sure that she's with *him*.

'My chair is dirty,' I say, my voice stronger now. 'I'd like to fetch another one.'

'Why?' someone says from a corner. 'You're just as dirty.'

'Trash,' someone else whispers.

'Please may I get another chair?' I say again.

'Sit down,' the teacher repeats. 'Sit down.'

'No,' I respond.

'You will be put in detention.'

I snap. 'You sit on the chair if it doesn't bother you, miss, and I'll take yours.'

Finally the teacher looks up, fury in her eyes. 'Do not speak to me like that. Sit down now and we'll talk about your punishment later. The headmaster will be told either way.'

'Good,' I say, and with trembling fingers reach for my phone.

'No phones in the class!' the teacher screeches. Some of the students rise from their seats, alarmed. I take a photo of the chair then stuff my phone back in my bag before anyone can wrestle it from me.

'I'm going now,' I say, gulping down tears.

I march out of the classroom, breaking into a run.

'Fern! Fern King!' the teacher yells at my receding back.

My first instinct is to go to the toilets, but given what's just happened that no longer feels safe. I simply have to get out of the school. I run past the receptionist and down the steps to the road. Passers-by stare at me suspiciously. Everywhere I go, I am being haunted and hunted by Medraut.

As I jog away from Bosco, I send the photo to Ollie without explanation. If the school catches me and, fearful of their reputation, makes me delete it I want to make sure the evidence is out there somewhere. I'm about to get on the tube when Ollie calls me.

'What on earth was that?'

'Don't ask,' I reply. 'Just keep hold of it for me.'

'Fern,' he says, 'is everything okay?'

'I'll see you later.'

I need to be angry about this by myself before I tell Ollie. A river breeze cools my flushed face. I decide to walk home instead. Ignoring the buzzing of my phone in my pocket, I think about Lottie. I'm certain she's behind what just happened. I can't reconcile this cruel prank with the girl who helped me to skive off school last year. This is her father's doing, but I don't know how to stop it. I don't know how to help her without putting myself in even more danger.

My phone buzzes again. This time, it's Dad. I let it go to voicemail, then wish I hadn't. He sounds furious.

'You'd better have a good reason for leaving school without telling anyone, Fern. You really think they'll let you stay on scholarship if you keep pulling these stunts? I want you home within thirty minutes, or I'm grounding you for a month.'

I laugh grimly. As if grounding me would be a punishment. I barely leave the house outside of school as it is. But now that he's told me to come home without hearing my side of the story, I don't want to. Instead, I take the scenic route wherever I can. I find myself walking along the canals that outline Victoria Park, and wonder whether the mural that Samson painted for me is still there. I'm heading in that direction when I hear it: an accordion.

The musician is a grizzled homeless man. The same one who gave me a message that changed the way I thought about myself. A note from Lord Allenby. Fishing in my purse, I drop a few coins into the man's paper cup.

'Thank you, girly,' he says.

I wait until he's finished his tune.

'You gave me a note, a few months ago,' I say.

'Oh yes,' he says. 'I remember.'

'The man who gave you that note – do you know where he lives?'

The musician throws back his head and laughs. 'He lives in a big place,' he says. 'Big as this whole city.'

'I don't understand.'

'He's like me, girly. We live where the coppers let us, don't we?'

'He's homeless?'

'That's about right. How do you know Lionel then?'

Lord Allenby? Homeless? I want to tell him that we're

thinking of different people. There's no way the Lionel Allenby I know could be . . . And then I think of that worn bear of a man, protective but pragmatic, and I understand that this is no lie.

With a few more coins, I persuade the man to direct me to the last place he saw my commander; under a bridge further along the canal. I know I shouldn't do this, but I can't help myself. Dad isn't on my side, and confiding in Ollie would shift the tenuous equality we have achieved, but I need to talk to someone about what's just happened. I can't think of a better person than the man who's guided me so well this last year.

Before I am ready, I spot the bridge and the bundle of plastic bags and blankets beneath it. The man inside that bundle is dozing, but not asleep. He is broad and tall, like the Lord Allenby I know, and there is still something of a bear about him. But his hair is greyer here, his face more worn. He hunches over his meagre belongings as though he's trying to turn invisible.

I had thought that I wanted to see him, and that he would be pleased to see me, but now that I'm here all the humiliation of what I've just endured at school melts away. I don't let myself pity Lord Allenby. I know that if he's anything like me, he wouldn't welcome it. I want to run up to him, offer him company and food, but something tells me that I shouldn't. He would be mortified. This is a secret I need to keep, for his sake. And I will. I turn around quietly and walk back the way I came, leaving the man I look up to more than anyone else huddled on the ground in a mass of cold blankets.

Chapter 44

I don't plan on ever telling Lord Allenby that I have seen him in Ithr. I try not to let it affect the way I act around him in Tintagel. Sometimes I find myself staring at him in our Excalibur meetings, wondering how on earth he ended up on the streets. I can't help but compare him to my dad, who's so lacking, despite having a relatively easy life. Lord Allenby, I know, would have *done* something about the people who pranked me at school. He wouldn't have fobbed me off with promises to talk to the teacher, like my own father did. It makes me admire Lord Allenby all the more: that he has retained his natural authority, when in Ithr he must endure incredible hardships.

Some of the others tease me about having a crush on him, which I vigorously deny. Samson gets it, though.

'He's like a father to me as well,' he says while we're out on patrol.

'Is your actual dad useless too?'

'No, not at all.' Samson smiles. 'Him and my step-mum – they're very protective. Never let me do anything for myself. Lord Allenby gave me a chance to be something . . . more.'

I nod. 'My dad's always around, but he's not always *present*, if that makes sense?'

'Perfect sense.'

We ride on in silence, listening to Rachel relaying the sentinels' observations. Ollie is chatting to Brandon behind us.

'I used to love Ostara,' Brandon is saying. 'One of the other veneurs is taking bets on whether Medraut pulls something this year.'

'He's doing what?' I twist round in my saddle. The thought that one of our own could be making a game out of something that every one of us fears makes me sick with anger.

'Don't worry,' Brandon says, 'I punched him.'

Ostara is supposed to be a celebratory night. But last year, we left Tintagel expecting to come back to a feast, and instead we returned with sixty dead friends. The shadow of what happened hangs over the preparations for this year's celebration. The reeves still decorate the castle, hanging garlands of honeysuckle and clematis from the walls and ceiling. They set long tables with crystal goblets and priceless china. But there's no anticipation. We have been waiting for Medraut to show his hand. If he's going to, it will be on one of the dates important to the Thanes: Samhain, Ostara, Beltane. The logical would say it's because the mysterious power of Annwn is at its strongest on these days. I say it's because he's a sadist who will want to ruin what should be a happy night.

Poor Sachi arrives at the stables on Ostara to me holding back tears. Ollie's hands are shaking as he tries to do up the straps on Balius's bridle.

'Why are these things so damn fiddly?' he snaps as I do them up for him. My hands are steady, even if my heartbeat is not. I keep seeing Ramesh's disembodied head, rolling along the ground. It's an image that's never far from my thoughts, but it's taken up full-time residence tonight.

'Are you guys okay?' Sachi says. It's a reminder to me that we can't ruin this for her. She's already missed out on some of the best aspects of Annwn. And if we're suffering, she's suffering more: it's a year to the day that her brother died. We should try our best to give her some happiness on tonight of all nights. If Medraut doesn't kill us before we get back, at least. I catch Ollie's eye and he nods, clearly thinking the same way.

There are two beings who aren't subdued. Cavall the dog, who pants excitedly around our feet, and Samson, who is boisterously, aggressively upbeat. It's slightly scary, to be honest.

'Right, welcome officially, Sachi! We're really glad to have you on board as a proper knight.' He smiles at her, moving as if to pat her on the back then thinking better of it and patting her horse instead. As we lead our mounts outside and swing into the saddles, Samson says, 'We're heading south, to the river patrol route. Everyone tuck in, we'll stay in the tortoise formation for now. Get cosy, get to know each other a bit better.'

Clever. Very clever. He's framing a protective stance as a bonding exercise. Without needing to say anything further, everyone moves their horses to surround Sachi and her cob: Lamb and I ride on her left, Ollie and Balius on her right, and Samson in front. The rest bring up the rear. It's these moments where we work together seamlessly, as though all of us have Ollie's mind-reading power, that make me love being a knight the most.

We're silent as we cross the drawbridge and make our way to our patrol route. We ride alongside Palomides and Lancelot for a while before they peel off. There's a lot of tight faces amongst their ranks – I'm not the only one having painful flashbacks. We cross the river and make our way along the Southbank, past actors in Shakespearean garb and trolls and other monsters that lurk in the concrete mazes here. We ride along the Thames, where dolphins and kelpies used to play in the lapping waves, and mer-people – tails covered in algae and hair thick with seaweed – would bask on the pebble beaches below. Now the river is dark, as though just beneath the surface a chasm of imagination lurks, poised to swallow the rest of the water.

We dispatch a few easy nightmares – a giant rat and some tricksters who are causing trouble with some young dreamers. Eventually we reach the elegant bulk of the Cutty Sark at Greenwich and turn south on our route, away from the water and down into the village. I can't help but remember that only a few miles to our east is the old Royal Arsenal, where Medraut set up his headquarters last year. The cloistered buildings that lead up to the park echo uncomfortably. Even the dreams of ladies in elaborate hats and layers of satin aren't enough to dampen the deafening sound of our horses' hooves. I use my Immral to cushion each step.

'Thanks, Fern,' Samson says. 'I was getting worried about hearing anything over the helmets with that racket going on. Usually there's more background noise, isn't there, so we don't hear the horses as much?'

Suddenly, an unholy noise erupts around the space, echoing off every surface. It's Cavall, barking like he's possessed.

'Quiet, Cav!' I hiss, but he won't. He's nipping at the feet of a statue.

I could have sworn that the statue should be of a military man – some long-dead admiral. But now the face that stares out at us belongs to Sebastien Medraut. The arrogance of the man. Or maybe it's simply that everyone's imaginations are replacing other statues with his image. Either way, it's driving the dog crazy.

'He's a good judge of character,' I say, coming to a halt behind the yapping creature. Lamb shoves Cavall with her nose. He yelps and rolls over, then licks Lamb enthusiastically. She doesn't seem to mind.

'Tell your horse to get a room, Fern,' Ollie says.

'Come on,' Samson says. We move on, casting uneasy glances back at the statue of Medraut.

Rachel's voice comes over the helmets. 'Bedevere? We've had sightings on the Round Table.'

My heart pounds.

'Violet inspyre. Immral. Up at the top of the hill, straight ahead. The Table's going crazy. Whatever's going on up there, it's big.'

We all look at each other. *This is it,* we are all thinking, *this is what Medraut has been brewing.* At least, this time, we're prepared.

Chapter 45

Sachi is gathering up her reins, her hands shaking.

I reach over to her. 'It's going to be alright,' I say.

'You don't know that,' she replies.

We urge the horses into a gallop as we cross out of the Naval College and into Greenwich Park. The horses' hooves are pounding on grass now, a hundred heartbeats meshing together. We canter around herds of deer, then gallop onwards past lone wolves and packs of hunting reptiles. As the grass slopes upwards, the observatory comes into view. A monument to stargazing. It's impressive enough in Ithr; in Annwn it is stunning. A shower of stars hangs perpetually over it like a canopy. Tiny, glinting planets spin around it. But something is wrong tonight. Something more wrong than the tell-tale metallic taste of Medraut's power. The inspyre that constantly ripples around me, waiting for me to use my Immral, is sinking inside me, as though it's frightened of what lies ahead.

'Samson?' I say over the helmets, so that only he will hear.

'What's the matter, Fern?'

'We need to be careful.'

Seeing me look so shaken, he holds up a hand. The regiment

instantly slows to a brisk walk. Another hand signal and Bedevere peels off into three separate groups: Samson continues on with Nerizan behind him, Brandon trailing them with his morrigan perched on his shoulder. Ollie takes Milosz and Vien, and I lead Sachi and Linnea round to the west of the observatory.

'Rachel?' Samson says. 'Can you get eyes on what's going on inside?'

'Negative,' Rachel replies. 'The harkers haven't been able to penetrate the walls. Medraut's work, we're guessing.'

Samson's voice comes over the helmets once more. 'Put the dome on standby.'

Sachi shoots me a look. The old Millennium Dome is where the nearest contingency of apothecaries is stationed. I smile back at her, trying to be reassuring, even as my very bones quake with the feeling of inspyre gathering into them, seeking a solid foundation to cling to.

'Fern?' Rachel says.

'What is it, Rachel?'

'I don't want any of you to go in there.'

'Why?' Samson says. 'Have you received further intelligence?'

'No,' Rachel says, her voice very small. 'I just . . . I don't want to lose any more of you. Please.'

There's a long pause, as we absorb this. Samson, when he speaks, is gentle. 'This is our job, Rachel.'

I lead Linnea and Sachi around one side of the observatory. There's nothing different about it at first glance, until I realise that it's absolutely silent. There are no dreams surrounding the building. Normally there would be flocks of dreamers, or dreams of mad scientists, aeronauts and astronauts climbing its bricks. There would be rockets escaping from its roof; aliens dropping from the sky.

'Anything your side, Fern?' Samson says.

'Nothing.'

'Ollie?'

'Nada here.'

'Okay, Fern, take the back entrance on my command. Ollie, reconvene with me at the front.'

Sachi, Linnea and I dismount our horses, and I send Lamb towards a clump of bushes, a good distance from the building. I don't want her caught in any crossfire. We slip along the side of the observatory, peering round the corners to ensure that no one's waiting to attack us. As we reach the entrance, I rest a hand on the wooden door.

A spark of inspyre flicks from my fingers and lands on the ground like molten metal. A shape forms there, just for a moment, pulled from the surface of my imagination. Ramesh's disembodied head. His gentle expression, his sweet face. Sachi lets out a low cry.

I flick the apparition back into inspyre. Shit. Linnea's expression is frozen on the spot where Ramesh's head appeared, one hand gripping Sachi's arm.

Sachi has a hand on her throat. 'He had marks here,' she whispers, devastation flecking her voice. 'Is that how . . . ?'

I force her to look at me.

'I'm sorry you saw that,' I whisper.

'Did Medraut make . . . ?' Linnea says haltingly.

'No.' I shake my head. 'It was me, by accident. I'm sorry.'

Sachi looks at me, breathing deeply and often, trying to keep her panic at bay. 'I don't think I can do this,' she says.

'You absolutely can,' I tell her.

'I don't want to end up . . .' Her eyes flick to the spot where her brother's head appeared.

'You won't,' I say fiercely. 'I wasn't ready that time. I didn't know it was coming. But I'm prepared now. I won't let anyone else die.'

'You can't promise that,' Linnea says.

'I bloody well can,' I say. 'I'm so fed up of that bastard killing my friends. I'm fed up of him turning the people I love against me. I am *never* going to let him win.'

Linnea nods tensely, but it's Sachi who I need to win over.

'Ready?' Samson's voice comes over the helmets.

'Give us a sec,' Linnea says quietly.

I make Sachi look at me again. 'You fight against them in Ithr, remember? I know you're tired of it all, and it feels useless. But in here, it's not. *Here* is where we make a difference. Annwn is going to be the place where we get our revenge.'

'We need to move now, before our cover is blown,' Samson's saying.

I ignore him. I bring my head closer to Sachi's even though I know that Linnea will be able to hear everything I say anyway.

'Your brother saved me once, did you know that? I should have been thrown out of the thanes, and he protected me. If he hadn't I don't think I'd have survived. He was my only friend, for a very long time. I know that my grief is nothing compared to yours, but I will *never* forgive Medraut for taking him away. Do you understand? *Never*.'

That seems to get through to her. Sachi nods, a spark returning to her eyes. She hoists her spear in one hand, the other coming up to rest on my arm.

'This is sweet,' Linnea says, 'but we've got a nightmare to face.'

'We're ready,' I say into my helmet.

'Go!' Samson commands. I fling open the door and we charge inside, adrenaline pumping. The observatory is a gallery of rooms that lead into one another. The lobby is empty, as are the next few rooms. Samson tells us to keep going, keep looking. If I didn't have the inspyre in my gut telling me something was badly wrong, I'd think that this was a false alarm. The light is dim in here, except for an unholy glow that emanates from the stars above the building; their translucence penetrating the ceiling.

'Central gallery,' Samson says. 'Everyone. Now.'

The shake in his voice tells me that he has found what we are looking for. Sachi and Linnea close in behind me as we head for the observatory's belly. The door is already open. I can see a few of the other knights frozen in the entrance. I push through them and stop.

The only source of light is an ethereal glow from the stars above. There are shadowy shapes on the floor, and at first I think they're snakes, moving sleepily. Then my eyes get used to the darkness and resolve what they're seeing. I put a hand over my mouth to stop myself from crying out.

Five dreamers lie on the floor. They are awake, and their eyes stare at us in unbridled terror and agony. For they cannot move. Their limbs, all four of them, have been lopped off.

Something is moving on their chests and heads and mouths. Grey, half-rat, half-cockroach, the creatures are undoubtedly Medraut's creations – and they're feeding. They're feeding on the hearts and minds and mouths of those helpless dreamers.

Nerizan pushes past me, and I hear her vomit onto the grass outside the entrance. Samson approaches one of the dreamers.

'Can you hear me?' he says.

The dreamer nods. He tries to say something but the creature gnawing at his mouth stops him from articulating anything but a pained groan. I move closer. Something about the dreamer is familiar.

'We're here to help you, sir, okay?' Samson says, his voice low and calm. The dreamer makes another noise, and suddenly I place him.

Constantine Hale. The leader of Shout Louder.

'What has he done?' Brandon says softly, kneeling down beside one of the other dreamers.

'Don't touch them,' Ollie says.

'I know,' Brandon says. 'I've seen enough horror movies to know how *that* one ends.' But he gets as close as he dares to the creatures. The morrigan on his shoulder takes flight, shrieking in fear.

'Another morrigan experiment?' Samson asks. 'Like the ear bugs?'

'I think so,' Brandon says. 'Poor things. We just need –'

But clearly he hasn't seen enough horror movies, because that's the moment one of the creatures leaps for his throat. Brandon cries out, pulling fruitlessly at the creature as it latches into the soft flesh above his clavicle.

Ollie tries to carve at it with his chakram as I reach for my Immral, commanding it to crush the beast. But nothing we do makes any difference. And Brandon's screams are attracting the attention of the other creatures.

'Get him out,' Samson says, and two of the knights half drag, half carry our friend from the room.

I pull Samson away from the creatures. No one says anything as I reach out a shaking hand, careful not to touch the things. I close my eyes, trying to feel what they are. There's inspyre there, for sure, but there's also something kalend-like about them.

'Ollie?' I say, and my brother is there in an instant, understanding that I need his part of our power too. He places his hands on my shoulders, and the familiar spark of energy joins us. Suddenly, the creatures are illuminated for me. Illuminated with emotion. Ollie gasps.

'Dear God,' he whispers. 'What's he done?'

I reach into the creature with my Immral, twisting and turning it this way and that as it snaps at nothing, unable to see what is controlling it. Cockroach wasn't a bad way to describe it at all. But instead of a head it just has jaws. Brandon had said these used to be morrigans, but there is no elegant morrigan beak: these are gnashing jaws that will chew through anything, regardless of whether it is flesh, emotion or the person's very soul.

'Some cross between a morrigan and a kalend,' I tell the others.

I open the jaws and feel inside with my mind. There's a mechanism in the mouth – a chute designed to expel something. I press on the opening, and the creature vomits.

'Urgh!' Linnea says, nearly breaking my concentration. I can't blame her. *Urgh* is putting it mildly. For the creature has vomited larvae; thick-skinned, grey cocoons that are covered in spikes. As they wriggle they embed themselves in the nearest warm flesh of another of the prone dreamers. Each spike is hooked, just like those roots on Medraut's rope of thorns.

'Can you remove them, Fern?' Samson asks, 'if we stay quiet so you can concentrate?'

The memory of Brandon, screaming, and me unable to help him, is still raw.

'Better yet, can you kill them?' Ollie says.

I press on the creature's body with my mind, squeezing it until it must surely burst. The thing flails, but no matter how hard I press it, it will not die. My inability to crush it has nothing to do with my concentration. Whatever pit of nothingness is at the creature's centre is too strong for Ollie and me to combat.

'We're going to have to remove them, then cage them, I think,' I tell Samson, trying to keep the fear from my voice.

'Sachi,' Samson says. 'Fetch the saddlebags. Fern, come back to us for now while we prepare. No point in you using your strength needlessly.'

I put the creature back down, and it immediately latches back on to Constantine Hale. The pang of guilt I feel is not at all lessened by Samson taking my shoulder. 'We need you to preserve your strength for all of them, not just this one dreamer, okay? If we get them all it will be worth a short delay.'

Sachi runs back in with handfuls of empty saddlebags. I set about strengthening them, turning them into solid cages, throwing meshes of inspyre around them.

'Brandon?' Samson says as I work.

Sachi shakes her head. 'He . . . did it himself.'

'But he could have . . .' Linnea begins, petering out as she looks at the dreamers at our feet. None of us can truly know what unimaginable pain the creatures are subjecting them to. If they had limbs still, who's to say that they wouldn't have decided that a quick death on their own terms was better than this slow erosion?

I feel the loss deep in my stomach. Sweet, animal-mad Brandon, who tried to kiss me and didn't hold it against me when I turned him down. Oh God. The blood on Medraut's hands. How can he not feel the weight of his victims pressing down on him the way they press down on me?

'Guys, be careful,' Ollie says suddenly, pointing towards the door. The larvae that we'd thought were slow moving are not. They are wriggling with surprising speed towards the light of the entrance to the observatory.

'They can't get out – they'll do this to any dreamer they meet,' Vien says.

Sachi looks round at the dreamers who are already being feasted upon. 'What about them? We can't leave them here.'

I abandon the cages I'd been making and throw my Immral out to the dreamers, pulling them up, trying to heft them with my mind. But some other power is pinning them down, making them heavier than they should be. 'I can get one, maybe,' I say, 'but not all of them.'

'That doesn't matter any more,' Samson says. 'We're never going to reach the door before them.' Sure enough, some of the larvae are nearly at the entrance, all the way down the hallway. Some have split off, heading for the closed back door that Sachi, Linnea and I entered by. A silent understanding passes between Samson and me.

'Nerizan,' Samson says into his helmet to the one knight still outside. 'Can you hear me?'

'Yes. Samson, Brandon –'

'Nerizan, tell Allenby what happened here, okay? Get away from here now.'

'What? Samson, no. Samson!'

Before she can finish, I throw my Immral at the distant door and shove it closed with all my might. There's the sound of hundreds of larvae hitting the inside of the door. We are alone. In this building, under the starlight. With those creatures. And the nightmare of the dismembered dreamers, their souls and brains and hearts being slowly devoured while they are still alive.

Chapter 46

I look at Samson. 'What do we do? I can't kill them.'

'Are you sure?' Samson says.

'Pretty certain, yeah.'

'Um, guys?' Ollie says. 'I think we should find somewhere else to have this conversation.'

He is pointing towards the now closed entrance, where the larvae, finding their way out blocked, have turned around and are heading straight for the only other new sources of flesh available: us.

'Back, get back,' Samson says, pushing Sachi behind him. We all race for the door opposite. The dreamers who are being feasted upon make incoherent sounds of panic, entreating us not to leave them behind. I tug fruitlessly at one of the bodies.

'I'm sorry,' I whisper as Ollie pulls me up. 'I'm so sorry.'

I follow my brother and the rest of Bedevere out through the opposite door, the wordless screams of the dreamers pulling at my conscience.

Ollie and Samson shove the door shut behind us as we go, plunging us into darkness. I conjure some inspyre from the little mass nestled around my bones and turn it into a light. It casts a pale blue glow on our faces.

'We have to go back,' Sachi says. 'You said we'd protect them. You said we wouldn't let him . . .' She's glaring at me, as though I've personally failed her.

'Back off,' Ollie snaps.

'What did it do to Brandon?' Samson asks Sachi. Everyone turns to her. Sachi's eyes are wide. 'We couldn't pull it off him. My spear – it didn't make a difference. That thing was eating him alive.'

I try to imagine Brandon being eaten by the very creatures he wanted to help. There has to be something I can do. Something *we* can do.

'He said something before he . . .' Sachi says. 'Something about a Cantabrian circle.'

'That's a battle formation,' Linnea says. 'Are you sure?'

'I think so. He wasn't very clear.'

'The most important thing is to keep those creatures inside this building,' Samson says, 'and to see if we can rescue the dreamers. Fern, did you sense any weakness in them at all? Fern? Fern?'

I have pressed my cheek against the closed door, throwing my power into the room beyond. I can feel the outline of the space: a perfect circle, just like a portal. A way to amplify Annwn's power . . . or the power of an Immral. The creatures are little black diamonds of inverted inspyre. They cluster around the five bodies, dots of darkness against the dreamers' dying imaginations . . .

Five.

I can't explain it, but I know, somehow, that Nimue's belt could help us. A circle, Brandon had said. I wonder . . .

The strands of everything I've learned over the last few months, both in Annwn and Ithr, begin to weave together. The whispered grievances; the arguments solved through compromise; the endless learning and research undertaken by a group of people I have come to trust, even if we do not always agree. And that number. *Five*. Five blank strands, a gift from a goddess, waiting to be written on.

'Sachi?' I say, my head still pressed against the door, 'there was a belt in one of the saddlebags . . .'

'A golden one?' Sachi says. 'I took it out when I brought the bags inside. I'm sorry.'

She looks devastated, even though she doesn't understand why it's important.

Through the door, I hear the moans of the dreamers, and sense more of the creatures vomiting up their larvae. The maggots writhe on the floor. I need to get that belt. It's only outside – that's a start.

'Follow me,' I say, and turn up a side corridor, looking for a way to the entrance that avoids the larvae. A set of steps leads up to a higher floor. Through another set of galleries and there – a window looking down over the grass outside. But the larvae are approaching from a room beyond the one we're in. They slither towards us, far too fast for creatures so small and eyeless. Ollie slams the door before they can reach us. They fling themselves against it on the other side, looking for a way in.

'Guard it,' Samson tells Ollie. I peer out of the window.

Down below, Nerizan has gone, taking her horse with her. Brandon's lifeless body lies on the grass below, his penknife clasped in his hand, a streak of blood ebbing from his throat. How could Nerizan abandon him like that? But then I realise that the creature that was eating him has disappeared – it's escaped into Annwn, looking for prey. Nerizan must have gone to try to protect any others it attacked.

Lamb and the other horses are still waiting for us. They watch the observatory restlessly, stamping their feet at the sight of Brandon's corpse. Cavall is lying next to him, licking his hand, as though he can't understand why he isn't cuddling him.

On the ground beside them rests a jumble of items from the saddlebags. There, in the middle of it, is Nimue's belt. I reach out with my mind, trying to call it to me, but there's some kind of shield around the observatory. It must have been this that prevented the harkers from seeing what was happening inside.

If only I could reach out to Cavall and make him understand me. Feeling foolish, I bang on the windowpane, as loudly as I dare. Even that clatter sends the larvae on the other side of the door mad with hunger. Lamb twitches her ears, but nothing more.

'Fern, what are you doing?' hisses Ollie. The door bounces, and he braces himself against it. I ignore him, and bang on the window a little louder. This time Lamb looks up and sees me, and so does Cavall. He barks wildly. I point to the items that I want. Cavall just wags at me.

'How solid is that door?' I ask Ollie. He kicks it. On the other side, the larvae kick back.

'Pretty solid, but I wouldn't want to . . . Fern!'

I disappear a small pane of glass in the window and lean out, so Cavall can hear me. 'Ollie, I need you here.'

My brother switches places with Samson.

'I need you to tell the dog something.'

Muttering about Doctor Dolittle, Ollie takes my hand and I turn myself into a channel for his power. I've never tried to wield Ollie's part of the Immral before. I have to concentrate in a different way. With my part of the power, I am always reaching out, manipulating things with my mind. Ollie's half is more about becoming a sponge; soaking up emotions and memories. Cavall is only made of inspyre, so there's not much to go on, but I am counting on there being enough in him for me to make a request. There are echoes of memories inside the little creature's trusting body, although I cannot see any of them clearly. And there's a taste, too – the kind I get when I'm manipulating another person – a sweet citrus tang; I feel as if I know it, although I can't place why.

I channel my command into Cavall, and he obediently trots back to the saddlebag contents. Halfway there I lose my connection with him. So that's the boundary of Medraut's shield. A moment later Cavall returns, carrying the belt. He deposits it at the foot of the observatory wall, then sits down and looks up at me, panting, waiting for his next order.

'Good boy,' I say, and send a little wave down that I hope he will feel as a pat on the head. I reach with my mind for the belt, and float it up and through the open window. Cavall lets up a howl of distress, placing his paws against the wall as if wanting me to float him up too. The noise sends the larvae on the other side of the door mad with lust.

'Shh!' I hiss, and to my surprise he quietens almost immediately. 'Just wait there,' I whisper.

Samson and Sachi are already untangling the belt, even though I haven't told them what I need it for.

'Where do we put it, Fern?' Samson says.

'I . . .' I look at everyone's expectant faces, and feel the weight of their hope. 'I'm not sure yet.'

'Well, let's figure it out together,' Samson says patiently.

'I think we need to separate the belt, each take a piece of it.'

I'm playing it totally by ear here, trusting my instinct.

'There's five strands of fabric and seven of us,' Sachi says, holding the last one out to me. 'Do you think that matters?'

'I think if Nimue gave us five, she meant us to use five,' I say, accepting her gift. 'Who doesn't have one?'

'Me and Linnea,' Sachi replies. I wind my piece of belt around my wrist. The inspyre inside my bones is growing restless. Maybe it is fearful of what lies in wait for us. Maybe it's excited at the plan that is forming in my head. I hope I'm right. If we're to stand a chance of defeating those creatures, I need this to work.

Ollie comes over under the pretence of helping. 'Do you really know what you're doing, Fern?' he says in a low voice.

'No idea,' I reply, 'but we've got to try something, haven't we? Otherwise we're going to be stuck here until we're too weak to hold off those creatures.'

Ollie grips his belt and nods. 'Okay,' he says, 'I trust you.'

'*Is this the faith, she said, and said no more,*' Samson quotes.

'What?'

'That's what your mum wrote. I don't think it was a message

just for you, Fern. I think it was for all of us. For what it's worth, you have my faith too.'

'And mine,' says Sachi, granting me a rare smile.

Our little band – what's left of Bedevere – nod in agreement. I look at the belt, feeling like a fool. Just as the thanes have hung all their hopes of survival on me, I am hanging my hopes of survival on five silken threads. Faith should be the key to making the belt work. That they all have faith in me. My wrist tingles with Immral, but nothing else happens.

Is this the faith, she said, and said no more.

It wasn't about them believing in me. It was never about that, I realise. Mum knew that people would have faith in Medraut – that would be too easy. But would Medraut have faith in others? Would an Immral set on their own path make room for the skills of their companions? It was always meant to be the other way around.

'And you have my faith,' I say, too loudly. 'All of you.' I mean it.

Something blooms inside my chest – belief and power. It comes not just from me, but from all of us, travelling through our limbs into the fabric wound around our arms. The inspyre crackles into life, bursting forth from my hands and sparking along the length of the belt. It winds around our wrists and turns golden silk into a length of rope that stretches between the five of us. A binding, a fence. Something to create a net.

I look round at my friends. 'Let's go.'

Chapter 47

We set off down the corridor, abandoning the other door, knowing it will not hold for long before the onslaught of the larvae. Back down the staircase towards the main gallery. I'm just praying that the dreamers are still alive. Our priority has to be to stop those creatures from escaping the building and then to save any survivors. There's a *boom* behind us as the door to the room we were in flies open. The wet sound of the larvae gaining on us reaches my ears far too quickly – we do not have as much of a head start as I'd been counting on. A cry goes up behind me: Milosz, at the back of the rope, has been caught. The larvae swarm up his leg, digging their thorny bodies into his flesh. Ollie pushes me forward.

'You can't help him now,' he hisses.

'Here, Linnea! Go!' Milosz says, thrusting the rope towards Linnea. She grabs it without hesitation, and the knight falls. The last I see of him, he is drawing his weapon – a grenade – and pulling the pin. Brandon is not the only one who refuses to be eaten alive. We run on, the panting breath of me and my companions the only noise above our pounding feet. The distant explosion of the grenade nearly throws us to the floor.

Soon afterwards, the sound of the larvae grows louder. The grenade did not harm them.

The door to the main hall is ahead of us. I reach out with my mind, trying to feel what lies beyond. There is life there still, but there are far more of those creatures.

'Fern?' Samson says, his voice wavering.

'Trust me!' I shout. 'We just need to hold them off for long enough to make this work.' I lift my hand up, and a shower of inspyre rains from it, casting itself wide over the heads of my companions, forming a protective shield – perhaps not strong enough to keep them out for long, but enough to buy us some time.

'Ready?' I roar above the sound of the larvae.

'Go!' the others shout, and with a thrust of my mind I push the doors to the main hall so hard that they are nearly wrenched from their hinges. Beyond, a sea of larvae falls out like water breaking a dam. They surge against my makeshift shield. Each time one of them batters against it I can feel my power ebbing. We have to move quickly.

'Make a circle around the dreamers!' I shout, and the others rush to do my bidding. There's shouting from another part of the room – Vien has been taken, the larvae swarming up his legs. I run to him, trying to bat the things away without letting them get their hooks into me.

'Stop!' he says, then more quietly, 'Stop.' He looks over to Sachi, who is swiping her spear at larvae and creatures alike, trying to keep them away from the rest of the team. 'Here!' he shouts, and tosses her the rope. She catches it, and we watch as he runs from the room, larvae following him. There are now only five of us left. If we lose any more, then my plan can't work.

'Get off!' Ollie shouts. 'Get off me!' He kicks out at the larvae.

No. Not my brother.

I run towards him but before I get there Linnea throws herself in front of him. She holds her hands out to the creatures swarming up his legs and they make the leap, digging into her with relish. She looks up at me. 'Gotta keep the Immrals together, right?' And she, too, runs from the room. Her rope falls to the floor and Ollie scoops it up.

We're down to four. We can't make it work. The power that was keeping the rope together starts to fade.

I look at Samson and at Sachi and at Ollie. 'There has to be someone else,' I whisper.

'Give . . . it . . . to me,' a low voice says, almost too quietly to hear. I look down.

Constantine Hale – what is left of him – is talking. His mouth is a mess of missing teeth and gnawed-upon tongue, but he can just about make himself understood. I hold my hand out and Ollie tosses Linnea's rope to me. Constantine has no hands, so I tuck it into his bloodied mouth, praying that that will be enough.

'I believe in you,' I tell him. 'You're going to get through this.' I know I need to mean it. I need to have faith in him, if the magic is to work. But how can I have faith in this dying, mutilated creature? One who has made his dislike of me so plain.

For the first time in my life, I try to think the best of someone.

I open up the part of me that I locked so long ago, the part I only allow a tiny group of people into. Yes, he may be patronising, he may act like he's a saviour to people like me who don't need saving, but at least he's trying to fight. At least he recognises what Medraut's up to. He may have believed I was a coward, but that's only because he didn't know about the knights. His heart was steering him true, even if it took the wrong course.

'I *do* believe in you,' I say, placing a hand on Constantine's chest. 'I *do*.'

At first nothing happens, then a little spark of inspyre ignites once more from the rope held in his teeth. I feel it in my bones; the power running between the five of us – four knights and a dreamer. It tastes of something – a familiar taste, and then I place it – the Round Table. The ancient power that binds the thanes together. Nimue has invoked the sacred bonds between those of us who protect Annwn and those who walk through it.

'Fan out!' I cry, and the four of us who can move span the width of the room, creating a five-pointed star. The rope, as if blown by an invisible wind, billows out as it sparks. It takes the shape of a circle. The inspyre inside me is trembling now with barely suppressed energy. It is building to something, although I don't think I'm in control of it any longer. Then the rope grows solid; a hard circle made of pure light. The strength of all my fellow thanes; the strength of the dreamer who has survived against the odds. I can feel all of it channelling into me. It is mine to command.

I use my Immral to find the creatures and the larvae in this building. They are everywhere, in every room. I pinpoint the specks of blackness at their hearts. I lift them up, wrenching them from whatever they were clinging on to. Beside us, the dreamers are suddenly revealed, free of their parasitic leeches. The full extent of what has been done to them becomes evident. Their torsos are empty cavities. Some of them have lost half their faces. The ones who are dead have had their skulls hollowed.

Ollie turns away, and Sachi closes her eyes. Samson, though, holds the gaze of one of the remaining living dreamers. His eyes are full of compassion.

A wave of anger and sadness rolls over me, and I force the new power granted to me to crush the creatures. But they only squeal in pain, and a rocket of agony sizzles around the rope and through each one of us. Whatever power Nimue granted me doesn't want me to destroy them.

An image from long ago, when I was starting to learn about my power, comes to me. A malformed, malevolent baby, turned inside out into a little girl. The moment that made Andraste believe in me.

Use inspyre for creation, not destruction.

I feel my way to the edges of the creatures first, teasing them apart, peeling them open. Even with the strength of my comrades channelling through me, the pain in my skull is excruciating. There are so many of them. Ollie is already bleeding through his nose. Sachi and Samson are in worse shape.

I wonder if I should stop, but then Samson catches my gaze. He shakes his head. *We can do this,* he's saying. *Keep the faith.*

I turn my attention back to the creatures. They are no longer squirming. For a moment I think they might be dead, but no, there is the little beating vessel that must be their version of a heart. I dig into the black seed at their cores, prising it away with infinite care and infinite power. With a searing pain that sends me to my knees, I excavate all of them at once. The seeds drop to the floor with a clang that echoes around the galleries. They do not roll. They are as heavy – and as deadly – as lead.

With another burst of energy, sapped from not just me but my companions, I send a river of inspyre directly into the creatures' veins, powering them with purest imagination instead of the inverted, stagnant stuff of Medraut's Immral. I do not try to alter their outer form, but when I release them to the floor they are like new creatures, still the same shape but now sparking with inspyre. Maybe I should give them a new purpose – a little seed of my own inserted into their stomachs. But no, I think – that's something Medraut would do. Give them free will. Let the inspyre lead them. They are no longer any more dangerous than a common dream.

I release the rope, and it drops, fabric once more, to the ground.

Golden silk amidst carnage.

Chapter 48

It is done. The headache coursing through my skull kicks up a notch, perhaps understanding that its work is over. I sink to the floor, and with me sink the others. Ollie crawls over to Samson, who is bleeding from his ears. Sachi has fared little better. She limps over as I hover over Constantine Hale.

'Thank you,' I say.

He nods, unable to respond.

'Will he be okay?' Sachi whispers.

I look into his broken face. 'We're going to try our best. Help me with him.'

Sachi holds his head tenderly as I lift his torso. We shuffle towards the doors. With a reluctant whine they open before my Immral. The sunlight streams in. Cavall is waiting there, as is Lamb. To her credit Lamb doesn't baulk as I lift Constantine onto her back. Cavall attaches himself to the only other surviving dreamer.

Then the apothecaries are upon us, asking us questions, pressing poultices to our heads and muttering exclamations at the blood coursing from my friends' ears and noses. Someone has placed a blanket over Brandon's body. There is only one face I look for.

'Lord Allenby is on his way,' Jin says, leading me away from the scrum.

She eases me down onto the grass and hands me a poultice. The cool herbs take the edge off my migraine.

'Did Nerizan find the one that escaped? The one that got Brandon?' I ask her.

'Don't worry about that now,' Jin says.

'They killed him,' I whimper. The faces of the dead dreamers – the faces of the living dreamers – and all the knights who I couldn't save – taunt me.

'It's not your fault,' Jin whispers. 'You can't carry it all. No one could.'

The sound of pounding hooves on grass shakes the ground, and I look up through tear-streaked eyes to see Lord Allenby gallop up on his charger. He leaps from his horse and strides straight over to me. He's going to want to hear everything that happened, and I know I need to be strong but I just can't. I can't face reliving it so soon. As if reading my mind, Jin plants herself in between me and him.

'I'm sorry, sir,' she says, 'but Fern can't talk to you right now. And, honestly? I know it isn't my place but you can't expect her to keep working like this. She's sixteen, for God's sake.'

Lord Allenby raises a hand. 'Jin, I'm not here to interrogate her.'

He kneels before me. 'It's okay, Fern,' he says softly.

'They killed so many . . .'

'Let's get you back to the castle, then get you some proper sleep.' On his orders, Jin summons a bicycle with a stretcher attached to its back and makes me lie down on it.

'No – Lamb . . .' I protest, but Lamb is already being led away by a knight from Palomides, Constantine's torso strapped carefully to her saddle. She whinnies mournfully at me. Jin drapes a blanket over my shaking limbs. Lord Allenby is helping reeves and veneurs to stow a few of the newly harmless creatures into vessels. Cavall is chasing the creatures here and there, snapping them up in his jaws to bring back to the team. Samson stands apart from everyone else, leaning against the wall of the observatory, his head bowed. Ollie is talking to Sachi in a low voice, tears streaming down their faces. Everyone else is suffering just as much as me and here I am being coddled in my stupid little stretcher and blanket.

'The others need seeing to as well,' I tell Jin.

'They will be,' she says, pushing harder on her bicycle as we crest the hill and join the path down towards the river and central London. As the bike moves this way and that, I slip into a zen state, watching the sky and trees slide across my vision. Everything I've seen tonight, everything I've done, should also have been leading up to completing the second task. But what was the point of it all? Was it worth our losses?

Mum, Andraste, Nimue – none of them could have known what I would be facing, but they should have known that it would be dangerous and they made it as difficult as possible for me anyway. If it hadn't been for us needing to run as one with that rope, would Milosz have been able to take a different route? Would he have lived? If we hadn't needed five people, would Linnea and Vien still be with us?

This anger at my mother is a new experience. She's been

on a pedestal for so long. I can understand her not wanting to trust that I would grow up to be a good Immral, but to put me in a position where I have to endanger other people's lives? That's unforgivable.

Jin cycles us over Tintagel's drawbridge, where apothecaries swarm around me, then she walks in between me and the wall of faces trying to see what happened to the girl with Immral. Inside the hospital tower, there are a dozen platforms studded into the walls at intervals, like shelves. Each one holds a bed. Mine is right at the very top. I'm grateful – I know it's to prevent people from trying to sneak a peek at me. From my bed I have a clear view of the turret: engraved stone decorated with snakes, and murals depicting men and women in white robes, tending to the sick. A sweet-smelling smoke falls like dry ice from a vent at the very top, making it feel as though I'm being cleansed by rosewater.

My head is still pounding, but the longer I lie here the more I think about the others who were in such bad shape. They're not used to channelling Immral. I shouldn't have left them there.

I am just sitting up to see if I can find an apothecary to talk to when I hear movement below. The wide doors into the hospital are creaking open once more and a flood of apothecaries enters, bearing more stretchers. Sachi is passed out on one of them, and Ollie looks like he's in a bad way. Jin and another apothecary are trying to restrain Samson who is slurring, over and over again, 'I have to get to Lord Allenby'. Then another crowd of apothecaries enters, surrounding two further stretchers bearing the maimed dreamers.

One of them is groaning constantly. Constantine is silent.

'No,' Jin says, landing on my platform.

'What?'

'You're wondering if they're going to be okay. I was pre-empting your question.'

One of the apothecaries surrounding the dreamers peels off to go into the pantry where the herbs and cordials are kept. I get a clear view, for the first time, of what they're doing. Someone is trying to sew the limbs back on to their bodies. Someone else is packing restorative plants into the caverns of their torsos and skulls.

'What happens if that doesn't work?' I ask Jin. 'They won't lose their arms and legs in real life, will they?'

'No,' Jin replies, 'that's an easy fix. In the worst-case scenario they'll have some marks where the limbs were cut off, and their arms and legs will be numb for a few days. It's everything else Medraut's done. It's what's in here that's dangerous.' She points to her heart and head. 'If we can't regrow those then they'll lose everything that really matters.'

'They'll become Medraut's perfect person.'

'Quite.'

'Can I see them?' I ask Jin. 'I might be able to help.'

'Not before I take a look at that rash on your face.'

'What rash?'

I run my hands over my cheeks as Jin fetches a mirror. The skin is raised, bumpy, almost like . . .

'Here,' Jin says, holding the mirror in front of me. It's faint, but unmistakable. This is no rash. It's my burn scar, starting to become visible in Annwn.

I touch it again.

'Does it hurt?' Jin says, producing a salve.

'Less than it does in Ithr, that's for sure,' I reply. I have to catch my breath when I feel the crinkled skin beneath my fingers, not because of the sensation – but because of the way I feel about it. Free. So, so, free. It's one less secret, one step closer to my friends. And I'm not ashamed of it, not any more.

'You look like that in Ithr?' Jin says, an odd expression on her face.

'Long story,' I say. 'You don't need to worry about it, honestly.'

She stares at me, words brimming at her lips until they spill out. 'I thought I had Immral, you know.'

'What?'

'When I first learned about it, I was convinced I had it. That's why I know so much about your power. I thought I'd be the first person to really do some good with it. The first person who wasn't a knight. I thought I could heal people instead of destroying them.'

Suddenly, Jin's animosity makes sense. All of her snide comments and knowing remarks. Simple jealousy. Or maybe not so simple. I try to put myself in her shoes: someone as fearsomely intelligent as Jin, believing she was the best at everything. I've never experienced it before because I've always felt that others are better than me: Ollie, Lottie, Ramesh, Samson . . . For Jin, it must have been a sobering moment. Disorientating.

'I guess it took me a while to realise that having Immral doesn't make things as simple as I thought it would,' Jin says. I think it's her way of saying sorry.

'You don't need Immral to be an amazing apothecary,' I reply.

'Without my Immral, I'm nothing.' And that's my way of saying sorry back.

A pain at my hip makes me wince: something's burning into me. I feel around in the pouch that rests there and produce the jewelled coin my mother left. I swear that only one of the jewels was coloured before: now there are two. One sapphire, one amethyst. Jin and I look at each other in astonishment.

What is going on?

Chapter 49

Jin helps me down from my platform to visit the two surviving dreamers, promising to tell Lord Allenby and Easa about the coin. Constantine moans quietly into his pillow. On the other side of the room a sheet is spread over a series of beds. The dead dreamers and the fallen thanes: Brandon, Linnea, Milosz and Vien. Nerizan is bent over her friends' bodies, sobbing silently into the linen.

I catch Jin's eyes. She's sombre, tense – holding herself together. I am beginning to understand what the apothecaries have to go through. Sure, the knights have had a rough time of it lately, but before last year it had been over a decade since a knight had been killed in the line of duty. The apothecaries have to deal with dreamers who've been attacked and maimed by nightmares far more often. It's not that often that a dreamer dies on our watch any more – or it hadn't been before Medraut – but when they're near death or have been hurt by a nightmare it's the apothecaries who have to try to heal them, or provide a warm hand and a comforting smile as they slip away, witnessing the ebb of a stranger's life.

Our confessions to each other make me bold: I slip my hand into Jin's and squeeze gently.

Where Constantine's ribcage should be is only the husk of a torso. The top of his skull has caved in, leaving his eyes shrunken and uneven. Where his mouth should have teeth and a tongue, there is only gaping blackness that dribbles blood with every breath.

I have seen my friend decapitated. I have seen my lieutenant torn in half and my other friend have her chest opened up before my very eyes. This is still the worst thing I have ever witnessed; the most horrific mutilation of a person that I can conceive of.

One of the apothecaries looks at Constantine with a mixture of disgust and pity, and anger wells up inside me. I have received that same look from people in Ithr, for my eye colour and burn scar. This dreamer doesn't deserve either emotion. I take his hand and close my eyes, sending what Immral will respond to my aching head inside him, probing the recesses of his empty body. I want to see if there's a way of rebuilding what has been taken from him. But the inspyre will not stick. There is too little left.

'Can you?' Jin says quietly.

I shake my head.

Constantine turns what's left of his head towards me.

'I'm here,' Ollie says behind me. He takes my free hand and I become a channel. Ollie isn't able to read many memories, but he finds something of what's needed. A woman's face. A little boy. A sense of fulfilment – a job he loves, and that he finds satisfying. There's an aftertaste of Medraut – but I suppose that's to be expected since it was Medraut's handiwork that did this.

A thought occurs to me. 'Can you bring the box?' I whisper to Jin, and a few moments later Easa is beside me holding the multi-coloured puzzle box. Constantine deserves to have his dreams matter.

I take some of Constantine's desires – for himself, for his family, for Shout Louder – and fold them gently until they soften. Then I siphon them into the vessel. It's harder than I thought it would be. The Immral that holds the box together revolts against my intent: it is already bursting with so many imaginations. But gradually, like injecting treacle into concrete, I push Constantine's dreams inside. The Immral there ripples. A taste of Constantine's imagination seeps into my mouth: it reminds me of books, new and old.

It is done.

'He's getting weaker,' Ollie says.

I turn my attention back to Constantine. I take his memories now, and weave them together, until they are a quilt of peace. I cover him with them; if I cannot fix him, I can at least make his last moments ones of comfort. There's another burning pain in the pouch at my hip, but I can't think about that now.

Constantine's groans become quieter. Then they die down altogether and there is only the sigh of him breathing in and out, in and out, slower and slower. Then he's gone. I can tell the exact moment of his death by the way the taste of old books evaporates.

'We've got him from here, Fern,' Jin whispers, pulling me away, giving me permission to leave.

I don't remember walking down the steps of Tintagel. The next time I come to myself I'm kneeling at the threshold of the herb gardens, gulping in great breaths of air. My whole body aches from what it's been put through tonight, but that's nothing compared to the ache inside my chest.

Strong arms circle me. Samson.

'It's not okay,' he says softly. 'It's not okay.'

'I don't want to keep crying,' I say, through my tears, 'I want to be able to do something about it.'

'You are,' he says, and when I shake my head he turns me to look at him. His face is more tired than ever. There's still a streak of stray blood on his cheek. 'It's not a scale, Fern. We don't put the dead on one side and the saved on the other and measure your worth by that. That's not how it works.'

He leads me to the platform back to Ithr, helps me to find my portal. He rakes his hands through my hair, and then, right as the portal whisks me back to Ithr, so quickly I think maybe I imagined it, he presses his lips to mine.

Chapter 50

The memory of Samson's kiss is still on my mouth when I wake, so sweet that I can half imagine it was truly a dream. It cannot replace the memories of everything else that happened last night, but that kiss, along with Jin's peace offering, blunts the spikes of injustice.

One of the first things I do is see if there is anything on the television about the night's attack. The Shout Louder website has already heard about Constantine. The obituary is colourless, and followed by a load of comments from other Shout Louder supporters. The first few are blandly sympathetic, but then something strange happens. Someone has written, *And I bet the One Voice lot will be singing in the streets*. It's followed by a flurry of vitriolic agreement. Then someone replies, *C'mon, guys, now's not the time to make this political. It's not like this is Medraut's fault.*

It devolves from there. I read the ensuing argument between people who are supposed to be on the same side with fascination and profound sadness. There's an irony, of course, in that his death was Medraut's fault, but there's no way that these people could know that unless they, too, are thanes. They've turned a tragic death into a political movement. I can't work out how I feel about that. I didn't understand Constantine well enough to know whether he'd have wanted to become a symbol for that one facet of his life, or whether he'd want to be remembered as a fully-rounded human who was more than just his beliefs. And that leads me down a new path of thought: *are* we just our beliefs? Medraut certainly is. And is there anything left of me that isn't focused solely on fighting Medraut?

I click away from the Shout Louder website and look for details of the other dreamers who were killed. There's barely any mention of them. No one seems to have made the connection that every one of them was a threat to Medraut's plans: a human rights lawyer; a woman he went to school with; a rogue journalist; a constituent with a well-founded grudge. He's getting better at covering up his crimes.

I can barely look at Lottie in school. She and the other students involved in the chair prank were only given slapped wrists, and they've taken that as a victory. But as I watch her staring straight ahead in class instead of taking notes, the memory of what her father did to those dreamers returns. We haven't been able to find Lottie in Annwn. Medraut must be experimenting on someone.

Hollow heads where the thoughts should be. Hollow chests instead of a heart. Has he broken the unthinkable taboo, and done those things to his own daughter?

When the bell rings, Lottie doesn't move. Her friends leave without her, used to her strange behaviour now. Soon it is only the two of us left. There was a time when I'd have considered revenge for what she did to me.

'Are you okay?' I say quietly.

She looks at me as though she can't quite remember who I am. 'You're not one of us,' she says, although there's no malice in her voice. I look into her eyes and even though I don't have Ollie's gift, I can tell that something's very wrong. I know that nothing in Ithr will get through to her, so all I say instead is, 'Stay strong.'

She just smiles, confused, and turns back to face the front of the empty class.

After school, I find myself wandering the streets aimlessly. I don't want to get on the tube, to be subjected to the glares and prods of the brainwashed. I don't want to go home, where Clemmie will probably be crowing over Constantine's death. I don't even want to talk to Ollie. He saw what I saw. He was there in the observatory, and afterwards in the hospital. I want this pain to be mine for a little while. I don't want to have to support someone else. Not yet.

But I do need to talk to someone. Desperately.

I do what I swore I never would. I go down to the canal in Hackney, to the bridge where I last saw Lord Allenby in Ithr. I tell myself, right up until the last moment, that he won't be there; he'll have moved on.

And then I see him. He's still hunched over his pile of blankets and sleeping bags. His beard is a little more bedraggled, his hair less combed, but it is him.

'Lord . . . Sir?' I say, stopping at a distance.

He looks up through bleary eyes, and recognition shoots across his face.

'Fern,' he says, in a voice unused to talking. 'No. No, you shouldn't . . .'

I step forward, knowing that I am trampling all over his pride and desperate to make it okay. I gesture to my burn scar. 'I guess neither of us is quite what we look like in Annwn.'

Lord Allenby turns away from me, one hand pulling at the blankets around him.

'I'm sorry,' I say. 'I just . . .' The tears well up as the events of last night catch up with me. 'I really needed to talk to you.'

In an instant, he is there, leading me to the grubby blankets. He sits opposite me, neither of us knowing how to navigate this new truth. When I imagined our conversation, the words came easily, but in reality I can't tell him how I feel. How on earth can I complain about my own pain when his is evidently so much greater?

It's only now that I notice his black eye – the shadows beneath the bridge had camouflaged it. 'Sir, should you go to a hospital?'

'No, Fern, no. I've had worse. It'll pass.'

I can't help myself. I have to ask the question that sits between us. 'How?'

Lord Allenby smiles grimly. 'What happened all those years ago, with the treitre's – Ellen's – attacks on us. It took a toll, Fern, even on the survivors. I kept it together in Annwn but in Ithr . . .' His voice catches. 'I couldn't handle it. I had such terrible rages. My wife, she didn't feel safe. She didn't want our children around me when I was like that. I never harmed them,' he adds, seeing my expression, 'I'd *never* hurt . . . But I wasn't myself. It was best for them if I left. So I started spending more time in Annwn, and before I knew it, I'd lost my job.'

He rifles through one of the plastic bags and produces an energy bar. He offers me a piece, but I shake my head.

'Couldn't you go back to your family?' I say.

'No, no. Can't have them seeing me like this, can I?'

'But it's just . . . age. Experience. There's no shame in that, surely? Even if they can't know the truth?'

But he won't be persuaded. 'That's the end of it, Fern,' he says. 'I don't even know where they live any more. They're better off without me.'

I want to hug him, but I know that when I was at my most vulnerable, the last thing I'd have wanted was compassion from someone who should look up to me. I stand, feeling his desire for me to not be here. I fish around in my purse for coins.

'No,' he says sternly, seeing what I'm doing. Some of the Lord Allenby I recognise returns to his features. 'Please, I don't want it.'

I nod, but scribble my address on a scrap of paper and give it to him. 'If you ever need it,' I tell him.

We both know he'll never come to find me. He hasn't asked me not to tell anyone in Annwn about this. Maybe he knows that I would never betray his secret. As I walk away, I feel keenly how self-absorbed I've been. I've always been aggrieved by the necessity for Dad's penny pinching, the distance between my scholarship-funded place at Bosco and the pupils with rich families. But that wasn't poverty, not compared to this. I think of the kind of people who gave him that black eye, and then

I think of Shout Louder, arguing about responsibility when they should be *doing something,* for God's sake.

'Fern?' Lord Allenby says.

I turn.

'Don't let the anger get too much.'

'Sir?' It's as if he read my mind.

'I told myself it was worth it – that I had to lose my family to be the best knight I could be, to make sure Medraut got his comeuppance.'

He takes a bite of his energy bar.

'I think about that choice a lot, now. I'm not sure, if I had my time again, that I'd choose the same way. Something for you to think about.'

Chapter 51

I have no idea how to behave around either Samson or Lord Allenby when I see them again. Do I run up to Samson and kiss him back? Do I act cool? The more I think about it, the more doubt creeps in. Maybe he kissed me as a way of comforting me, and is already regretting it. Even if he doesn't regret it, how are we supposed to work so closely together in Bedevere while this – whatever it is between us – is going on?

And Lord Allenby . . . Knowing what happened to him to bring him to that bridge, only makes me admire him more. I can't help but make the comparison with my dad. Dad will do anything for a quiet life. Lord Allenby gave up his for the sake of the thanes. Dad sugar-coats everything. Lord Allenby is gruff and honest, sometimes brutally so.

By the time I arrive in Annwn, I've worked myself up into a tizzy. I linger in the cloisters, wondering whether I can delay going to the knights' chamber by talking to Rachel. But Rachel isn't at her desk. A pile of papers sits neatly on one side, pens on the other. I lift the cover of the top file, curious.

Lost contact with Bedevere, Rachel has written. *Attempted multiple times to make contact.*

At third sunset, sentinels reported veneur Brandon Wilson exited the building with a nightmare attached to his throat. Attempted to speak to veneur Wilson. Informed him that apothecaries were en route. Veneur Wilson did not reply. Knight Halder attempted to help Wilson, but he pushed her away and drew his knife. Attempted to persuade Wilson to wait for the apothecaries. He . . .

The handwriting blurs.

He wouldn't wait, even though I begged him to.

The account ends there. A seed of worry buries itself in my chest, but before I can go looking for Rachel, a reeve approaches.

'Lord Allenby wants –'

'. . . to see me. Sure.'

I look down at Rachel's notes again. 'Listen, can you do me a favour?'

The reeve nods eagerly.

'Can you check on the harker who sits here? Rachel? I'm worried about her.'

With the reeve's assurances that he'll find my friend, I jog on to Lord Allenby's office. The door opens as soon as I've knocked. Samson is standing there.

'You . . .' I stutter. My fears about Rachel had driven my fears about Samson from my mind. But now he's here, looking handsome and sombre and handsome, and I don't know what to say. If I'd been worried about seeing Lord Allenby and Samson separately, I'm doubly worried about seeing them together. I suppose I'd better rip the plaster off.

'Miss King.' Lord Allenby walks into view. 'Come in.' He looks as steady as ever, as though our conversation earlier today had never taken place.

I move past Samson, acutely aware of our proximity. His hand brushes my elbow. I don't dare to look at him.

'How are you now, Fern?' Lord Allenby says softly.

'I've been better, to be honest,' I reply.

'So, we think you completed the second task.'

'Yes. Or, well, I think so.' I realise something. 'I didn't see a third clue.'

'Given how the other one manifested itself, I'm guessing it will appear at the observatory somewhere,' he says. 'I'm sorry, Fern, I know it must be the last place you want to go but . . .'

'It's okay,' I lie. 'We can head over there now.'

'I'll send a party with you,' he replies. 'I have to talk to the other lords and ladies. I'm worried that Medraut's done this in other parts of the country. They'll need to be on the lookout.'

I don't get a chance to talk to Samson alone even when we're walking to the stables. Easa, Jin and Ollie are waiting outside the office for us and cleave to me as we move through the castle. It feels strange not having Brandon amongst them. He may not have been an original member of the Excalibur squad, but he had become indispensable with his encyclopaedic knowledge of animal behaviour.

I spot Rachel at her desk. She looks fine. Maybe I didn't need to worry about her after all. Just in case, though, I run over and hug her.

'Fern?' she says, surprised.

'Thank you for caring,' I whisper into her ear. 'You help us remember that it's not just a job.'

I rejoin the others before she can respond. By the time we

reach the stables, Samson has had to peel off to lead Bedevere out on patrol.

Lamb seems to understand that I'm fragile, because instead of butting me as she usually does, this time I get a tender nuzzle. I wish I could ask her whether she's worried for me or for herself. I wouldn't blame her one bit. I understand what's going on and my mind's still unravelling. Lamb and the other animals never had any choice over being part of Medraut's power games, yet they're still affected by them.

We set off together over the drawbridge. A garland of flowers tumbles out of the guardhouse, reminding me that only yesterday it was Ostara. Once again those celebrations have been ruined by Medraut's attacks. I haven't yet had the opportunity to sit with my friends and feast and laugh and enjoy being a knight. It seems like a petty thing to get angry about given everything else Medraut's done – but I know that he's done it on purpose. He gets grim satisfaction from ruining this moment.

Ollie reaches over and grips my arm hard. 'You were shaking,' he explains. 'It was irritating.'

I push him off. My heart is hammering. The faces and bodies of the dead dreamers, of those knights being eaten alive and choosing to end things on their own terms, keep flashing before me. I really, really don't want to go back to the observatory.

The doors are still wide open from yesterday. The whole place is silent.

'See anything?' I ask into my helmet.

'You're clear,' a harker's voice replies – it feels strange not hearing Rachel, but she's busy with Bedevere's usual patrol. 'We can see inside this time. Whatever shield Medraut placed over it has gone.'

We might not be safe, but there's a chance that Medraut doesn't have something else even more horrific waiting for us. Jin reassures us that the apothecaries and reeves have cleared the place of the other bodies – what was left of them.

'Will you bury them?' I ask, realising that I have no idea how this works in Annwn.

'No,' Jin replies. 'We place them next to a bridge – it doesn't matter which bridge. And within a night or so they'll disappear. Or sometimes they'll get up as dreams and fade away as they cross the bridge. It's pretty intense to watch.'

Lamb is not happy about me going into the observatory again. She follows me all the way to the entrance and even tries to step into the lobby until I tell her, gently but firmly, that I'll be fine. I don't think she believes me, but she walks off in a huff as if to say, *Well, if you get yourself into trouble again don't come crying to me.*

The harkers are right – the observatory is blessedly empty, showing no sign of what happened here just a day ago. We wander through the galleries, looking for any message from my mother. We meet up again in the main hall, shaking our heads. Nothing. Then Ollie runs his hands over the walls, and they erupt in light.

The second task you have fulfilled,
A trial of faith, a trial of love.
The third and final task you must complete

Before Excalibur is yours.
No power this time, but show what you are,
Five united in one, from deepest enmity.

'At last, one that makes sense,' Ollie jokes.

I try to erase the lines, knowing that there's a chance Medraut will see them. Hopefully his mind will be on other things; like why his experiment didn't go to plan.

As we ride back to Tintagel, the conversation ebbs and flows, but always around one purpose: what the final clue could mean. *Five united in one*. I pull the coin from my purse. Five jewels on one coin. Could it . . . ? I hold the coin up to the light, and my heart gives a little jolt. Three jewels are now coloured – blue, purple, green. I show it to the others.

'Maybe it's showing you how close you are to getting Excalibur?' Easa suggests.

I shake my head. 'I think it's something to do with the last clue.'

As we come into sight of Tintagel, though, all thoughts of clues and quests are driven from my mind. Because there, waiting for us beside the walls, are the Fay.

Chapter 52

Andraste and Nimue aren't amongst them. Puck is, though, and several others who I couldn't name. All of them Fay who were outraged at my mother taking Excalibur. Is it a war party?

'Fern?' Easa says. 'What do you want to do?'

'Chrissy, what's the deal with the Fay?' I say into my helmet to our temporary harker.

'Sorry?' the answer comes. 'What Fay? Where? Should I get Lord Allenby?'

So no one else can see them. What are they plotting? As we come closer, I take my scimitar out of its sheath, just in case. The Fay are barely moving.

'They don't look like they're about to attack us,' Jin says.

'It could still be a trick,' Ollie replies, echoing my own thoughts.

There's a bundle in their midst – human-shaped, but the limbs are twig-thin, and sprawled this way and that, like a spider that's been trodden on.

'Is that . . . ?' Ollie breathes.

Merlin. I dismount Lamb and approach the group. Puck raises his hand, a sign of surrender.

'What do you want?' I say, keeping my distance.

Puck seems to be warring with himself. It takes another of the Fay – an old woman with three eyes – to speak for him. 'Your help, girl. We need your help.'

'Why should we help you?' Ollie says, his chakrams poised.

'Please,' the woman says, gesturing to Merlin's prone body. Reluctantly, I approach him. He stinks. His ribcage was always prominent, but now a bone has broken through the skin, a white thorn protruding from his torso. I can't help but remember the dreamers last night, hollowed out. If the Fay had helped us all those months ago, then those dreamers might have lived.

'What can I do?' I say. 'Medraut's the reason for this. I can't help any of you without Excalibur.'

'Please,' the woman repeats. 'He is our all-father.'

'Arthur would have been able to help him,' Puck says. 'You must too.'

Merlin is pitiable. I kneel next to him, handing my scimitar to Easa for safe-keeping. I don't want the Fay trying to steal it from me when I'm distracted. I place a hand on Merlin's prone form, and instantly sense his age. The layers and layers of stories that have gone into his creation, all of them withering like a plant without water.

'*Can* we do anything?' Ollie asks.

Footsteps approach – Lord Allenby rounds the corner and stops dead as he surveys us. So he is able to see the Fay. They only made themselves invisible to the wider thanes. Jin fills Lord Allenby in on what's happening.

'We can help you,' he tells them, ignoring my shocked expression, 'but we want something from you in return.'

'Excalibur?' Puck says, his mouth twisting in disdain.

'Do you know where the Ladies Nimue and Andraste are?'

The Fay glance at each other, and, finally, they nod. 'They fled this country,' the old woman tells us. 'We are at war with them.'

'Well, not any more,' Lord Allenby says. 'They are not your enemies, and neither are we. So. Do you want Fern's help or not?'

Before I can reprimand Lord Allenby for making promises that I might not be able to keep, he stops me. 'Jin and I have an idea, Fern. I think it will work. Trust me.' And as the Fay converse, he tells me his plan. Well, Jin's plan, really. Born of all that research she did into Immral years ago, when she was my age, still trying to work out the limits of what she could do in this world. And born of what we've created in our puzzle box.

At last, the Fay turn back to us. 'We agree to your demands.'

Puck opens a wound in his palm by forcing it onto one of the spikes on his head, and shakes my hand firmly. Delightful.

I kneel beside Merlin, take Ollie's hand, and feel the force of our Immral flowing from my brother, to me, and into the ancient being before me.

'Jin, you first,' I say. And Jin begins to tell a story. A tale once told to her as a toddler, about an old woman giving her life for her grandchild. Then Lord Allenby picks up the thread, talking of a man who thought he knew what was best for his family, and how he ended up losing them instead. Easa begins to understand what is happening and tells his own stories. I pull some from Ollie's mind, too, feeling the push-pull of his imagination and memories. Together we give up so many tales, ones passed down from parents to children, ones absorbed through books and films, in the cadence of symphonies and the eurekas of scientists. I take all of them, and I add my own, spinning them into substance, sending them deep into Merlin's flesh.

His muscles begin to reform. His rib draws back inside his torso and the skin heals. He breathes deeper and deeper, his ribcage heaving with new strength. Until at last, when the sun is setting and my ears are bleeding, he sits up.

'You,' he says in wonder.

'We're not all evil,' I tell him.

Puck mutters to the old woman. She presses a hand upon her chest and, closing her eyes, murmurs words I cannot understand. A moment later, there's a flash of white light, and a rip opens in the fabric of Annwn. Through it, two figures appear, their silhouettes familiar.

Andraste and Nimue have returned.

I limp over to them. Andraste folds me into a hug, her half-face resting uneasily against my forehead. I touch the emptiness there. 'I could heal this too, if you want?' I say. 'I know how to now.'

She smiles. 'Perhaps later. There are more important things to do first.'

'Are you going to tell me about the third task?'

Nimue is kneeling next to Merlin, talking to him earnestly.

'Do you have the coin?' Andraste says.

I pull it from my pouch. 'I can't work out what it means . . . Oh.'

For there are now four coloured jewels. Only one remains clear.

'You are nearly there,' she tells me. 'Have you solved the final clue?'

I shake my head. 'It's impossible.'

'But it is not,' Andraste says, 'you have nearly completed it. *No power this time, but show what you are*.'

'*Five united in one*,' I say. 'So something to do with the five stones here. But how do I get the last one if I don't understand how I got the first four?'

'*United from deepest enmity*,' Nimue says, looking from Merlin to me.

Easa, understanding dawning, recites the verse he found on the pill box all those months ago, '*When all men saw mortal foes so friendly to agree*.'

It begins to slot into place. 'You mean I have to make people who were my enemies . . .'

'Into your allies. Without manipulating them with your Immral.'

I look at the others as we try to figure it out. Merlin was one. 'Constantine Hale,' Ollie says. 'He hated you, and then helped us last night.'

'And me,' says Jin. 'The second jewel got its colour after you and I became friends.'

'So who was the first?' I ask.

'Me.' Ollie smiles. 'I was the first.'

'The more important question,' Lord Allenby says, 'is who will be the last?'

'It will need to be big,' Andraste warns. 'A greater enemy than any of the others. Someone who truly hates you.'

I look up at the castle, an idea forming. 'I've got just the girl for the job.'

Chapter 53

I may see her every day in school, but finding Lottie in Annwn remains impossible. We try everything we can think of: I even delve into the mechanics of the Round Table again, instructing it to look only for her. The other thaneships are on alert too, but she seems to have vanished from this world. And without her here, I have no chance of completing the final task.

'Maybe we can find someone else for you to convert,' Ollie remarks. 'Quite a lot of people don't like you.'

'No,' I say, 'Andraste said it needed to be someone bigger than the others.'

But our time to find Lottie is running out. Medraut's influence is veering dangerously close to home. Much as I've sneered at Clemmie in the past, she has proven herself a loyal, sweet woman time and time again. These days she hums with unspent rage.

'Troublemakers giving us extra work again,' she spits as she lets herself in one evening when we're setting the table for dinner.

Ollie and I exchange a glance. 'Shout Louder?' I hazard a guess.

'You understand then,' she says, her irritation flowing off her in waves. 'And of course they know exactly what to do so that we can't arrest them. Push us far enough to send a message but not so far that we can actually charge them.'

'What have they been doing this time?' Dad says, more calmly, bringing stew to the table and taking Clemmie's coat.

'The usual. Shouting at anyone wearing the One Voice badge. Putting up posters and handing out leaflets.'

'Sounds truly criminal,' Ollie says, sharing a smile with me.

'Oh yes,' Clemmie says, 'I'd forgotten your *boyfriend* is one of them, isn't he?'

She says it with such disdain that Ollie shrivels. I gape at her.

'I like Kieran, love,' Dad says, patting her hand.

'So do I,' I say, rather more heatedly, 'and it doesn't sound like he's doing anything near as bad as what One Voice have been doing.'

'Well, I should have known you'd be one of them too,' Clemmie says, spearing a chunk of parsnip with her fork and tossing it into her mouth.

I start to retort, but Dad just says, 'Enough, please. I'd like to have a nice, quiet, polite dinner.'

Clemmie continues to eat in resentful silence. My brother is staring at his plate, his jaw clenched. Dad is placid as anything. And I see it – the two different sides of Medraut's army. The ones who, like Clemmie, are fully on Medraut's side and hate anyone who is remotely different to them. And the ones like Dad, who feel as though they should remain neutral in this war, thereby inadvertently handing Medraut his victory.

I squeeze Ollie's hand across the table. Clemmie's eyes

narrow and Dad sighs, acknowledging my small act of rebellion. From that moment, I know that I cannot trust her. It's a desolate feeling – I had come to think of her as a benevolent aunt. She might not understand me but she would at least look out for me. I wish I'd spent more time talking to her when she wasn't under Medraut's influence. Maybe then she'd have been harder for him to brainwash.

That night, I log on to the Shout Louder website and read some of their news. It's full of the stunts they've pulled – protest groups standing outside the One Voice offices; people lying in the street with tape over their mouths; banners and placards being held aloft at any gathering of Medraut's supporters. I spot Kieran at the forefront of most of them, and occasionally I'll get a glimpse of Sachi's black hair and boots. Then I click onto another page and see Ollie next to Kieran, hands held high together, shouting in the faces of One Voicers, who are holding their fists over their mouths. It's a video. I click the *play* button.

'Sheep!' Ollie is shouting.

'Degenerate,' comes the reply from the One Voicers, so quietly that it's hard to hear on the video.

'What did you say?' Kieran responds.

The man doesn't reply. Kieran takes Ollie's face in both his hands and kisses him, hard, on the mouth. I pause the video. So this is what Ollie's been up to in his spare time.

'I didn't realise you'd joined Shout Louder again,' I say to him later.

He shrugs. 'Just after Ostara. I wanted to do something to honour Constantine.'

'Are you finding it less pointless than you did before?' I ask, leaning forward. If Ollie says it's changed, that it gives him a purpose, then maybe I should reconsider too.

'I don't know,' Ollie says. 'Sometimes I worry that we're playing into Medraut's hands. We shout and he can just point at us and say, "Look, they're young troublemakers, making a lot of noise but not doing anything useful." But then what's the alternative? Just sit it out and hope we're not the next targets, like Dad?'

'Or me.'

'You're different. You're doing enough in Annwn.'

'Does Kieran think that?'

'You really want to know what Kieran thinks?'

'Of course.'

'He thinks you're so used to not wanting people to notice you that you're avoiding doing anything that would get you noticed.'

Maybe that is part of my reticence, but it's not all of it.

'Do you agree with him?'

Ollie shrugs. 'I don't think he's *wrong*, but I also don't think that's the main reason you're not joining. I can't tell him about that reason.' He grimaces and looks away.

'It must be hard,' I say, 'not being able to tell him about Annwn.'

'Yeah,' is all the reply I get. Given that I'm supposed to be the monosyllabic one, Ollie can sure give me a run for my money.

The next morning, I get up to find Dad in the kitchen pulling sweet batter out of the oven and drizzling it in honey. I'm still feeling bruised from last night, and he's not so far gone down Medraut's path that he doesn't notice.

'What is it, Ferny?' he says. 'Boy problems?'

'Not really,' I reply.

'It's not Clemmie, is it?' he says, sliding a slice of the batter onto a plate for me. 'I did tell her that she was out of line. She's just very stressed at the moment, love.'

'That doesn't really excuse it, but okay,' I snap back, but not so sharply that he might take my breakfast away.

'You're all so full of fight at the moment,' Dad says, tucking into his own plate, 'I can't keep up with you.' He looks at me piercingly. 'Did you join, in the end?'

'Shout Louder?' I say. 'No.'

'Good.' He catches my gaze. 'I know, I know, you don't like Medraut. But honestly, Fern, I'm pleased you're not getting involved in all that.'

'What, not standing up for what I believe in?

Dad looks surprised. 'Of course you should stand up for what you believe in. But you don't have to join a club to do that, do you? You were never a sheep, Ferny.'

He says it with something akin to pride, which knocks me. I suspected that Dad was trying to do right by me in his own way, but I never thought he really understood me, let alone was proud of me. I want to ask him whether he knows that Ollie is in Shout Louder, but that feels as though it's something old Fern would do, to try to get her brother in trouble.

Something in his words sticks, though. I'm on the tube to school, trying to ignore the fact that a girl not much older than me is holding her breath in disgust at being in such close quarters to me, when I hear a couple of blokes discussing Constantine's death.

'All of them are wrong 'uns . . .' one of them is saying.

'I'm not one to speak ill of the dead, but he got what he deserved if you ask me.'

I am suddenly aware of the polarisation in the carriage. It's gone very quiet. A handful of people are tense, casting angry looks at the couple. Most are smiling into their tablets and newspapers, offering tacit agreement.

'That lot were barely human in the first place,' one of the men is saying. 'Animals, more like.'

'That's right. No one blinks an eye when you shoot a rabid dog, right? Same difference.'

I can't help it. The tiniest gasp of shock escapes me. Immediately, a dozen eyes are trained in my direction.

'Got a problem, love?' one of the men leers.

I catch the eyes of one of the other people who were pursing their lips in disapproval, and they shake their head. I won't get any backup from them. Everyone else is either glued to their phones or books or meeting my gaze with open hostility. I should back down. *Be small, Fern, be insignificant, then maybe they'll lose interest*. That's what I've always done.

Look where it's got me, the girl with the burn scar.

'Yeah, I've got a problem, love,' I say. Energy flows through my chest, my arms, my hands.

The man smiles slowly. 'Did I hurt your feelings, little girl?'

'No, you didn't hurt anything,' I reply, my voice deep and quiet. 'I've faced down way worse than you. How dare you call innocent people who've died animals, when as far as I can see you're the only beasts here.'

The man snorts, and opens his mouth to say something, but his friend nudges him with a gruff, 'Leave it.' I still catch the flash of unadulterated hatred that crosses his features, but there's a shift in the mood of the carriage, and I think he's felt it too. A lot of the people who were silently agreeing with him have gone back to their own business, not so full of hatred that they're willing to back him openly. The ones who were on my side are now the ones smiling. My heart is hammering with nerves, but something is running through my blood. If I didn't know I was in Ithr, I'd mistake it for Immral.

Chapter 54

Samson's been avoiding me since the night he kissed me. Not overtly, of course – he still talks to me on patrol. He still smiles at me in a way that makes my insides twist. But he makes sure we're never alone together. He tries to make it subtle, but I can tell, and it hurts like nothing else. It's not the rejection – I could handle that. I can understand that he might have kissed me in a moment of needing a shared comfort. That would be far more understandable than him genuinely fancying me. It's the loneliness. The feeling that I've lost more than hope – I've lost a friend.

I try to distract myself by focusing on the quest for Excalibur.

'If you find the sword, you could smite Samson into the abyss,' Ollie jokes in Ithr, and I laugh, but part of me quite likes the idea. Jin, Easa and Rachel throw themselves into trying to find Lottie, unaware of my resentment towards my captain. In return, I spend more time in their company.

In the end, though, our lead to Lottie comes from the unlikeliest of places. We are heading away from our usual route to investigate reports of nightmare activity over in the film studios on the borders of west London. Our detour takes us past Bosco College. I've seen it once or twice in Annwn. It used to glitter with inspyre; all the knowledge and excitement for learning drawing the imagination to its bricks. Now, though, it sits silent and grey on the busy road. Utterly unremarkable. Except that it makes Cavall go crazy.

His barks even attract the attention of the nearby dreamers.

'What's got into him?' Nerizan says.

'He must hate Bosco even more than you,' Ollie jokes quietly, so that only I can hear.

But his reaction sparks something. I leap off Lamb's back. 'Cavall, here,' I say. 'Let me look at your tag again.'

I belong to Charlie.

Could it be? I have a distant memory – something Lottie once said to me – something about skiving off school to train her puppy.

'Cavall,' I say to the dog, 'are you Lottie Medraut's?'

Cavall wags, barks and licks me.

'You're shitting me,' Ollie says. I conjure an image of Lottie from my memory and hold it in front of the dog. He barks joyfully and tries to leap for the spectre of Lottie's face. I look up at Samson, astounded.

'All this time,' Samson says, shaking his head ruefully. 'No wonder he cottoned onto you, Fern. He could probably sense you knew her.'

'Cavall,' I say, 'can you find her? Can you take us to her?'

As Samson leads the rest of Bedevere onto patrol, Ollie and I tell Rachel of our plan and follow Cavall in the opposite direction.

'Are we sure this is going to work?' Ollie says. 'If not even the harkers can spot her, how is her dog going to?'

'Aren't dogs supposed to have a sixth sense for this kind of thing?' I ask.

'I think you're referring to smell,' Ollie says, 'which is very much part of the five.'

But Cavall seems to know where he's going. He presses his nose to the ground, never once distracted by the squirrels and other chaseable creatures who cross our path. He leads us across the river to a stretch of scrubland, empty but for clumps of dry grass, and a small concrete structure. An old bomb bunker.

'Rachel?' I say into my helmet. 'Can the sentinels see anything in there?'

The answer comes back a moment later. 'Nothing. Literally, nothing. Sorry, Fern.'

'Don't apologise, that's actually helpful. We know something's going on in there then.'

Ollie and I look at each other in trepidation. Could this be where Medraut is breeding those leech-like creatures we found at the observatory?

'Do we wait for reinforcements?' Ollie says.

'Do we want to risk Medraut finding us here?'

'Good point.'

We jump off Lamb and Balius and approach the bunker. I have to clench my fists to stop them from shaking. We round the corner and there, inside the open entrance, is Lottie. She is bound tightly to what I can only describe as a torture chair. Syringes with huge needles are inserted into her skull and back. Her eyes and mouth are sewn shut. She does not – cannot – move.

'Be careful of traps,' Ollie says. 'We don't want to get caught by a kalend gun like the one at their house.'

I close my eyes, using my Immral to search for spots where a weapon might be hidden. But there is nothing. Maybe Medraut thought that his shield and the remote location were enough. Cautiously, we untie Lottie and pull the syringes from her body. I don't dare unsew her eyes and mouth. That will be a job for the apothecaries. Through it all she remains silent, compliant. Cavall whimpers at her feet.

Then, taking a side each, we drag her out of the bunker and on to Balius's back.

'Go,' I say to Lamb, and the horses spring away towards Tintagel.

In the castle, the apothecaries do their best to patch Lottie up. There is some discussion over whether it's wise to unsew her eyes.

'I don't think I'm the only one to worry about how easy it was to get her out of there,' Lord Allenby says.

We all nod silently. None of us can shake the feeling that this is somehow a trap. But we couldn't leave Lottie there. Not like that. Ollie and I may have tracked her down to try to pass the third task, but once we saw what her father had done to her, our priorities shifted. She needed to be rescued, Excalibur or not.

Rachel has the idea to keep her in an empty tower room, heal her eyes there and lock her in, where it will be harder for her to escape. Two knights are assigned to guard the door at all times. It takes Jin a long time to remove the stitches. When Lottie finally opens her eyes, there is a white film over the pupils.

Ollie and I place our hands on Lottie's shoulders. The last time we did this, we ended up torturing this poor girl. We must be gentle with her now.

Lottie doesn't react as Ollie probes her memories. It's all familiar – every single one is of her father; brightly, sickeningly positive, as though he's expunged any hint of his wrongdoing – or as though she's done that herself to try to rationalise his torture.

'There's nothing here that's going to help you,' Ollie says eventually, and I'm forced to agree. We pull away, and I kneel in front of her, taking her hands in mine.

'Lottie? It's Fern,' I say softly.

Lottie's head turns sharply, as though she's trying to flick away a fly.

'Lottie, can you hear me? Can you see me?'

As if from a great distance, Lottie says, 'Yes.'

'Do you know who I am?'

Her eyes are still not focusing on anything, but she frowns, as though she's trying to concentrate. 'You are wrong.'

'Wrong? What does she mean?' Rachel says.

'I'm an aberration. That's right, isn't it?' I say.

'Yes.'

'That's what your dad's told you. But it's not what you really think,' I say. 'That's not what Charlie thinks.'

'Charlie?'

'That's you, isn't it?' I say, nodding at Ollie. 'You were Charlie once. Before your dad got his powers back. Charlotte Medraut.'

Ollie opens the door, and Cavall bounds in. He runs straight up to Lottie without pausing, and covers her face in licks, clambering into her lap with the kind of pure love only a dog can show. Lottie pushes Cavall away from her, as if she doesn't recognise him.

'You once told me that you skived off school to train your dog,' I remind her. 'What happened to him, Lottie? What happened to your dog?'

Lottie frowns again, but this time she genuinely sees Cavall. She looks down at him covering her hands in kisses and slowly, ever so slowly, raises one hand to cup his head. He leans into her grasp, encouraging her to scratch his ear. I keep watching Lottie, though. Because something is changing in her. It's not just that the white film is disappearing from her eyes; her whole demeanour is shifting. The Lottie I know is old for her years. There was always something lost in her eyes, as though she was playing a part. Now, her face opens up.

'Loco?' she says uncertainly. Her voice is different, too. Deeper, softer than the affected, high-pitched rah of Bosco Lottie.

Cavall – Loco – pants at her.

'What happened to him?' I ask again.

'I came home from school one day and he . . . Mum said he'd got sick. Dad said I must have left out something bad for him. He was always eating things he shouldn't have.'

'Do you think you did?'

'I don't remember but I must have.'

'I don't think you did, Lottie.'

'Dad said I did.'

'Loco likes to bark, doesn't he?'

Lottie nods, growing upset. 'I tried to make him stop, but he got excited.'

'Your dad didn't like that, did he?'

Lottie shakes her head, her lips a taut line. 'He was too loud.'

'Lottie. Charlotte. Charlie.' I make her look at me – she finally actually, really meets my eyes for the first time, and I can see the answer and the knowledge there before I have even asked the question. 'You didn't kill Loco, did you? You know what happened to him.'

Lottie stares at me for the longest time. I can sense the conflict inside her; the warring parts of the true Lottie, and the person her father has forced upon her. But I don't do anything. It is crucial that neither Ollie nor I use our Immral on her. She has to do this of her own free will. At last, ever so quietly, she says three words.

'I hate him.'

She folds over Loco, hugging him, smiling through tears when he starts licking her face, and then she begins to laugh. It's a free laugh, one I've never heard from her before. It comes easily – a throaty sound I can't imagine her father ever permitting.

I look up at Ollie, who just shrugs at me, nonplussed. 'Lottie?'

'Charlie,' she says, hugging Loco again, breathing him in. 'I used to prefer Charlie.'

'Charlie. Will you help us?'

'Help you what?'

'Kill your dad.'

Charlie wavers – the old mask clouds her features. But I have to tell her the truth if this is going to work.

'Really?'

'Do you know what he's planning on doing?' I ask.

She frowns again, then nods. 'Silence.'

'Silence. Everywhere. In here too,' I say, placing a hand over my heart. I feel it swelling in my chest, clamouring to be heard.

Charlie nods. 'Yes. Yes, I'll help you.'

I take the coin from my pocket and watch it, hoping that I'm right. Then, so gradually I hardly notice it, colour seeps into the final stone. Gold. The coin grows hot in my grasp, and melts, reforming into a new shape.

A key.

Chapter 55

The key rubs against my sternum as we canter towards central London. Every movement sends a jolt of its power through my flesh; a cold chain, a hot key. Andraste's arms are wrapped tightly around my waist, her body so slight now that Lamb barely feels the extra weight. Samson and Ollie ride on my right; Lord Allenby and Sachi on my left. She had seen us saddling up and insisted on joining. 'If you're going to bring him down, I'm going to be there,' she had said, in a voice that brooked no disagreement.

Andraste had showed me how to find the place, although she no longer had a voice. She had staggered to the Round Table and crawled a spindled hand to the centre of the mahogany, to a wide square where lions prowl. Then her palm came to rest on the building next to it. A building I know almost as well as my own house.

'Nearly there,' I tell Andraste every few minutes. And then we're passing down Charing Cross Road and we *are* nearly there. The looming buildings open out to reveal the majesty of Trafalgar Square. I have always loved this place, in both Ithr and Annwn. In Ithr not even the crowds of tourists can dampen the splendour of the huge marble lions guarding Nelson's Column.

In Annwn pixies leap into the fountains, trying to ride the dolphins and giant koi that swim there. The lions are not marble beasts but real, giant cats of beauty and terror – some of them tame; some of them less so.

But we're not stopping in Trafalgar Square. I leap from Lamb's back and help Andraste down. Ollie follows us up the steps of the National Gallery. I used to come here every week on my way home from Bosco and wander the corridors, dreaming that one day someone might think to place a Fern King artwork in these halls, long after I'm dead.

Andraste doesn't lead me so much as lean me to the right place. Soon we are deep in the bowels of the gallery, in the Renaissance hall, standing before a painting that I don't remember seeing before. It's gorgeously depicted in watercolours. A splash of blues picking out the energy of a stormy lake. Prostrate knights on a shore dashed in greys. And in the centre of it, an ivory arm reaching out from the water, clasping a sword that gleams gold and silver and copper under the candlelight. A shiver runs up my spine. *It's nearly done.*

As soon as I touch it, I know that this is no painting that exists in Ithr. It has been created by the Fay – I can taste the same age behind it. There's something else there, too – a consciousness that is waiting for me to work the right spell to bring it to life. The adrenalin that drove me from Tintagel to this spot seems to coagulate in my heart. Excalibur is here. Our chance to defeat Medraut. The ending to a story started by my mother sixteen years ago.

I drag the key from around my neck and run my hands over

the paint. In the centre there's a change in the texture of the watercolours, just where the hand grips Excalibur. A shifting of sands beneath a strong current. Under that, there's a surge of power waiting to erupt.

Something isn't right.

I can't explain it, but suddenly, every sense I have is telling me not to do this. But what choice do I have? This is our only chance of defeating Medraut. Mum had planned for me to have Excalibur. She can't have been wrong.

I press the key against the painting, and the image shifts. The sword sinks into the canvas, forming a keyhole. The key slips inside easily, but when I try to turn it, it's stiff. It's as though the painting itself does not want me to claim the sword. Against my better judgement – *something is wrong, something is wrong* – I use my Immral to force it.

When the lock finally twists, the image morphs. Watercolours melt and swirl. The sun pulses with incredible heat and becomes real, blinding light.

When the heat fades, and it is safe to look again, the painting is no longer there. Instead, the wall is bare except for an ornament protruding from the wall. No, not an ornament. It's the hilt of a sword. The pommel is golden, engraved with enamel of all colours. It is hypnotically beautiful.

'Take it then,' Ollie says shortly.

My hand hovers over the handle. Panic overwhelms me. The same doubt and fear that took hold of me when I was changing the Round Tables all those months ago. The throb of warning builds in my head, battling with temptation. The hilt is so very beautiful.

'What are you waiting for?' Sachi says.

In one swift movement, I pull the sword from the wall.

My brain explodes.

My hand, my arm, my entire body is on fire. Excalibur is burning me alive.

Through my agony, I hear someone entering the gallery. There's a scream, but I cannot move. I am lying on the ground, my fingers trapped around Excalibur's hilt as its power rages through me.

Soft footfalls approach.

Sebastien Medraut kneels, nudges my head with his foot so that I can see him.

'Well done, child,' he says.

I lurch back, pulling Excalibur with me despite the pain. 'It's mine,' I say thickly. 'You can't have it.'

Medraut smiles indulgently. 'Shall we test that theory?'

He pulls Excalibur from my grasp, as easily as if he were plucking a flower. The sword wanted to be wielded by him, I realise. The pain subsides, and I scramble to my feet. I have lost. We have all lost.

Jin lies on the floor, a puddled lump. Her foot twitches. She's alive. Ollie and Samson and the rest are pushed up against the other wall, Medraut's Immral too strong for them to overpower. I cannot see Andraste.

Mum was wrong. So were Andraste and Nimue. It didn't matter that I passed the test – somehow, Medraut has bypassed whatever controls they placed upon the sword. And he doesn't seem to be in pain. He hefts Excalibur with one hand, sweeping it through the air, and inspyre dances around it like aurora. He looks complete.

'How?' I whisper.

Medraut looks at me. 'This time it is *you* who underestimated *me*. I know more than Una ever did.'

He holds out his spare hand and twists it, and the puzzle box materialises. His endgame, so close now. All he needs to do is to climb to a great height, and then it will be time for him to put his plan into action. I can't give in to despair, not yet. I have to delay him, until I can work out a way to wrestle Excalibur from him, whatever the cost.

'How did you get into Tintagel?' I ask, nodding towards the box.

'Why don't you ask your dear leader?' Medraut says, looking at Lord Allenby, who is still frozen in place. For a sickening moment I think that our commander has betrayed us all, but the confusion on his face cannot be an act.

'Not like you to forget things, Lionel,' Medraut says. He flicks his head, and I am inside someone else's memories.

I see the clues Medraut put in place to nudge me to complete the tasks; the tasks he knew were meant for me and not for him. I see him place Lottie just so, understanding that he would never truly break her will and realising that he could use that to his advantage, ripe for Ollie and me to turn to our cause. I am watching a thousand experiments at once, each one refined until there is no way of telling that he is controlling someone – each one a reaction to the very processes we put in place to detect his Immral.

Then the trick of planting invisible seeds in the right minds. Catching them when they left the castle grounds, or sending an innocent, injured dreamer in to infect them. Testing on lesser targets: like showing someone how to reach the archives undetected . . . Until he was ready to take back what was his: Lord Allenby, zombie-like, handing his keys to Natasha. Natasha, her eyes glazed, trudging up the stairs to the turret and taking the box from its safe. Then the final truth. Rachel taking the box from Natasha and wrapping it in her tunic. Leaving the castle and walking a few streets to where Medraut is waiting. He manipulated all of them, made them do it without them even realising. He knew that if I could get Excalibur that he could take it from me. Mum knew him, and his weaknesses, and made sure he wouldn't be able to pass her test. But Medraut knew Arthur, and he knew that the sword would answer, ultimately, to power.

Suddenly, I am so very afraid for Rachel. I have to pray that Medraut is only allowing those of us in this room to see these memories. Rachel must never know what she has done.

'No,' Lord Allenby whispers, 'I didn't . . .'

But Medraut is done. He sweeps Excalibur once more and points it at me. Execution time.

Then something falls on him from above. Andraste, what is left of her, wrestles with Medraut for the sword. 'Go!' she hisses at me. 'Run!'

Her attack has startled Medraut enough that the others are released from their positions against the wall. Ollie and Samson take my hands and race for the door. Lord Allenby, Jin in his arms, isn't far behind us. As we reach the door I turn, determined to wait for Andraste. She might not be strong enough to kill Medraut, but she's Fay – she'll escape, she'll do something to buy herself time.

But Medraut is holding Andraste by her throat, lifting her bodily from the floor. She cannot fight him off.

I try to go to her, I do. I try so hard but I'm weak, and Samson and Ollie won't let go of me. All I can do is watch helplessly as my darling Andraste, my second mother, struggles against his grip. Then he does something, and she stills.

His words are quiet, almost a whisper, but I can hear them as clearly as if he was saying them right into my ear.

'*Your stories are forgotten.*'

He clenches his fist – the one holding Andraste's slender neck – and she crumbles. Just breaks apart into fragments of dust and metal shards, as though she was never alive, as though there was never a beating heart and a wilful mind inside her body. Andraste is no more.

Chapter 56

She couldn't even look at me. I couldn't say goodbye.

I reach for the dust that was once my guardian angel.

Ollie wrestles me to my feet. 'Fern, we've got to go or he'll kill us too. Come on. Come on!' A dozen hands half pull, half carry me from the building. Behind us, Sebastien Medraut is preparing his final victory. I can feel his presence from across the hall, even when Ollie and Samson drag me into the open air. The urge to obey his command. The voice at the back of my mind, telling me to *just give in – it would be so much easier, so much simpler*. I have never felt this way before – not even when I stood right in front of Medraut and listened to him speak. His power now is unimaginable.

We race across the landing outside the National Gallery, down the steps towards Lamb and Balius and the other horses. One moment, the square is nearly empty. The next, it is full. Bubbles of inspyre burst across the concrete, signalling an arrival. In a matter of seconds, the square is packed with dreamers, every one of them silent. Every one of them facing the gallery. Waiting for their leader.

We move to the side, trying to see a way out, but the dreamers move as one, blocking our way. Lamb whinnies, trying to reach me, but I can no longer see her. I try to send a mental message to her, telling her to return to the castle, to stay safe.

I feel Medraut's presence before I hear his footfall. Fearfully, I turn to face him. In one hand he holds Excalibur, the sword's blade alight with inspyre. He surveys the dreamers who have answered his telepathic call. The streets beyond the square are now full too. There is going to be no easy escape for us.

He raises Excalibur aloft, and the mouths of every dreamer in sight disappear.

Then he turns towards me and my friends. 'Don't worry,' he says softly, 'I haven't forgotten about you.'

'Go!' I shout, pushing the others away with my mind as well as my hands. Excalibur emits a burst of light that leaves a deep pit in the stone steps where we were standing. I fling myself into the air, avoiding another blow from Medraut. Lord Allenby and Samson are ushering Sachi and the rest of the thanes away from the crowds. Hopefully they'll be able to get to safety before Medraut turns his attention to them. Let's just hope I can stay alive while he's focused on me.

I think about diving into the crowds, but that would only sentence others to death as well. Medraut won't hesitate to kill dreamers alongside me. I could justify killing the treitres last year – they were paid assassins, fully aware of what they were doing. These dreamers may well turn on me, but they are being manipulated by Medraut. I have no doubt that many of them would be devastated to find out, if his influence were ever lifted, what they had been made to do.

I fly up, up, trying to make myself as difficult as possible to reach. I swoop over the National Gallery's roof and out of Medraut's eyeline. Hopefully that will buy me some time.

'Fern?' I hear Samson's voice over the helmet. 'Fern, are you there? Are you okay?'

'I'm here,' I whisper. 'Where are you?'

Samson begins to answer, but then another voice – one who shouldn't have access to the helmets – speaks.

'*Too loud,*' Medraut taunts.

'Move, Samson!' I hiss, unsure whether Samson heard Medraut or whether that message was for me alone.

There's a low boom from the direction of Trafalgar Square, and a flash of bright blue light. A strange wind passes by me – *through* me. It tastes of Medraut's Immral. Inside the wind is a command. *Listen to me. Obey me. Come to me now.*

It reaches far across the city and beyond. This is the power of Excalibur – it magnifies Immral's normal scope, but only if you have the strength to wield it. For like power itself, Excalibur demands a price for its potency, and I was lacking. Across the country, maybe even beyond our shores, Medraut is extending his influence over anyone whose minds aren't able to withstand him. I imagine my dad, already so soft and avoidant of conflict, appearing in that square, his mouth disappeared, ready to do Medraut's bidding.

Racing across the rooftops, I peer down, trying to spot Samson and Ollie and Sachi and the rest. All I can see are dreamers stretching into the distance, every one pushing to get to Trafalgar Square, to be closer to their new god. Maybe my friends are hiding amongst them, but if they are I can't see them. I can't feel them either, in the clamour of bodies below me.

'*Fern!*' I hear to my left.

There they are, hiding on a neighbouring rooftop. I fly over to them, kneeling down behind a chimney. Jin is weak, but awake.

'We have to get Excalibur off him,' Lord Allenby says.

'How?' Ollie says. 'You saw how powerful it made him. He'll kill us in a second.'

'If we don't he'll kill us anyway,' I say. 'Maybe not today, but at some point he'll end up hunting us. Or he'll get his followers to. We're never going to be far from death as long as he has that sword.'

We look at each other, trying to work out how to do this when we know we don't stand a chance.

'You figured out how to defeat the treitres,' Jin says quietly. 'You can work this out too, Fern. I know you can.'

Jin's belief is supposed to make me feel stronger, I know, but it has the opposite effect. It was chance that I worked out how to defeat the treitres. I've never been good at planning – I work impulsively.

'Okay, Jin, you need to get back to Tintagel,' I say, thinking on my feet.

'No, I can help –'

'You can,' I tell her, then lower my voice. 'You need to make sure Rachel's okay.'

She looks stricken that it hadn't occurred to her, then nods. She limps away, finding an air vent that will take her to the ground and out without being noticed.

'Backup's on its way,' Lord Allenby says, predicting my next question. 'They should be here soon, if they can get around the crowds.'

'Look.' Samson points to the sky, where every knight in Tintagel is flying through the air to reach us.

'Yes,' Sachi breathes, but there's another noise from Trafalgar Square. A fireball. There's a moment where I can see it heading straight for the knights, and the next second it explodes, knocking three from the sky.

We're all on our feet in an instant, focused on the steady stream of fireballs heading towards our comrades. I reach out towards them with one hand as Ollie takes my other without hesitation. His power joined with mine gives me just about enough strength to swing the first fireball out of the way, diverting it towards a neighbouring building. I have to hope there aren't any dreamers inside when it hits.

Medraut anticipates my move with the other fireballs, because nothing I do changes their course. They hit true, taking down knights and, when they drop to the ground, dreamers too.

'Get down!' Lord Allenby says through his helmet. 'Come through the crowd, just try to blend in.'

We have to wrestle Excalibur from Medraut's grasp. I have to get back to Trafalgar Square. I have to face him.

My own despair is mirrored in my friends' faces. 'I'm sorry,' I say. 'I'm just going to have to go over there and hope . . .'

'No,' Ollie says fiercely. 'He'll kill you.'

'Well, I'm all out of ideas,' I say.

'This isn't all on you, Fern,' Samson says quietly. 'It never was. You might be the most powerful one of us, but you're not the only one with a brain.'

'He's right,' Lord Allenby says gruffly. 'You're not alone in this Fern. We're here. Use us.'

So I do. We find an air vent and hunker down in it as a group, trying to ignore the growing sense of energy that is emanating from the square. At last, we are ready.

'Shall we?' Samson says, looking at me and Ollie.

I nod. 'Let's go.'

We run, staying as low as possible, over the rooftops, back towards Trafalgar Square. Lord Allenby, who is coordinating the rest of the knights, maintains a constant volley of information through our helmets, quietly keeping me sane and focused. No matter that Medraut can probably hear us. Let him. Let him hear Lord Allenby and Samson and Ollie and me. Let the chorus of our voices deafen him.

My head is pulsing with the energy that Excalibur is emitting.

We crawl over the roof of the National Gallery once more, and see what Medraut has been up to. He is standing atop Nelson's Column – the commander who once rested there, and whose statue exists there in Ithr – has vanished. Medraut has found his great height. A place not only tall in reality – but tall in people's imaginations too. He is holding Excalibur aloft, and inspyre is crackling from it like lightning striking a mast. The puzzle box is before him, ready to be opened.

We are out of time.

Chapter 57

'Go,' I say, and a dozen knights break cover from the streets, trying to distract Medraut from what Ollie and I are doing. I throw myself from the side of the building, into the depths of the crowd below. To my left a hubbub begins. This was Sachi's idea – to remind dreamers that they *do* and *should* have voices, and that they must use them.

'Rise up!' they shout. 'Rise up!' Then Sachi begins to sing – a heartfelt aria about grief and loss and trying to find the courage to keep on going through it. My heart floats to meet her voice. She may be singing about despair but suddenly all the hopelessness that was inside me is being sucked from my body. Then Niamh and the other knights take up the tune, and their harmony swirls with the futility in the air around us, filling the void of Medraut's majesty with a different kind of power – one made up of many voices, not just his.

I push through the dreamers, raising my hands in the direction of the fountains. *Remember what you did inside his fortress?* Samson had said as we plotted and planned. *You showed the inspyre what it was capable of. That's the only way to make it forget his command*. I make dolphins and krakens that erupt from the water in joyful play. The lions, which now are solid stone, as they would be in Ithr, shake their manes and become golden, living beings once more. They stretch and roar, and the dreamers who had been so focused on Medraut inch away. Some of them have the outlines of mouths returning to them.

We can do this, I think, right before a pack of mouthless dreamers bears down upon me.

They are clawing at me, tearing at my clothing, my hair, my ribs. One of them places his fingers over my eyes and presses down. I kick out, knowing that despite the pain these people aren't my enemies. They aren't acting of their free will. But I also know that that won't stop them from killing me. I try to throw them off with my Immral, but Medraut's control over them is too solid.

Knowing that if I survive this my soul will be scarred with guilt, I free my scimitar from its sheath and rake it upwards. There's the silent sound of falling bodies, and the pressure on my eyes eases. I struggle to my feet, surveying the carnage. Sachi's song is still there in the background, but it's being drowned out by the sounds of my friends battling their way to join me at the base of Nelson's Column.

I call to the living lions with my mind, and because all of Medraut's power is focused on influencing dreamers, they hear me. That's good to know – Medraut wants the people, not the inspyre. For someone who can control imagination, he has only ever been interested in the basest aspect of his power.

The lions stride towards Samson and Ollie, protecting them. I look up. Medraut is unbothered by our rebellion. He holds Excalibur aloft, and I'm sure that he smiles at me as I leap upwards, trying with all my might to throw myself in the way of that sword. But I'm not strong enough – a surge of dreamers grabs my ankles, pulling me to the ground. With a sonic boom Medraut brings the sword down upon the box, plunging it into the mahogany as though the wood were oil. For a moment everything, everywhere, stops. I can feel the change in the marrow of my bones.

When Ollie and I had read the puzzle box before, we'd seen glimpses of what Medraut wanted for Ithr and Annwn. It's nothing like so neat now. Now there's just a sensation, a fundamental shift in the atmosphere. In the way of thinking. I can feel it everywhere, like a cold wind blasting through the square, except now the wind is malice, singularity of voice, sole purpose.

Any dreamers who still had mouths instantly lose them. They turn on the knights, but this time they are coordinated in their attacks. Medraut's targeted hatred has given them an ability they wouldn't normally possess.

'Help!' I hear someone crying. The dreamers have Natasha. Great chunks of her flesh are being torn from her body. A gouge is taken from her cheek, another from her shoulder.

'*No!*' I cry, directing the lions towards her. But they are not needed. Niamh swoops in, one hand directing her wheelchair through the air, the other flinging the wheels like discs at the dreamers who hold Natasha. She grabs my friend from their clutches and takes out a whole swathe of dreamers with one sweep of her weapon.

But even with Niamh's skills, everywhere I look, my fellow knights are being torn down. They're pulling their punches, even though they have to fight to survive. It's been trained into us to protect dreamers, no matter what their nightmares are making them do. Samson has not, as far as I can tell, killed anyone even though he's more than capable of it. But it's beginning to show on him – he's bloodied and weary. If he doesn't put his principles aside, they'll kill him.

I try to fight my way over to him, but Sachi reaches me first. A cut glances from one side of her face to the other.

'We've got to get the sword, Fern,' she pants. 'Nothing else matters.'

'But –'

'No one. Else,' she says. She knows what I was planning.

She's right. I might be able to protect Samson momentarily, but that's all. Sachi and I brandish our weapons, since my Immral is useless against the dreamers. As I slash left and right with my scimitar, as Sachi punches the dreamers back with her spear, I call to the inspyre around me: every piece that is still left in the paintings inside the gallery. I call to the horse statues in Piccadilly Circus, and the soldiers and noblemen and women who adorn the pedestals of Buckingham Palace. Everything that still has some remnant of artistry and imagination. I call to it and I tell it to rise up against the man who would destroy it.

Nothing happens.

'Climb up!' Sachi shouts, pushing me up the column and holding the dreamers off with her spear. I clamber up, imagining claws on my fingertips to help me find purchase in the rock. The dreamers are wrestling Sachi's spear away from her.

'Here!' I shout, and throw her my scimitar. She wields it

inexpertly, but it's enough to keep them from tearing her down as well.

From my vantage point, I can see my friends still fighting. Ollie throws himself out of the scrum, landing on the other side of the column. I press my hands against his, giving him the same spider-like abilities.

'Come on!' I shout down to Sachi. She swipes once more at the dreamers and clambers up. Ollie is above me now, gaining height quickly. I follow him. Then I look back down, and my heart stops.

Sachi is clinging on to the stone, but the dreamers have her legs. I reach down, trying to pull her up with my Immral, but the dreamers, imbued with Medraut's power, are too strong.

'Take my hand!' I shout at her. She looks up, reaching for me. She grasps my outstretched fingers, clinging to them as the dreamers tear at her feet and legs. She does not scream. She doesn't make a sound.

'Fern!' Ollie shouts. 'Fern!'

I look up, my shoulders straining with the effort of holding Sachi. Ollie is at the top of the column, waiting for me, but as I watch Medraut bodily lifts him from his place. The sounds of my brother's screams rake at my heart. I have to get to him, but I cannot leave Sachi.

'It's okay, Fern,' she says.

I look down. She is calm, despite the terror in her eyes. I can feel it in her bones, and that's strange because I shouldn't be able to feel her emotions at all. That was always Ollie's strength.

'It's okay,' she says again. She smiles at me. A sad, accepting smile.

'No,' I whisper. Ollie screams again. 'No, Sachi . . .'

She lets go. I reach down, trying to grab her arm, her wrist, anything, but I'm too slow. The dreamers fall upon her. The last I see of her is her closing her eyes, folding her arms, permitting the inevitable.

Chapter 58

I cling to the column for a second and no longer. I cannot think about what's just happened. Sachi did this so that I could save Ollie and get Excalibur, and that's what I'm going to do. With a cry of rage I clamber up the column and over the precipice. Ollie is pinned to the floor, the stone that supports us moulded into spikes that are pushing their way through his body. No quick death for the rival Immrals. Medraut needs us to understand, before we die, exactly how useless we are.

The stone forms into spikes around me, too, trying to imprison me. In the centre of the pedestal is the puzzle box, Excalibur still thrust through it. Medraut has one hand on the sword, leaching its power for his own. The other hand is manipulating the stone.

Ollie reaches for me, and I reach for him. Our fingertips touch.

'Sweet,' Medraut says, and brings a boot down on our conjoined fingers with such force that our hands are crushed. I close my eyes against the pain, against Ollie's screams, and I focus on the call I made earlier. *Rise up*, I plead, *I know you're still there. I know it.*

My brain bursts, and that tells me that it's worked. Whether it will be enough is another matter. The crushed fingers that are still touching Ollie's prickle with our shared Immral. There's a distant noise. Medraut snarls.

A huge wave of inspyre is crashing through the streets –white light flooding, ready to drown us all. I welcome it, I call to it, and it answers me as inspyre has never answered me before. With the remnants of my broken brain, I forge it into myriad monsters and a thousand dreams. Flying horses to replace the ones we cannot reach through the scrum; hulking, many-limbed beasts that provide a canopy to my friends; and in the centre a snake, as strong as I can make it, that flings itself at Medraut and wraps around his arms and legs, stopping him from doing any further damage.

We still need to wrestle the sword from his grip. A vulture made of inspyre lands on the pedestal and rips up the stone shards pinning Ollie and me to it. We scramble to our feet. Our Immral isn't strong enough to hold Medraut for long. He manages to free one hand, and uses it to grasp the snake's body. I feel the power in his grip. I reach a hand out to try to grab the snake myself, but it retreats from me, its loyalty wavering before Medraut's command. Before my eyes, the inspyre creating the snake unravels, untwists itself, and bursts into green flame. Medraut locks eyes with me, and though he says nothing, I can tell what he's thinking.

See how I destroy this thing you have made? This is how I will destroy everything.

I am almost lost in those violet eyes, when there's a *twang* and Medraut is knocked off balance. An arrow from a crossbow, embedded into his shoulder. They are there, all of those still alive: Samson, Niamh, Natasha, Lord Allenby and the rest, each of them astride one of the flying creatures I made. Each of them directing their weapons at Medraut.

Medraut snarls again. He raises Excalibur. I can feel the power building in his wrist. He's going to knock my family out of existence. Ollie and I leap on him as one, wrestling his arm down, away, while the others shoot their bullets and arrows at him. Medraut uses his other hand to shield himself, disintegrating their missiles before they hit. But then we're not alone on the platform. The dreamers have clambered up and are ripping us apart.

We cling on, desperately trying to tear Excalibur away from Medraut. Ollie is weakening. He catches my eye.

'Don't you dare,' I say.

He's struggling to reach his chakrams, and my scimitar was lost when Sachi fell. I try to reach them for him, but the dreamers have my arms now. They are pulling me away from my brother, from Medraut, intent on throwing me off the platform into the chaos below. I try to wrestle them off with my Immral, but everything I have is concentrated on keeping my friends alive.

'Help him!' I shout, trying to raise my voice above the commotion. 'Help Ollie!'

'No!' Ollie shouts. 'Help Fern! Help Fern!'

There's another *twang* and the dreamers holding Ollie fall away, one with Samson's arrow in his chest; one with Lord Allenby's. It's enough time for Ollie to pull his remaining chakram from his belt before more dreamers attack.

'Catch it!' he shouts, flinging the chakram towards me. Then he is gone, pulled from the platform.

'Ollie!' I scream, but I manage to wrestle one arm free and catch the weapon by its blade. My hand oozes blood as the metal cuts deep into my flesh, but I don't let go. I slash at the dreamers holding me, and they fall back.

But with Ollie and me no longer holding Medraut, and Lord Allenby and Samson focused on helping us, it's given Medraut time and strength enough to ward off the others' attack. I can't get to him before he raises his arm. Excalibur emits a pulse of impenetrable light. Vast power is building inside it. I don't have time to get to Medraut. But I do have my brother's chakram. I release all the Immral I've been using for the others. I use all of it instead to guide the chakram as I throw it towards my enemy.

The blade hits Medraut's arm at the elbow, and I force it onwards; on through the flesh and the veins, on through the bone, through the cartilage and muscle, and out the other side.

The pressure in my head lifts immediately. I kick the remaining dreamers away; without Medraut bolstering them, they have lost their superhuman strength. They tumble off the column to the ground far below. Medraut is bleeding from his severed arm but like Sachi, he is silent. He is already reaching for the sword with his other hand. He kicks at me as I scramble across the bloodied, slippery stone to reach it.

'No, you don't, Sebastien,' Lord Allenby growls, and there's a thud as one of his arrows hits Medraut in the other shoulder. Medraut grunts, and tries to bat away the flurry of missiles coming towards him. He manages to erect a shield with his

Immral, but he must be in such pain that that's all he can manage. And then I'm there, reclaiming the sword. I don't have time to think about what it might do to me. I just have to make sure Medraut doesn't get hold of it again.

I fling Medraut's disembodied forearm from the weapon, and seize the hilt.

So. Much. Pain.

The power of Excalibur flows through me. Its ancient might takes hold of my meagre half-Immral as though it were a wolf shaking a rabbit. I am prepared for it this time.

Medraut knows that I cannot handle the power I've grasped. He smiles, leans down as if to pluck it from me once more. With what's left of my strength and my sanity, I wrestle my Immral into focus, and channel it through Excalibur. The sword listens, for a moment. It looks outwards instead of inwards. It leaches my power from me, greedily using up everything I have.

I point Excalibur's tip at Medraut. *Kill him*, I think.

Medraut's eyes widen, as though he's heard my thoughts. Maybe he has.

Light bursts from Excalibur's tip. But I'm too late. Medraut has activated his portal and disappeared before I can finish the job.

It was all for nothing.

I sweep Excalibur round, trying to return the dreamers' minds to them. I see them differently with the sword in my hand. Some of them are black holes where inspyre can no longer penetrate. Others flicker with red spots – the promise that imagination could still be born. Those are the ones I focus on, trying to reignite that flame. I have to try to undo whatever Medraut did. But it's so painful. Excalibur is draining my life force.

'Fern, stop!' Lord Allenby says. He's on the pedestal beside me.

'I have to –'

'Fern, it's going to kill you.' That's Samson.

He takes hold of my arms, but my skin sparks with Immral, burning him, warning him away. No one can touch me. I am on fire, I am immortal, I am . . .

'Hey. Hey. Fern.' My brother. He's safe. He places his hands on me and doesn't draw away. The fire runs into him as well, cooling me, sharing the burden of this mighty sword. He pulls my arm down.

'Ollie, we have to.'

'Fern, listen to me,' he says, drawing me in to a hug. 'You need to let go of Excalibur, okay?'

'But –'

'Trust me.'

With a great effort, because it feels as though it is cleaved to my flesh, I drop the sword. It clatters to the ground, and my eyesight returns. The pain lingers, as though the fire is still ravaging my bones. I raise a hand to my face and realise that I must have been bleeding from my eyes again. That must be why Ollie told me to stop.

I look around at the devastation in Trafalgar Square. The dreamers that just a moment ago were attacking us now mill aimlessly, wending their way through London, or through portals to other parts of Annwn. So many of them still don't have mouths. Some of them have the backs of their heads entirely eroded. I could not reverse most of the damage Medraut did.

I am so tired. So very tired. I look back at my friends, wanting them to carry me back to Tintagel. They recoil in horror.

'Fern, your eyes,' Samson says, 'they're . . .'

'They're not red any more,' Lord Allenby finishes.

'What?' I open my hand to conjure up a mirror from some inspyre. Nothing happens.

I'm just tired. I call to the part of my brain that houses my Immral, taking deep breaths – it will only work if I'm calm. I just need to calm down. *Calm down, Fern.*

Silence. I stand there like an idiot, trying not to panic.

'Here,' Samson says, passing me one of Ollie's chakrams – the one still covered in Medraut's blood. He rubs it clean and holds it in front of me, turning the weapon into a mirror. I stare at myself. My burn scar is still there, faintly. But my irises are no longer red. They're the colour they would have been if I never had Immral. They're beautiful. They're hazel.

Chapter 59

I am numb as we return to Tintagel. Medraut's eyes changed too, when the morrigans took his power from him. It took him more than a decade to regain his strength. I barely hear Samson's muttered reassurances, or see the shocked faces of the harkers who greet us as we ride over the drawbridge. I avoid their eyes. Everyone else retreats to the castle, either to care for the wounded, to mourn our losses, or to spread the news of what happened in Trafalgar Square tonight.

Me? I stay in the stables, grooming Lamb long after the others have melted away. She keeps nuzzling me, checking I'm okay. My first instinct is to give her a sugar cube, and I keep having to remind myself that I can no longer make sugar cubes for her. Every realisation is a new jolt of emptiness: I might not even be able to ride the same way – so much of my riding talent was tied up in my Immral, in my ability to override Lamb's former riders' memories. What if I no longer have that bond with her? What if –

'It's time to go in, Fern,' Ollie says softly. I hadn't even realised he was still here. I know he's right – I'll have to face it all at some point, and there are others in the castle I need to check on. Jin and Rachel and Natasha. But I can't bear the thought of people staring at me in pity. Or will they be angry with me? Angry that I wasn't strong enough to wield Excalibur the way we'd all hoped?

As I walk up the steps and through the huge doorway, I shrink, turning back into the hunched girl who hid inside her hoodies. Ollie may be beside me, but I am alone. We have been separated yet again, brother and sister.

The walk to the knights' chamber is endless.

Then I sense someone walking on my other side. Rachel. Pale, red-rimmed eyes, but alive. She takes my hand. 'Chin up,' she says, smiling softly. Someone else joins us, next to Ollie. Samson. He looks down at me with such intensity that I blush. And then others are coming forward to flank me: Niamh, Easa, Amina and Nerizan, Jin and Natasha, both limping and bloody. Their presence bolsters me.

We come to a halt in the grand hallway under Tintagel's dome, where a group of thanes is listening to Lord Allenby. 'We have to be more wily,' he is telling them. 'We have to remember that the only way we'll win this war is by working together. This was never about just one person . . .'

I know what he's doing, and why he's doing it – he wants to reassure them that I was never going to be the saviour. It still stings. It's as though he's erasing everything that I was and did.

Later, in private, Lord Allenby tells me, 'You must remember that your Immral will come back. Don't lose hope.'

I watch him write a message to the Fay and burn it in the little shrine in his office. Neither of us talk about what we saw Medraut do – the way he killed Andraste. The memory of it is a permanent rebuke. All that faith Mum put in me – the lengths she went to in order to deceive the Fay – all for nothing. Worse than nothing: if I hadn't looked for Excalibur, maybe Medraut would never have been able to find it by himself. And now, without my half of the Immral, Ollie and I have no way of bringing Andraste back. She is gone for as long as it takes for my Immral to return. If I survive that long.

Lord Allenby hands me a glass of fiery lotus juice, and knocks one back himself. I remember how devastated he had been to learn of the part he played in returning Medraut's puzzle box. I am not the only one Medraut tricked. I think of what happened to Lord Allenby in Ithr the first time Medraut made it clear how powerless the thanes are to stop him.

'Are you alright, sir?' I ask him.

'I should be asking you that,' he says, the wrinkles around his face deepening into rivulets.

I shake my head. 'I don't think any of us are going to be alright, are we?'

'Not for a while, maybe,' he replies, 'but there is always light, somewhere, even in the darkest of places.'

I'm not sure I believe him.

For the first time since I joined the knights, I am looking forward to returning to Ithr. There, at least, I know who I am. In Annwn I am lost.

As Ollie and I traipse towards the platform portal, Samson catches up with us.

'Can I talk to you, Fern? Before you go home?'

I look at Ollie, who shrugs and carries on walking. Samson gestures towards the cover of a willow tree that sheds its leaves onto the roof of the stables. We wander over, and I watch as the leaves fall to the ground. Gently, but continuously. Medraut's power is getting stronger – the willow tree is dying.

'Fern,' Samson says, 'are you listening to anything I'm saying?'

'What? Yes. Sorry. No. What?'

'Oh.' He shrugs. 'Here I am, just confessing my undying love for you, and you're not even listening.'

I stare at him. 'You were?'

'Well, no.' He says ruefully. 'I was making small talk until you were able to concentrate. But I was going to. And now it looks like I have.' He is uncharacteristically nervous.

'But I'm useless,' I say.

Samson places his hands on either side of my face, his palms touching the coarse skin of my burn scar. 'Don't ever, ever say that, Fern.'

'It's true,' I whisper, tears falling. 'How can you love someone who's broken?'

'Fern, you've seen the videos of Medraut after he had his Immral taken, haven't you?'

I nod.

'You saw what he was like. For him it was more than a breakdown. It was more than being broken. There was nothing left of the person he was.'

'I guess . . .'

'People like Medraut, people who've never had to face any difficulties before, can't cope when their power's taken from them. But you and me – we've faced down so much, even before we came to the knights. We were warriors before we learned how to fight. That's why you're still you, even without your

Immral. That's why you're going to get through this. Maybe you are a bit broken, maybe you always will be. But you'll still be Fern. You never needed your Immral to be brilliant.'

'I don't know.' I say, despite the spark of hope rekindling in my chest. 'Maybe you think I'm stronger than I really am.'

'I'm wrong about a lot of things,' Samson says, 'but I'm not wrong about you. I was wrong for worrying about falling for another knight. I was wrong to worry that you'd think I liked you just for your power. I was wrong to distance myself after kissing you the first time.'

'That's a lot of wrongdoing, Captain.'

He smiles, a shy, rakish smile I haven't seen before. It suits him. It suits him a lot. 'Then I'd better do a lot of right to make up for it.'

I allow my hands to touch his chest and his neck and his chin and his cheeks. 'What were you saying about confessing your undying love?'

Samson closes the gap between us, and kisses me again, at last. There's no seamstress skilled enough to untangle the web of my emotions in this moment. Fear is there, a red ribbon twisting through everything, and anxiety and anger. But everything is wrapped in joy and warmth and the softness that comes from another person's heart pressing against mine, holding me, telling me that he has wanted me for so long and kissing me in a way that promises he wants to do more.

I wake up to a pillow covered in blood. At least that will be the last time it happens. No power means no more migraines or nosebleeds or haemorrhages. Small mercies, I suppose. It's hard for me to feel truly sad about losing my Immral when I have gained . . . a boyfriend? No, the word is too insubstantial for what Samson means to me. For what we've been through together.

I bring the dirty linen downstairs to wash, and find Ollie already sat at the dining table. The TV is on, turned to the news. Ollie nods bleakly to the screen.

Mobs of One Voicers surround the Houses of Parliament. They are all silent, staring with stoical faces as MPs pass between them to enter the building. Then the camera pans back, and I realise that this is no ordinary One Voice protest. The crowd wings back, through the streets of London, stretching out and out and out as the helicopter the camera is mounted on takes flight.

'There are stunning scenes across the country this morning,' the news reporter says, 'as the public make their unhappiness with the current government clear . . .'

The camera cuts to shots of similar scenes all over the country. All the cities that Ollie and I visited last year, trying to find a way to detect Medraut's Immral. Everywhere, people stand in silence outside the municipal buildings, waiting not for their voices to be heard, but for Medraut's voice to be heard.

Then there he is, his handsome face filling the screen as the interviewer stumbles over their questions, in awe of his presence. As is the way with Medraut, it's hard to remember the substance of anything he says. He talks of honour, and of the people being heard. He says something about humility and pride, and mentions his wife and daughter and how everything he does is for them.

I think of Charlie and the experiments he submitted her to, and the anger fills me like water overflowing a tub.

When the interview comes to a close, he walks away, and I'm gratified to see that his left arm – the one I cut off with Ollie's chakram – hangs limply. A small chink in his otherwise impenetrable armour.

At some point, Dad joins us. Later, Kieran comes over too. We watch in stunned disbelief as MP after MP stands to voice their lack of confidence in the prime minister who, only yesterday, had commanded their full support. We should be in school, but there is no question of us leaving the house. The footage makes it clear that Bosco is inaccessible today – the streets too filled with protestors for me to make my way through the throng. Ollie simply refuses to leave home.

Instead, we sit together, sometimes making dinner or tea, sometimes holding hands silently across the table as history lurches on its axis.

Before the week is out, Sebastien Medraut is the ruler of the country.

Chapter 60

August 2005

Una slid the portrait into place, standing back to allow the Fay to work their power on the keyhole.

'The key is where we agreed?' Andraste said when it was done.

'Yes, this is the last task,' Una said. 'My final deed for the thanes. For Annwn.'

She was exhausted. Night after night of slipping into Annwn to lay the breadcrumbs. Lying to the two women who were helping her – the women she had worshipped. Day after day of watching Fern, hoping that she would find the clues and be able to decipher them. Or better yet, that Una herself would be able to show Fern the right path. Una would be able to make sure that her daughter grew up to be worthy. Strong enough, open-hearted enough, clever enough. For she knew, from the spark in Medraut's eye when she had met him in Ithr, that he would be back. That was why she did all of it. This was why she was lying to the Fay. It wasn't for Una's sake. It wasn't because she needed to vanquish the man who had cost her so much, and know that he knew it was she who vanquished him. She had outwitted him this time, she was sure of it.

With a burst of inspyre, the keyhole vanished, replaced by an image so beautiful Una could have imagined Ellen had painted it. She didn't let herself dwell in melancholy. Normal life for the next fifteen years. A normal life, nursing her secrets, and then the truth could finally come to light.

'Here ends our work,' Andraste said.

'It's the right course,' Nimue said, more to herself than to the others. Her eyes flickered towards the painting. Una wondered whether she suspected the truth.

'Please, my lady,' Una said. 'I have been your acolyte, have I not?'

'The sword is safe. Only those who love stories will be able to reach it now,' Andraste said.

Nimue nodded, and together the sisters turned towards Una. 'And now we say farewell.'

The Fay kissed Una on both cheeks. 'Go well, dear heart,' Andraste said.

'Keep him close.' Nimue smiled; their shared secret.

Outside, on the terrace, the women mounted horses: Andraste a stallion, Nimue a palfrey. They raised their hands once in a farewell, then turned their horses and urged them into a gallop. As they leaped down the steps, a rip opened in the fabric of Annwn, conjured by Fay magic. Horses and riders vanished into the ether, and the rip closed behind them. Una was alone.

She turned and wandered back through the gallery, reluctant to leave now that her time had come. Annwn had become a craving. One she needed to ween herself off. She knew how much she would miss the thrill of it, the possibilities, the ways her body moved in this world. It had been a darker addiction of late. She had found herself enjoying the deceit – the power of knowing that she was lying to two of the most formidable beings in this world.

It made her worry that she wasn't a good person. That was why she had to leave. She had to find her way back from this place.

Una took her time exploring the gallery, running her hands over the artworks in a way she'd never be allowed in Ithr. When she had exhausted every room, she moved back towards the main entrance. In the grand hallway, painted birds fluttered and watercolours bled up the walls, forming vines and trees that morphed and became real and unreal in the space between heartbeats.

It's time to say goodbye.

Una broke into the fresh air of Trafalgar Square, throwing her face up to the sun. Every moment was a eulogy to this world and the woman she was inside it. She bobbed down to the fountains and let the dolphins splash her.

Just as she had decided to head back to her portal at Tower Bridge, she heard it.

Tap tap.

Una spun around. Was that . . . ?

Tap tap.

The golden treitre emerged from behind the fountain, its pinprick eyes darkly fixed upon her. She had tarried too long.

The chase had begun.

Chapter 61

A lethargy spreads through Tintagel, but it's not a surrender. It's a pause. A gathering of strength. We do what we can, for now. Charlie is kept in Tintagel, away from her father's influence in Annwn, although we cannot protect her in Ithr. She has moments of lucidity, but for the most part we keep her in her tower, with her dog, Loco. It's a pitiful existence for her, but I like to think that it affords her more freedom than her father did.

Charlie may stay in Tintagel, but Excalibur does not. Merlin and Nimue answer Lord Allenby's call at last, stumbling across the drawbridge, shedding pieces of themselves with every step. They are the last of the Fay. All the rest have crumbled.

'We can't risk him finding it again,' Lord Allenby tells them. Excalibur has been wrapped in thick cloth. I'd be happy never to see it again, but Merlin looks at me beadily. 'You might need it yet, girl,' he says. 'We'll put it somewhere you'll be able to find, even if we're gone.'

'If you like,' I say heavily, then, as he turns to leave with it, add, 'Just don't give me three impossible tasks again, okay?'

He nods, unsmiling. Nimue runs a scaling hand down my face, across my eyes.

'I'm sorry I couldn't save her,' I say.

'She is in you,' she says, then she looks at the others in the room: at Natasha, Niamh, Rachel, Jin and Easa. 'I see my sister in all of you.'

My brother is never far from me in the weeks that follow. The old Ollie would have crowed over the fact that he now has power and I don't. The Ollie of last year would have tried to hide his Immral, so cautious that he'd end up making me feel worse.

This Ollie does neither. He simply is. He will use his Immral to reassure me, but never tell me my own feelings. He will hold a spark of inspyre in his hand, as I used to, and make it play with me. This is a new feature of his Immral – Ollie is beginning to gain my part of the power.

'It will only ever be limited,' Jin tells us. 'He'll never be able to do things the way you could, Fern.'

'Might be enough to hold the fort until yours comes back, though,' Ollie says, looking at me with wide eyes, trying to say the right thing.

'You did still stop Medraut from keeping Excalibur, remember,' Rachel reminds us.

'Yeah,' Ollie says. 'Mum would be proud of you, you know.'

I look at him, and I don't need Immral to tell how much that comment costs him.

I may be useless as a knight, but there are still some things I can do. Being an artist means I'm a pretty good handwriting mimic when I want to be. I've spent long enough staring at Mum's spiky script to do a decent imitation. It's time I set right something that she should have done when she left me that letter telling me about Excalibur. It doesn't have to be her that does it.

Later, I find Ollie. 'You'll never guess,' I tell him, hoping I'm a good enough actor to pull this off. 'I was tidying my room –' I ignore his snort – 'and I found this compartment under the floorboards, just like the one in Annwn.'

'Cool,' he says. 'Anything juicy in there?'

I shrug. 'Just this. It's for you.'

I present Ollie with the letter, his name on the envelope. I did a good job of ageing it. Dad will never notice one missing teabag. Ollie's hand shakes as he takes it from me.

'Cool,' he says again, and excuses himself to his bedroom. I don't follow him in, or ask him what the letter says. I already know.

Dearest Ollie,

Don't ask me how or why, but there's a chance that I won't be able to see you grow up, my darling. I'm so sorry. I am doing important work, to try to make the world a safer, more open place for you and your sister. I never want you to be afraid to be who you are. I never want you to have to lie about what's in your soul. Fear can be useful, and so can anger, but honesty is the most powerful emotion we have and I want you to be able to use it.

Ollie – you and your sister are so precious to me. I want you to know that, whatever happens, whatever paths each of you take through life, I love you both so, so much. Protect each other in my absence, please. You're twins, and that has to count for something.

Love,

Mummy

Not as eloquent as she'd probably have made it, and maybe I shouldn't have mentioned myself, but I need him to stay by my side. I'm not strong enough yet to stand on my own.

The second note I push through the letterbox of a house not too far from here, and not too far from the cemetery I visit afterwards, where two fresh graves sit side by side, bearing the same surname. I'd probably be turfed out of the thanes if anyone found out. But they need to know that their children died for a reason.

There is a place not far from Tintagel, where dual monuments of amber and gold reach up to the sky. Inside them rest the precious pieces of the fallen thanes. A graveyard of those who tried to stop Medraut over the last sixteen years. About a month after the Trafalgar Square battle, we gather to erect a third one.

Inside it, amongst the many tokens of the fallen, is a pen identical to one in the monument next to it. Ramesh and Sachi, joined in so many ways even though they didn't know it.

There is one last thing to place with the monument. My puzzle box. *Our* puzzle box, for it belongs to all of those who walk through Annwn. I won't be able to use it now – not for many years, by which time whatever war we're still trying to fight will be decided. A part of me died that day too. It feels only right that this should rest alongside our fallen friends and their broken dreams.

After the ceremony, most of the thanes trudge back towards Tintagel, but a few of us tarry in this spot. It doesn't feel like London – it feels like one of those in-between places, like Stonehenge, where time is meaningless.

Samson and Jin help me dig a hole for the puzzle box at the base of the new monument. Ollie brings it over, and together we form a circle around the little dent in the ground.

'Do you feel anything?' Niamh asks my brother.

He nods. 'It's so loud, guys. Like a concert of different music, but all the notes fit together.'

'I wish I could help us all to hear it,' I say.

'We can hear it,' Samson says, coming to stand behind me, so my back rests against his chest. 'We made it, didn't we?'

Natasha smiles and closes her eyes, 'I hear rock. Proper mosh-pit stuff.'

Easa's next. 'Jazz.' He smiles.

'Folk,' says Rachel.

'Nineties pop,' Niamh says, to general laughter.

They keep going, throwing in suggestions and singing snippets of their favourite songs; musical butterflies that take wing inside us. Samson kisses my hair, his hands snaking around my waist. Ollie laughs at one of Easa's jokes. Rachel looks at me, her eyes shining with renewed purpose.

For the first time in years, I feel no anger. But that doesn't mean I've given up. I place a hand on the monument next to me, as Ollie lowers the puzzle box into the ground and the others throw earth on top of it, still singing-talking-laughing.

Medraut thinks he's won, but as long as we are here, together, as long as we remember what brings us joy, then the war is still raging.

'It isn't over,' I say quietly, to the monument beneath my fingertips. To Ramesh and Rafe, Phoebe, Vien, Linnea and Milosz, Sachi and Brandon.

This isn't over.

Acknowledgements

A Gathering Midnight is a book of the pandemic. It was written and edited during lockdowns and tiers and beneath a shadow of grief, fear and anger. I suspect that it shows in the writing – but you, dear reader, will be the best judge of that.

These acknowledgements can never do justice to the many people who had a part in creating this novel and guiding me through the privileged and odd process of publishing a book. Even more so because many supported me generously despite their own struggles during this strangest of years.

My first thanks must always be to my agent, Anna Dixon at WME, and to my editor, Georgia Murray at Hot Key Books. Thank you both for your extraordinary ability to simultaneously make me feel as though I *am* a proper writer, while also making it clear just how much work needs doing.

Thanks also to the editorial, marketing and publicity teams at Hot Key and Bonnier: Jenny Jacoby, Melissa Hyder, Sasha Baker, Amy Llambias, Molly Holt, Emma Quick and Sophie McDonnell. To Gavin Reece, who managed to make the cover for *A Gathering Midnight* just as stunning as his cover for Midnight's Twins, which I didn't think possible. And to the rest of the team at WME: Hilary Zaitz-Michael, Janine Kamouh, Laura Bonner, Florence Dodd and James Munro.

The world of UKYA is overwhelmingly populated by a group of very generous authors and readers. Thank you to the tweeters, bookstagrammers and bloggers who shouted about *Midnight's Twins* and sent me theories on what could happen next – I hope you won't be disappointed! Many writers have given me invaluable advice, cheerleading and quotes, even in the midst of scaling their own drafting mountains. A particular shout out is due to Rachel Burge, Alexia Casale, Katharine and Elizabeth Corr, Bex Hogan, Michelle Kenney and Menna van Praag; brilliant authors all.

Now for the WhatsApp and Facebook groups – who knew that they would become such a lifeline! Thank you to the members of Netflix Party, Quaranteam, Cambridge(ish) Parents, the D20 Authors, the Savvies and to my ever-wonderful Faber Academy group, for your memes, sarcasm and raw honesty.

Then there's the host of friends, some of whom I haven't seen in over a decade, who got behind a little urban fantasy released during lockdown. I can't tell you how wonderful it has been to get a message from a familiar name telling me how much you enjoyed my writing – the possibility of reconnection online has been one of the highlights of this year.

Chris Massey, my man of honour, was the mastermind (aided by Tara Beattie and Juliette Burton) behind a spectacular surprise online launch for *Midnight's Twins*. The memory still brings a spark to my heart. To them and to all the other friends, near and far, who participated – thank you so much for making a depressed writer feel immensely loved.

Thank you again and again to my parents and my husband, who let me be weak and angry and afraid. You and Ada – our little bubble – are my everything, for ever.

Finally, thank you to the readers. Without you, there are no stories.

Holly Race

Holly worked as a development executive in the film and TV industry for nearly a decade. These days, when she isn't writing, she can usually be found either script editing or baking. She is a Faber Academy graduate, and the first book in this trilogy, *Midnight's Twins*, was her debut novel. Holly used to live in Fern and Ollie's neck of the woods, but now resides in Cambridge with her husband and daughter.
You can find out more about her and keep up to date with her book news at www.hollyrace.com